FIREBLOOD
THE FIRST FLIGHT

SAM
STEWART

Firefly

First published in 2023
by Firefly Press
25 Gabalfa Road, Llandaff North, Cardiff, CF14 2JJ
www.fireflypress.co.uk

A CIP catalogue record of this book is available from the British Library.

1 3 5 7 9 8 6 4 2

ISBN 978-1-915444-19-6
ebook ISBN 978-1-915444-20-2

This book has been published with the support of
the Books Council Wales.

Cover illustration © Keith Robinson
Typeset by Elaine Sharples

Printed by CPI Group (UK) Ltd, Croydon, Surrey, CRO 4YY

THE FIRST FLIGHT

Sam Stewart was born in Zambia, grew up in South Africa and now lives in the UK with her two children. She has been fascinated by fire since a very early age when she accidentally set her bedroom alight, and though *Fireblood* features some spontaneous blazes and a fair amount of unexpected flame she has been very careful with anything burny ever since.

For John Edmund Charles Richards,
who has fire in his soul

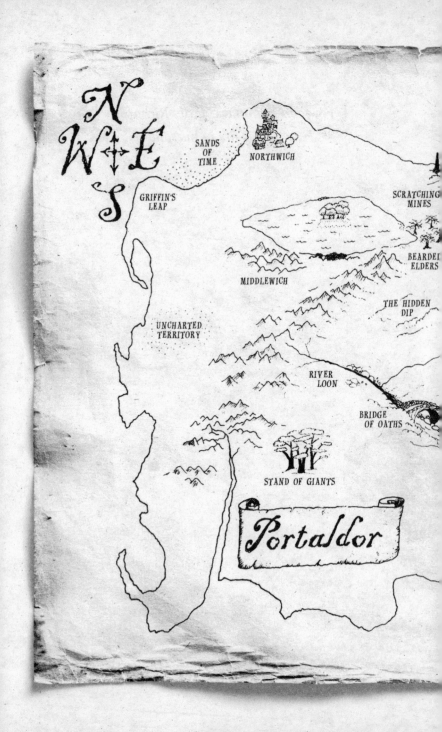

Running along the bottom of the pages of this book is a hidden chapter which reveals the secret history of how the fireblood world began. Use the translation of the chapter-heading numbers to crack the code, and discover this ancient story for yourself...

PROLOGUE

ᑭᒥᓯᑐᕕᎬ

Augustus Flint stood listening to the silence of the rock and the glass and the steel all around him. He was a tall man, wiry, with sinewy muscle, and every bit of him hummed with a strength that was almost visible even though he stood as still as the strange stone that lay on the kitchen counter.

'I don't want to leave them,' he whispered, picking up an old and battered canvas rucksack from the floor. His words echoed in the enormous space of the open-plan living area, though he was trying to be very quiet. It seemed to him that the word 'leave' bounced back over and over from the huge vaulted ceiling, the enormous facets of glass that looked out onto the dark gorge below and the steel girders that connected the walls around him.

'You shouldn't be leaving them,' replied the Stone. It was an uneven oval of frosted crystal that had quite lost its shine, about thirty centimetres long, and half that in width. It looked like a huge lump of very, very old sea glass, but you'd never say that to her. She'd be

ᕆᐁᒥᒥᎬᔕ ᕦᑐᖈᔕ ᕦᔅᕝᕋ ᐱ Ꮎᕝᐱᒥᕝ. ᕴᕡᔤ ᕦᔕᒥᔕ ᒥᑐᐱᓫᔤᐁᎾ.

furious with that kind of observation, though, frankly, furious seemed to be her usual state of mind.

'Definitely should not be leaving them,' she added. 'Do something else instead.'

'Something else?' Augustus heaved a heavy sigh, his breath catching in his throat. 'How are you—' His voice cracked. He cleared his throat and swiped a hand across his forehead, then quickly down across his eyes. With the same hand, he pulled hard on his moustache and beard, considering what to say next.

'How am I never helpful?' prompted the Stone.

Huffing a mirthless laugh, Augustus replied, 'I don't feel good about this mission. Something's off. Even though this place' – he gestured to their home, carved into the cliff face – 'is protected from within and without, and even though I've taught them the hidden entrances and exits, and to be quick and strong and clever, I worry for Finn and Tula. They've only ever been out with me, at night, and very rarely then...'

'The last time you felt something was off,' said the Stone, her voice hard, almost strident, 'your wife, the mother of those two children, was killed in cold blood.'

Before Augustus could reply with the breath he'd sucked deep into his chest, his eyes wide with hurt

ᐱ≡ᐠᚱθ ᕊ≡'ᑫ ᐁ⅄ᒡ�≡ᑫ, ᑲ≡θᛑᐯᚱ⟩≡θ, ᛑᐁᛑ ᛑᕊ⟩θ ᐁ⅄θ ᛑᕊ≡

and shock, she added, 'Trust your instincts, you stupid, stupid man! Why is it that the grown-ups of this world always make such terrible mistakes?'

'It's different this time,' muttered Augustus, leaning towards the Stone, his fists clenched at his sides. 'I have more gifts from mythic and frailskin creatures now. I can speak any language, stop my own blood, control the portals. If I don't go, we are looking at catastrophic consequences. This planet will die—'

'It will not die! It will sleep for an age, then recover again, as it has done before. Forget the volcano, Augustus! Think of your children!'

'My children are part of the planet that will die if I don't leave now and complete the task.' He put the bag on the kitchen counter and reached for the Stone.

'Leave me here,' blurted the Stone. Then, 'No!' she shrieked when he withdrew his hand. 'Take me with you.' He frowned and she cried out again. 'No! Leave me here!'

Augustus sighed. 'Milady,' he said, hesitant, 'you always come with me. What if I need answers?'

'The children will need answers,' said the Stone, and her voice was softer now, 'especially if you don't come back.'

'*What?* There's n—'

'I will need to tell them, Augustus.'

⊿∠□⊿∖≡Θ�. ‡ΛჰΘ ⊽⌐λθ ჰ⌐, Θ□ ⊲□⊽↓⌐. Ⴙ≡ ΘⲢⲆλΘΘ ⌐□

'Milady! I—'

'I'll need to tell them everything you've kept from them, because if you don't get this to work, it'll be up to them to save the world, and they won't have the first clue how.'

1

Finn and Tula Flint slipped into the shadows behind a noisy row of restaurants near Bristol Temple Meads train station. Finn could smell fire, the waft of woodsmoke in the night air, and the scent of it both terrified and intrigued him. There was so much going on around them that he was struggling to focus. He had to concentrate on making sure they looked normal, instead of like children who'd never been allowed out of their house in daylight. Ever.

How far north can the trains take us? signed Tula. *How will we get tickets? I'm starving.*

His sister hadn't spoken aloud since their mother died eight years ago – she'd been barely a year old and Finn had been three. No one but Finn and his father understood her subtle sign language. A twitch of an eyebrow meant *Where are we going?* and when she added a slight flick of her finger, with a tiny dragging motion of her hand, well, that became *Where are you taking us?*

It was all a bit complicated, but Finn was an expert at understanding her, even better than their dad, though sometimes, like now, he wished he wasn't. He tried to ignore the urgent expression around Tula's eyes, how she was biting her top lip and touching a thumb to her stomach. He knew she didn't realise it was making him feel bad about what a terrible job he was doing looking after her – she was only nine – and somehow that made everything worse.

Tân is starving too, she continued, and patted her coat pocket gently. It wriggled then went still. *Tân is sick of walking around. He wants to sleep now.*

'Stop!' whispered Finn, holding his hand up at his sister, wincing at the noise of all the millions of things going on around them. 'Please just *stop*. I can't think with you going on and on at me. Tân is not walking around. He is *sitting* around – fat lazy lizard – while *we* do all the legwork.' He grimaced at the bright-green crested gecko peeking out from Tula's inside jacket pocket, and the creature glared balefully back at him.

Why are you so cross? Just because Dad's been gone for ages doesn't mean we have to be all stressed out! Aren't you glad to be out on an adventure instead of stuck inside like always?

ᐁᔑᑊᔖᐊ ᐃᑲᕐᘊᘊ ᕋᔖᘊ ᘊᕋᐤᐧᐸᑫ≡ᕐ, ᕋᔖᘊ ᘊᔥᐧᐱ≡ᕐ ᕋᐃᔖᕐ ᐃᐡᕐᐱ.

Finn was about to speak again when a rectangle of light flooded across the ground. A door opened and someone came out into the alley.

The children shrank against a wall into the shadows.

Tula drew closer to her brother, breathing in the scents from the alley. *Oh, WOW, Finn. That guy's throwing out fresh boxes of leftovers! I can smell … pizza!*

Finn grinned, thankful for once that no one could hear his sister. If she'd spoken aloud, attracted attention, that would have been dangerous, out here on Bristol's streets on their own.

On their own.

For the first time ever.

His grin faded as Tula moved forward. 'Wait,' he whispered.

For what? she signed impatiently. *Stop being such a scaredy-cat!*

'Tula, we've got to be careful because we have no idea what we're doing! We've never gone anywhere without Dad! Never gone to the shops, to school, never run in parks, never walked on pavements, never been on a bus or met anyone other than Aunty Myra.'

Not complicated, Finn, signed Tula. *We've found some food, we're hungry, we're going to eat it. And*

ꝫᴑ θ≡ᑲᴑᴑꝺθ, ꞙᴀ≡ θꞙᴑᐯꞙ ↲≡ㅅꞙᴀ≡ꝿ Ꞁᴑᴑꞙθ ⅁‾≡ꝿ≡ ᴑᴑ ᴀꝫθ

there's no need to be so cross because Dad's only been trying to protect us. The outside world might be mean about your hunch and me not speaking out loud and—

And we're going to be just fine, signed Finn fiercely, standing up straighter. *Just fine.*

Tula grinned back at him, motioned to the bins outside the restaurant kitchen door and did a show-off backflip, landing right next to them.

We're already fine! she signed. *Dad says no one can climb or jump or decipher a code faster than me and you. He says he's trained us well.*

Finn pulled a face. 'He said never to tell Aunt Myra about you icing things up just by breathing or waving, or that magnetic thing you do with locks—'

That's because Aunt Myra is always pestering him to send us away to boarding school.

'For help with our "oddities, where they could lead a normal life, for snakes' sakes, Augustus",' said Finn, mimicking their aunt, and Tula did her silent laughing thing with her hands in front of her mouth and her eyes all crinkling up.

I'm glad we don't know how to contact Aunty Myra, signed Tula, *so we've got no choice but to go search for Dad and eat pizza by ourselves.*

'Cheeky,' said Finn in his best stern voice, but he was smiling and feeling better at the smell from the

ᒥᐦᒥ ᐊᐤᐅ ᖏᐡ Ꮁᐅᐊᕆᕗᑦ Ꭶᐴᑊᑊ ᠴᐤ ᕕᠻᐤ ᖎᐊᐤᐅ.

boxes left on the bin. 'When we find him, he's going to be so impressed that he's going to let us do everything from now on.'

They each grabbed a few boxes and moved soundlessly further down the alley where they could eat in peace.

'I hope there's a cucumber or something in this lot,' Finn whispered, 'otherwise Tân is gonna have one of his hissy fits.'

You know nothing, Finn Flint, signed Tula, her fingers moving quickly. *If you listened to* Desperate Diners *just once instead of playing Flybynight Warrior all the time, you'd know pizzas definitely don't have cucumbers. One of Dad's rants about fast food was…* Tula trailed off. A siren wailed in the street behind them, and traffic noise swelled as a light went from red to green. Finn hadn't thought that cars would be so … loud.

How long do you think it'll take us to find him? Tula asked as she stared up at the graffitied wall at the end of the alley. *It's been ten days…*

Finn swallowed. 'Dead end,' he said, changing the subject.

Look, signed Tula. *We can hide in those boxes over there.*

'Okay,' replied Finn. Tula's hand on his arm was

'8ᕁ≡◌,' ᕁ≡ ᒥᐁ⦵ᕈ≡◁, ᕁ≡ᐱ⫸◌ᕽ⦵ ᒦ◌ᒥ ᕼᕁ≡ ◁◻◻ᒥᒥ. '8ᕁ≡◌⌐

cold, and it scared him. The two of them were usually a whole lot warmer. It would be good to stop and eat.

Within minutes they'd arranged a rough shelter from a huge refrigerator box and some pieces of cardboard. Tula found a wooden crate, and the pair sat inside the box, the crate between them as a table.

Lovely, signed Tula, her hands dancing in the shape of a heart. *Bring it on, bro.*

'Okay,' murmured Finn, but then came a soft call down the alley that froze the siblings instantly.

'Oi, oi! Someone hiding down there, then?'

Finn and Tula locked wide eyes.

Let's take a look, signed Tula, blinking.

Finn nodded, and his sister turned slowly to lift the top of the box behind her so they could both see through a crack. A man dressed entirely in black from top to toe was coming down the alley. Three thugs shambled along behind him, attitude in their walk and attitude in the pulled-up hoods of sleeveless tops, though being December it was absolutely freezing.

Uh oh, signed Tula.

Tân climbed up on to her shoulder, and went completely still except for his tail, which had curled up behind him in a movement that also meant *uh oh*.

The guy who'd spoken was probably the man in the suit. He had slicked-back hair and a huge signet

ᗯᐱᖇ≡⅃ ‡�A≡⅄'ᖇ≡ ᑲᗐᐞ⸏ᔓᗩᎾ ᖶᗐᖉ ‡�A≡ ᖲᖆᕐᗝᗐᗺ.'

ring on the index finger of his left hand. You noticed it straight away because of how his fist was clenched round the handle of a nasty-looking whip.

The three behind him were enormous. Colossal. About seven foot tall and at least three foot wide. The muscles in their arms bulged and rippled under heavily tattooed and scarred skin. Even though Finn hadn't been out much in the real world, he was pretty sure these guys wouldn't be able to merge casually in crowds of happy families and peaceful do-gooders. Definitely not. With their bunched fists and snarling expressions, they looked distinctly like do-badders, and the *stink* of them…

Eat quickly, signed Finn. He passed Tula another slice of pizza, ramming one into his own mouth. *We need a distraction*, he signed. *Fuel up fast while I think*.

'They came in here…' said the man in the suit. He lifted his nose to the air and sniffed.

Huh? They came in here? *Is he talking about us?* thought Finn. He swallowed hard and Tula's hand crept over to his, holding it tightly. The glare from the kitchen door caught the edge of the man's face in a grim white light, throwing his quivering nostrils into sharp relief.

Before any more thoughts could enter Finn's head, Tân flung himself into the alley, skittering round the

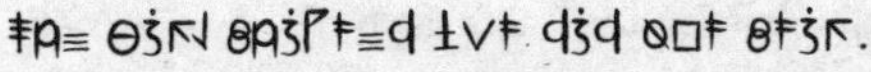

pointed shiny shoes of the suited man, past his three sidekicks and straight towards the rubbish bins.

'Eeeeee!' squealed the biggest of the thugs in a voice too high for his hulking size.

Tula clapped a hand to her mouth in horror.

Call Tân back! mouthed Finn to Tula.

She shook her head violently. *No! If he comes back here, they'll grab him AND he'll bring them to us!*

The suited man put a hand on the shoulder of the biggest one. 'Compose yourself, Jed,' he said in a silky voice. 'You all right, Carl?'

The smallest of the thugs grunted. 'Yes, Mr Craven, sir.'

Craven took a step forward, and the light from the back door of the restaurant moved across his face, revealing the pointed teeth of his triumphant smile. He was staring right at the box in which Finn and Tula were hiding.

'Found you, kids,' he said. 'At last. Wondered how long it would take to flush you out of your lair, and now here you are, running to Daddy.' He gestured with his whip to one of the three massive forms behind him, who were shifting from foot to foot, looking nervous or eager, Finn wasn't sure which. 'Rafe, go get them.'

'Yes, Mr Craven, sir.'

The one in the middle moved forward reluctantly.

'ᐘᑫ═ᐅᒧ' ᑫ═ ᐅᐃᕦ═ᑫ. 'ᐘᑫ═'ᕮ ᖠᑫ═ ᒡᐃᕮᖠ ᐅᕩ ═ᐅᒥᖠᑫᒧ ᐂᕮ ᐃᔾᐁᕮ

A knife handle just above his belt flashed in the light.

Okay, signed Finn to Tula. *Get Tân to come to us, then we sprint back up the alley.*

Tula's eyes flickered. Finn watched as Tân peeped out from the rubbish bins, and then there was a yelp from Rafe, and Tân was heading back their way. In the blink of an eye he was on Tula's lap and wriggling into her pocket.

Finn took a deep breath. He nodded, and he and Tula burst out of the box in a tangle of fast-moving limbs and bright-eyed determination.

Shielding Tula, Finn ran hard down the right side, knowing Mr Craven's thugs were huddled on the left. Even though Finn was fast, Rafe still reached him, clouting him on the jaw with furious strength.

'Got him, Mr Craven—'

Finn jumped and spun away with lightning cracks of arms and legs. His eyes caught snapshots of everything as his head whipped round – Jed, still gaping in astonishment, frozen at the far end of the alley … the close-up eyeballs of Carl … Rafe swiping at him desperately—

Then the flavour of fresh-struck flint flooded Finn's mouth, stopping him in his tracks. He skidded

θ⅄∧≡ Ⱥ≡Ɐ⊥'

to a halt, whipping round to see where the taste of fear had come from.

Tula! No!

Mr Craven was holding his sister, twisting her up by her long pale hair, twisting, twisting, twisting it back till her arms came round and clenched at his arm. He laughed – a high-pitched, breathy wheeze – but that was the only sound in the alley. Tula could not scream.

Finn's fists clenched at his sides. 'Let go of my sister,' he rasped, his chest heaving.

Run! mouthed Tula.

Craven laughed, soft and low. 'Dearie me,' he murmured. 'The boy has no manners.' His eyes narrowed and he yanked on Tula's hair again. She hung limp, unmoving, as Finn stepped closer, closer.

Don't, Finn, she begged, her face moving too subtly for the thugs to notice. *Please. Calm down*.

Finn stopped a metre from Craven. 'Last chance,' he said. Finn's voice was low for a twelve-year-old. And measured. He faced up to the thug like a person three times his age. 'Otherwise,' he continued, 'you're going to get hurt.'

'Oh, really,' drawled Craven. 'You have a secret weapon, then? Better than mine?' He flicked his whip in the air like a cheerleader with a ribbon stick and laughed again.

ᒥᐊᑐᑊᔦᐸ, ᑲᗕᑕᏅᗕ ᐁᗇᐸᐟ 8ᑫᗕ᙭ ᗕᗿᔔ ᗕᐁᗕᗕᑭᔇᏅᗕ ᐧᗕᑊ ᒥᐤᗕ ᑭᑕᒥ

Finn did not reply. His body angled back and down, like a big cat getting ready to strike.

Craven sneered again and gestured to the others. 'Time to take this little squirt apart,' he hissed. 'Gargan is going to be very pleased with me for finally finding these lovely treasures.'

Finn's vision zeroed in on Craven. The man's pointed teeth seemed somehow longer than before and anger came off him in waves, but it was his eyes that made Finn's heart freeze. They blazed a dark ruby red now, as if filled with blood, and they were focused on Finn, and Finn alone.

What the—? he thought.

Then, just as Carl's big, hairy fingers came for the back of his shirt, he saw his sister shout *NOW!* with both hands, and he gave it everything he had.

2

Heat raged up through Finn's body and blasted from his hands in a torrent of scorching brightness straight into Craven's face. It took a second for the man to register that this boy was *actually throwing a nuclear blast of light at him* before he felt the agony of burning. He shrieked and threw his arms up to protect himself, dropping Tula to the ground but holding tight to his whip, which, in the shock of the moment, he did not even think to use.

Finn spun to face the other three, and in the face of that white heat the hooded thugs scrambled screaming to their feet, rushing to get away, and pulling Craven with them. When they reached the street, Craven threw one last glance back, and the rage and hatred on his face shocked Finn from white heat to white ash.

Tula was still on the ground, still clutching Tân.

ᛏᚨ≡ ᚩᛃᚻᚦ, ᚥᛝᛏᚪ ᚥ�□ ᚼᘁ□□ᚥ ᚼᚥᛩ ᚥ□ ᚦᛏᚼᚱᚦ ᛏ□ ᚦᚢᛝᛞ≡ ᚩᛃᚼᚼᛝ,

The world seemed to hang motionless for a moment, the only movement the clouds of mist that billowed from their heaving breath into the icy air. Then she sprang to her feet, placing Tân carefully in her pocket.

Finn! she signed. *What was that? What did you do? How did—?*

Finn's mind cleared.

'They were looking for us,' he said. 'Those people. We're not safe here.' He lifted his hands slowly to his face, staring at his shaking fingers in disbelief. Soot from his skin dusted to the cobblestones, and he hurried over to his sister.

In that moment, the world on the road beyond seemed to whoosh suddenly to life, tyres sending dirty spray into the air, horns loud, another distant siren somewhere, the pounding footsteps of Craven and his crew already inaudible in the city noise.

Finn? signed Tula, her arms moving in a mad windmill around her head. *Answer me! That light from your hands? What was that?*

'I-I don't know,' stammered Finn. '*Did you see their eyes? Did you hear what they said? They'll be back for us!*'

A voice with an Irish accent echoed down the alley. 'And there'll be more of them next time.'

Finn snapped back into his cougar crouch, facing the exit to the road to see who had spoken,

ᘚᐻᎾᑊ ᖨᎻ≡ ᘚᐯᐯᎷᓀᔔᎾᎾ ᒍᔔᎾᎻᑊ ᑎᖨ ᖨᔔᎾ⅄ ᒑᒍᐃ⅄≡Ꮎ ᑎᖨ ᖨᑎᖪᗝᎻ≡Ꮎ

his arms out wide, while Tula leapt to her feet just behind him.

A dark figure was silhouetted against the streetlights, legs apart, hands on hips. Despite the bright light behind the man, Finn and Tula could make out every detail of his form. Short black hair, immaculate goatee beard, one earring, chiselled features, chiselled muscles in tight black T-shirt, fitted jeans, black combat boots.

'Who are you?' demanded Finn. 'What did you say?'

The man stayed put. 'You're right. Those idiots are going to come straight back here.' He glanced at his watch. 'In about, oh, I reckon … eight minutes. They've got a lot of friends. And I'm not sure you've got a lot of firepower left.'

Firepower? signed Tula. *Finn? What does he mean?*

'I'll explain everything,' said the man. 'Come with me.'

Finn's cougar stance melted and he straightened his knees to standing again. 'Y-you understood her,' he stammered. 'You understood my sister.'

Shh, Finn! commanded Tula.

But Finn's chest was heaving with emotion. 'How did you know what she said?'

Be quiet, Finn! gestured Tula, her face furious.

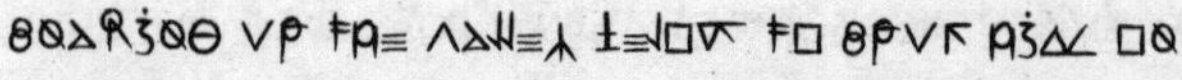

ᎾᎥᎡⴝᎾᎾ Ꮙ�P ᛏᎡ≡ ᏞᎥᏚᐊ≡Ꮮ ⟘≡ᛁᏫᢦ ᛏᗡ ᎾᏢᏉᎦ Ꮧⴝᐱ⟋ ᏏᎾ.

'I think,' said the figure, 'it's time we got going.'

No! signed Tula. *No, Finn! He feels strange. I – I can't read him.*

'Often you can't read your father either,' said the man, 'yet you trust him.'

'Tula!' gasped Finn, whirling to face his sister. '*Tula!*'

No! signed Tula again, her eyes wide with fear.

'I'm your only chance,' said the figure. His face shifted sharply into profile as he looked up the road. 'Here they come.' Turning to face them, he said, 'I know this is strange, me arriving unannounced like this' – he looked hard at Tula – 'but we've been searching for you because these idiots are the least of your worries. There are … others. Aren't there, Tula?'

Finn looked from the man to his sister then back to the man. Neither of them had anything more to add.

'Tula?' Finn grabbed his sister's hands, but she had nothing to say.

'Tân has been telling her, but she won't listen.'

'Tân? What do you m—?'

'Come,' urged the man, and he extended his arm. 'Don't forget your bag. It's in the box. You need your bag.'

Finn's heart pounded as he stared at the figure's

ᐃᖃ≡ᐤ ᖃ≡ ᒥ≡ᐃᑲᖃ≡ᑫ ᖼᖃ≡ ᖱ�ⴱᖱ ᑳᐱᐱ≡ᕁ, ᕁᐃᘁᑎᖰ≡ ᐁᐧᐃᕁ ᑲᕐᕁᠯᣘᕁᕁ

face. He felt his eyes do that weird thing where they zoomed and held an image in his head. The image now was of brown eyes, softer than you'd expect in a guy like this, and worried-looking. He was for real. No doubt.

Then the clincher: 'I know what happened to your father,' said the man. Even Tula looked startled, her expressions dancing in hope and fear across her face. 'We must hurry back to his office to pick up his, er, letter opener, then we'll have all we need to get him back.'

Finn tasted hot orange juice in his mouth, which always happened when people told the truth.

'Letter opener?' he asked.

The man shrugged. 'It's the key to a locked place that'll help us find your dad. I'll explain later.'

Finn raced back to the box and grabbed his dad's old khaki fishing bag. The thick canvas of it was stained with rust and dirt, but the inside was pristine and carefully padded for its precious cargo. He pulled the straps over his shoulders and snatched up two pieces of pizza on his way out.

'Come on, Tula,' he said, holding out a slice. 'It's going to be okay.'

He tugged her with him out of the alley. Parked at a hasty angle on the pavement was a Jaguar Mark 1, the driver's door still open and the radio blaring with a news broadcast about volcanic activity escalating in Russia.

'Jump in,' said the man. 'Hear that? Sounds as if we need to hurry.'

'He thinks Dad is in Russia,' whispered Finn. 'Probably getting readings from Mount Elbrus, like we thought!'

'Yes,' came a voice from the bag on Finn's back. 'That's what they all think.'

Tula's eyelids fluttered, but she came to the car and climbed in, staring around her at the luxurious interior.

Finn felt hope flicker in his chest, and it felt good. He shut the car door and the man pulled off into the traffic. The newsreader had stopped talking about Mount Elbrus being ready to erupt and was moaning about gangs on the streets of Bristol instead.

Finn signed to Tula: *This guy definitely knows where Dad is.*

He just wants the bag, replied Tula. *And Dad's letter opener.*

'Everyone wants the bag,' said the man up front, driving expertly through the traffic. 'Everyone *always* wants the bag. And the opener. Could you kids please keep your greasy fingers off the upholstery?'

Finn, I can't feel where Dad is at all, signed Tula,

ˈŌ⌐꒚≡�յ⌐ ꟼꗺꝱꝱ≡ꝗ Ꝕ≡◻⌐Ꝋ≡. ‡ꟼ≡ʎˈ⌐≡ ꟼ≡⌐≡⊥ˈ

on the verge of tears. *I don't know about Mount Elbrus. We're losing him…*

Finn bit his lip. He found his gaze locking with those brown eyes observing him in the rear-view mirror.

'Hey,' said the man. 'My name is Patrick. Some prefer Patrick the Mighty, but I don't like to insist.'

'Hello,' said Finn, his voice barely a murmur. He squeezed Tula's hand and then wrapped his arms tightly round the bag. 'Where is our dad?'

'I was hoping you two could tell me that.' One of the brown eyes winked at Finn, but Finn couldn't smile back.

'But you said—' he blurted, a sense of unease shifting the hairs on the back of his neck.

'I said I knew *what had happened* to him. He's been captured by bad people who want information from him. I don't know *where* he is, though we've got a lead from the Ministry of Defence.' Patrick grinned. 'You should know that I'm one of the rare firebloods who can read minds and project the occasional message to the—' Patrick stopped abruptly.

'Hang on,' he said. 'Let me do this properly otherwise my boss, George, will flay me alive.'

Patrick cleared his throat and continued in a robotic tone. His Irish accent lilted more strongly.

ᐳᑕᖼ ᗷᐁᖼ〓 ᢃᒉ ᖺᗡ〓 ᐸᖸᐞ⊖◖ᗡ ⊤ᢃᖺᗡᣚᗴ � ᕿ〓ᐞᖽᐸ ᕿᣚᐞᐸ⟋¸ ᕿ〓

'Your thoughts may be interpreted, not just for training purposes. If you do not want your thoughts to be interpreted, transmitted or communicated in any way, and if you do not want to be contacted by the finest fireblood mind, then please tick the box.'

'What box?' asked Finn, his voice a bit whispery.

Patrick laughed. 'Yeah, I know, it's like I'm being all reasonable, but actually, er, not at all. Don't worry, though. I'm the only one at the fortress who can intrude on your minds. Sir George says it's because I was closest to the dragon's head when she…'

Finn thought quickly while Patrick began talking – like he actually believed it – about some strange legend that would fit right in with the Flybynight computer game he played, but not here in the real world. Tula's hand crept over to hold her brother's. Finn felt shocked at how icy she was.

Scarcely had the thought entered his head than he saw Tula shift closer to the car door. She placed her other hand against it, and her fingers twitched. She didn't have to sign anything to him – he already knew what she was doing. Inside that door the locking mechanism was clicking softly open. Finn squeezed Tula's hand hard, ready and waiting. Then, as Patrick braked to a crawl, coming up to a set of traffic lights at Temple Meads station, Tula signed: *MOVE!*

ᖇ=ᑭᕴ ᎾᑲᖸᐱᐱᑯᕼᣲᎾᎾ ᕹᣲᎾᕱ=ᖸ. ᎢᎢᖸᣲ=ᒪᒪ ᎢᎢᖸᣲ=ᒪᒪ

The car door shot open and both children barrelled out at the speed of light, dodging taxis, bikes and buses, with the outraged shouts of Patrick fading behind them.

3

‡ΑΓ≡≡

Fifteen minutes later, just as the Exchange clock clicked round to 6pm, two ragged shadows hurried from Temple Meads station up out of the city towards Princes Lane. Despite the absence of moonlight and the pockets of darkness, the children moved with a surefooted certainty, closer and closer to home. They agreed they needed to get this 'letter opener', no matter what it opened, before anyone else, and they'd sneak in through the back door, hidden several streets beneath their actual house.

Over to the left of their hurrying feet, the cliff plunged to a busy road thirty metres below, the usual rush of cars loud at this time of night. Beside it, the River Avon flowed powerfully towards the sea, and just ahead, nearly a hundred metres above the river, slung the familiar arches of Clifton Bridge. Its elegant curves shimmered with hundreds of lights that usually delighted Finn, but this evening the shadows

⅃ ⅃Δ∨ΘႶ Θ∨ΓΘ⅃≡Ⴖ ロ∨‡ ‡ロᖦᴧΓႶႶ ჩᰥ∆ᒄ. ˙8‡ᖦ⅄ ‡∆ᑲ𐊕,

seemed too long, and a stench of sewage made him feel sick.

He was the first to reach a small door with a dramatic tableau carved into its surface, thickly painted in glossy blue. It was wedged into the clifftop along the high cobbled road to the bridge, scarcely noticeable. Above it was the back of an old, sprawling hotel, and, beyond that, townhouses stretched all the way along the road to the bridge. Though lights were on in many windows, no one was about.

Tula nodded, and Finn leaned into the door, listening. A few seconds later, he quirked an eyebrow at his sister, placing two fingers on the head and heart of a huge leaping creature in the carving. She stepped forward, resting her hand over the ancient keyhole. The wood around it was scarred and gouged, as if a hundred beasts had sought entry there, but under the lightest touch from Tula's fingertips the mechanism behind it clicked and groaned. When she turned the heavy iron handle, the door opened, slow and silent.

Despite Finn's restraining hold on her shoulder, she stepped, unhesitating, into the pitch black beyond, and Finn followed quickly after. Only when Tula had closed and locked the door behind them did Finn dare to speak out loud.

'What is that *stink*?'

ᐅ═□ᒐӨ≡. ㆍ'ᐱᒼ ᐁᐣ᠘ᙘӨӨ.'

Both children lifted their noses and sniffed the air.

'Probably Mrs Juggernaut's drains,' decided Finn. 'Again. Dad is going to have to fix that situation the second he gets back. It's disgusting.'

Finn and Tula had no trouble seeing every nook and cranny of the underground room in the inky blackness. Three niches had been hollowed out of the craggy rock walls. They were about half a metre tall, quite narrow, and a carved stone figure stood in each.

The niche to the left of them held a young Chinese woman wearing an old-fashioned kimono. She had a beseeching expression on her face and one of her hands was slightly outstretched, as if asking for something.

The figure to the right was that of a young man. It was difficult to make out his face, obscured as it was by a knight's helmet that reached down his nose. His posture was that of a person coiled for action, as if about to jump into battle. He wore chain mail, and his left arm held a decorated shield.

Finn and Tula ignored both of these and walked straight over to the stone dragon in the niche ahead.

'This place always gives me the creeps,' muttered Finn. 'Why can't we just go through the front door like normal people? Maybe we should have jumped on a train and—'

ᑲ=ᑎᒥᎾ= Ꮛᛏᑎᑭᑭ=ᑫ ᙎᎧ ᑫᏰᎾ ᛏᚱ⅄ᑲᏒᎾ, ᛏᑫ=Ꭷ ᑫᒥᑎᑭᑭ=ᑫ ᛏᑎ ᑫᏰᎾ

Finn, admonished his sister. *We've got to get that key thing before anyone else does.* She gestured towards the dragon.

It was sitting back on its hind legs but reaching forward with the clawed foot of its right foreleg, talons fully extended. Its mouth was slightly agape, showing curved fangs and a long tongue that seemed ready to lick its lips and speak. Narrowed eyes were masterfully carved, and they appeared to watch every movement with keen interest.

As ever, Finn took a moment to catch his breath – he'd once run into an outstretched claw and still bore the scar on his chest, a small black circle just below his collarbone – but Tula strode fearlessly forward and clasped the taloned paw, the fingers of her right hand alternating with each claw of the fearsome beast. She had the same dark scar from a similar accident, but their dad had still refused to remove the dangerous statue.

Come on, she signed to Finn. *Unless your hands hurt?* She looked at Finn's fingers with suspicion. *Was it painful, what you did back in the alley? Did Dad teach you to—*

'NO! That's never happened before and it's never going to happen again. I don't want to talk about it. Probably another reason why Dad kept us locked away, because I'm weird and ugly and danger—'

ᖆᐤ᙭ᙰᕁ. 'ᖠᐊᐳᔓᏔ᙭'

Tula whirled round. *Stop it, Finn.* They stared into each other's faces, hearts thudding at seeing how afraid the other was. *It's the same as my icy magnet hands*, signed Tula, *but the opposite. Don't worry about it.*

Finn swallowed and made himself smile at her. 'I wish Dad had explained how…' He trailed off.

Tula bit her lip, her eyes wide with anxiety.

'Forget it,' said Finn. 'Plenty of time for that once we've found him. Let's hunt for this letter-opener key and get some sleep. Then we'll leave tomorrow with a better plan.'

He stepped towards the dragon reluctantly, and Tula reached for the claw again. It always seemed to Finn that the statues were on the brink of springing to life, this dragon in particular, ready to tear him to pieces. Gritting his teeth, he helped Tula turn the statue, she pushing one way on its claw, and he pulling hard on its tail. A grating sound echoed into the small room and a part of the rock to the left slid open. It was just wide enough to slip through, though Finn caught his ankle as he squeezed past to the other side.

'Ow!' he muttered, pulling up the leg of his jeans to examine the damage, but it was already healing fast. In five seconds not a trace remained of the painful graze and his golden blood. He'd got better at healing

ᒐ○□ᛏᕕ≡ᒃ ᐊᐁᐯ○ᕕ. 'ᒐ≡ᕲ. ᙖᛏᐊᒉ ᛏᐊᕝᖆ.'

himself as he'd got older, but Tula had always been faster than him.

You okay?

'Yeah,' replied Finn. 'Remember the code?'

Mmm. Tula tapped seven digits into a keypad just inside the opening, and the gap in the wall closed behind them, leaving them in a dark, rocky tunnel that was too narrow for comfort, and so low in places that Finn would have to stoop more than he already did.

'Let's go,' he murmured, and they hurried along the tunnel. It wound uphill about five hundred metres or so, the ground beneath them rough and uneven, until at last it ended abruptly. Tula's face gleamed with sweat, Finn noticed, but when he reached for her hand she felt cold and shivery again, probably because that stench was much worse here. Her eyes were raised to a wooden trapdoor in the rocky ceiling just millimetres from her nose, but just as he was about to ask her why they weren't going straight into the vast room above, she lifted a finger to her lips.

Shhh.

There. A voice raised in anger, the sound coming from the room above them. Both stood, listening, and when Finn realised who was speaking the taste of flint flooded his mouth again.

4
FOUR

he voice barked another question: 'What are you searching for?'

'It's Patrick,' whispered Finn, 'the man from the car… How did he know where we live?'

'Why are you here?' came Patrick's voice again.

Who is he talking to? signed Tula.

There was a noise upstairs like breaking glass, and a shrill shriek that made both Finn and Tula jump. They stared at each other in bewilderment as a far-off tearing noise echoed through the rock.

What was tha—? Tula was staring up at the trapdoor.

Before she'd even finished signing, that sewage stink flooded the air, a hundred times worse than before. The sound of running footsteps – those of hard, huge, heavy feet – pounded the floors above them, followed by an exclamation from Patrick, and in that moment his voice filled their heads:

Okay, you little miscreants. You got me into this –

ᑫᗑᒋᏔᎬ ᖴᏉᏔᏔ�ᑫ ᗅᎦᏔ ᗰᎦᎠᏞᏞ Ꭲᗑ ᗅᎦᏔ ᕼᗅᏔᎦᎢ. 'ᏞᗑᏉ ᕼᗅᎠᗑᗑᏔᎬ

you'd better get me out. I need you to help defeat this horde of Venomous.

'What?' whispered Finn, his forehead creased in a frown. 'How did he know we were—?'

We should stay here, signed Tula to Finn. 'Venomous' – she did quote marks in the air with her fingers – *does not sound good! We're safe in here – we're all Dad has. If we don't get to him—*

Come on! came Patrick's voice in their heads again. *COME ON!*

The pounding footsteps had slowed to an uncertain shuffle and tramp, but noises of clanking metal and what sounded like blades being pulled from sheaths were clearly audible.

'Venomous are made-up monsters from Flybynight Warrior,' whispered Finn. 'They're not *real*…'

An unexpected silence settled, as if every creature above was filling its lungs in a slow measure of what was to come.

And then all hell broke loose.

The roar of fifty voices shook the building, along with the sound of more unsheathing blades and stampeding feet. They could barely hear Patrick's yell, but somehow they could feel it in their heads, and it sent a surge of adrenalin coursing through their veins.

'TULA! We *must!*' cried Finn.

ᖚᐤᓱᑌᕬᐟ ᖚᐤ ᐡᐊᐧ ᐡᐤᐁᕐ ≡ᎾᎾᕲ ᐡᐤᐁ ᐊᐟᐁᖚᐟ Ꮎᖚᐤᕒ − Ꮎᖚᐤᕒ

Tula gritted her teeth, already thrusting her hands towards the trapdoor. She blasted it open with air from her hands in one spectacular explosion, and the carpet that had covered it in the room above flew back with such force that four of the creatures attacking Patrick were thrown hard against the wall.

Finn, emerging from the trapdoor with a determined bound, stopped abruptly.

'What…' he gasped, struggling to breathe air so thick with stench. This was not Mrs Juggernaut's drains at all. He gagged.

Before him, in the cavernous space of their living room, stood a horde of massive greasy monsters, hissing at him and Tula, assessing their next move. They wielded axes, clubs and broken glass bottles.

The stink of them pulsed from mottled and broken maggot-white skin. They looked as if they'd once been the biggest of men who'd been submerged in boiling oil until they'd half melted and swollen to gigantic proportions. Livid tattoos and patterned scars the colour of oily blood writhed from the top of their hairless heads to their gnarled ankles. Most were naked from the waist up. Trousers made of leather strained over their enormous legs, and many wore no shoes, their feet too wide and hairy and big to fit into any human kind of footwear.

ᎤᏂᏴ – ᎢᎯ≡ ᏒᎮᏣᎤᎯᎢᎾ ᎠᎢᎧ≡ ᏒᎤᎥᎤᎦ ᎴᏂᏴ. ᎴᎤᏴ ᏒᎤᎤᏴ ᎢᎯ≡Ꮄ

Venomous was a good word to describe these monsters: evil rolled from them in such strong waves that Finn and Tula could almost feel it poisoning the air, slithering over their skin. Their mouths, wide and lipless, resembled those of a cobra, with tongue and fangs to match. Their goat-like eyes bulged either side of nostril slits. The irises were blood red, exactly like those of the thugs in the alley, and seemed to move and flicker like flames.

Just like in the game, signed Tula, and Finn nodded.

One of them barked an order, and their clawed toes scratched against the floor as they shuffled slowly closer, heaving their breath in and out as if they'd climbed the gorge to this point in a matter of minutes. And they probably had.

The four Venomous thrown back by the carpet began picking themselves up, dazed and disorientated.

'Behind you!' yelled Patrick, whirling to face the monsters. He was now wearing enormous gloves with claws, the kind you'd buy in a dress-up shop for Halloween. The surface of them gleamed with black scales and at the end of each finger curved a ten-centimetre talon that looked able to slice through solid steel.

Finn and Tula stared in horror at the writhing mass of monsters swarming in through the windows.

Ꮲᐱ∨≡ ᑫᐅᐱ∠≡ ᖵᐁ ᎾᏢᏋᎥᏔ ⅄ᐁ∨ᖵ ᖾᏆᎾᎾᑫ. Q̄∨ᵻᑫᏝᏒᏞ ᎾᏋᵻ≡Ꮣ, ᏓᏒᵻ≡Ꮱ'

'I said *behind you*!' shouted Patrick again, and the siblings spun to find themselves face to face with an eight-foot Venom, with two more at its shoulders.

Finn was only dimly aware of Tula's lightning-fast signing – *Finn! Finn! Use that light from before! Now! Now!* He was already dropping into a crouch, his fingers angled upwards and, in an instant, white-hot beams shot in a torrent from his hands. But the creature coming straight for him merely raised its forearm in a cry of rage as the light licked its eyeballs.

'*Tula*,' yelled Finn as the Venom roared again, thudding another step closer, the two behind him already barrelling forward, their mouths open in a frightening hiss, tongues flicking and fangs dripping poison.

Patrick was a blur of movement, holding off the monsters, whirling, weaving, whirling again, as his clawed hands slashed with mesmerising precision. Every movement drew screams of pain and gouts of thick black blood that stank of burnt meat and sewage. Venomous thudded to the ground around him, but there seemed no end to their onslaught.

Finn's body shook with the effort of blasting the strange light from his hands. The shouts and yells and guttural grunts, along with the clash of steel against steel as Patrick battled his assailants, crowded out any sensible thought. He felt fear pull his heart into a

ᠣᒥᘥᕊ ᑊᘥᕊᑖᕊ ᒣ ᐴᕊᑯ ᑖᐷᢢᘂ ᒥᔑᕐᕐᕊ ᒣ ᒣᐱᘂᐴ ᕀᕕ ᑫᐴᐴᕊ᠈

tight knot, but breathed it away with shallow panting, gritting his teeth against the shakes that wracked his frame. He had nothing left.

Your turn, he signed to his sister in desperation. Tula was already drawing a painful, ragged breath. With her eyes narrowed and focused, she exhaled, long and slow, out into the room, crackling the air with a freezing cold. Instantly, every creature around them was frozen in place, unable to move – unable, even, to blink. All sound was silenced, all motion stopped. A thin frosting of ice dusted every surface.

Finn fell to his knees, sagging with a relief so intense it made him feel sick. 'Whoa,' he moaned. 'That was close.'

Close? CLOSE? Tula whirled on him, her eyes flashing, fingers flicking. *We should never have come up here, Finn! Dad needs us!*

'Patrick would have been a total goner if we hadn't helped!' said Finn, outraged.

That bumbrain can look after himself! signed Tula, her fingers making snapping sounds with the anger and the speed of her response.

'I dunno,' said Finn, getting up slowly. He walked over to where Patrick crouched, motionless, just centimetres from the lethal blade of the biggest Venom of them all. 'You saved his life.' He looked back at Tula.

†⌐ꝫⱣⱫꝫꝎ ꝫⱣ†⌷ †Ꝓ☰ ꝏꝫⱣꝒ Ᵽᴙⱶ ꝫⱣ ⅄ Ᵽᴦ☰⅄† ⱶ⌷∀◁.

'This monster over here was half a second away from lopping off his head.'

Tula did not reply, just stared, astonished, at Patrick.

His heart in his mouth, Finn turned back to look at the Irishman.

'You have got to be kidding me,' he breathed.

Ice was prickling and cracking in tiny fragments that fell to the floor with a chiming sound as Patrick began to move. He eased his limbs slowly until he was standing. Flexing his hands, he coughed and suddenly the glove claws were gone, seeming to melt back into his human skin. He sighed, as if with relief, and put his hands on his hips.

'You broke Tula's ice,' murmured Finn. His eyes skittered around the room, but all the Venomous were still frozen solid.

'I always break the ice,' said Patrick with an ironic quirk of his eyebrow, 'and actually,' he added, 'I was perfectly fine.'

Finn shot a look at Tula, and her *yeah, right* expression made him want to laugh.

'Huh.' Patrick stepped forward and flicked Finn's ear with his forefinger. He looked around him and swore. 'Any of you see a guy in a suit with an ugly ring on his left hand?'

ᑰᑎ₠ᒥ ᑯᑍ ᒣᕁᐞᒣᒧ ᑊᶘᏪᏪᵕᑫ ᏪᵕᑎᒥᏪᵕ. 'ᒣᕁᐞᐞ ᑊᐞ Ꮺᵕᵕ ᐞᑎᐱᒥ

'Noo…' said Finn slowly. 'Are you talking about the man called Craven from the alley?'

Tân bobbed up and down, and Tula glanced at him sharply. *Tân says he left with one of the monsters,* she signed as Tân whisked back into her pocket.

'A Venom.' Patrick sighed. 'I *am* a bumbrain.'

He reached for Tula's shoulder, looking into her eyes. 'You ready to come with me this time, missy?' It seemed he got no answer, because he added, 'It's going to carry on like this, you know, just like Tân said: Venomous everywhere you turn, rising up out of the gutters to fight you, never stopping till they've got your precious blood, got what's in your bag.'

Finn tasted the truth in his words – hot orange juice again – and when he looked at Tula he found she was waiting for his reaction. He signed, *Oranges,* and she nodded.

'I didn't think the Venomous were real,' said Finn to Patrick.

Patrick looked confused. 'But that's why your dad kept you hidden away in here. They're very real, and someone betrayed your family. Now it's time to stop hiding. Ready?'

Finn squared his shoulders, cleared his throat and asked, 'Telling Stone, should we go with this man?'

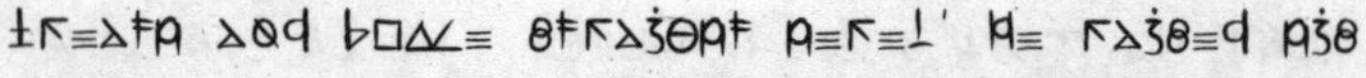

ᒪᕑ≡ᐱᵻᗄ ᐱᕀᑫ ᖲ�口◿≡ ᗕᕀᕑᐱᔓᎾᗅᕀ ᗭ≡ᕑ≞ᒪᐟ ᕼ≡ ᕑᐱᔓᗷ≡ᑫ ᗭᔓᗷ

A sigh came from the bag he carried on his back, and then the sound of someone clearing her throat. A reluctant smile crept across Patrick's face as a low musical voice replied: 'I'm afraid so, Finn and Tula. Only through him can you stretch your wings and fly.'

5

ᒦᐧ᠎ᐁᐧᐱ᠎ᐩᐁᐧᐱᐁᐧᐱ≡

'Okay,' said Finn to Patrick. 'We're ready. Let's get the opener and go find our dad.'

'Yes,' said Patrick, but he stood still in the middle of their house, looking at everything with a clenched jaw – and Finn followed his gaze, seeing their home through a stranger's eyes.

It was a space five storeys high with no stairs, just steel girders, thick ropes, titanium wires and iron pegs in the walls. It had swings, chains and moving platforms, and suspended cabins hung high in the air. Irregular panes of glass were set top to bottom, left to right all across the front wall to make up an immense cathedral-like window. One of them had been smashed by the Venomous, and the shards on the floor glinted in the light from the bulbs of Clifton Suspension Bridge. From the other side, the facets of glass looked like the rock faces of the River Avon's gorge. They could see out, but no one else could see in.

Finn didn't like Patrick's disapproving expression.

'Dad made space in here to run and jump and climb,' he said to the Irishman, 'because we don't go outside.'

Patrick sighed and Finn tasted the cloying taste of rosewater in his mouth.

Pity.

Finn frowned. 'We like it. It's home to us.' And immediately the taste of rust at his lie was so strong that he walked over to the kitchen area and poured a glass of water. He drank without stopping. Patrick had turned away and was making a call with a minuscule device, which had appeared from behind his ear as if by magic.

'Move in, aviators,' he said. 'We got fifteen down.'

Finn's eyes widened as, with another sound of breaking glass, twelve black-clothed figures dropped in through the upper windows of the building, whirling and vaulting their way across the beams as if they'd lived here all their lives. They carried with them an assortment of ropes that whipped and cracked with a sparking electric light. With each expert flick of the wrist, the ropes lassoed the monsters and reduced them to the size of hairless guinea pigs. They were bundled into a large sack that one of the figures carried effortlessly over her shoulder, and Finn wondered what would happen to them.

⊢�`==◻=θ ʒꝺ ⊢ꝯ= ⊢`==θ. ⱱꝺꝒ θʒθꝒ⊢ λʒᚱ θ==Ꝓ=ꝺ ⊢◻ᐁλᚱꝺθ

'They get sent back beneath,' said Patrick as all but one of the aviators – the one with the sack – disappeared just as swiftly as they'd come. Finn blinked and could see no sign of a broken window.

'Beneath?' whispered Finn. 'This is crazy.'

It's like we're trapped in that weird game of yours, Finn, signed Tula. *Monsters, aviators, whizzy whips…*

'Game?' asked Patrick.

'Flybynight Warrior,' croaked Finn, staring at the aviator with the sack of Venomous. Tula wasn't wrong. His favourite fighter in the game, Angelina, looked exactly like the woman standing in black ninja clothing near Patrick. She'd pushed her hood back and stood tall and strong, with long brown hair, big brown eyes and a look of simmering intensity that hinted at a terrible temper. She held the heavy sack with ease, and was twirling a whip around like she wanted to shrink Patrick too.

'Hey,' she said to Finn and Tula. 'You guys all right?' She sounded American.

Finn nodded and Tula crept closer to him, keeping her distance from the aviator.

'There's nothing in here that can burn,' murmured Patrick, touching the huge leather sofa facing the glass wall. 'The entire building is built to maximum-security, dragon-lair specifications. It has undetectable

Ꭿᏸᐟ, ᐁᎥᑫ Ꭷ≡ ᎾᏔ≡Ꮲᵻ ᎯᏸᎾ ᎾᵻᏗᏔᏗ ᐊᏂᎲᎾ≡ Ꭿᏸᐟ, ᏢᏔᎲᏸᎾ ᵻᎯ≡

technologies and every millimetre of it is firewalled – in every sense of the word – inside and out.' He turned slowly, still looking around him and thinking. 'Hmm… This game of yours,' he said, turning back to Finn and Tula. 'Does it also have dragons and firebloods and people that—?'

Finn nodded. 'It's great. There's even a character called Aria, like my mum, who has a cool water dragon sidekick who's supposed to be dead but has this massive hoard of gold that she still guards.' He swallowed. 'There's a fighter called Angelina who…'

Who looks a lot like you, signed Tula to the aviator woman, who frowned and ignored her as if she hadn't noticed that Tula had said anything at all.

'Patrick!' she said. 'We gotta go. Let's take Augustus's kids and move out right now.'

'I'll show you another time,' said Finn. 'Dad won't mind. He says it's actually his favourite story.'

Tula nodded. *The story about how Saint George wasn't slaying dragons – he was protecting them, because—*

'Dragons guarded us from the Underworld,' interrupted Finn, babbling with nerves, 'by keeping the forces that turn us round the sun perfectly balanced. They could blast fire with fire, forcing volcanoes to subside, earthquakes to settle, tectonic

⌐ϡᎧᑫ ⊦ᕂϡᎦ ⌐ᕐ⅄ ⅄Ꭷᑫ ⊦ᕂ⅄⊦ ∨Ꭷⵚϡᒾ ⊦ᕂ≡ Ꭶ⅄∠Ꭷᴿ≡ ⌐ᕐ⅄Ꭷ ᎦᎮᎧ≡.

plates to stay still… It's a great game. We've got the book too.'

'Game?' The woman hefted the sack of Venomous to her other shoulder. 'Book?' Her expression was hard to interpret, but it wasn't happy. 'Patrick, the Venomous are gonna get all big and smelly any minute now, and George is in a hurry for these kids to open the watchtower.'

'Angelina!' Patrick laughed. 'Are you listening to these two? Augustus didn't forget us! He built a game – with you in it, and George in it, and Oriel!'

Angelina frowned. 'Oriel?'

'The last dragon,' whispered Finn. He stared at Angelina.

She stared back at him. 'Yes, boy,' she snapped. 'Yes, I really am Angelina Tempest, and, no, you can't have an autograph. I'm working.'

Tula looked astonished and Finn swallowed convulsively, starting and stopping questions and finally stammering, 'S-S-Saint G-George—?'

'Yes!' snapped Angelina, her perfect brow deeply furrowed. 'Real person! Like me!'

'I don't understand,' blurted Finn.

'*Ugh*,' growled Angelina. 'George is actually the actual factual Saint George who is the famous dragon-slayer but truly, properly, a secret dragon-keeper. He's *a real person.* He'll give you an autograph any time.' She turned to Patrick. 'Augustus didn't tell them anything?'

'We should focus on getting to Augustus,' said Patrick, a reassuring smile pasted to his face. 'Come on, guys, let's—'

Finn waved his hands around in the universal sign of *just hang on a sweet second!* and blurted, 'St G-George is alive? But … but *the dragon legends are from two thousand years ago!*'

Patrick frowned. 'Yes, of course yes.'

Tula's jaw was literally dropped in open-mouthed shock, and Finn would have laughed at her if his mind hadn't been so thoroughly blown.

Angelina adjusted her grip on the sack, and threw Patrick an astonished look. 'Augustus didn't teach them *anything*?' she repeated.

'They know nothing of the firebloods,' said Patrick. He looked across at Finn and Tula, his smile fading. 'Nothing of George or any of us…'

'Oh boy,' said Angelina, and she whirled round, examining the children's home with lightning-fast glances before pointing at a plug socket next to the door that had exploded recently. Scorch marks blackened the wall all around it and stretched three metres high.

⸸∨⸸ ⸀ᴨ≡ ⥥⸠∧⸵ᴑꟼ⸵өⴱ ⎰⸝⥥⸝≡ө ꟼ⥥⸝ ∧⸵өꟼᴨ≡ꟼ.

'No control yet,' she said, sounding upset, and Patrick frowned at her.

'What's going on?' asked Finn. Tula had taken his hand and was holding it tightly.

There was a silence while Angelina and Patrick looked at each other, not saying anything but somehow communicating because at last Patrick sighed and said, 'The thing is … your Flybynight Warrior … it's not just a game – it's a history, and … a reality.' He stared intently at Finn, waiting.

Finn tasted hot orange juice, and his eyes grew wide with astonishment.

What? signed Tula to her brother.

He's telling the truth!

'Of course I'm telling the truth,' scoffed Patrick. 'You two are firebloods. You're not safe here. You need to come with us.'

Tula's fingers signed it out slowly: *Fire … blood?*

Finn clenched his jaw so hard his teeth hurt. 'In the game, firebloods are the knights who got splashed with the last of the blood from the dragon that Saint George was trying to protect. They, and their descendants, all inherited different combinations and strengths of the dragon's powers: being able to fly, shoot fire from their hands, never get burned … and a few other things.'

ᑯᓚ ᘐᘯ Ꮎᆖᆖ ᖴᗑᆖᐞ, ᑫᆖᘯᖇᎾᆖᕐ ᐞᔅᖇᆖᑫ ᐅᖇᔕᆖᓚ.

Finn and Tula stared at each other. *The light from your hands*, signed Tula. *Is that a fiery dragon thing?*

'What? No...' Finn held his fingers up and stared at them. 'It's a ... weirdness thing, like my hunch. Something I was born with that's ... that's not ... normal. In Flybynight Warrior the firebloods throw fireballs. They don't have weird shiny fingers.' He swallowed and looked at Patrick with a question in his eyes.

Is Finn a fireblood? signed Tula.

'Yes, and you are too, Tula,' said Patrick. 'He's probably from the fire house of Kellan, but you're likely to be the house of Brann, with your control of air. Your mother commanded the Vulkan house of earth—'

'Stop!' shouted Finn. 'Just stop! None of this makes any sense! This fireblood stuff is all just a story, a game!'

Patrick shot out an accusatory arm at the plug socket near the door. 'Who did that?'

Finn, signed Tula at the same time as Finn said, 'No one!'

Patrick pointed at him. 'You have the fireblood gift of fire, from Kellan.'

'I don't like fire!' yelled Finn.

He's very scared of fire, agreed Tula.

Finn was making wild gestures of denial. 'I never... We're not—'

ᗩᗴᑎᔑ ᔑᗝ ᐃᒪᓍ ᑫᓳᔑᖱ' ᖢᓳᑭᒍᔑᖱ ᗷᓳᗝᖋᗲᓍ. ᗯᓵᓳᐁᓵ ᖋᐁᗝ ᗝᐁᖴ

'Flints.' Patrick took a step forward, and the children took a step back. 'I appreciate this is a lot to take in, but you can't argue with the facts: Tula has scrying skills, yes? Sensing where your dad might be? The house of Brann will invite her to develop that talent – it's hard to get right. Finn, you blast things. That's a fireblood skill. You both have golden blood, you don't ever get burned, you smell things better than any human, you can see in the dark: these are fireblood powers that we all have in various strengths. Electrical things near you explode when you lose your temper... Your fingers light up – that's gotta be a kinda fire, right? – and your sister *breathes ice*. Not normal in the world of frailskins. In, you know, the nicest possible way. Okay?'

'Frailskins are people who have no fireblood,' added Angelina.

Finn and Tula stood still, unable to speak. *All this time*, thought Finn, *we were hiding this stuff from Dad. And he's so obsessed with his work that he never noticed ... never worked it out for himself.*

Patrick's jaw clenched. 'And if you'd talked about this with Augustus, perhaps he'd have explained things to you, maybe shown you a thing or two about the powers we have: creating fire, healing, flying—'

'Seeing in the dark, not getting burnt...?' whispered Finn.

⊓ᚑ ⴾᔓ△∠≡. ⴽᕼ≡ᚺˈᚱ≡ ᕆ≡ᚷᚱ⅃ᚴ ᕼ≡ᚱ≡.'

Patrick nodded. 'Exactly. And that's not all. There are rarer things that only a few firebloods can do, like reading minds or the scrying or creating fidgets or whispers.'

'Like your Aunt Myra,' interrupted Angelina, 'who should never, ever be trusted.' She threw a meaningful look at Patrick, who shook his head.

What? signed Tula.

'Ignore her,' said Patrick. 'She's just jealous. Myra can create a fidget, an enchanted creature that can find information and bring it back, or a whisper that can carry a message far and wide.'

'Lies, more like,' snapped Angelina.

Patrick rolled his eyes and continued. 'You'll learn about the houses, like Siarad too, who are the strongest, and about the singing...' He sighed. 'Can't believe your dad didn't explain. Families. Unbelievable. That's why I'm so attractively single.' He turned his head and winked at Angelina. She rolled her eyes at him, and was about to speak, but he continued, saying, 'It is a lot to take in, and there's no time to explain more because there's a bit of peril going on. That power the dragons had to stop the Earth falling apart? The most important one of all? Your father is the only one who has it.'

Angelina turned her gaze to the children. Tân

‡ꔹ≡ꔵ ⊢◻◿∠≡ ꖎꔵ,' ꖟ◿ꖴꖴ ꕒꕤ≡◺.

whisked inside Tula's shirt, leaving only the tip of his nose and a curious eye blinking out from behind her collar. 'And your dad is the only one that Telling Stone in your rucksack will trust.'

The musical voice from the backpack suddenly spoke again. 'I'm glad I haven't been forgotten in the mists of time, Angelina, thank you. Information: the Clifton Bridge tunnels are closing in five minutes, and those Venomous are waking.'

Angelina bowed. 'Thank you, milady.' The sack she was holding suddenly bulged. 'Okay. Gotta go.' She fixed the children with a clear-eyed stare and leaned closer, speaking in a quiet voice, 'Do whatever Patrick says – he's one of the original knights, your father's best friend and the bravest fireblood I know: one of the last of the immortals.' Tula nodded straight away – which surprised Finn – and Angelina smiled, which changed her face from Scary Warrior Queen to something else that made Finn feel more courageous somehow. 'Don't tell him I said that. See you at the fortress.'

She was gone before they could say goodbye.

6

8ϧ⋊

With a deep bow in Finn's direction, Patrick said, 'Milady,' in respectful tones, which made Finn frown.

He's talking to the Stone, bumbrain, signed Tula, *not you*, and Finn pulled a face at her.

Patrick coughed and stood straight again. 'Milady,' he said, 'is there any equaliser hydrant in this house?'

There was a resounding silence from the bag.

'It would be nice,' said Patrick tightly, 'really quite lovely, milady, if you could let bygones be bygones. I made a mistake. Are you going to make me pay for it forever?' More silence. He sighed and gestured to the children. 'C'mon. Show me your father's office.'

What mistake did you make? asked Tula, pointing out their dad's study on a mezzanine level above, *and what exactly is this equaliser hydrant?*

'In the game, equaliser hydrant is the stuff the

ϼ≡◻⌈⊖≡ ⊽⊿∖ꓤ≡ᑯ ⊖�≡⊿ᑯϧ⅃⋏ ϧ⊖ᖪ◻ ꓕϥ≡ ϼ⋏⋏≡. ꓕϥ≡ ⊽⊿ꓤ⊿

alchemist has to throw down volcanoes or into tsunamis or over earthquakes to calm everything down,' explained Finn. 'Fighting fire with liquid fire.'

'Exactly,' said Patrick. 'Your dad is not just some egghead geology professor – he's the reason this planet hasn't disintegrated into a gazillion lava flows and broken bits. When we ran out of Oriel's blood to control the Earth's forces, *he* came up with a potion to use instead.'

The equaliser hydrant, signed Tula.

'Yep.' Patrick's expression was deadly serious. 'It's probably in the watchtower back at the fortress – the opener will unlock the door. We need it desperately. It does what you said, and then some. Just a few drops of it into a volcano?' He made a spreading gesture with his hands. 'Mellows the whole mess out – no one dying, no disasters, happy planet – but without your dad to make more of it for us, or to tell us exactly where he left the last bottle, and without the precious Stone to tell us the answers we seek, we're all in a world of trouble because the Venomous are rising up, wanting the chaos of their underworld to take over up here.'

'Oh, now he calls me precious!' came a grumble from the bag.

Patrick frowned. 'She's got into a bad habit since the Last Battle of not giving us advice that could lead to our harm, which is ridiculous! Her job is *telling*,

ᎾᏐᏪᑱᎬᎾ ᎾᏐᏯᎤ ᎢᎡᎪᎢ ᏉᎾᏅᏊᏗ ᏒᏝᎢ ᎢᎡᎬ ᏴᏗᏛᎬᎡᎾ ᏊᏗᎾ ᎾᏐᎤᎬ.

thus *Telling Stone*, and it's up to us to decide what to do from there.'

'Such disrespect!' shrieked the Stone. 'If I could be assured your decisions would be the *right* ones, I'd certainly be doing telling, telling, telling. But you make stupid decisions all the time, don't you? *Especially* you, Saint Patrick of the Green Isle, with your unsuitable girlfriends and—'

'Okay, okay,' interrupted Patrick, his hands out in front of him as if warding off actual arrows. 'I—'

'And if you're not careful I'll never speak to you again!'

'The hydrant!' blurted Finn. 'It could actually be in Dad's office.' He pointed to a rope hanging down in the middle of the room. 'You can climb to it over there, or up the wall here with Tula and me.' He began scaling it quickly, his fingers and toes gripping the grooves between the cracks with ease, still talking to Tula over his shoulder. 'The hydrant is a secret recipe of different ingredients and the whole point of level five in Flybynight Warrior is working out what the ingredients are and how much you need of each one.'

At the top of the wall, Finn and Tula leaped on to a cable traversing the space, then walked a tightrope up to a mezzanine level with a steel door.

You got past level five? signed Tula while they waited

⅃Ш �⊟ ⅃�ⱱ⊓ⱱ Ꝗ θ== ⱱꝗⱱθ ꝲꝗ= θꝲ==θ � ꝲⱱ⎓ ꞇꝶⴋθAꝲ =⅄=θ

for Patrick. He was climbing the rope impressively fast for an adult. *You know what the ingredients are?*

Finn heaved out a shaky breath. 'No. Remember the time I got so cross I blew up the plug? The last day Dad was here?' Tula nodded. 'It happened because I was getting frustrated with the game. That other gamer who sends the messages—'

Flybynight Solo.

'Yes, him, he kept defeating me.'

You were behaving like a spoiled brat, signed Tula with some satisfaction. *All that shouting and yelling.*

'Dad said it was important that I worked it out for myself. He wouldn't do the ingredient list for me. He said—'

He said anger was dangerous, and you had to stop being so angry.

Finn bit his lip, watching Patrick swinging across to them. 'You think Dad saw what happened with the plug?'

Um, signed Tula, looking over at the huge scorch marks. *I'm kind of confused about how you could think he didn't?* She tugged his hand. *In the game the firebloods have wings!*

Finn put up his hand as if to stop her moving forward. 'They're born with them.'

Patrick landed with a thump.

ᎥᏲ ᖴᎪ᙮ ᖶᐞᎩ ᖶ᙮ᐞᏏᎩ᙮Ꮎ ᗡᖰ ᖶᎪ᙮ ᑫᐞᎩᏒ ᏏᎩ᙮ᐱᎥᏏᏏ᙮.

So we can't have them?

'Can't have what?' asked Patrick. He stopped short, staring up at their dad's office door. It was a three-metre-tall slab of solid steel, and a strange mirage of images seemed to flow across it – like a moving satellite picture from outer space. 'Wow. This is it? The famous Augustus's laboratory?'

Tula frowned at Finn – *famous Augustus?* – and pushed the door open. They all trooped inside. Patrick's jaw dropped. It felt as if they were stepping into an enormous inside-out globe. Walls stretched up, up, round and back down again, seething with a vast image of the Earth's surface. In the middle of the room was a round table with no legs. It was ancient and wooden and stained and scarred. Names had been carved along the outside of it – a bit like the graffiti you see on old school desks. On it was a scattering of personal things, including a letter opener that had a blunt blade for slicing envelopes neatly. Its golden handle was shaped to look something like the end of an enormous key, with grooves and holes and complicated patterns carved into it. Finn went straight to it and put it in the front pocket of the bag so it wouldn't scratch the Stone.

Patrick walked around slowly, staring at the walls. 'It must be, somehow, a satellite image,' he breathed.

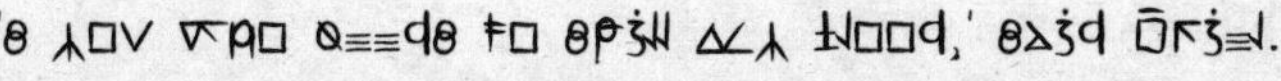

'Augustus, you genius… Look here, how it shows the clouds, ocean currents – oh, for snakes' sake, look at that – the detail! You can see the heat from the Iceland volcano. Must tell George, and…' He ran out of words, turning this way and that, amazed.

Tula watched him closely. *We're not usually allowed in here*, she signed.

'But you searched the place when you realised your dad wasn't coming back,' replied Patrick.

Finn nodded. 'The Telling Stone told us we'd need something of Dad's to find him.'

'Hmm,' said Patrick, distracted by a trail of smoke emerging from the sloping hill in Iceland. 'I wonder if the scryers have seen this activity from Hekla.'

'Why did the Venomous monsters come to our house?' asked Finn. 'Was it for the letter opener – the key?'

Patrick looked over to the children. 'This particular troop was hunting you and the Stone too, so you'd tell them where the hydrant is. That Craven guy has been after it for a long time. He's got some Venomous skills and a dangerously hypnotic whip that he got from who knows where, but he prefers life up here, wheeling and dealing. There's a lot of money in having the answers to everything.'

He came over to the table and stared at a huge

book on the desk, open at an image of a dragon's head, eyes wide and bright, seeming to stare directly into theirs.

'Oriel,' said Finn. 'She's in the beginning of the game, but she dies.'

Patrick began examining every millimetre of the table. 'She's the dragon I was talking about, the last one – Oriel. She trusted your ancestor 'Andrew' with the most precious of all her hoard of treasure, the Telling Stone that you carry in your bag. It caused a lot of trouble with David, but that's a story for another day.'

Finn exchanged a glance with Tula, and she gave a small nod. 'The Stone usually sits on the table,' he said. 'In the middle. We didn't realise that she spoke until Dad went missing and we found her on the kitchen counter.'

Patrick pulled a face. 'Over the centuries, the Stone has grown stronger and wiser than any scryer we've ever had, and your family has always cared for her. Like I said before, she only speaks when her words can save lives without endangering any at all, and even then she's choosy about who she chats to and what she says.' He glared at the rucksack on Finn's shoulders. 'Have you asked her where your father is?'

'⅃θ⎮≡≡ዖ.'

'That's what she said after Dad had gone. That's how we realised she talks.'

The Irishman's eyebrows flew up to his hairline, and his voice went high and squeaky. '*She said where he is?*'

'No,' replied Finn hastily. 'She said, "The Underworld has your father, but I don't know where he is. Don't bother asking."'

All the light went out of Patrick's face. 'Oh,' he said, an expression of fear visible for just a second.

Just that one word sent the taste of struck flint into Finn's mouth. It was strong enough to raise goosebumps across his skin. Tula was watching him carefully, so he smiled as best he could.

'And she also said to take something of his?' queried Patrick. 'Milady,' he said, addressing the rucksack. 'Would you care to explain?'

'No! Absolutely not,' came a voice from the bag, and Patrick sighed.

'Tula has his amulet,' said Finn, 'and I put on the bandanna Mum gave to him.' He waved his wrist to show a piece of cloth wound round his wrist. Patrick had resumed his fruitless search of the table. 'Maybe we should just get going,' Finn added, restless. 'Tula will be able to find Dad. She has a connection with him.'

'Υοv θθο∨dϼʌ∧≡ ŧℾο∨ፀϼŧ ϼ≡ℾ. 8ϼ≡ Ϸο∨dϼʌ∧≡ ϼ≡lϼ≡d.'

Patrick looked at Tula sharply. 'I thought you didn't know where he is either.'

The connection comes and goes.

'It's better than nothing. Shen will help to strengthen that connection.'

Who is Shen?

'Jingshen, actually. The fortress's oldest scryer. She's been by George's side since even before Oriel was killed.' Patrick grinned at Tula. 'Don't worry. You'll like her. She's sweet and gentle and always making sure we do the right thing. The Stone loves her. Don't you, milady?'

Finn felt warmth against his back from the bag and took a breath to ask another question, but Patrick had turned away and was pointing a finger at a mountain in Russia, with smoke drifting from its summit. 'Did Augustus ever say anything about Mount Elbrus?'

'That's where we were heading,' said Finn. 'Our Aunt Myra came to see us before he left. She was talking to him about Elbrus and wanting to send us away, as usual.'

Patrick had gone very still at the mention of Aunt Myra, so Tula explained.

Aunt Myra is…

'Our only living relative,' interrupted Finn hastily, throwing Tula a look. 'We didn't want to worry her with

ᚦᚯ≡ ⚼⟋∨ᚢᚻ∖≡ᚦ ⚼⌒ᚩᚨᚩ ᚦ≡▢ᚱᚦᚩ≡'ᚢ ᚵⱶⴸ ᛏᘔᚩᚹᛏ≡ᚩ≡ᚴ ⴸᚨᚴ

anything. She and Dad don't get on, but sometimes she looks after us when he has to go away...'

We wouldn't know how to get hold of her anyway, clarified Tula.

'Elbrus,' said Patrick, his smile growing big again. 'Fantastic. We're just going to do a quick detour so the experts can skill you up, source your weapons and find you a creature to keep you safe.'

Detour? signed Tula.

Finn frowned too. 'Then we'll go straight there and get Dad back.'

'Easy peasy,' agreed Patrick, and the Stone snorted rudely as Finn's mouth flooded with the taste of rust again.

7

8≡∧≡◊

They were nine hours into the 'quick detour'
when Finn next opened his eyes. Tula was
staring out of the car window at the pitch
darkness outside, and she had the rucksack on her
lap. Finn saw that her knuckles were white and her
jaw clenched as if she were grinding her teeth. Her
ratty black coat could not have been keeping her
warm, even though the car was toasty, because she
was shivering ever so slightly. Tân was tucked into her
neck, one of his tiny feet on her cheek.

'Tula?' murmured Finn. 'Are you okay?'

He noticed Patrick's eyes slide to him in the rear-
view mirror, but he said nothing, and neither did
Tula. Finn swallowed, his mouth feeling dry and furry
from the pizza all those hours ago, and he cleared
his throat. He pulled on Tula's hand, but she didn't
respond.

Tula? he tried again, this time just signing.

₹∨∆⌐≡٩. ׳∆ ⅄Ⱶ ⅄◻∨ ◊≡≡٩,' Ᵽ≡ ∆⌵Ⱶ∆⌵Ⱶ≡٩.

She blinked once, and Finn got the feeling that was the only response he was going to get. He didn't let go of her hand, though, just shifted a little to the left so he could see out of his window.

He saw they'd left the motorway and were travelling on a small road overhung with trees bent under the weight of thick snow. He had a sense of water nearby, and every now and again caught sight of a dancing reflection, but it was mostly dark.

'Where are we?' he asked.

'Far north of Scotland,' replied Patrick. 'Just looking for the parking near the shore. There it is.' He drove quietly on to a pristine white track, deep snow crunching under the wheels. Finn squeezed Tula's hand, but she just looked at him with huge, frightened eyes, as if she were seeing something far away that he couldn't.

Patrick parked the car deep in scrubby bushes, hidden behind trees, and shifted in his seat to look at them. 'We've got to be very quiet, okay? Very quiet. Old McKay won't be pleased if we make a disturbance. Tula?'

There was no response.

Patrick looked over at Finn. 'I don't want any running off, or any funny business. You must believe that we're here to help you. And that you can help us. If you want to.'

ᐧᐁᐟ, ᖠᐄᐧᐤ. ᑌᑕᐤ, ᒣᐡᖕᑕ ᠵᐟᐦ ᖠᑕᑕ ᐧᐊᐟᑕ.

The taste of orange was reassuring, but the flavour of rust tinged Finn's tongue also, and that told him there was something in what Patrick had just said that wasn't quite true.

We're here to help you. No, that seemed true enough.

You can help us. Yes, true.

If you want to. The taste. So, not true. Whatever it was that Patrick and his people wanted, Finn and Tula may not want to give it. His eyes slid to the bag, and he saw Tula hunch over it again.

The Telling Stone. Were they going to have to fight to keep the Stone?

Patrick rolled his eyes. 'Don't be daft, laddie! I don't want to open up any communications with that Stone, thank you very much.' He lowered his voice to a barely audible whisper. 'She was rude enough the last time she had an actual conversation with me. Made horrible allegations. Caused all sorts of unnecessary upset.'

Patrick got out, opened Tula's door and walked down to the shore. Finn realised when he tried to get out that the rear doors had been child-locked. They'd been trapped all along, just like before. He took a breath to still the choking thud of his heart, and slowly let go of Tula's hand. Climbing stiffly over

ᕐᐂ.' ᑫᐁᐅᕐᏇᗷ ᏸᑲᒐᐴᐟᏝᏇᐤ ᐃᐧᏋᏒ ᒪᐅᐧᑫᏝᏒᏋ ᐴᐊᑫ ᏒᐃᑲᏰᏋ Ꮭᐅ

his sister, he got out of the car, sinking up to his knees in snow, and pulled the door wider.

'Come on, Tula,' he whispered, and in the freezing moonlight he saw his breath fug out into a curling mist. *Maybe Patrick is taking us to a hotel. A hotel with a pub downstairs, with sausages and mash and bright green peas. Plus gravy.*

The thought of a square meal just minutes away made him start towards Tula. He pulled her gently from the car, taking the bag from her. She resisted, keeping it close, but Finn whispered, 'It's okay, Tu. I'll strap it on my front, all right? And you stay with me.'

She might have nodded – he wasn't sure – but she came reluctantly, keeping on his right side, moving slowly and jerkily through the snow as if in terrible pain.

Patrick glanced at her and frowned in a worried sort of way. He met Finn's gaze and they didn't need to say anything to voice their concern, not just for Tula, but for Augustus too.

'Hurry,' said Patrick, closing the car doors quietly and setting off down a gentle slope. The moon was high in the sky, but every now and again it was blotted out by clouds, plunging them into darkness. All around them was scrubby, scratchy green gorse, just visible through thick drifts of white powder. A freezing breeze drifted over to them, and Finn realised he could hear lapping waves and smell the dense cold of deep water and, at the same time, salt, and the tang of what had to be seaweed.

The children drew up to Patrick's side where he stood at the top of the small rise. Finn could see a rusty fishing boat tethered to a post driven into the shore.

'Come on, you two,' said Patrick, crunching over to the boat. 'Hop in. Will you take my jacket?' He took it off without waiting for an answer, and said, 'You need to make for Portaldor.'

'What's Portildoer?' asked Finn.

'*Portaldor* – it's that island over there.' He pointed into the distance, and Finn's eyes recalibrated to see a glimmering on rippled water.

'That's miles and *miles* away!' said Finn, startled.

'Nearly four hundred,' said Patrick, sounding very Irish through his smile. 'I'm glad you could spot it in the dark. You've got impressive fireblood sight, Finn Flint. Now, get a move on, will you? This is old McKay's boat and he'll need an explanation we don't have time for, if you get my drift?'

Finn looked more closely at the boat. Despite living on the banks of the Avon all their lives, they'd never messed about in its waters, never got in a boat.

ρšᑫ≡ ᐃΘᐃšᗺ. Ӈ≡'Λ≡ ᑫ◻ᗺ≡ š� ⊥≡Γ◻ᖀ≡.'

Besides which, this was the *ocean*. 'There are no oars,' noted Finn. He swallowed. 'Where are the oars?'

'Well, you're right there, lad. No oars. This is a fishing boat and I'm not sure the engine is up to much. If you had an invitation from the house of Siarad you could summon the sea creatures to help you, but… You should try a little fire power. I've got to get to the island right away to debrief George and rally the aviators. See you later.'

With that he tossed his coat into the boat and jumped into the air. In that instant two huge black wings sprang from his back with a sound of tearing cloth, and – *THWACK! THWACK!* – he was off.

Finn gaped. He whirled to face Tula, whose face remained expressionless, even her eyes appearing glazed now. 'Tula? Did you see that?' Twisting back, the gravel of the shore grating beneath his boots, he scanned the sky. There it was. Someone *flying*.

Never!

Despite knowing now that everything about firebloods was true, it still felt impossible to believe that a person could just jump from the ground and *fly*.

No way.

He rubbed his eyes, hard, and blinked at the silhouette winging across the sea. A gust of midnight

ᐱᐅᐁ ᗤᕼᖴ ᑭᗌᗤᐃ' Ꮎᐁᡲᖴ ᖴᖰᐁ �585ᖤ6ᐃ8᠐, ᒪᐁᖴ ᖰᐁᖴ ᐱᗤᡰᖯᐁ ᐁᐳᐁᎾ

air tossed cloud across the sky, and Patrick was lost from view.

'Wow...' said Finn slowly. 'Tula, I'm...'

Scared, he thought. But he didn't say it out loud. He didn't like how quiet his sister had got, and she still hadn't stopped shaking. He put his hands either side of the bag and asked, 'Milady,' as Patrick had done, 'please tell us where our father is.'

The bag vibrated with a long, slow sigh. 'He has shielded himself from us because he does not want you to go to him. It is too dangerous.'

'But you know he is in Mount Elbrus, right? You can tell us if he's okay?'

Tula was still staring into the darkness that had just swallowed Patrick. He could actually hear her teeth chattering. The Telling Stone was silent. Tula touched the bag, lightly, carefully, and took a step towards the boat.

'Okay, Tula,' said Finn. 'This is you deciding now, right? You can't blame me for this later.' He nudged her shoulder with the flat of his hand. 'Tulalula?'

She walked away from him, and got into the boat, settling calmly on Patrick's jacket.

'Fine,' sighed Finn. He took the bag off his shoulders, and held it out to Tula. 'You hang on to this and I'll get us going.'

⊕⊓ᒋᖇ ⅄⊕ᑫ ⦿⅄ᑫ. ⅃⧵◻⅄⩶. ◌̄⊕⩶ ᑲ⅄ᅡ ⅄⊕ᑫ ⅚ᅡ'⦿ ᑫ◻⊕⩶.'

Tula took a firm hold of the bag, despite her shaking, and Finn turned to the rope tied to the post. It was hard and icy, and his fingers fumbled this way and that, but at last it was loose. He pushed against the boat, and splashed and scrabbled on slippery shale beneath the seawater until it was floating free, and then he jumped in. He took a moment to catch his breath. Even though he was numb with cold, Finn could feel minuscule legs and minuscule wingbeats landing on his face and hands.

'Great, just great,' he said, eyes squeezed shut with irritation. 'Bugs.'

He opened his eyes to bat them away, but what he saw silenced him entirely.

'Whoa,' he breathed, completely mesmerised. He and Tula were surrounded by a cloud of flitting lights, dancing their short lives away around them. Fireflies. Hundreds of them. The longer he stared at them, the more the uncertain feeling within him faded.

Just then a shout from the trees onshore startled him into action.

'Hey! You there! What do you think you're doing!'

In a flurried whirl, Finn flung himself over the stern. Taking a deep breath, he plunged his fists underwater, flicking his fingers out hard. In an instant there was a small flash, as if something were igniting,

‡ค= ◻ld ⌂⊿ΔΘ dξd Θ◻ꟊ ꟊ=ꝑ\⅄. ꓤ= Ꝓ⊿∨=d Ꝓξ⊿∠Θ=lꝒ ◻Θꟊ◻

and then from his hands a torpedo blast of white light propelled them away from the shore like a rocket. Out of the corner of his eye, he saw Tula grab the tiller and trail a hand in the water, turning the boat sharply in the direction in which Patrick had flown. Finn wriggled his fingers and the boat leapt forward a little faster. Somehow all the buzzing energy of the flitting insects was giving Finn a restless power he'd only ever had after his dad's special chilli, and he was going to make the most of it while it lasted.

The voice shouted out again, but they were already fifty, sixty metres from the shore. Finn blinked water from his eyes. He could see a rotund figure leaping on the shale in a rage, shaking his fists and shouting.

The next sound in his ears was of another *whoosh* as he flexed his fingers into a steady torrent of bubbling heat that was fast motoring the boat across the water, like a shooting star across the sky.

8

ᗱᔑᏅᑎᎢ

Finn's finger power ran out just before they reached the island, leaving him feeling empty and exhausted. He thought he'd just close his eyes for a second, and rest… He was so tired. No way he could get them to the shore right now.

It was then that he heard it. A sort of a grumble sound from somewhere, and it seemed as if the ocean shifted beneath him in a tremoring swell.

'What was that?' whispered Finn, fear squeezing at his chest. 'Tula?' he asked. 'You okay?'

No reply.

He stared out at the water around them, filled with fresh urgency. His sister needed help. Small waves coasted them gently to the shore as adrenalin fizzed through his veins, sending his mind into overdrive.

Why didn't I ask Dad about how I blow things up, about how me and Tula never get burned, about how she can breathe out air so cold that it can freeze living things?

� decorative script line

He answered the question himself, straight away, tears pricking at his eyes.

Probably because we were afraid he'd do what Aunt Myra wanted: send us away to a school or a hospital to fix those things, along with my messed-up back and Tula's speech.

He reached round and felt the weight of the heavy hump that curved out from the bottom of his shoulder blades. The skin was tight and hot there, always, and got even hotter when he was angry or afraid or upset, like he was now.

Not his spine, Dad had said. He'd been injured in an accident when he was three and the scar tissue—

Well, look, at least Finn had survived, Dad would say. And then he'd always give him a too-tight hug, and then they'd wrestle, with Dad winning, even when Tula leapt in on Finn's side, and it would end in laughing and Dad making his spiciest dishes and Finn and Tula listening to funny stories from the world of Flybynight Warrior...

Dad.

So obsessed with his work that he never noticed that we never seem to get hurt? Never even saw that our blood is golden, not red, like the rest of the world's?

Impossible.

Or was Dad just waiting for our powers to show so he could explain everything?

⌐∧≡ᒋ ꓥ˘ꝋ ꝋᵻ⅄ᒋᒋ, ᵻꓕ≡ ꓥ∨⅄ ⌐ᒀ ᒀᒋꝋᵻ≡ᑲᵻ˘∧≡ ˘ꝋᐳ⅄ꝋᵻ⅄ᵻ˘�□ꝋ�

Would they ever get to ask him? Finn blinked back the tears and glanced over at his sister. She was bent over the bag again, her eyes open and shaking so hard he could hear the chattering of her teeth louder than before.

He jumped to his feet and the boat rocked wildly. 'Tula?' he asked again, his heart thudding hard with worry. 'Put on Patrick's coat!' He shook her gently by the shoulder. 'Tula? Pass me the bag and put on the coat.'

Looking up, Tula's glazed eyes took in the darkness around them, outside the glittering edge of the cloud of fireflies. Slowly she uncurled her fingers from the straps of the bag and straightened a little. Finn pulled Patrick's coat over her arms, zipping it up in front, and pulling the collar up to her small, pinched face. The sea breezes had whipped her hair into a halo of fuzz, and he wasn't entirely sure there weren't a couple of bugs caught up in it.

Shouldering the bag with renewed purpose, he stared out in front of him, breathing quickly. He could hear enormous waves crashing against rock, great booming explosions of powerful water pounding over and over, but all he could see was gently lapping water and swirling mist. He realised the boat had drifted into a wide, rocky chasm that stretched up to the sky

ᒥᔑᑐᕪ ᖬ᙮ ᐵᔑᒥ᙮

until it seemed as if the cliffs met at the top. The water was choppy and Finn pushed away the thought that it looked as if it were being churned by some enormous monster beneath. In the distance there was a strange glow, as if someone were holding a burning branch up in the air. Suddenly, it winked out.

Finn didn't know whether to feel relieved or afraid. While he did not like burning things or fire of any kind, it would be good to have someone helping them ashore.

Tula crept closer to him, and he put his arm round her, and she put hers round him. He tugged at the straps of the bag to make sure it was secure. Whatever happened, they could not lose the Telling Stone. A thought flashed across his mind that he wished it would do a bit more telling and a bit less sitting around, silently weighing him down, but he pushed that away as the boat neared the end of the chasm.

When it began scraping on the rocks beneath the water, Finn jumped out into the lapping waves, and turned to pull it on to the pebble beach, hauling hard with both arms, the water splashing messily to his knees.

'Need a hand?' A young voice came out of the misty gloom, followed by the crunch of boots coming towards them. Squinting through the dancing lights

Ɪⴸⵟ ⴲႶ≡◊ ◊≡×ⵟ Ⴖ≡ ⴸⵢⵏⵟⵟ≡◖ Ⴖⵢ☷ⴱ Ⴖ≡⅄◖, ⵟⴲ≡⋀∧≡ Ꭱⴱⵢ☷ⴱႶⵟⴱ

of the fireflies, Finn could see a boy, about two or three years older than him. He had his hand up at his eyes, as if he were making a sun visor to ward off bright light. 'Good thing that tremor was so tiny. Not sure you would have enjoyed being thrown at the cliffs by the ocean, huh?'

Tremor? signed Tula.

'That was the big swell in the sea?' asked Finn.

But the boy was looking above their heads. 'I thought you guys had lanterns or something. How did you do that with the bugs? You should know it's dangerous to attract attention when coming to the island. The mist is here for a reason.'

Finn concentrated on the boy's energy instead of his grumpiness, and tasted his words on his tongue. Good.

'I don't know,' he said to the boy. 'Fireflies. Gazillions of them.'

'Yeah. Never seen *that* before.'

Finn watched him loop the boat's rope expertly round a post blasted into the bedrock, pulling the craft even further from the water, and reaching to help Tula ashore.

His sister took the stranger's hand without hesitation.

'You recognise me?' he asked her with a glimmer of a smile.

Ꭿᐱᕼ ᆖᎾᐪᆖᒦᆖᕊ �aᎯᆖ Ꮟᐱ∧ᆖ. ᒦᎯᆖ⅄ Ꮎ�ᕼ ᆂᆖᒦᏫᒦᆖ Ꭿᘰ∆ᔑ

'Oh,' said Finn. 'We've not met you before. You must be thinking of someone else. We've not really met anyone before.'

Tula blinked, and gently pushed the closest fireflies away so she could look at the boy more closely. Finn squinted at him. There *was* something familiar about him, but…

'She's Tula,' said Finn when the boy's forehead began to crease in a frown. 'She's my sister.'

'Like you had to tell me that,' said the boy. Finn had an overwhelming taste of dark chocolate and salted peanuts in his mouth, and with it came a wave of sadness that he didn't understand.

Involuntarily, Finn looked over at Tula. Yes, they had the same pale, pale skin, untouched by the sun, and the same white-blond colour hair, but hers was a wild, too-long tangle and his was cut short by himself with rough swipes of the scissors. Possibly they had the same sharp features in their face, but Tula's eyes were ice-blue and his were grass-green.

'I'm Charlie,' said the boy, and he turned towards the snow-laden trees that crowded the shore beneath the cliffs. 'Follow me.'

'I'm Finn,' said Finn, distracted by the two leathery rolls of skin that he could see hanging in tightly curled cylinders from the top of Charlie's back.

⊥ᠴ═ᐁᎾᖴᑭᐯᐁᖴ═Ꮎ ᑦᕐᑊᎾᠦᎾᎾ ᐃᐊᑫ ᎾᕽᎾᖀᕽᎾᎾ ᐁᕼᑊᑫ ᎾᐁᎾᑭᕽᎾᎾ ᐁᕽᕐ.

'I know.'

'How?' asked Finn. 'Where are we?'

Charlie threw them a swift look over his shoulder. 'Didn't Patrick explain?'

'Not about this place.'

'You've come to the fireblood fortress. The people on this island are mostly unknown to the rest of the world. Safer, given the whole blasting-fire thing.' He paused, and a ball of flame appeared between the cupped palms of his hands. He bounced it from palm to palm, as if to demonstrate, and Finn's eyes went huge. Tula squeezed Finn's arm and he knew she was telling him to be brave, to ask Charlie more, but the boy had already moved on, the fire lighting the way. 'Because obviously most parents drop their firemakers at birth like a hot potato. This is where we come when no one else wants us.'

Finn tasted the salted peanuts in his mouth again and swallowed it down. His heart was hammering at being so close to the swiftly moving flames.

Up ahead, Charlie threw the fireball high and far. It had an eerie blue light that made everything appear scary and ghostly. It hit a stone wall and winked out.

'What are you doing?' croaked Finn, glad the flames were gone.

'Releasing the crank for the lift,' said Charlie.

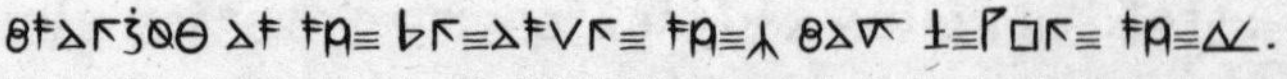

'There's no electricity on the island, except buried very far below. It's to stop people finding us by spotting any electrical charge or activity.'

He made a fist, and another fireball grew when he unclenched his fingers. He narrowed his eyes, took his time to aim and then threw it. It arced as high as the one before, but when it hit the wall it seemed to stick there, glowing gently like one of the bulbs that hung over the Clifton Suspension Bridge.

'*Agored*,' murmured Charlie, and the fireball fizzed with lightning crackles then went out. At the same moment there was a scattering of snow and a crunching, grinding sound. A flurry of bats took off from crevices in the stone that Finn saw were elaborate carved images of dragons with fiery mouths and long, twisty tails. A shrill creaking squealed through the air. Two parts of the wall slid open to reveal a metal cage with a number of chains and ropes swinging gently above it.

'It's perfectly safe,' said Charlie, stepping into the cage and gesturing for Finn and Tula to get in with him. 'Patrick said you don't fly yet so we need to use the lift. It takes us up to the fortress.'

Finn tasted hot orange juice so when Tula threw him a questioning look he nodded, and they got in, standing close together. Finn could see the shape of

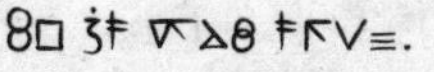

Tån hiding up Tula's sleeve, unwilling to come out, and the cylinders on Charlie's back made a rustling sound then stopped.

'Can you fly?' he asked Charlie. 'Are those wings on your back?'

Charlie grimaced. 'Yes,' he said, 'unfortunately.'

Finn drew breath to ask another question, but the stone doors closed in a racket of noise, revealing runes carved on the inside that shone with a golden light. One was an eye, another a burning fireball and another graphic looked like two fanged jaws. Charlie breathed on a symbol of two rectangles close together and stepped back quickly. A metal grate slammed down from above, and the cage began to rumble slowly upwards.

When it stopped and they got out, Finn saw they were walking on to an enormous square area, like an Italian piazza, cleared of snow. They were so high up that the noise of the crashing waves was subdued behind chest-high crenellated walls. Finn squinted through the drifting mist and saw that the piazza ended in a series of wide shallow steps, probably a hundred of them, each thirty metres wide. The risers glittered with the colours of myriad gemstones. As he stared at them, the stones began to glow.

'Wow,' said Charlie and Finn at the same time, and

ǂﾁ≡ɔ⌐ ≡⅄≡θ ⌐≡⌐≡ ⌐ɔˊq≡ ⌐ɔˊﾁﾁ qˊθﾱ≡ǀˊ≡⌐ ⅄θq ⌐≡⅄⌐ ⅄ǂ

Tula gasped in wonder. It was as if the Northern Lights were chasing around inside the stairs, desperate for release. Soft rainbows shot from the gems into the night sky, lighting up the air all around them.

And then, just as suddenly, the lights winked out, leaving only the cloud of fireflies still dancing around Finn and Tula. There was a strange rush of noise, and the children held their breath in amazement as a tall, narrow house on the edge of the piazza began to move. Its weathervane of a pouncing dragon spun so fast that it let out a piercing shriek, almost as if the dragon were warning them all that danger was afoot. The house shifted to the left, squashing the home next to it so hard that some of the plaster from its elaborate facade fell off. Then it tilted to the right, snow tumbling from its roof, reaching right across the street.

'What the hell…?' murmured Finn.

The house leaned forward, then back, and at last with a deep groan it uprooted itself from the street entirely, pulling up from the ground on long, dark, bricky legs. It turned down the road with a great deal of creaking and groaning, the dragon weathervane still shrieking, and swiftly disappeared from view, leaving a gaping hole behind.

'Great, just *great*,' muttered Charlie. 'That was

ᎢᎭ≡ ᎾᏣᎾᎯᎢ ᏆᏛ ᎢᎭ≡ ≡ᎾᏆᚱᎠᏆᎾᏛᎾ ᏘᚱᎠᎾᏍᎾ ᎤᏣᎢᎯ ᎾᏓᏄᐧ≡Ꮎ ᏆᏛ

Rudimenta's house, which obviously doesn't feel very safe out here with a sea view now that you two are here.' He looked up into the sky, as if searching for more of the light, but everything was dark, inky and still. 'Come on,' he said, and gestured towards the stairs. 'We'd better hurry before anything else notices your arrival.'

9

ΦϡΘ≡

'What is this place?' whispered Finn to Tula.

She shrugged in reply, still shaking slightly. Peering into the drifting moonlight, they saw that the snow-topped wall behind them stretched to the east and west as far as they could see. To the left of them, casting shadows across the piazza, was the crowd of jumbled buildings from which the tall house had just removed itself. Some were old, some new; a few were big, but most were small or medium, leaning this way and that either side of a downhill road as far as the eye could see. A scattering of homes were many storeys tall, others more modest with grassy roofs, or odd turrets, or covered in slate tiles just visible beneath the snow. Many had lots of windows, some had none. Most glowed with warm orange light and smoke plumed from the chimneys that created a higgledy-piggledy outline overhead.

ΘΑϡ∠∠≡Γϡ⊖Θ ⊖□Ⅰϙ ϡ⊙ϙ ≡⅄≡θ □Γ ≡∠≡ΓⅩⅠϙ ⊖Γ≡≡Θ.

Between them ran narrow streets and lanes hung with lanterns of flickering flame.

Finn swallowed again, hating himself for his fear of fire. Tula squeezed his hand with her own shaking fingers, freezing cold. He had to get her somewhere warm, get some food. He pulled her closer to him as they struggled to keep up with Charlie.

People hurried by in the distance, and their laughter chimed clear as a bell in the icy air. A few paused at the hole left by Rudimenta's house on the edge of the piazza, but soon walked on as if this were a commonplace occurrence. Finn could hear the rattle of cartwheels on cobblestones, subdued by the slush of trodden snow, the braying of a donkey somewhere and a group of people calling out to each other in what sounded like an African language with clicking noises. Someone somewhere was singing what had to be a sea shanty in a Spanish dialect and a mother crossing the piazza was comforting a crying baby wrapped in a sling pressed tightly to her chest.

A gust of wind blew drifts of mist away, revealing snatches of an enormous building at the top of the stairs: half castle, half fortress. It had walls of grey granite and stretched high and wide, reaching for the sky with its turrets and crenellations and fluttering flags. A vast golden clock above the entrance showed

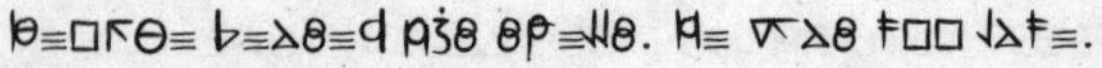

ᑲᆖ�口⌐Θᆖ ᑲᆖλθᆖᑫ ᑭｾθ θᑭᆖᐟᐧθ. ᕼᆖ ᐁᐧλθ ᖴ口口 ᐟλᎰᆖ.

the time as seven o'clock – an hour and fifty-four minutes before sunrise. A three-headed stone dog shrouded in mist hung down from the battlements above it, seeming ready to savage anyone who dared to change the time.

Carved into walls, curved round pillars, peeking out from various corners were more mythical creatures – griffins and unicorns, multi-headed serpents and dogs, pegasi and bakus, and even a phoenix. Most of them formed elaborate gargoyles that were strangely beautiful, but Finn and Tula were drawn to the most common creature of all...

Dragons.

Moulded, sculpted, carved and crafted into the smallest and biggest of spaces were the stone, wooden and metal coils of these ancient creatures. Sitting, lying, writhing – tongues lolling, eyes winking, fangs bared, nostrils flared – they stretched down banisters, across walls and over battlements.

Everywhere.

Charlie's voice floated down from some distance away: 'Come *on!*'

He was already at the top of the stairs to the front door of the castle fortress. 'Hurry!' he called, heading for a huge arch of carved wood set deep into the stone. 'George is waiting!'

ꓕⅤꓕ ◖◻ꓕ ꓕ◻◻ Ɩ⅄ꓕ≡ ꓕ◻ Ⴆꓝ⅄△◖Θ≡ ꓕꓥ≡Ꝫꓲ △¿Θ◖Θ.

Finn and Tula staggered up the last few steps after him, but before Charlie had a chance to knock, the door swung open on silent hinges. A strong, stocky man with dark brown eyes, ice-white hair and a close-clipped beard and moustache stepped out of the doorway's bright arch of light.

'Ah,' he said, and smiled out at them.

'Here they are, George,' said Charlie. 'As you can see.'

'Good lad,' said the man.

Charlie swept into a bow. 'Finn and Tula, meet Saint George, patron saint of England, defender of dragons and all that is good.'

Tula pushed her tangled hair from her eyes, jostling past her brother to stare. Finn was staring too. He wasn't sure what he'd been expecting, but it wasn't a man around a grandfather kind of age, strong and fit, in black jeans and a black leather jacket that had a rip across the shoulder blades.

'Welcome,' he said to Tula and Finn. 'We—'

Are you really THE Saint George? signed Tula, her eyes enormous.

George grinned. 'Yep, the actual patron saint of England, for something I never did. Slashing dragons with swords?' he shuddered. 'Never.'

Tula's fingers flew, her facial tics and gestures wilder than usual. *You're nearly two thousand years old?*

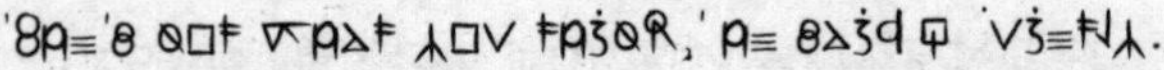

George laughed. 'Immortal sounds better, yes? Patrick is too, and Shen, because of being splashed by Oriel's blood.'

'And you can understand my sister?' blurted Finn.

'She speaks like many creatures without language, and a fair few firebloods here understand the curve of a lip, the twitch of an eyebrow, the wiggle of an ear. You children find each other easily?'

'Wasn't hard, sir.' Charlie stepped inside so Finn and Tula were in full view on the stone step outside. The fireflies still crowded round them, shimmering in the glow from the open door, and followed them in when Finn and Tula came into the shadowy hall.

Though tired lines creased George's face, his smile grew wider.

'Well, I never,' he said. 'Never in all my days.'

'That's what I said.' Charlie levelled a look at Finn and Tula. 'And did you see the heartstones in the stairs?'

'I did,' George replied. He shook his head, still smiling. 'That hasn't happened in a long time. It's a good sign.'

'The houses didn't think so,' said Charlie, crossing his arms. 'Rudimenta is going to go nuts at me again because hers just up and left.'

George shrugged. 'She knows her house is anxious. She can't blame you for that, Charlie.'

ᕼ᙮ ᐤ᙮ᕯᐟᐁ⨯ᕂ᙮ᑫ ᐟ�口 ᐟᕤ᙮ ᒲ᙮ᐱᐁᐟᑐᒣ⋁ᕟ ᑲᕂ᙮ᐱᐟᐁ⨯ᕂ᙮ ᒲ᙮ᕤᕑᐤᑫ ᕤᕑᐃ.

'She can and she will,' blurted Charlie.

Finn looked at the boy properly for the first time. He was tall and lean, with hazel eyes that seemed to see everything all at once, and he had a nervous energy. His thick, dark hair fell across his face and he pushed it aside impatiently. His skin was pale and clear, his lips curved and generous. He looked like a boy who laughed easily, but who hadn't for a very long time, and there was a crease between his eyebrows that Finn didn't think a smile could ever reach. He thought it might be there permanently, and not just because of this Rudimenta person.

Charlie's feet were big, even for his height, though he'd moved silently through the trees down at the shore. He wore a longish black jacket with a worn collar and big square pockets, and threadbare jeans. Finn still couldn't work out who he reminded him of.

George folded Charlie into a big-armed hug and slapped him gently on the back. 'There, there, you silly muggins,' he murmured. 'It's not really about that, is it?' He talked more quietly to the boy, not whispering – that would be rude – but Finn felt he didn't want to be overheard so he and Tula stepped towards the portraits hanging beneath the gaslights on the walls. There was George, looking like he did now, but with a much longer beard and ancient-looking

ᎤᏍᎨᏹ ᏂᏝᎦᏤᏥ ᎬᏓᏫᏗ, ᎠᏒ ᎪᏫᎬ ᏉᏚᎦᏈ ᏞᏫ ᎤᏒ ᏆᏡᏇᎤᏌ,

clothes. There was Patrick, wearing a funny floppy hat. A young woman stared out of the newest-looking portrait. It had a black frame instead of gold like the others, which matched her black modern clothing and her long, dark hair. She was unsmiling and her gaze was focused and intense. It was Angelina, the woman who'd taken the Venomous.

Finn thought he heard Charlie say, '...might remember...' and George made a comforting sound, saying, 'We talked about this, didn't we?'

Tula pulled Finn over to two darker rectangles on the wall where clearly other paintings had been before. A smaller painting hung in the place of one of them, but what it lacked in size it made up for in ostentation. The frame was very ornate and a very bright gold. The man in the picture was smiling broadly from a little round face with twinkly eyes. His dark hair was very neatly combed with a precise side parting, and it looked as if he'd spent some time clipping his moustache.

Finn noticed that George was releasing Charlie from a hug.

The old man bent his head to look intently into Charlie's eyes. 'You okay?' he asked.

Charlie nodded. 'Yes, of course. Thanks, George.'

Finn sensed Charlie's discomfort and coughed,

ᏏᎣᏉᎾᏓᎾᏎ ᎭᏍᏈ ᏝᏎᏛᏉᏓᎩ. 8ᖰᏎ Ᏽ═ᏕᏝ ᎠᏅᏔ ᏬᏏᎥᎣᎾᎾ ᏝᏉᏅᏀᏈ

pointing to the shiny-looking man in the new frame. 'Who is this?' he asked.

George answered. 'That is Simon Veritas. He is a valuable ambassador for the firebloods to the government officials of the world – the United Kingdom's Ministry of Defence, in particular. That's why he has a place in our Hall of Heroes.'

Charlie snorted. 'The only thing that's valuable about him is that solid gold frame he's got round his stupid portrait.' He raised an eyebrow at George. 'Did you know he's already commissioned a bigger picture? Silly man.'

George shrugged, and smiled. 'Simon can be a little vain, but you have to admit, Charlie, that he's good with the frailskins.'

Charlie frowned, unconvinced, and Finn asked, 'Whose portrait was here before?' gesturing to the darker square on the wall behind Simon's picture. 'Did they die?'

'Augustus's,' said George when Charlie did not answer. 'Your father's.'

His father, gone. From here too. Finn felt a hard thump to the chest that choked his throat.

'He took it when he left,' said Charlie in a rush, adding, even faster and louder: 'The time of the Last Battle here when someone betrayed the firebloods and

ᗷᔕᎾᏗᎢ Ꭲ�口 ᗰ≡� Ꭲᗰ口ᐯᎾᗰ ᗷ≡口ᖇᎾ≡ ᖇᎾ≡ᐁ ᎢᗰᐱᎢ 口Ꮎ≡

the Venomous got in and they killed Aria, because Augustus couldn't save her in time and he was angry and sad and out of his mind. So he vanished, taking you two with him and thinking of no one but you and himself, and very few have seen him since.'

'Charlie,' said George softly, putting his hand on Charlie's shoulder, but the boy moved away.

Finn looked at Tula, his eyes wide. *The accident*, he signed.

Her nose twitched, the fingers of her left hand fluttered and her right hand touched her ear: *I feel like we have no idea who our father is.*

George sighed. 'He took your mother's portrait too. We still miss her. She was the most powerful singer we've ever known. Her Welsh charms are still the most magical words used today.'

Finn exchanged another look with Tula. She didn't sign anything but he knew what she was thinking.

Singer? Welsh?

'Let's go upstairs,' said George. He gestured towards a wide staircase that led off the entrance hall, curving up high above them into the darkness.

Tula was the first to turn towards it, but as she did so the fireflies flew towards her and she gasped, an expression of pain flitting across her face.

I've been stung, she signed to Finn. Tân peered

ᒉᐊᑭ ᑯᑉ ᖦ�Iᐊᐤ ᑐᑯᐃᑯᖅ ᐅᐴᖦᖦ ᖦ�≡ ᔎᕏᕂᐴᖅ≡ᕀᕀᖇ ᒉᕂᑐᐴᖦ ᕀ≡ᕀ

cautiously out from her shirt pocket, pushing aside the collar of Patrick's coat with an impatient foot.

'What's happening?' asked Charlie.

Tula made a small sign, a fingertip pressed quickly to her clavicle.

Finn, have I been scarred again?

She tugged her shirt to one side, showing a short line of tiny black images that ran across her collarbone, the first being the dark circle left by the stone dragon in Bristol. The fourth image at the end of the line was a pair of minuscule insect wings. Her skin looked hot and red there, as if she'd been bitten, but it soon faded to a black tattoo-like symbol like the others in the line.

Tân scurried away round the back of her neck to stand on her opposite shoulder.

'Ouch!' said Finn as the fireflies swarmed to him. He pushed his shirt to one side, as Tula was doing. 'Yes, and me too,' he said. The mark on his skin was the fourth or fifth in the line – it was difficult to tell – and an instant later the fireflies flitted towards Charlie. He yelped, waving his hand around his head to bat them away, and they swarmed out of reach, off into the night sky.

'Well, you three,' said George. 'The fireflies have marked you with another gift. Bioluminescence?' Finn and Tula blinked with confusion.

ᏏᏗᏠᗕ ᔦᏍ ᖴᏕᗕ ᏂᎦᏍᏍᏴᎡ ᗡᏞ ᐱ ᏉᏴᐱᏐᎦᏍᏍᏴᏴ ᗕᎩᗕ᎐ 8Ꮥᗕ ᏉᏍᏙᏖᗕ᎐Ꮰᗕᒑ

'Gift?' asked Finn.

'It's a very great honour,' said George, 'when a creature bestows their power to you. They're not scars – they're marks of significance.'

Power? signed Tula.

'That mark of the dragon that I can see at the top of your marking line is very rare,' said George. 'And it could mean you have the gift of invisibility, for instance, though that would be unheard of.' He smiled. 'Did your father tell you anything? Or explain about your other marks?'

I breathe ice, signed Tula. *But I didn't know it was because of the mark.*

Maybe, maybe not, George signed back. 'Powerful stuff. You're living up to the legends already, Tula. These other marks – the owl, the snake, the fruit fly – probably give you powers over the air, of healing, of magnetism, and now you have this from the firefly. It feels important.' He turned to go up the stairs. 'Come on. You'll learn more about your marks if Augustus lets you stay for schooling here on the island.'

'Bioluminescence,' muttered Charlie in disgust. 'I bet that means we light up like a firefly just when we need to stay hidden! Is it time for breakfast? George? George, wait!'

But George was already striding to the foot of

ᐱ≡ᖇ ᐱ≡ᐃᑫ ᔒᐤ ᐥ Ꮤ≡Ᏼᐟᐻᖇ≡ ᗕᒥ ᑭᗕᒡᔥᐟ≡ ᐁ≡ᖕᗳᗕᐃ∠≡.

the stairs. 'Otto won't have opened the kitchen yet, Charlie, and we've got urgent business. Come on, Finn and Tula. Let's see if you can unlock your father's watchtower with that key. No one has been inside these past eight years, and we're hoping to goodness he left enough hydrant in there to save the world.'

10

'No interest in saving the world,' said Charlie, rubbing his chest. 'Sorry, George. Call me when you need me for something important.'

George turned back to look at him. 'But—'

'I've got to go,' continued Charlie, pointing through the half-open doors. 'The minions will be hunting me down for their flying lesson. Whoa—' He leaped back as the doors slammed wide open and Angelina appeared, surrounded by a motley crowd of panting children, aged between three and seven.

George's eyebrows shot up. 'Minions?'

'He means this swarm of kids,' said Angelina, her tone sour and her nostrils flared. 'Loud, disrespectful, unruly children, who for some reason have latched on to Bad-boy Charlie Stupidhead in a ridiculously adoring way. They fling themselves off the battlements in their quest to be the best fliers ever, fill up Shen's clinic with their injuries, wake up the elderly and generally drive this island round the bend. They call themselves Charlie's minions. Ridiculous.'

'Ahh,' said George, and his face softened. 'That is really sweet. Hello, children.'

The crew of youngsters chorused hello, still catching their breath, and shuffled closer to Charlie, staring wide-eyed at Finn and Tula. The tallest of them, sucking her thumb, butted up against Charlie's hip, grabbing one of his hands in her own in a possessive gesture.

'The parents don't like their children in peril, missing their tutor sessions, not listening, behaving badly. We get complaints daily. The admin is off the charts,' added Angelina brutally.

Charlie sighed, this time sounding more like forty than fourteen. 'For the record, I did not ask this lot to come to me. They just started *arriving* at my morning workout. They're actually a pain in the bum.'

The little girl released her thumb and yelled 'Hey!' at Charlie, her face furious. '*You* bum! You bu—'

'Okay, Vida, okay,' said George, patting her carefully braided hair. 'Does your mother know you're here?'

Vida blinked at him solemnly. 'Mum says Finn Flint will be a great flyer,' she said, then looked curiously at Finn, 'and I wanted to see, but how will you fly with your back broken?' she asked.

ᕈᔑ⊲= ᛏᕈᔑᎦ ⊥=ᕼᎦ⧻Ꮶ ᛋ= ᛏᕈᗅᐁᏫᕈᛏ ⅄◻ᐁ Ꮻᐁᕁᖇᐸ=⊲ ᛏᕈ= ᐱᔑᐻᐃᏫ=.

Finn flushed red. 'I—'

Vida frowned, not waiting for an answer. 'How will your wings sprout? Where is your dad? Why haven't you brought him? We need him to stop the volcano otherwise we will all die and—'

'Die! Die!' yelled a boy much younger than Vida. He whirled his arms around and a fireball from his fingers blasted into the air. It would have obliterated the Simon Veritas portrait, but Angelina deflected it with the gauntlet on her forearm and it only caught the edge of the frame.

'Small George!' yelped Charlie. 'Stop that!' He caught the boy by the back of the collar and flung him up and round on to his shoulders. 'Fly! Fly!' yelled Small George, bashing at Charlie's head.

Charlie grabbed his hands. 'Settle down, Small George, otherwise no flying.' He lunged for a dark-haired child, about five, who was pulling at Tula's arm. 'Stop that, Morty.'

'I am Mortimer Jones,' said Morty to Tula, still tugging on her sleeve. 'Best flyer! Will you sing Elbrus to sleep?' he asked. 'Is that your plan if you can't find the hydrant? Just three days before it erupts! Can I come with? I love volcanoes. I can protect you with my flying and my su-superior strength.' He flexed a bicep and a chorus of voices from six or seven other

ᖚᕓᔕᐃ ... ᖚᕓᔕᐃ ᔕᐃ ᖚ᐀ ᐁᘲᕵᐊᖚ ᖚᕵᗓᐅᑫᕓᗓᕵᐩ.' ᖚ᐀ ᐃᐁᕵᘲᕵᑫ ᔕᐃ

children behind him filled the Hall of Heroes with promises of skills and talents to help the Flints save the world, raising their voices with questions too:

'Have you got your questing licence?'

'What house are you in? I'm in Vulkan – be in Vulkan, be in Vulkan!'

'Be in Brann! Can you scry? How high can you fly?'

'Out!' shouted Angelina. 'All minions out!'

'What's all this noise?' came a voice from the doorway, and Patrick appeared with a young Chinese woman at his side. Her long dark hair was pulled back into a bun, secured with a pencil and a hypodermic syringe, and she was wearing a high-necked top in ice-blue silk, with a skirt of cascading dark-pink ruffles that fell all the way to her soft boots. She looked as if she should be in a fashion magazine instead of here in real life. The sun chose that moment to tip up over the horizon, bathing the mist with a golden glow and sending sparkles dazzling across the snow. The clamouring children squinted at the silhouettes against the brightness and quietened at once.

'How did you know the Flints had arrived, eh?' laughed Patrick, picking Small George off Charlie's shoulders, and pulling Morty away from Tula. 'Did you see them in your bowl, Vida? You will all make

ᑭᔑᕿ ᕴᐊᕁᑫ ᑫ ᐧᕈᔅᐱᐁᕉᐁ�ᒧ ᕈᔓᕀᕴ �𖼾ᐁᐨᕉ ᐊᕁᕿ ᕒᕎᕓᔆ.

excellent spies and investigators, but for now off you go back home, you miscreants.'

'No lesson today,' echoed the Chinese lady in softer tones, ushering the children back out through the front doors. 'Tula looks very tired.'

'But, Shen!' protested Morty. 'We can help!'

'I know,' said Shen, nudging him outside. 'Thank you, Mortimer. We will call for you as soon as we've worked out next steps.'

Ignoring their protests, she shut the doors gently but firmly behind the last of them, and the heavy timber instantly muffled the outrage from the other side. She turned to stare at Finn and Tula, a smile growing across her face. 'Welcome,' she said with a bow. 'We are so happy you have returned. You made good time across the sea – we weren't expecting you so soon.'

Finn bowed awkwardly in return, conscious of his hunched back, not knowing what to say. Tula put her hand in his, and Finn's brow furrowed. Her fingers were icy again, and her lips were turning blue. As Shen asked George something about the watchtower and the Telling Stone, he bent to stare into his sister's eyes. They were wide and unfocused.

'Tula? You okay?' he whispered.

Her face crumpled in pain. *They're hurting Dad…* she signed, her knees buckling. *He's— He needs us—*

ᑊᐁᒧᒥᖬᗕᐁ ᗕᕮᐁᑊᕚᕚᐁᑫ ᐃᐁᕐ ᕐᕌᗕᐃ ᕐᕮᐁ ᕮᕕᐃᕹᑫᗕᕐᗕᕮ· ⅃ ᕮᘉᐱᐁᕚᕐᕼ·

Finn clutched his sister to him as she sagged to the floor, her eyelids flickering as if she were seeing a million things at once. 'Tula! Talk to me!'

Charlie swore, but no one reprimanded him as he leapt to help Finn hold her up.

'George? Shen?' exclaimed Patrick, springing to Charlie's side. 'What's happening?'

Shen dropped to her knees, the back of her hand on Tula's forehead. 'Did she say something about your father?'

'She said they're hurting him—'

'Quick! Up to the watchtower,' commanded George. 'It's the closest space with a pool. Hurry.'

Finn cradled Tula to his chest, already heading for the wide stone steps.

'Pool?'

'Best scrying source on the island. We'll be able to see what she's seeing, so we can help her,' replied Patrick.

They hurried after George and Shen, who had already disappeared from sight, and Angelina took up the rear. 'She say who's hurting your dad?' she asked Finn as they took a sharp left off the landing on to a spiral staircase.

'No,' panted Finn, his heart beating too hard to speak easily. He scarcely noticed the stained-glass windows that seemed to shift and move with ancient tableaus, the dancing light across the walls, how they got larger and more elaborate the higher they climbed. His eyes were fixed on the stairs ahead, praying he could make it to the top. His arms were in agony.

'You're strong,' said Patrick. 'Come on, Finn.'

'She'll be fine,' added Angelina. 'Shen is the best healer, the best scryer, and your mother had the most powerful scrying pool in the city.'

Patrick threw a glance over his shoulder. 'We just need to get into the tower…' and with another burst of speed he disappeared round the next turn, his voice echoing behind him '…which we've not managed for eight years.'

Finn's legs were burning and his mind racing when at last he emerged in a square room. *Eight years?* George, Shen and Patrick were waiting at a pair of carved wooden doors that stretched all the way up to the high painted ceiling.

George raised his staff and knocked gently, then turned the handle. The door did not open.

'Come, Finn,' he murmured. 'Did you bring the opener?'

Finn hurried to the door, delivering Tula into Patrick's arms. He tugged the rucksack off his shoulders and reached into the front pocket for the

⏃⎐⏁ ⟋⏃⎅ ⏆⏃⎐⟊⏃ ⏁⎍ ⏚⎍⎐⎁⎁⎍⎐⏃⎅ ⏁⟊⌁ ⎅⎁⟋⏃⎅⎅⎍ ⏁⎓⎅⏚⎅⎅ ⎅⏚⟋⟍.

letter opener. He slid it into the keyhole, turned it and rotated the brass handle. The door did not budge. He groaned, and twisted the handle harder, shoving against the door in frustration.

'Stop,' whispered Shen. 'Look.' She gestured to the carving and Finn saw it was a picture of a fight of some kind. 'There's a clue in here for you.'

Finn rattled the handle, impatient, and shoved against the door again. 'A clue? What—'

George drew breath. 'This carving has changed to show a tableau of the Last Battle. That is your father.'

Finn took a step back, his eyes widening at the familiar image of a man standing on a watchtower balcony reaching out to a woman flying in the sky, fighting a monstrous creature.

It's the same picture as our back door!

Without thinking, his left-hand fingers slotting between the claws of the dragon-foot door handle, Finn pressed two fingers of his right hand to the Venomous attacking the woman: one on its head, one on its heart. He gasped when the wood beneath his touch moved and the carving changed, like a muscle moving beneath the skin, as the monster twisted and turned, falling to the bottom of the carved panel.

And then, with a distinct click, the door opened.

11

The room into which Finn stumbled was overgrown with plants of every kind. He pushed impatiently through creeping vines and whispering leaves towards dim light at the back of the room.

Pool! Where's this pool?

Mosses and lichens carpeted the floor, ferns reached out from the darkest crevices and soft fronds touched his face and hands, as if inviting him in. More green things grew from the teacups on a table to his right, from the shelves of books to his left, from the seat of an overturned chair in his path. They wound round a huge stone dragon rearing from the wide stair banister, and thick-leaved vines crept across the walls and stained-glass windows, right up to the ceiling that soared into a glass dome overhead.

'I can't see it!' he called back over his shoulder,

hoarse with anxiety. 'The pool in here to help Tula – where is it?'

'You'll have to invite us in,' said George, tapping his staff on an invisible barrier in the doorway. 'By name. Your father put a locking charm on—'

'Please come in, George, Patrick, Angelina, Shen and Charlie,' replied Finn so fast that the words blended into one.

Charlie was the first over the threshold and at Finn's side in a moment. 'It's over there near the balcony windows, under the flying carpet.' He hurried past and bent to tug at a woven silk rug at the far end of the room. It was almost completely covered in soft moss and took some effort for Finn and Charlie to pull it away. George helped Patrick lower Tula to the edge of the rectangular pool that had been hidden beneath it, and Shen dipped Tula's hand into the black water, murmuring words that Finn could not hear.

The surface of the water flashed with whirling, blurring images. Finn saw himself, and Tula, and then a flashing sequence of fighting and resistance, close-ups of red eyes, yellow teeth, then darkness again. Some of it he recognised, a snapshot of his father's hands, though they shook, his boots—

'Everything Tula is thinking is there?' he asked, kneeling beside his sister, her other hand clutched in his.

ᖀ≡ᐸ, ᐳᎸᕻ ≡ᐱᔑ� ᐁᔑᐱᔑ ᖋᗒᐃ≡ ᗒᒻ ᔑᖴ. ᑫᒪ≡ᐳᎧ≡, ᔑ ᖶ≡Ꮎ ᐱᗒᐯ. ᖶ≡ᖴ

Shen sat beside him. 'Not quite. See these shadows? Your sister has shielded herself. How can we get her to let us in?'

'We'll see inside her head?'

'I know it feels like an intrusion,' said Shen, 'and I'm sorry about that, truly I am, but Tula's link with your father is dangerous for her. We need to pull her out of it to keep her safe.'

'But Augustus needs our help,' said Patrick, 'and he's left nothing behind to lead the way to him. Just these kids, Shen, and we need to reach him—'

'We can find him without hurting Tula!' interrupted Finn, as Tula began to shake, her breath coming in short pants. 'Help her, please!'

'Steady,' said George, his eyes on Shen. She nodded back to him, and he took a breath, choosing his words carefully. 'If we can see exactly where Augustus is, right now, then we can retrieve him, yes?' He looked intently at Finn, and Finn nodded back, swallowing hard, 'and, most importantly, save your sister too.'

'Agreed,' said Angelina. 'Get the intel and sever the link with Augustus before this child is finished.' She gestured at Tula. 'Look. The connection is draining her fast. You've got a few minutes, max.'

12

ᚦᚢ ᛋᛁᚾᛖ

Tula's mind raced beneath the cloud of static air that she'd pulled around herself. She wished Finn would sing to her. That always helped her feel better. Tân was asleep inside her shirt, curved into her neck, but it wasn't the same.

Feelings. So many feelings.

I can feel Finn being scared, she thought, *and Dad is lost … somewhere … but everything is slippery. Normally, I can grab on to things with my mind as if … as if they're pieces of rope – like their voice, or their smell, or the look of their hands from their own eyes – something like that, some little thing. I can usually hang on tightly, and that way get inside their head. I can track them down, see through their eyes. Or else just talk to them from where I am, but now the pieces of rope have turned into slippery spaghetti and I cannot hang on to anything.*

I feel as if I'm close to Dad, though, and getting

ᛁᚾᛖ ᛖᚲᛈᛚᛁᚾᛋᚦᚾ.

closer, but I'm so scared that I won't be able to find the thread that leads me back to Finn. It's getting darker and darker. I'm out here all alone, and I'm too busy looking for Dad to be afraid, but deep down I am.

I really am.

13

‡ꝆꞀꞂ‡══Q

hen placed her hands either side of Tula's head and began to murmur the same words over and over in a language Finn did not know, but the shaking did not subside.

Tân suddenly emerged from the folds of clothing at Tula's neck, running down her arm to touch Finn's hand with one of his tiny feet. Finn gasped as Tân leapt to Charlie's hand, tapping it three times.

'Wow,' breathed Angelina. 'She's already got a creature of her own.'

'Watch,' said Shen.

Tân lifted his leg and tapped Charlie's hand again, lifting his foot slowly up, then down. When Charlie didn't move, he repeated the action.

'Oh,' said Finn, reaching for Tula's hand and holding it tightly.

'Oh, okay,' said Charlie, slowly moving his hand, with Tân on it, to Tula's shoulder. His angry frown

⅃Ꝋꝙ⌐══Ʌ Ꝇ══θꙧ‡⅄‡══ꝙ, Ꝏ⌐Ʌꝏ θꙧθΘ.

softened into an expression that Finn couldn't read as he placed his hand on her other shoulder.

Shen bent her head to Tula again, and whispered something different, low and quiet, almost a chant, and Finn suddenly noticed that the pool was no longer so dark.

Is that a light over there on the right? Is it a lamp?

Tula's thoughts in the water became less shadowy, more defined. The light on the surface of the pool sharpened into an image of a window about thirty centimetres tall and fifteen wide with two thick iron bars running from top to bottom.

In the dim glow below it sat a man with his back against the wall, his legs drawn up to his shoulders, his arms loosely laced above his knees and his head hanging down. He was entirely motionless, and it would have been impossible for anyone else to tell who this person was, but Finn's heart thumped with recognition.

A shout coming from the pool made his heart pound even harder, and the man slowly raised his head to see who was calling to him. There was a rattling sound of a bunch of keys, and then one of them turning in the lock. The man under the window tried to stand, but fell in a jumble of arms and legs, too weak to remain upright. He pushed himself up into

ᏔᎪᎧᎢ — 'ᎪᏍ ᏖᏍᎾᏝᎾ, ᏖᏉᎢ Ꮧ ᏒᎤᏉᎾᏑᏗᏞᎦᏔᏍᏟ ᏒᎤᏡᏌᎾᏔ ᏖᏍᎾᏡᎾᏑ

sitting as quickly as he could, running a hand through his hair, as if wanting to present the strongest, most composed force possible.

'Dad,' whispered Finn, horrified. Immediately the scene in front of them zoomed wider, wider, and the images lightened still further.

Finn heard the cell door bang open. Then, as the image enlarged, he could actually see the door, and he could especially see the huge creatures marching through it towards his father, though once they'd passed he could only make out the back of their heads.

The first of the Venomous was the biggest – a huge monster – completely bald with his head patterned in geometric tattoos. He barked a word at Augustus – '*Tala!*'

Finn's father shook his head and said, '*Þú munt ekki ná árangri,*' and without a pause the Venomous drew back his massive leg and kicked Augustus hard.

'Dad!' screamed Finn, clenching his sister's shoulder. 'DAD!'

The Venomous shouted something else, but Augustus was coughing so loudly his voice could not be heard.

They watched as the scene before them began to shake and the Venomous howled as dust rained down around them. A few seconds later the water of the

ᕐᓴᐠ Ꮺᒂᐯᐠᐟᐟᑌᕧ ᒐᏫᕐᗷᐟᕧ ᕐᐢᗘᖅ ᐢ Ꮺᑫ ᐯᑌᐢᒧ, Ꮺᕐᓴᕧ

pool rippled the image away as another tremor shook the island, fading away as quickly as it had begun.

Tears were pouring down Finn's face, but his horrified gaze never left the pool, until he felt Tula's fingers begin to freeze beneath his hands. Shen was mumbling something soft, low and calming, the words getting faster and faster, and Tula's eyes had flown wide open.

It was as if someone were pulling her skin back from behind her head, freezing her from the inside out. Her mouth was slowly opening now too, lips going purple, her skin losing colour fast.

Before he knew what he was doing, Finn leaned into her face, stared into her eyes, and whispered, 'Come back, Tula.'

Not really knowing why, he concentrated on releasing all his white heat through his fingers into his sister's frozen frame. With his breath warming her face, and his hands powering up the fire within her, he felt his toes go tingly, then numb. Soon his legs felt like lead, and so did his arms. At last his own breathing became shallow and short, and his heartbeat slowed. Finn felt his eyes fluttering closed, and he thought he heard, '*That's enough, son, that's enough…*'

His eyes flew open to find the pool reflection had

ᖴᐋᔭᐁᐸ.

smoothed out again, showed his father standing – no, not just standing, but *confronting* a dark fig—

No! he thought. *Focus!*

He got a picture in his head of his sister in the dark, a long way away, and imagined that he was holding a rope down to her and she was reaching for it.

Stretching…

Higher…

Higher…

In his mind, he saw her frightened face focused on grabbing hold of the sturdy rope he was lowering to her, and then her fingers tightened round it and suddenly – in the blink of an eye – his rope became a twisted cord of two ropes, double the thickness and strength, full of knots and twists and tangles.

Easy to hold.

Easy to climb. Just like Dad had taught them.

He grinned to her and said, 'Come on, Tula. Get up here.'

And she smiled back and clambered towards him, her movements slow but sure.

14

ᒥᐅᐏᑭᐁᕁ

Finn's eyes opened to find Tula looking up at him, her face back to normal. He wrenched her up into a rough hug and held her tightly.

'No more of that, Tula,' he said.

'No more,' agreed Shen. 'We don't need to – we have those Russian words to translate. *Þú munt ekki ná árangri.* They'll tell us something.'

'We can ask the Stone,' said Finn, letting go of Tula slowly. 'Milady…' he began, but the Stone interrupted him immediately.

'Sorry,' she said. 'No can do. Everybody needs to stay here and find the hydrant. Those words are too confusing for you all.'

No, signed Tula. *No, no, no, no!*

'That Stone—' started Patrick, but he swallowed his next words under Shen's stern gaze.

George sighed. 'The Stone is overprotective,' he said to Finn and Tula.

ᐁᕁ ᒥᐄᐟᐁᐧᐏ ᑭᐧᐁ ᐁᕈᐅ ᐤᒥᐟᐅ ᐧᐁ᠈ ᐄ ᐅᑭᒥᐊᐟᕁᐢᐧᐞ᠊ ᐧᐸᐅᒥᐅᕁ᠈

'Patrick said she was,' said Finn, 'but she's right, isn't she? We need the hydrant before we go get Dad!' He sprang to his feet. 'What does it look like?'

'A small blue bottle of glass, wrapped in flames of gold with a gold stopper.' George frowned. 'But I don't sense it in this tower, Finn. I would know if it was here – it has your father's blood in it, and that has a magnetic pull.'

Finn's face flared with hope. 'You could find Dad yourself?'

'No, my boy. He is too far away, even for such powers as mine, and the scryers have had no success either.' George patted Finn on the shoulder and got to his feet. 'But we have a clue from the words Augustus spoke, and your sister shares a link with him.'

I can't always feel him, signed Tula, swallowing back her tears. *Mostly, I think he's blocking me out. And we don't know what those words mean.*

'We can check with Drishti,' suggested George. 'She can do an online translation once the systems are back up.'

'The systems are down?' asked Angelina. 'Again?'

'Drishti blames the earth tremor,' explained George, 'but she usually sorts it out fast, doesn't she? Then we go to Augustus, and I'm certain the link with your father will strengthen the closer we get.'

⅃ⱯⱰ ʒⱰ ⱯⱰ ʒⱰⱰϝⱯⱰϝ ϝⱯ≡ ᏒⱰʒⱰⱰϝⱰ ▽≡ᴦ≡ Ɒ▽ⱰᴦⱰᴦⱯ⌀ʒⱰⱰ ∨ᑭ

'The hydrant must be here, George,' said Patrick. 'Maybe he shielded it. He did that a lot when they all lived here, but I know all his hiding places.' He whirled away and began searching, teasing away plants, pressing wooden panels, leaping from table, to stairs, to shelves and back to the table again, his movements quick and sure, but a little frantic.

How will we come with you if we cannot fly? signed Tula.

'What did she say?' asked Angelina.

'They can't fly,' said Charlie.

Patrick paused briefly in his search to note, 'So they cannot come on this quest.'

There was a stunned pause and George was just about to say something when Angelina cried, 'They're Augustus's children! Of course they c—'

'He has no *wings*!' interrupted Patrick, sweeping aside a jumble of scientific instruments from the table and pulling open the lid of a wooden box. 'They won't grow from...' He gestured at Finn's hunched back and trailed off.

There was silence in the room.

Then Finn spoke and his voice was bleak. 'It's true. I have no wings and Tula wasn't born with any either.'

The adults stared back at him blankly.

'A-and,' stammered Finn, shifting uncomfortably,

ᏔᎠ≡ ᏞᏧᏤᏧ≡ᖆᎾ ᏂᏂ ᏫᎪᏏᏏᎠ ᏔᎠ≡ ᏧᏒᎦᎾᏂᏂ ᏙᏗᎩ.

'I was wondering if it's because I have this hump and if there's anything that can be done to … to fix it…'

There was another stunned silence, even Patrick halting his search to walk slowly back down the stairs, and for some reason Finn felt his throat close up with a hurt that smarted his eyes.

'You do not need *fixing*, Finn Flint,' said George, his voice gravelly with the intensity of what he was saying. 'Like all of us, you just need to grow – in a different way. Different people have different strengths, different powers – you are more powerful than you know.'

Tula's hand crept into Finn's and he swallowed hard, unable to speak.

'Er…' said Charlie. 'Oleksiy down in the town does flying rigs for … for injured firebloods, and maybe… Well, we could ask him if there's anything that would fit over…' He gestured at the hump on Finn's back, and flushed, then spoke quickly as if to undo his awkward words. 'But don't you know that wings come for the first time only when you first really need them? Some firebloods never grow them – they prefer Oleksiy's options – and yours—'

'Maybe they will still come?' blurted Finn. 'And Tula's!'

There was a split second of silence, then: 'See?'

ᔊ᙮ᑯᒥᏇ᙮ ᒥᐁᐁᐧᏆᏇ ᏘᔉᏇ Ᏹᖑᔭᒥᒥ ᐁᏘᏛ ᐊᏛᏇ Ꮧᐁᖑ, ᏘᔉᏇ ᔍᐃᐁᐧ ᒥᐁ᙮᙭᙮ᑯ

Patrick exploded. He gestured to Finn with a wide, frantic arm. 'This is all pointless. You were right, George, the hydrant is definitely not here. The children know nothing of it, or of Augustus's whereabouts. We should just be leaving for Elbrus to get him, right now.'

'Charlie,' continued Shen with a narrow-eyed look at Patrick, 'we're running out of time. You stay with Finn and Tula, teach them to fly with Oleksiy's rigs so they're not grounded if things go wrong. Yes?'

'No!' yelped Charlie. 'I want to come! You need me—'

But Shen gave him a stern look, a hand held up in the halt position, and said in firm tones, 'Charlie, you're the best for the job, and you know that, truly, don't you?'

'But—' spluttered Charlie.

'I'll fetch the medical supplies that Augustus will need,' continued Shen. 'Angelina, you will need to exercise all your patience in waiting for that translation from Drishti.'

'Simon might return with news from the Ministry of Defence sooner than Drishti's technology is back up,' said George. 'Charlie, I suggest breakfast first—'

'Hang on,' interrupted Angelina with a deep scowl that threw two deep grooves from the bridge of her

⨂ᚼᚦᙠ ᐱ ᑯᗕᖡᗕᖣᐱᘎᙅᐱᖣᘜᙍᙅ ᖠᙅ ᙖᐱ∧ᙍ ᖠᙠᘜᙅ ᒒᖣᙍᐱᖠᐺᖣᖣᙍᠶ ᙅᙍ

nose to her forehead, 'Charlie Flybynight is really going to be the actual tutor of Finn and Tula Flint?'

Patrick grinned at her. 'Charlie is gr—'

'Do not say *great*,' snapped Angelina. 'Do not! He has not turned out well!' Her nostrils flared at Charlie. 'He may have some decent flying skills, but he is feral! He doesn't do what he is told, he's a terrible ringleader and I'll bet he knows zero songs!'

'I do too!' replied Charlie, sounding four instead of fourteen.

'I bet not a single lyric stays in your head!'

'I know the important song – the song that matters.'

'Everyone knows "*Canu I Ni*"!' protested Angelina.

Dad's lullaby? signed Tula, exchanging a glance with Finn.

'Not like I do!' retorted Charlie, incensed. 'I can do more melodies than anyone else, and I know our history better than most—'

'He does,' interjected Patrick, 'and his flying skills are not just decent – they're … well, they're nearly as good as mine.'

Shen put a hand up to hide a smile.

'Ha!' barked Angelina. 'If anyone can get Finn and Tula flying, it's Grey Griffin—'

'I'm afraid, Angelina, that Grey Griffin would refuse

△∠⊃ᔑᒷᒐ ᒣᔑᒷ ᒐ𝔯ᒐᒷᖇ ᒣᗕ ᗷᒲᒷ ᗕᐁᔑ ᒍᒪᒷᒷ≡.

outright, besides being far too dangerous to be charged with their care,' said George, 'and in any event we will need him for the retrieval of Augustus. Patrick, you will do your best to persuade him to come with us now?'

'Simon Veritas should be back any minute with information from London,' replied Patrick. 'And I'll do my best to convince Grey Griffin to help us find Augustus, but—'

'He's still really angry,' said George. 'I know.'

Shen smiled. 'All is not yet lost. Don't forget he was Augustus's greatest ally.'

'Hmm,' replied George. 'Don't forget that Grey is very unpredictable.'

'Well,' said Angelina, 'I value an unpredictable griffin more than the information Simon Veritas brings us from London. When have the frailskins ever known more than we have?'

George shrugged. 'We should remember that we have the ancient magic and great power of these children on our side,' he said. 'Even if they don't know how to use it yet.' He leaned forward, chucked Finn beneath the chin and squeezed Tula's hand gently. 'Good luck, you two. By the time we are back with your father, you'll probably be better aviators than me.' He turned and left, the door swinging closed behind him.

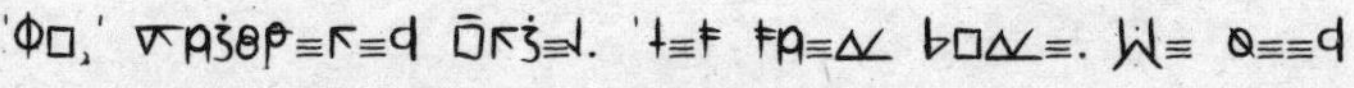

Orange juice? signed Tula. Tân, perched on Tula's shoulder, blinked his round eyes, also looking hopeful.

Finn shook his head. Fresh-struck flint.

George, the most powerful fireblood of them all, was afraid.

But he didn't tell Tula that.

15

Shen, Patrick, George and Angelina left in a rush of silk, leather and linen, talking urgently and leaving Charlie with his arms crossed, frowning at Finn and Tula.

We should follow them! signed Tula. Her gestures were wild and urgent.

'Yes! Where do we get the rigs?' said Finn.

'I can't teach you how to fly in a day,' Charlie ground out, once the last echoes of the closing door had faded. His hands were clenched in angry fists at his sides. 'Impossible. Not even with Oleksiy's rigs.'

'Patrick said you're the best, that you were taught by the best,' said Finn, his throat tight.

'A pity my teacher couldn't teach you!' replied Charlie. 'This is just *wrong*! I bet they're making me do this just to stop me from leaving Portaldor!'

His eyes were bright and Finn wondered suddenly what was so awful about Tula and him that Charlie felt they were a lost cause. His hunch? Tula's silence? His heart clenched and his bones protested as he pushed his shoulder blades as far back as they would go, standing as straight as he could. This was why his father had kept them away from the real world. To protect them from this horrible feeling of shame and sadness and humiliation that was squeezing up his chest right now. He had a terrible fear that he might cry, and he—

He cleared his throat. 'I wouldn't want to teach me either,' he said, his voice croaky.

Charlie looked startled, jolted out of his fury and frustration. A long vine trailing from the ceiling moved slowly and gently, swatting him across the face. His eyes narrowed as he glanced up at it. Leaves overhead moved and rustled though there was no air that came through the windows high above them. He released a shaky breath.

'I'm sorry,' he muttered, and Finn's mouth flooded with an uncomfortable swirl of flavours: flint, chocolate, peanuts, caramel, orange juice, more flint, flint, flint…

'He's feeling overwhelmed,' came a voice from the bag.

Charlie flushed. 'I am not!'

'It's because there are more important things to know than flying,' explained the Stone.

ᑊᙰᎮᏕᎾᙰ ᎾᏗᐺᑫᑫᙰᏕᙰᑫ ᐃᙰᎱ ᗱᙰᏕ ᐁᙰᐁᏕᐃ ᒻᏕᙰᐃᑊᗱ ᐸᙰᐺ ᐃᐁᐃᐃᏗ

Like what? signed Tula.

'Like how to ask for a house invitation, the best way to carve a weapon, what all the fires mean, never ever say *marw*—'

'Mahwoo?' repeated Finn.

'Nearly,' said Charlie. 'Softer at the end: *marw*.'

That's what he said, signed Tula.

'Stop!' said the Stone. 'Put your hand down, Finn! Welsh is a magical language for dragon people – use it carefully!'

Tula's fingers flew again. *What did you mean about an invitation?*

'Look into the windows,' replied the Stone.

Charlie frowned. 'There's no time for invitations from the houses.'

The Stone made a rude sound. 'You stupid boy! You're just afraid you won't get an invitation to join a house of power, which is ridiculous. Get me out of this bag.'

Finn shrugged off the backpack, put it on the table and lifted out a smooth oval of frosted crystal that seemed to glow from within.

'Wow,' breathed Charlie. 'It's true. All the descriptions are true. It's just like a big bit of sea glass when actually it's one of the most powerful pieces of the planet. Think what we could do with this!'

‡ꟼ= ⅃ӡϴꟼⵑ ꟼ=᛭ᑫ �664ϴꟼ ᐱ⵿ϴⵑ‡ ‡ꟼ=᠘. ‡ꟼ= ᑫⵑⵜϴ◖ϴ ꟼⵕⵤ

Tula put her hand protectively on the surface.

'What are you doing?' asked Charlie as Tula pulled the bag open.

'She's putting the Stone away,' said Finn. 'I'm not sure "think what we could do with this!" is making me or Tula feel very comfortable about sharing her with you,' he added in a rush. He reached for the Stone, about to help Tula put her back in the rucksack, but a low, musical sound filled the air.

Laughter.

'Thank you for protecting me, Tula Flint and Finn Flint, although I'm not sure I'll forgive you for choosing such a stinky old bag for me,' said the Stone.

Charlie blinked.

'And you, Charlie Flybynight,' said the Stone to him. 'You even *think* of taking a scraping off me to put into some hydrant alchemy and I'll spontaneously combust.' And as she spoke, the light in the room changed.

'I don't think the houses will be extending invitations n-now—' stammered Charlie. 'Look!'

They stared in silence at the four huge stained-glass windows placed north, south, east and west in the walls of the watchtower. Though the morning sun now lit up the room, each of these windows seemed dark and shadowy. They held pictures of people in

◁═b⅗ᑰ═◁ ᐁ◻◶Θ Θ⅗Θb═ ┠ᕈ⅄┠ ⅄∠◻ᖴ═ ▽═ᖴ═ Θ══◁═◁ ⅗Θ ┠ᕈ═

ancient clothing, and they did not seem to be very inviting at all.

Invitations to what? asked Tula.

'To join them,' replied Charlie. 'Each house holds a power of dragonkind – frugality, fire, force, flight – and every fireblood has an invitation from at least one of them.'

'Your mother and father had invitations from more than one,' said the Stone. 'That's why they were so powerful, and everyone forgets the glass dome, which still stands even though it was bombarded by Venomous in the Last Battle— Argh!' And then she went suddenly quiet.

'Oh boy,' said Charlie. 'I learned about this last term in History. The Telling Stone hates talking about the Last Battle. We won't get any more information from her for a while.'

Bum, signed Tula.

'Tula!' said Finn. *Bum* was much ruder in Tula's sign language than in words.

More happened in that Last Battle than people are telling us, said Tula.

Finn glanced at Charlie. 'I don't suppose you could explain?'

'Not before breakfast. Come on. Errol Ember will be hoovering up a stack of pancakes right about now

ᒋᐱᗷᐁ ᛏ�口 ᑭᒋ口ᛏᗱᑲᛏ ᛏᑫᐁ ᛍ口ᑭᐱᑫ ᒋᑭ口ᐱᛜ ᛏᑫᐁ ᛍ口ᑭᗱᛏ 口ᒋ

and we'd better ask him for help because there's no way Grey Griffin will talk to Patrick, but he might listen to Errol. Errol has a way with the mythics that means we won't get eaten alive. Then we'll get you flying, with or without rigs.'

16

8ȝ×ł≡≡Q

Charlie waited just a few seconds to check Finn and Tula were behind him before clattering at speed down the spiral staircase. After a few dizzying turns, he pushed hard against a small iron door, and the three of them emerged on to a stone walkway sparkling with icicles and drifts of snow.

Finn's jaw dropped at the shock of freezing air and an incomprehensible cacophony. 'What the…' he breathed, instantly transfixed by the chaos two storeys below. Hundreds of people were crowding through the cobbled streets and alleys that wriggled and curved through random rows and lines of clustered buildings rising at various heights all around.

'Morning market,' noted Charlie. 'Used to wake me up at sunrise that did, until I moved to the treehouse.'

Tân scrambled to the top of Tula's head for a better view. Finn and Tula stared out at a multicoloured tableau of people who looked as if they'd arrived here

≡∧ȝ¡θ. łⱵꞀ≡ … ŁⱴŁ ᒡł ⱴ ꝒꞀȝᑊ≡ Ⱶ≡ⱵꞀϴ≡ łꝑⱷⱱϴꝑł łⱽⱵ

from every corner of the planet. They were buying and selling things from market stalls, from barrows, from shops so old they seemed to sag and bulge onto the streets into which they were crammed. Like the houses around the piazza, they leaned every which way, some tall, some wide, some low and squat. There were stone arches, many with huge scorch marks searing up the front of them, and the buildings had windows of every kind: round, rectangular, big and small.

Through swirling snowflakes and patches of mist, Finn could see that some roads were wide and straight, others narrow and dark, twisting secretly between buildings. There seemed to be a wall of impenetrable cloud, banking up into the sky from about a hundred metres out, so thick that he could look directly into the shimmer of the sun.

Below them, chimneys leaned, most wisping smoke from their stacks, and wherever possible the shops and homes and courtyards hosted balconies that offered access to the outside. From the balconies hung lines of washing airing in the pale sunshine, pairs of … were those … *wings*? Pieces of chain mail? Faces, infant and old, peeped over the balustrades, their voices calling down to those below.

'Mama!' yelled a child clutched in her grandmother's arms. 'Me too! Me too!'

ᴘᶱᴑᴀ ᵻ▢ ᴘ⅄⅄.

A woman in the crowd with a basket on her hip waved back with a smile and was soon haggling with a man selling piles of strange fruit and vegetables, some of them completely unrecognisable to Finn's amazed eyes.

'Tula,' he whispered. 'Look over on the right!'

He pointed to a vast man with enormous tattooed arms and a piratical beard standing on his shop's doorstep above which read the sign:

It's a Wing Thing!
None better than Oleksiy's expert fixings!

The man held up two vast scaly feathers for all to see.

'Wing extensions HERE!' he bellowed in a Ukrainian accent. 'Forged with lava lathes from FINEST materials! Two for one! Two for one!'

'Who'd buy *one*?' snorted Charlie, jostling against Finn for a better view. 'You'd go in circles forever. Look, there's Angelina, arguing with Patrick as usual. She's head of the House of Brann. Patrick says he's the best flyer – he's captain of the aviators – but people say Angelina can fly further than him, though he'd never admit it, and she can do arch spins that I've never seen Patrick try. What are they doing? They should be hurrying to Drishti and the labyrinth.'

⊕ᕼ□ρ⊥'ᑲᖋᔑ◁ᑫ ⅃ᖴᑯᖋ≡� ᖴᑌ ᗷᔑ⊖ Ɽᴏᔑ⊖ᗺᖴᖶ⊖. 'Ⱶ⅄ᔑᖶ⊥' Ⱶ≡ 57ᐳᖴ⊖

'Sold out of flying rigs!' yelled Oleksiy. 'But still stocking harnesses from Hungary! Best on the island! No chafing or rubbing of the jiggly bits!'

'No flying rigs!' said Finn. He and Tula stared at Charlie in horror.

'Don't worry – we can borrow some if we can't get you airborne without them. I'm sure lots of people would be happy to help,' said Charlie.

Finn was startled by a taste of rust. *Why's that not true?* he thought. *Why wouldn't people want to help us?*

The three of them turned to watch Angelina bark something at Patrick. They banged on the door of a shop selling fire pellets, firecrackers, fire bombs, fire blades – and the heavy steel door was opened by a tall, statuesque woman with high cheekbones and skin as dark as the night.

Finn took a breath in, and released it, filtering out all the noise around him until it was almost as if he'd tuned in to the specific frequency of this particular conversation.

'Hello, Edith,' he heard Angelina say above the throng. 'I need more arrows, please, and this imbecile needs a new brain because he thinks he can sweet-talk you into giving him all your precious yew berries for Grey Griffin.'

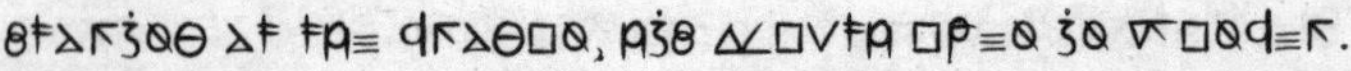

ΘⴼⴸⴼⵀⵣꙨ⵿ ⵣⴼ ⴼꙨ≡ ꝖⴼⵘꙨⵑꙨ, ꝖⵣꙨ ⵘ∠Ꙩ⵬ⴼꝖ Ꙩⴼ≡Ꙩ ⵣꙨ �384Ꙩ⵿Ꝗ≡ⴼ.

There was the sound of laughter. They went in, and the door slammed loudly behind them. The sign above read:

The Arsenal

It had no shop windows at all – it was just a patchwork of metal sheets riveted together – and the windows above it were closed with copper shutters that were turning green.

'What are the yew berries for?' Finn asked Charlie.

'You heard that?' replied Charlie. 'Who taught you *gwrando mewn sŵn?*'

'What's gwrando min soon?'

'*Gwrando mewn sŵn*,' said Charlie impatiently. 'It's *listen in noise*, being able to hear things others cannot – it's a rare dragon skill unique to the House of Siarad.'

Finn shrugged at the same time that Tula signed, *Dad always taught us to listen properly. You just have to breathe and concentrate. Does this mean we're from the House of Siarad and not Brann or Kellan?* But Charlie was already leading them further down the walkway and did not see her questions.

'The berries are a treat for Grey Griffin, and the tall lady is Edith Ember, Errol's mother – she's the best arms maker we've got, and that's where the Ember family live,' he continued, 'in the Arsenal. They have always been allies of the Flints.'

Finn noticed that across the way from it gleamed the windows of

THE FORTRESS APOTHECARY
TAHIRA'S TONICS CURE EVERY AILMENT

and there was a restless queue lengthening through the market stalls towards its entrance. The people shuffling closer and closer to its doors mostly had the same anxious expression, and many of them were deep in intense conversations.

Why are they so scared? signed Tula.

Charlie traced her stare down to the queue below, a small frown wrinkling his forehead. 'The people lining up are mostly from the scrying families. I'm guessing they've seen that Augustus has disappeared and that you two have arrived, so they're stocking up on potions and poultices to cure Venomous wounds.'

'Venomous wounds?' said Finn. He dragged his eyes away from what looked like the world's oldest treat shop, filled with mountains of brightly coloured sweets and perfect chocolates.

⊥=ᴧẟꝋd ꞁᴧ=ẟᴦ Əᴧẟ=�itꝋ ẑⱱꝋꞁ ⅄ᴧᴦdꝋ ᴧ⊽ᴧ⅄ Ꞁᴦ◻ᴧ ꞁᴧ=

Lolly's Pops and Sugar Drops

'There's going to be an attack?'

Charlie paused, staring grimly down at the shifting queue outside the pharmacy. 'You've felt the earth tremors. There's news of Mount Elbrus in Russia showing volcanic activity, Hekla in Iceland is blowing smoke and Vesuvius is gusting ash. It's not normal. A lot of people are expecting a Venomous invasion of epic proportions. There are debates about the next world war starting this month or soon after. Also, a wyrm egg has been stolen from the labyrinth, so everyone knows that someone's launching a secret quest of their own to find Augustus.'

'Why would the quest be secret? Doesn't everyone want to find him? What does a wyrm do?'

Charlie sighed. 'Feelings about the whole Flint family, and especially Augustus, are complicated, but mostly based on pure fear. Some people want what he knows and then they want him dead. Other people really believe he's the only one who can stop the earth blowing apart.'

Dad can do that? signed Tula, but Charlie did not reply.

'Wyrms are ancient creatures that can tunnel through to the scent of their target, even if they're a

ᎾᐃᎮᏒᎨᎤᎾ ᒵ≡ᐱᎾᎸ.

hundred miles away. They're like a sat nav with road-building capabilities, right? Very rare. One going missing from the labyrinth is a big deal.' He looked back at Finn and Tula impatiently. 'Let's have breakfast, then we'll get on with your first flight. Don't look at anyone. Don't talk to anyone. Especially not any mythics. Those who want Augustus dead would quite like to see the end of the pair of you too. Stay close.'

17

8=∧=θ†==Q

Charlie led them on to a street with stone balustrades and high arches that overlooked the ocean on their left. The air was full of the sizzling smells of hot food, and the noise of cooking and conversation was loud. Finn and Tula stared at the series of counters, hatches and the open doors into restaurants and cafés all along the right-hand side of the walkway. Tân patted Tula's face urgently and she smiled down at him.

We'll eat soon, she promised him.

The figures who were crowded into noisy groups eating pancakes, sausages in rolls and bacon baps mostly looked like people, but here and there Finn saw some had horns on their heads, or reptilian skin, and a few even had wings hanging down from their backs.

The children stepped out of the shadows and the hubbub faded as the people and creatures turned to

 Þ=□┌Θ=˙θ Ꟁ=∆┌† Ꟁ∆∆∠∧=┌=ꟼ šQ Ꟁšθ Ҍꟁ=θ†: Ꟁšθ ∆┌∆∠θ

stare at them, their loud conversation reducing to fearful whispers.

'Oh boy,' muttered Charlie. 'There's Liberty Fairview from the *Town Scryer*. Somebody's obviously tipped her off that you've arrived, and she's already spread the word. Remember, don't talk to anyone.'

'The Flints!' exclaimed a beautiful woman. She was standing close to them with two of her friends, all of them wearing colourful floaty chiffon dresses, with wings like butterflies and bright hair piled high on their heads. 'You *are* the Flints, aren't you?' She put a wooden tub of what looked like falafels down on the balustrade near her, and took a step forward.

'Just passing through, Miss Liberty,' said Charlie respectfully, but she remained firmly in their path and ignored him entirely.

'We've been waiting for your return for a long time.' She gave them a very bright smile as her friends stepped back, and then very quietly the walkway began to empty of people. Conversations were hushed, food orders hurried and in a few minutes no one was left but Liberty Fairview, a few curious stragglers and Charlie, looking grumpy.

'Hi!' said Liberty to Finn and Tula. 'Could I trouble you for a quick snippet on how you plan to save the world?'

 θ†ξ‖ ≡×†≡θd≡٩ ξθ ⋀⋏ξθ ⊦ᒋ�口†≡ᑏ†ξθθ. ﻬﺎ⋏⋏†δ ﻬﺎ⋏⋏† ⋀⋏θ †⋀≡

She smiled brightly again and whipped out an intricately carved wooden handle with a crystal ball as big as her fist on the end of it. Finn blinked. It looked a bit like a microphone, but at the same time not at all. The end of it swirled with mesmerising colours.

Tula frowned.

'If that's a tricky question right now' – Liberty's voice was still light and chirpy – 'then we could start with whether you've heard anything from your father? Most people here believe he deserves everything that's now befallen him.'

Tula gasped, and her face went from confusion to anger. Finn's eyes narrowed, but the woman continued saying terrible things in her friendly, musical voice.

'Augustus abandoned us when we needed him most, when we were terrified and even the mythics were afraid. So many blame him for worldwide catastrophes, and fear him and fear his pow—'

Tula pushed forward with sudden strength, startling Finn.

Fear him? Blame him for what, exactly? He is kind and gentle and thoughtful! You want to know what real fear is? She was flushed and her fingers were flying. *Real fear is not knowing if we'll ever see our father again! Actual fear is watching him die and not being able to save him! Fear like that is so big that it stops us*

ᖇ◌ξ◌⊦† ⴲ══◌ᓄ ≢⋔═ ◻Ⴑᑫ ⋏⋌ᕆ⊖ ᐁ⋔ᔑᒑᐱ═ᑫ ᒥⵔⴸ◌ᑫ ᕁ◌ᑫ ⴲ⋌⋔

caring about whether the world is going to explode or not! We just want our dad back! Tula blinked, took a shaky breath and seemed to notice the crystal ball for the first time. It glowed for a second, then went *pop*.

The breakfast-burrito vendor hatch came down with a slam, and Liberty winced. 'Thanks so much,' she said, dropping her crystal-ball microphone into her bag. She grabbed her falafels and hurried away as more doors closed, shutters rattled down and curtains whisked shut.

Finn's forehead was creased in incomprehension. 'What just happened?'

The ocean view to their left was suddenly obscured by a thick bank of stormy cloud that gusted out from the open mouths of stone gargoyles on the other side of the balustrade.

'*What just happened?*' snapped Charlie. 'Not a good thing! I said head down, don't look at anyone, don't talk to anyone. I didn't think I had to spell out *don't talk to the paparazzi*. Ugh. Liberty will be broadcasting her own interpretation of everything you've said in the *Town Scryer*, and it won't be anything like what you meant.'

Finn and Tula did their best to ignore the curious stares of the stragglers staring at them from a safe distance as they followed Charlie. Some dashed away once realisation dawned, while hurrying people and storybook creatures retreated with urgent whispers and wide eyes. All of them stared at Finn and Tula curiously.

One man who definitely, *definitely* had a two-metre tail called out, 'Charlie! Is it true that pair is the fiercest firebloods the world has ever seen? You testing them? When? Where?'

Charlie grinned at him and waved. 'No one is fiercer than me, Hairless! Not before breakfast, at any rate!' and the tailed man's laughter echoed behind them down a narrow stone walkway that opened into a quadrangle of uneven flagstones.

'Testing?' asked Finn. 'And what's the *Town Scryer*?'

'Technically,' said Charlie, 'you can't leave the fortress until you've got a questing licence to prove you can handle yourself should a bit of trouble raise its melted head. You've got to prove yourself in a fight with a weapon of your own making, be able to fly really fast, disappear, partner with a creature and a bunch of other stuff.'

I don't like the sound of this licensing, signed Tula. *It's full of things we can't do.*

Finn was about to ask Charlie how firebloods were trained in these things, but he'd beckoned them impatiently down a steep stone spiral staircase, so he bit back his questions, and he and Tula hurried after him.

ᛏᚱᛄᛉᚻ ᚱᚨᛉᚻᚹᛏ ᚢᚨᚦ᰻ᚱᚻᛏᚥᚨᚦᛚ ᚻ᰻ᚱᚦᚥᚱᚻ –

After what felt like a hundred turns, they emerged into an enormous courtyard. It was enclosed by the leaning walls and balconies and verandas of tall, tightly packed buildings lining the quadrangle, and it was full to the brim with children of all ages.

'The school dining room!' announced Charlie, arms flung wide. 'Much better food here than the boulevard above. Fewer judgy grown-ups too. These kids won't have heard about your arrival yet, so enjoy being anonymous. It won't last.'

'What…?' whispered Finn. 'This isn't a room…'

Faces of all kinds looked out from windows on to the flagstoned space, but they didn't stay long – it seemed the gathering of kids to eat was not much of an event. But every available niche and balcony seemed to have a child teetering, sitting or hanging from it, like bats in a belfry. They made a noisy racket, calling across the square: insults and information, jokes and jibes, some with bowls of porridge or fruit or cereal, others held plates piled high with pancakes and some had nothing but crumbs on their lips and grins on their faces.

Finn stood stock still in amazement. All around them wings unfurled, flapped and sliced the air from children as young as four or five. They swooped here and there, but most went back and forth to a long,

ᕼ= ᖴᐁᖇ⦿=ᕲ � ᒪᐁᕮ ᑫᕼ= ᣒ⦿ᣕ⦿ᑫᖴ ᐃ⦿ᐁᣕ⦿, ᕟᣕᕼ ᒪᐁᕮ= ᐃᒪᣕ⦿ᕼᖴ

busy hatch in the eastern wall to pick up bowls of what looked like summer berries dusted with ice. Old-fashioned caravans were shoved into walls and corners, serving THE BEST WAFFLES! and PILES OF PANCAKES! YUM! and CHURROS, CHURROS, CHURROS alongside stalls of so many other delicious things he'd only ever heard about. FULL ENGLISH! and CONTINENTAL CROISSANTS had queues of rowdy children going round the tables, with an argument about maple syrup breaking out near the back. The sounds and smells of all the different foods were overwhelming, and the chaos of all the different languages and accents, all the whirring wings, clashing dishes and spoons, running feet and laughter – mostly laughter – was astonishing.

On the hard-packed ground, mismatched tables and chairs were crowded about in no particular arrangement, and it was a struggle to keep up with Charlie, who moved forward through the throngs quite effortlessly, ignoring swarms of little kids clamouring for his attention. They reached a table near the western wall where a gap in the buildings showed glimpses of the sea beyond, and Charlie gestured to Tula and Finn to sit. A boy on the opposite side of the table glanced up, his brown eyes blinking curiously from behind thick-rimmed rectangular glasses before

ᐁᒉᑊᗄ ᗅᗄᑊᕄᐧ ᖬᗄᐢ ᖯᐧᐱᐧᕄᖉ ᗅᐺᐞᐞᐧᕄᐧᑫ ᐁᒉᑊᗄ ᖬᐧᕉᕉᒉᐡᐧ

attending once more to the notebook in which he was scribbling furiously.

'Hey, Errol,' said Charlie.

'Hey,' said the boy. Finn thought he looked wary and guarded. His skin was smooth and brown, and his mop of unruly black hair needed desperate attention. One of the birds from a noisy dovecote high on a wall above swooped down to land on Errol's shoulder, and Tula's eyes widened.

'Simon Veritas brought you the stabiliser you wanted for the plane yet?' asked Charlie, surveying the main serving hatch on the far wall with interest.

'No,' said Errol, stroking the pigeon's head. 'Hello, Steve. How's your phantom leg?' The bird cooed, hopped about a bit on his one leg, then flapped away again, back to the dovecote. Errol threw a glance in Charlie's direction. 'I've given up on Veritas. Gonna make my own.' He turned a page in his sketchbook and began drawing a diagram of what looked like a matchbox with something small in it.

'Huh,' said Charlie, without interrupting his scrutiny of the food being served, 'you had breakfast yet?'

Errol stopped scribbling and started paging frantically through a leather-bound book that seemed as if it should be in a display case somewhere instead of in an impatient pair of hands.

= θ=ᒋΘλ, θ⊓† λ θ□Ⅵ θ℘□ᖇ≡, λθd †≡ɒ˧θd ᒐθdᒋ≡⊼

'Errol. Pay attention,' said Charlie. 'This is Finn and Tula.'

Errol muttered something under his breath that sounded like Latin to Finn. He was not paying attention.

'Errol! What are you looking for in *The Book of Mythics*, you big swot?' Charlie narrowed his eyes. 'You didn't have anything to do with the wyrm egg going missing, did you?'

'No!' Errol rubbed his forehead, and finally glanced up at Charlie. 'Of course not! I'm just researching the labyrinth. The recent wave swells round the island, the dimensions between the last of the passages and my workshop … I've been wondering if the water dragon might still be on the island somewhere.'

Charlie shook his head. 'The labyrinth is out of bounds for a reason, Ezza. Stop going down there.' He half turned as the crowd at the FULL ENGLISH stall drifted away with steaming plates. 'Anyone want bacon and eggs? I'll see if there's ketchup. Looks like Chef Otto is in a good mood.'

'Yes, please,' said Finn, his stomach clenching. 'For me and Tula, please.'

Errol glanced up at Finn. 'You feel the tremor this morning? We're gonna need escape routes, or maybe other ways back in here, through the labyrinth. We're going to need support from the mythics…' He

ᗑ═ᑕᖿᏫ═ �827dᑫ═ᏗᖵᎩ ᏴᒪᏠᐈᏢᗑ═ᑫ ᏘᏕ═Ꮧ, ᏘᏗᏠᏛᏅ═ᖿᏠᏫᏫ ᏠᏗ ᗑ═ᖿ

stopped his agitated page-turning to say, 'Code red – no flying. So you'd better not, Charlie.'

Charlie laughed disbelievingly. 'Errol's a total worrywart,' he said to Finn.

Finn frowned, feeling a prickle of unease, and the taste of fresh-struck flint in his mouth. 'What do you mean by "current level of threat"?' he asked Errol.

Charlie ignored the question and strode over to the serving hatch, but Errol put down his pen and stared at them curiously.

'Code red is one step away from full lockdown. With the disappearance of Augustus, we're expecting a Venomous attack somehow, somewhere, of epic proportions. Heads of Brann, Kellan, Siarad and Vulkan are meeting with Simon Veritas as soon as he's back from the frailskins today to discuss what he's learned from the Ministry of Defence. Top secret, but everyone here knows, of course.'

Finn and Tula exchanged glances that said the same thing: *We cannot get stuck here.*

He added, 'We're all in terrible peril,' just as a blood-curdling howl came from a metal grating beneath their feet. Tula jumped and Tân flung himself safely inside her shirt collar. The howl chilled Finn to the bone, filling his mouth with a rush of flavours so intense that he was nearly sick.

18

�674ᴛ══ᴏ

'ᴀROOOOOO!'

'What the—' blurted Finn. He stepped back quickly, pulling Tula with him, but no one else blinked an eye at the awful sound.

'Now *that* is a mythic creature having a moan.' Errol closed his notebook and sighed. 'Steve says they're not happy right now.'

'Ha!' said Charlie, returning with armfuls of plates, condiments and cutlery. 'They could use their skills and powers to protect us and the world, but most of them prefer a peaceful life retired in the labyrinth or outside on the island.'

'You can't blame them after what happened in the Last Battle,' replied Errol.

What exactly happened in the Last Battle? signed Tula at the same time as Finn asked, 'Can we meet them?'

'No,' said Errol, looking away, picking up his

ᴏ674ᴛᴡᴏᴛ4═θ.

pencil again. 'The mythics insist that their labyrinth is closely guarded.'

'Dunno why when their guards are such idiots,' Charlie chipped in.

'Rude,' said Errol. 'You don't like anyone except George and Drishti. That's why you haven't got your questing licence.' He bit his lip, as if he suddenly regretted what he'd said.

A shadow crossed Charlie's face. 'I can't leave here to go questing because I can't hide my wings, Errol,' he retorted. 'They're stuck.'

'*And* of course because you can't hide your fine and magnificent wings – of which I'm really jealous,' said Errol, and his face transformed in a grin of cheeky mischief that made Charlie laugh.

'They are very impressive,' said Finn.

Charlie flexed them up and out and a pocket of small children across the way whooped and cheered. He grinned and waved at them. A tall girl with wavy blue hair and green-tinged skin was settling them down for breakfast and she called out, 'Never taking the minions for you again, Charlie. This crew is impossible!' but she was laughing, and began making her way over to them.

'Good old Drishti,' said Charlie, his wings stretching even wider, the light catching the inky

Ɪ≡ᒉ�≡ ⅃ᴇᕊ≡� ᒉᴐᔑᕊ9ᴇ72≡ᴧᴙ ᴧ04ʒ0, ᴛᴧ≡ ᒉᴐᴧ04·ᒉᴧᕊ≡ᕊ

blackness of them so they gleamed in turquoise, emerald and sapphire blues.

Wow, signed Tula. *Do they really not go back in ever?*

'No,' said Charlie. He sighed, and his wings dropped back down into two neat furls against his back like rolled-up umbrellas ready for the next storm. 'I'm a laughing stock.'

'You're not a laughing stock, Charlie!' said Drishti, sitting down at the table next to Errol. Finn saw she was covered in pale scales from head to foot. 'You're the best aviator on the island.'

'Hi, Drishti,' said Errol, closing his notebook hurriedly as if he didn't want her to see his diagrams and notes.

'That's definitely not true, Drishti,' said Charlie as they did a complicated handshake. He shrugged at Tula. 'Wing retraction is an instinct. I stopped being able to do it when I was about seven, so now I'm stuck here on Portaldor with a boring code-red level of threat.'

Errol pushed his glasses up his nose. 'Code red because rumour has it we've been found even though Brann has hidden us in cloud and mist for hundreds of years. That's the reason for the grumpy, moaning mythics.' He put his head slightly to one side and blinked at Finn and Tula slowly from behind his thick glasses. 'Who are you? Are you new or just visiting?'

'Just visiting,' said Finn. 'Hoping to leave today or tomorrow. Clouds really hide Portaldor?'

Errol took a plate of food and a bottle of ketchup from Charlie. 'Yeah, well, the breathers are a powerful lot,' he said. 'Thanks, Charlie.'

Charlie thumped four more on the table, followed by plates of pancakes piled high with summer berries and lashings of maple syrup. 'I got some for you too, Drishti, as promised. Your computers up and running yet?'

Drishti shook her head, and long tendrils of her blue hair swooped and swirled around her head in a strangely hypnotic dance as if completely immune to gravity. 'So frustrating,' she sighed. 'I'm sorry this keeps happening, but it doesn't matter because—'

She stopped abruptly and looked at Tula, with her head on one side, who was signing, *What are breathers?*

'House of Brann,' said Charlie, throwing himself down in a chair at the head of the table, already hungrily eating his food. 'Airheads. They control things like clouds, mirages, a haze, a screen of sky. Easy for them to keep us all hidden.'

Drishti reached across and clouted Charlie playfully on the head.

ᐯᕼᒧᕠᕕᕁ ᕁᕮᒲᕕᕁ

'It's not easy at all, you ignorant boy.' She drizzled syrup on her pancakes and offered the bottle to Errol. 'I'm guessing Steve has already told you that Simon Veritas is back and he's confirmed that Augustus is being held under Mount Elbrus in Russia?'

'No!' yelped Errol. 'That pigeon! He's useless. This is huge news!'

Drishti nodded. 'Brilliantly huge,' she said with her mouth full, eating fast. 'I've got to go try rebooting the systems again to check that translation, but we don't need it now really, I guess.' She leaned forward, speaking quietly to Finn and Tula while a gust of wind rattled round the courtyard. 'Is it true you cannot fly?'

'Where did you hear that?' asked Charlie.

Drishti winked at him, swallowing her last mouthful. 'It's my job to send and receive all messages here, Charles, and don't worry – I'm very discreet. If people found out that the children of the Portaldor legends didn't have basic transportation skills there'd be even more panic than there currently is.'

'*Children of the Portaldor legends?*' queried Errol. His forehead furrowed. 'Who *are* you?' he asked Finn and Tula.

'The world's unluckiest kids,' said Drishti, getting up from the table. 'Everyone wants a piece of them, one way or another.' She paused, staring at Finn and

ᵀᴬ≡ Ᏸᐱᐱ≡ ᏔᗱᎾᏗ≡ᑫ ᶾᎾᵀ□ ᐱᏰᵀᶾ□ᴑ ᴧᎾ ᵀᴬ≡ ᎡᎾᶾᎾᏗᵀᎾ

Tula. 'Never thought I'd see the day you two came back here,' she said, her heavy eyebrows drawing tightly together as she turned to go. 'Bye, Charlie,' she said before disappearing through the stone arch, leaving Charlie smiling a stupid smile after her.

Errol pushed his plate away. 'I keep telling you, Charlie, she likes you. What was she saying abou—'

'We're just friends,' said Charlie, flushing.

'Ask your *friend* for access to the labyrinth and the tech room, Charlie!' pleaded Errol. 'I reckon I'd crack Augustus's *exact* location faster than anyone if I got half the chance to talk to the mythics without supervision! No one understands them better than me.'

'That's why we came to find you,' started Charlie, but Finn interrupted with, 'You could find our dad?'

'Your *dad*?' asked Errol, taken aback. 'Really? Augustus Flint is your dad?'

A group of teenagers at the next table looked up with sudden interest, and Finn held his tongue. A few other kids had turned to stare too. A girl and a boy with matching orange hair, about Finn's age, exchanged glances and walked up to the table.

'Where were you when he left?' asked Errol, his face alight. 'Wh—?'

'Errol,' said Charlie, pointing his fork at him. 'Augustus kept these two locked up in his house for

ᏋᎥᎥᏏᎡᏜᎤᏪᏇᎤ ᏆᎤᏂᎥᏜᏏᏜᎡᏏᎤ. ᏢᎦᎤᎡᏬᎦᎦ ᏋᏟᎡᎥᏜᏜᎲᎦᏪᎤ ᏖᎤ ᏅᎤᏂᏝᏇᏐᎥᏋ

eight years – hiding – you think they're just going to spill their postcode to you now?'

The spark in Errol's eyes dimmed.

'No one cares about their postcode,' said a voice behind Finn, and another chimed in with, 'Our father says Elbrus is protected by legions of Venomous, hordes of them, the likes of which London's Ministry of Defence has never seen before, so there's little chance of an Augustus retrieval anyway.'

Finn tasted a flood of orange juice in his mouth, and whirled round to see the flame-haired girl and boy smirking behind him.

'Our father is Simon Veritas,' continued the girl, 'and he has connections to all military and political intelligence the world over.'

'We-ell,' drawled Charlie, collecting up all the plates on the table, 'not sure about how *intelligent* his intelligence is if it's suggesting there's no hope for Augustus.'

'Oh please,' said the boy. 'Everyone on the island already knows Augustus is a lost cause.'

'Don't listen to Bestivo,' said Charlie to Finn and Tula, his jaw clenched. 'Or his silver-tongued twin. They know nothing.'

'We know how to get into the labyrinth,' said Bestivo, his smirk widening. 'And we know the griffin is in there, still, *and* me and Meritas –' he nodded to

ᑫᐊᐳᑫ, ᖖᖕᐱᣔᖬᎾᎾ ᗪᐴᖢ, ᒻᏎᎾᎾᣔᎾᎾ, ᙿᎾᖢᖕᐊᖢᣔᎾᎾ, ᐁᐴᐱᣔᎾᎾ

his sister – '*we* know that's because Patrick has failed to persuade him to rescue the mighty Augustus.'

'Yes,' said Meritas with a triumphant smile.

'Oh, shut up!' snapped Charlie, flushed with anger.

'Make me,' taunted Bestivo, and he laughed as he dodged the huge, messy ball of blue flame that Charlie hurled at him.

Charlie's fire roared again, but Meritas and Bestivo flung their arms up in defence, and the next ball of flame shattered into dancing stars that spun in the air, making squealing noises before bursting into showers of sparks with a rude raspberry sound. The twins leaped into the air with a showy explosion of colourful wings.

'Forget about Augustus,' yelled Meritas.

'Forget about the griffin,' called Bestivo, laughing openly now.

'Instead we go to war!' they both shouted as they zoomed straight up out of the courtyard, disappearing into the shifting clouds above. 'WAR!'

Their voices echoed in the sudden silence of the courtyard:

WAR, WAR, WAR…

And Finn, though he'd not once stopped to think about feelings since their father had disappeared, felt suddenly emptied by a wave of grief so immense that it was strangely hard to breathe.

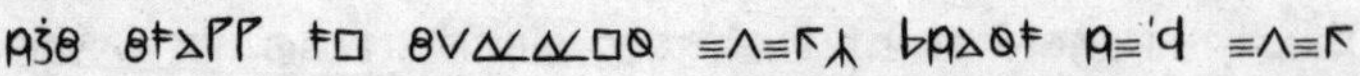

19

'**D**on't listen to them,' said Charlie again. 'They're mean to everyone, think they're better than everyone and probably reckon you're about to take their place as this year's favourites to join the aviator squad, so they'll want you *gone*.'

Errol nodded. 'They've always hated the Flint family. They're jealous of the bloodline's power, though they're powerful enough in their own ways.'

But they were telling the truth, signed Tula. *Finn tasted it.*

Charlie's eyebrows shot up in surprise. 'You can taste truth?'

And more, signed Tula proudly, but Finn jumped in to ask, 'Errol, will you help us persuade this griffin to take us to Dad? If Charlie can get us into the labyrinth?'

'Yes!' exclaimed Errol. 'Oh, yes, yes, YES!'

Charlie grinned, already moving quickly out of the courtyard, Errol close behind him, and Finn and

Tula had to run to keep up. The crowds of children parted to let them through, but at the huge arched exit the little thumb-sucking girl from the Hall of Heroes jumped out at them, her arms full of leafy branches with red berries.

'Vida!' exclaimed Errol. 'You genius! Thank you!'

He bent to give her a hug, cramming the branches under the flap of his backpack and securing it with a knotted length of string he pulled from his pocket.

'My sister,' he said to Finn and Tula over his shoulder. 'She's a scryer and can see stuff ahead of time. Grey Griffin loves yew leaves and berries.'

'Be careful,' whispered Vida to Errol, 'and you too, Manchego,' she added, kissing a mouse that had appeared from his pocket. 'Good luck,' she said to Finn and Tula. 'Please don't die.'

'Vida!' exclaimed Errol, but she'd already slipped away into the courtyard and Charlie was calling up ahead for them to hurry the hell up.

When they'd chased him down three side alleys and a long dark passage, they found him standing at a small wooden door with a rune glowing on it.

'Charlie is a wayfinder,' said Errol, 'which is handy because the labyrinth tunnels shift and move, a bit like the buildings in the town, so nothing is ever recognisable again. No reliable maps here, obviously.'

⊥≡Ʌȝөˤ, 8Ʌ≡ө, өρˤ⫲≡ᖰ Ꮁᒋ◻⋏ ⫢Ʌ≡ˤᒋ Ꮁᒋ◻▨≡ө өⱡ⋏өᖶ≡,

'*Agored*,' said Charlie, tapping the door with a small twig he pulled from his pocket.

'Welsh for "open",' whispered Errol to Finn and Tula.

The door opened and through they went, treading quickly but cautiously down steep steps into a rabbit warren of complicated passages. When at last they came to a stop, Tula grabbed Finn's hand and squeezed. He peered ahead in the darkness to find that the corridor in which they found themselves ended in a set of vast steel doors covered in hundreds of glowing symbols.

'The entrance to the labyrinth,' murmured Errol.

Two surly characters stood to attention either side of it: a young man with a shaved head and a dark and twisty beard that fell to his waist, and a young woman with the same olive-skinned complexion and dark and twisty hair that snaked to her hips. Both had matching scowls, furrowed foreheads and bright yellow eyes that glinted beneath thick, dark eyebrows. They wore baggy trousers and little tops in rich purples and blues. Their exposed midriffs were lean and muscled, and their piercings numerous.

'You!' snarled the woman at Charlie.

'Oh, great,' said Charlie with open animosity. 'Just great. It's the spindly ones. Better outside the labyrinth

ᎾᏴᖇᐁᐱᐟᏫᎾᎾ, ᏞᐁᐱᑫᏮᎾᎾ, ᐁᎾ ᏢᎪᐁᎩ ᎾᏓᏴᐱᐟᏞᐁᑫ ᏆᎾᖇᏑᐱᖇᑫ

than inside, I suppose. The mythics must be grateful.
How are you today, Padmakshi?'

'Gshnarr,' snarled the young woman. 'You cannot
enter without a permit and I'm guessing that, as usual,
you do not have one.'

'Hello,' said Errol to the young man before Charlie
could reply. 'Is Grey Griffin in today, Baha?'

'Such disrespect!' snapped the young man.
'Address me properly, youth!'

'Bahahahhaaahhaahh!' laughed Charlie, startling
Finn and Tula, but Errol was already saying, 'O Baha
the Magnificent, could we please visit with Grey
Griffin?'

'Unngrr,' growled Baha, but, at that moment
something snarled and thudded the steel doors from
inside, and deep claw marks embossed themselves on
this side of the door, making him jump.

Tân chirped something bravely from Tula's pocket
and the snarling stopped.

'LET … THEM … IN…' said a growly voice from
behind the doors, and Baha the Magnificent reached
hurriedly for a massive ring of keys at his hip. He
unlocked the doors, and he and Padmakshi stood back.

'Better let me go first,' suggested Errol. He pulled
a branch from his bag and frowned when one of the
little red berries rolled off.

⌐∧⹀ᒣ ⱦᔿ⹀ ᣳ⋋∧⹀'8 ᒣⴷᏏᕑᎧ ⋋ᗝᑫ ⱦⴷ∨Ꮷ⹀ᕑᎧ.

'Wow,' said Finn staring at the claw marks on the door. 'That is … something … *big*.'

'Huge,' said Charlie. 'Massive. Tempting to let Errol go first.'

'Wait!' commanded Padmakshi. 'We must follow proper protocols!'

'There are no proper protocols,' retorted Charlie, 'except maybe doing our best not to get eaten alive. Ready, Errol?'

'Yep,' said Errol, but Finn thought someone trembling this hard was probably not ready at all.

The door opened. There was an ominous pause of complete silence, then a rushing sound, as if a blast of breath were being sucked deep into a cavernous chest, and then an outraged roar, half lion, half eagle. Huge claws snatched the slow-moving door, flung it wide open and then the creature was gone, followed again by a silence heavy with fury and rage. The metallic taste of blood flooded Finn's mouth.

Whatever it is, it's really angry, he signed to Tula.

'Grey Griffin is always angry,' muttered Charlie.

Padmakshi produced a notebook. 'I am recording for the record that you should not enter at this time. The mood is not good. It is not safe.'

'We are entering at this time,' growled Charlie, and Errol, Finn and Tula dived into the labyrinth after him.

ᚾᐯᚻ ᚴᚦ ᐁᐁᚨ ᚠᗌ ᒍᐁᚻᐧ

Inside, the light was dim, even though iron sconces held balls of roiling flame. Strange creatures and unusual people stared out from the doorways, niches and passages that they passed. Tula made a motion near her forehead to Errol.

'Yes,' he said. 'Unicorn – the silvery one you just saw is called Francis.'

Francis? signed Tula, her eyes darting here, there and everywhere. *You know a unicorn called Francis?* From that moment she bombarded him with questions about the labyrinth inhabitants, and Errol replied in a mixture of whispers and sign language until after what felt like hours Charlie said, 'Stay close. This part of the tunnels is confusing. We'll be climbing to higher ground. Nearly at the arena now.' He grabbed a torch from the wall, and Finn veered away from the flames.

'The arena is like a colosseum, an open area where all the tests and battles are held,' explained Errol. 'Each year we are allowed to enter for tournaments, the Flybynight games, to grant the questing licences and to celebrate everyone's skills.'

They turned a corner and Finn could see the tunnel opening out up ahead, light spilling almost to where they were walking now.

'Except you, Errol,' said Charlie. 'You should

enter this year instead of just slaving away behind the scenes.'

'The creatures don't want me to,' replied Errol.

'They worry for you because you have no fireblood magic,' replied Charlie.

Errol was about to blurt a reply, but they had reached the end of the passage, and Charlie held out his arm.

'Careful,' he said. Finn and Tula approached slowly and found themselves looking over the edge of a void thirty metres deep, a hundred metres wide and completely open to the dark and moody sky above.

'Wow,' breathed Finn.

He stared. All around, galleries had been carved into the sheer faces of the gleaming rock surrounding the space. Tier upon tier of them circled the arena below, like the royal boxes of an old-fashioned theatre. Within them, Finn saw movement and shadows and flickering light from flames in sconces lighting up the darker corners on all the levels where the light pouring down from above did not reach. Along the galleries were hurrying, strolling, flapping, flying creatures of indescribable shapes, sizes and proportions. Down below in the massive arena space, strange beings and oddly dressed people were hurrying about their business too, disappearing into the tunnels that led off in all directions.

ᐅᒥᖻᔪᎾ ᕟᔕᎾᕟ ᔔᎾᖲᓚ ᖵᕟ☰ ᐅᔔᕞ, ᎾᕒᐚᕘᎾᕟᔔᎾ ᖵᕟ☰ ᎾᕒᔔᎾ ᐅᕝ

'We should fly to the bottom and wait for Grey there.' Errol grimaced and gestured towards a rope slung carelessly on the ground near them. 'But I generally go down this because I haven't got my wings yet.'

'*Yet?*' scoffed a voice behind them.

Charlie whirled round. 'Meritas. And Bestivo. What are *you* doing here?'

'We came to laugh at you all,' sneered Bestivo.

Meritas leaned into Errol's face. 'If you haven't got your wings by now, you never will, you buffoon.'

She turned her back on them as if to walk away, but shoved Finn hard as she went.

Finn, used to heights and a world of cables and steel girders, threw his weight backwards, wheeling an arm gracefully to keep from plummeting to the flagstones far below, but Meritas was already dropping her knee into the back of his, and tapping his ankle with the side of her foot, just hard enough to send him pinwheeling into the air. Tula snatched for her brother, her mouth wide in unvoiced panic, and she would have fallen too, but Errol held her back with a yelp of alarm.

Finn tumbled into the void beneath. Anger at Meritas's mean jabs and kicks fuelled a fire in his belly that threatened to blast from him like a furnace from

≡∧≡ᒥ⅄ ᒠ≡ᒥⴱⴱᵍ � Ϝᒠ≡ ᗢⵌ∧≡ ⵌⴱꝺ ⴱⴱⵌⵌⵧⵗⴱⴱⴱ Ϝᒠ≡ ⴱᒠⴱⵡⴱꝺ

the depths of the earth. Sucking in a desperate gasp of cooling air, it was all he could do to swallow it down as the ground rushed up to meet him.

Just as he braced himself for the oblivion to come, there was a flurry of movement, and he saw Charlie flying towards him, his black batwings scything the air, his face fixed in grim determination, his arms outstretched like a weird cameo of Superman. Then at the last second Charlie wheeled away, the air sizzling beneath him.

Sssssszzzzzzzzzip!

Before Finn could gasp in shock at being left to fall to his death, he felt himself swooped out of his freefall by someone or something, zooming high into the air.

'Stay still!' called Errol as Finn flailed about, feeling sharp edges and a choking softness against his eyes, face, hands. 'Don't move!'

Something in Errol's voice made Finn obey instantly. And then when at last he felt all movement come to a stop he slowly lifted his face and stared in amazement to what had saved him.

20

t first, Finn couldn't work out what had happened, but once he'd pushed himself to his knees he realised he was on the wing of an impossibly huge...

What is this creature?

At his feet and knees, and almost to his waist, was the softest sea of downy feathers, but above them, surrounding his shoulders and brushing against his face and arms, were strong quills of inky black. He stood slowly and unsteadily, careful not to trample or pull anything around him, his mouth hanging open in complete astonishment. The feathers around him flattened as he moved to standing, but Finn hardly noticed. He was completely mesmerised by the regal head of an eagle staring back at him along the arch of its wing.

He did not notice the rush of people and creatures on the balustrades all around them. He did not hear the excited exclamations or muffled murmurs that rose and fell, as if trying not to be heard. He did not realise that with every passing second the motley crowds were growing, gasping and pointing at him and the creature that had stopped him crashing to the ground.

Caught up in this moment, oblivious to all else, Finn suddenly realised that it was possible to connect with another being *instantly*. To look into their eyes and know that there are many, many things about which you will both agree. Important things. Like whether to run or hide, to sink or swim, to choose song or silence.

And when those eyes are the size of your own head...

Well.

Staring into the bright, glowing orbs of this creature's owl-like irises, Finn knew that if nothing went disastrously wrong, if nothing interfered, if he were true to himself and to those around him, this mythical beast would be important to him, vital, in some way.

And then the world around him began to intrude. Finn heard a distant shout – Errol? – and the voice was laced with fear.

'Please put him down, Grey Griffin.'

Yes, definitely Errol, and he heard Tân chirp too.

8ᕂ≡ ⴷ⅄ϑ ϴ□ᕂ≡, ⅄ϑ� ⅄Ϻ ╀ᕂ□ϑ≡ ╀□ⴴϸᕂ=9 Ⱶⴷ ╀ᕂ≡ ϴ⁊Γ╀ □Γ

Finn blinked. He looked over his left shoulder and saw that instead of a feathered body and tail he was staring down the torso of an enormous lion, the lightly furred golden skin rippling with enormous muscle and power.

With a sudden movement, the griffin arced his wing high and Finn instinctively tensed every muscle he had to keep his balance as the mythic held him out, like an auctioneer displaying a product for bidding.

Without thinking, Finn signed, *Thank you*. He was about to draw breath immediately thereafter to voice it, but the griffin signed, *You're welcome*, back to him with a blink of an eye and the quirk of a brow.

Finn thought he'd imagined it, but then the griffin signed, *Where are your brother and sister?*

Before Finn could explain that he only had a sister, there was a shout of warning, and the huge rope from above fell down next to them. Shinning swiftly down it were Tula and Errol. Meritas fluttered to the ground with her wings of bright red and gold scales, while Bestivo zig-zagged with wings of a startling bright green. He did a show-off swoop directly into Charlie who, caught off-guard, tumbled hard into Grey Griffin's wing.

A snarl – there is no other way to put it – erupted from the mythic.

ᐅᓐ ᒪᔦᕐᓚᑭᐳᐅ ᐁᓐᕐᓭ ᑲ ᑲᓪᔭᐊᐁᑫᐅᖅ ᒪᑕᕐᓭᐱᓭᕐ.

'*Snoooooaaarrrrfffffssyaaarr!*'

And in the blink of an eye Finn and Charlie were tossed high in the air and left to plummet towards the ground. Charlie wrapped himself in his wings and rolled harmlessly, but Finn landed hard, skidding for several metres, skinning his elbows, hands and a cheek.

'What did you do that for?' Charlie yelled at Bestivo, who had landed with an unnecessary flutter of his wings.

Snatching a branch of yew leaves and berries from Errol's satchel, Bestivo turned to the griffin and said, 'I apologise for the accident, mighty mythic. It seems some of our friends do not afford you the respect you deserve.'

The griffin dipped his beak to the yew branch and in one snap it was gone.

Respect, he signed. *Hmm*.

Tula ran to Finn. She snatched up his arms, examining his elbows, hands, face. His wounds were weeping painfully now in a steady stream of golden blood. She shot a dark look at Grey Griffin and, dropping Finn's arms, she signed a string of rude exclamations and curses at terrible speed.

'No, Tula!' called Errol, hurrying to her side. He spoke in a fierce whisper. 'The griffin can understand every bad thing you just said.'

'You!' Charlie shouted, striding towards the griffin, his wings hanging dusty and scraped behind him. 'You are so *grumpy* and so *mean* all the time! What the hell is going on in your head? Everyone thinks you're great and legendary, and all the infants in this place want to see you, to touch you, to be with you, and yet you … you –' he hunted for the word '– you *skulk* down here in the gloom! Never flying, never teaching, never hunting, never protecting!' He flung his arms wide with rage. 'You are abandoning a world that needs its warriors! What is *wrong* with you?'

The griffin's eyes narrowed. He opened his beak, just a little, and though Finn and Tula and seemingly no one else could hear a thing, Charlie dropped to his knees, clutching his ears and screaming. In a flash Finn was shoving Charlie behind himself and holding his hand up high in the halt position to the griffin.

STOP, he signed.

The griffin's beak snapped closed. He blinked. He dipped his head. There was a soft thud behind Finn as Charlie rolled on to his side, releasing his head, crying quietly.

To his horror, Finn saw thick trickles of blood oozing from Charlie's ears. Tula knelt beside him, taking Charlie's head in her hands.

No one said a word. High above, the open sky had darkened with more black clouds, and heavy wet snow began to fall in splattering sheets. The quick and hurried movements in the galleries all around had slowed to a halt, with beings that had frequented childhood dreams and storybooks and legends of old, some tiny, some vast, staring down at them. Meritas and Bestivo were gawking openly.

I cannot help Charlie, signed Tula, squinting up through the whirling snow. *He is not healing*.

Finn placed his palm between Tula's shoulder blades.

'Try again,' he croaked.

She raised her bloody hands to Charlie's ears once more and held him still though he tried to jerk away. Finn focused on sending Tula all the energy he had, like he'd done at the pool in the watchtower. He felt the rising heat despite being battered by flying ice and sleet all around, and when he opened his eyes he saw Charlie's shoulders sag, his hands stop shaking and his breathing return to normal. With a relieved sigh, he swiped the tears from his eyes and the snow from his face. Tula dropped her hands.

'Can you hear again?' asked Errol, raising his voice above the squall.

'Yes,' said Charlie, 'and the pain has gone.' He

turned his head warily, as if afraid the agony would return. 'Thank you, Tula.'

It was nothing, signed Tula.

The griffin splashed across the puddled ground to Finn and spoke aloud. His voice was deep and rumbling, yet even in the whirling storm it had a sighing quality that echoed breezes from the highest cliffs, the rustle of leaves from the tallest trees.

'Boy. You have been damaged and cannot fly.'

Feeling the brush of the mythic's feathers across his hunched back, Finn looked up, then kept very, very still as the griffin nudged Tula's hands aside with the tip of his beak. Her fingers were slick with icy sleet and blood and her expression frantic.

The griffin bent down, his enormous eyes the size of her head. He blinked at Tula and twitched a few feathers above where his own ears would be.

'Girl,' he said, 'you too have suffered, but why do you not speak or sing when you can do so with such power?' He cocked his head at Charlie. 'And you, young man. Why so full of rage and rudeness?'

Staggering slightly, Charlie pushed himself back up into a standing position, a hair's breadth from Grey Griffin. His hair was slicked to his head, his baggy clothing stuck to his frame. He seemed suddenly younger and smaller than he usually did, yet the steam that lifted from his body hinted at reserves of a mysterious strength.

The sky lit up with lightning as thunder rumbled overhead, which seemed to slow the sleet. It softened into drifts of fast-falling snow and an immense hush fell into the vast arena once more with no one – not a creature or a person or a child – speaking or moving at all.

Charlie cleared his throat and stared the griffin straight in the eye. 'Well,' he said. 'That was humiliating.'

An intense sound of rustling leaves grew louder, then died back slowly into a fading sigh. Finn realised it was coming from the griffin, and he held his breath, but when the griffin spoke it was tinged with such regret that Finn was overwhelmed by the taste of cold soot and ashes.

Grey Griffin bowed his head low. 'I am sorry I lost my temper. You are a rude and unruly brat, but I misjudged you. There is a courage in you that we will need in these desperate times. I thank you for reminding me of air and sky and space, and of others around me. I had forgotten, lost in my own misery.' He raised his head, and his voice echoed all around. 'Call me when you need me, and I will come. This is my promise to you.'

Meritas and Bestivo hurried over, but Charlie ignored them and sank to one knee. All around, the creatures, the children, the people, all quietened again, yet Charlie's murmur curled and folded into this small group's ears only, like the distant rush and hush of faraway waves in a seashell.

'I am calling now. We need your help, Grey Griffin. Augustus Flint has gone missing, and we need him back before Elbrus erupts.'

Before Grey Griffin could reply, Meritas stepped forward and said, 'Pardon the interruption, Your Magnificence, but our father is back and begs your assistance in retrieving Augustus. These children' – she gestured at Finn and Tula – 'cannot fly to his rescue.'

Do you taste their truth? signed the griffin to Finn and Tula.

Yes, admitted Finn, *but we were hoping you could take us to him.*

The griffin bowed his head. *I would fly faster and stronger alone. I feel certain your father would not want me to take you into danger.*

'Tell me this isn't happening,' growled Charlie.

'What is happening?' asked Bestivo.

The griffin blinked at Finn slowly, then winked at Charlie. 'Take care of these two while I am gone,' he said, and he placed one of his enormous paws on his chest. 'Never again will you be deafened,' he said, and Charlie drew in a sudden breath with the pain of acquiring another mark. 'Even whispers will be clear to you now.'

Charlie signed his gratitude, and the griffin turned to Tula.

'Remember there is great power in silence,' he said to Tula, moving his paw to her shoulder, 'but not always.' She flinched at the pain of another mark, but still stared at him wide-eyed. *Thank you*, she signed.

'I know you will not use it unwisely as I just did,' he said, then turned his golden gaze to Finn.

'And you, Finn Firefearer, have forgotten too much. Use this gift when you are ready to remember.' He tapped Finn's chest with his claw, and through the searing agony Finn saw flashes of a life lived years before, but they were gone in an instant, along with the pain, and all he could see was Grey Griffin flying up, up, up in the softly falling snow, out of the arena and away with Meritas and Bestivo swooping gleefully behind him.

21

The departure left a strange, soundless vacuum, as if their leaving had sucked something else away with them, and the snowfall eased to drifting flakes, though the clouds stayed black and ominous. Then, little by little, the people and creatures in the square and on the balconies towering above them began to whisper, then mutter, then talk and debate, and flurries of movement began again. Charlie, Errol, Finn and Tula came closer together and Errol punched Finn lightly on the shoulder.

'What did Grey Griffin mean by remembering? Has he given you the power of photographic memory?'

'I don't know.' Finn pushed his clothing away and they all stared at the curved shape of a griffin claw on his chest. He lifted a finger to touch the mark, which was already turning black, but paused.

'Don't activate it until you feel ready, is my advice,' said Charlie, pulling his own shirt aside. 'See this one here? One of Steve's mates gave me wayfinding after I helped stop those Veritas brats from destroying their nest last year, and for two days I was cooing like a turtledove at everyone.'

'Ooh, I remember that,' said Errol, trying not to laugh. 'Side-effects can be unpredictable. Maybe now's not the time. Tula, I'm guessing you got the earsplitting thing Grey Griffin just did to Charlie?'

Tula nodded. *How do you know how to use it?*

'Instinct,' said Charlie, 'and the next time someone is whispering a mile away from me, I'll be able to hear it.' He made a face. 'Thank goodness it has to be activated. I'd rather not hear Rudimenta moaning about me all day every day.'

'Not sure you can do much about Rudimenta's moaning, Charlie,' said a deep voice from behind Tula. 'Not until you stop leading her Morty astray.' The children turned to see a big, tall man with dark smiling eyes walking towards them.

'Dad!' said Errol. He pushed past them all and threw his arms round the man's waist in an oddly childlike way that made the muscles in Finn's throat clench so hard they hurt.

'Looks like you've made new friends who are human, for a change,' said Errol's dad with laughter in his voice.

Errol came out of the hug and flung his arm out: 'Finn and Tula,' he announced, 'this is my father, Idris.'

'I'm so glad to meet you,' said Idris. 'Welcome. George sent me to express immense gratitude for the griffin, though the Veritas twins are taking credit.' He chuckled when Charlie groaned. 'The aviators are ready. We leave for Elbrus in twenty minutes. I'm going to take you back to the Arsenal, Errol, and you three to the watchtower, where I'd like you to stay until we're back.' Errol began to protest, but Idris held up a finger. 'Otto will deliver food, so consider yourself the luckiest abandoned children alive, and Shen will check in on you all. We can't take any chances.'

'I need a few things from my house,' said Charlie.

'Oh, please take us there quickly, Dad,' begged Errol, sounding suddenly younger. 'I've never seen the treehouse, if that's okay with you, Charlie? And we've not had a flight for ages, and Finn and Tula never have! It might help them fly themselves...' He trailed off looking suddenly uncertain.

'Flying rigs, Idris,' said Charlie quietly. 'That's what I need to get from my place. Oleksiy has none left and we can't go asking around for any because islanders will get panicky.'

Idris nodded. 'The treehouse is good for privacy. You can try them there without upsetting anyone. I can take these three now if you get them back here before nightfall? I've got to return right away to lead the squadron to Elbrus.'

When Charlie said, 'Yes, sir,' Errol whooped, and sprang onto his father's shoulders.

Idris grinned. 'Come on, Finn and Tula. The famous treehouse awaits.'

He held each of them in a one-armed hug as his wings unfurled. They were the most spectacular Finn had seen by far, covered in huge inky-black feathers with an iridescent glimmer of deep green. Tân dashed swiftly into Tula's coat pocket. Idris bunched his powerful legs into a crouch and then pushed off hard from the ground, his wings deafening them in a series of thunderclaps that took them straight up into the air, higher, higher, until they were out in the open sky and soaring silently. Charlie flew like an arrow ahead of them and was soon a speck in the distance.

'Show off,' laughed Idris.

The children gasped at the sight of the island laid out below them. It looked huge, with the fortressed city below them, punctuated by the watchtower and the four turrets of Brann, Kellan, Vulkan and Siarad. Far beneath, the houses hugged the piazzas, walkways and narrow alleys of the fortress, as if seeking comfort, warmth or safety from the lengthening shadows.

They stretched out in a curve all the way to the cliffs, then round and down to a harbour reflecting the dark clouds overhead. The natural landscape of the island beyond the cold stone and beaten metal of all the buildings, and the shining water of the harbour, was a startling contrast, because whatever wasn't white with snow was as black as night: scorched, burnt, broken.

The ground, the grass, the trees stood out in sooty greys and the charcoal black of a burning so intense that it had left not an iota of life behind. Beyond the blackened wastes to the north ran a stretch of water from one edge of the island to the other, and beyond that were the feet of mountains wreathed in cloud.

'Why is everything burnt?' called Finn to Idris. Even though the desolation was blanketed by snow, it made him feel a keen sense of loss.

'You do not remember?' asked Idris. 'Your father told you nothing of the Last Battle?'

'No,' said Finn, 'but Charlie said the firebloods were betrayed and the Venomous killed our mother. He said that's when Dad left the island.'

'Yes, eight years ago,' Errol said, 'when the whole island got blasted in the Last Battle.'

All across the island, everywhere they looked, was evidence of it. Even after so long it still smoked. It struggled. It lost. The saddest thing to see were the trees. Their many-pronged branches seemed like arms stretching into the sky for some kind of relief that would never come, and to the north and the west these burnt silhouettes stretched on and on, softened only by clods of snow. The furthest trees from the fortress crowded closer together, in the way forests do, and then the hills rose up behind, hiding the next horizons.

'Must have been some battle,' said Finn, his voice croaky.

'Yes,' said Idris. 'Your mother died while flying very, very high, and she was in full song. Your family was attacked by Venomous and badly hurt. You were at the age, Finn Flint, when firebloods begin to fly, but after that you never did.'

Finn could not reply. His throat was suddenly too tight to ask more questions and his eyes too full of grief.

'You, Tula, had just begun to speak, but after that you never said another word,' Idris continued, his voice gentle. 'But no one believes you were destined always to be speechless or flightless. Your mother was the most powerful singer the world has ever known, belonging to all four houses, and your father belongs to all four too, like George. It was inconceivable that the Venomous could defeat them.'

'Straight after the battle,' said Errol, 'your father left here, swearing never to come back, and without his potent alchemy, things started to fall apart. Tsunamis. Earthquakes. But the Venomous beneath did not grow strong enough until years later. The most dangerous and strategic volcanic eruption in centuries began in Finland, and Augustus stopped it single-handedly.'

'How?' asked Finn.

Idris barked out a short laugh. 'Ha! We wish we knew. We'd all feel a lot less vulnerable.'

'But the world was saved?'

'Yes.' Idris flexed his wings for more height again, then soared on a cold wind and the rush of air in their ears quietened once more. 'That went some way towards re-establishing the trust lost between Augustus and the firebloods. For a long time, we had no idea what had happened to you, though our sources told us that you were safe in the west country, but—'

He stopped short, suddenly suppressing what he was about to say.

'But?' questioned Finn.

'But now no one is safe, least of all you, because you cannot fly, Tula cannot sing, and it is rumoured that neither of you have the power of flame.' Idris chose his words carefully. 'Legends say you are the ones, that you will save us all, but I worry that we have run out of time to teach you what you need to know, if indeed it can be learned.'

His arms tightened round Finn and Tula as if to give them comfort, and Finn tried to reply, but his voice came out in a strangled sound.

With a polite cough, Errol pointed to the foothills in the north-western mountains. 'There is the obscura tree,' he said, 'Charlie's treehouse.'

Finn and Tula squinted ahead to see a tree standing all by itself in the scorched meadows and patchy snow to the north-west. It seemed less of a silhouette, less statue-like somehow than the other tree skeletons, and twice as tall as the biggest of them.

'Though the great burning happened so long ago, hardly anything will grow here again,' said Errol, 'but that tree lives on somehow. Most of the amazing mythic beasts that lived in the green forest left, though a few of them came to live in the labyrinth. Plants that do sprout grow black and stunted – even the grasses.'

'Ready?' asked Idris, and he began the descent. They landed in a quick running stop that seemed to come naturally to Finn and Tula, and Errol jumped easily off his father's shoulders.

'Thanks, Dad!' said Errol, his face alight. 'That was so good!'

Idris smiled back at him before hugging him tightly. 'Look after your sister, Errol. Look after the Flints. Get up in that tree and tell Charlie—'

He was interrupted by a loud cooing from above and Errol's bird, Steve, came tumbling quickly towards them. He landed messily on a branch above them, skidding through the snow, and sending clods of it rattling down on their heads. A small grass snake poked its head out of Errol's pocket, slithered up his chest and hung round his neck like a broken necklace, and the little mouse called Manchego that they'd seen in the dining room emerged from his hair. Steve did a little side-to-side dance, cooing urgently again.

'Steve has news,' said Errol.

He says Liberty gave the aviators my message for Dad, signed Tula. *What message is he talking about?*

Steve cooed and did a dipping back-and-forth movement.

'Oh boy,' said Errol. 'Steve says Liberty did a *Town Scryer* interview with Tula? They've taken it with them as proof to Augustus that you're here, to be sure he returns with them.'

Finn frowned. 'The woman from the fast-food street, the one wearing floaty clothes.'

Steve cooed and flapped three times in agreement. 'Proooooo-prooooo!'

'What is the written message Steve brings, son?' Idris was already buttoning his coat and pulling a knife from the front pocket to hide it in his boot as if he were preparing for battle.

Errol reached for the bird, cradling him to his chest as he pulled a tiny coil of paper from the elastic band on his leg.

'Proooooo,' went Steve.

Errol looked up at his father, dread in his eyes. 'The Venomous are on the move,' he said. 'George is asking for you.'

Idris nodded and hugged Errol again. 'Must fly,' he said with a wink at Finn and Tula. 'Get that Charlie to the fortress before the Clanging Bell. He cannot stay out here.' He flexed his wings and began to run. 'Stay safe, all of you.'

22

Finn, Tula and Errol tramped round the base of the tree, their sodden feet making mud and slush of the soot and soil.

The sky had darkened, creating shadows and silhouettes where before there'd been nothing. A faint rotten smell kept drifting across the icy wasteland, but each time Finn turned, trying to pinpoint where it was coming from, it disappeared.

It's nothing to worry about, he thought, but even so he shivered and slowed to a stop, staring all around.

Somewhere out in the twisted trees on the horizon a creature howled, the echoes rolling down the slopes towards them, laced with a dreadful warning, and Finn's heart was pounding when they finally crunched through the snow towards what Errol had called 'the obscura tree'.

It grows, signed Tula, looking for a way in.

'Yes,' said Errol. 'The House of Vulkan can't explain why.'

The vast and ancient yew tree was scorched, yes, but still very much alive. Even though it was deep midwinter the branches held fat berries amongst the profusion of leaves. About halfway up was a…

'Is that a *house*?' murmured Finn.

Tula's signing was quick but clear: *There are no steps. No ladder. No doorbell. Not even a bell or a knocker or … or even a door.*

'Charlie?' called Errol softly. 'You want us to climb up or come in through the front door?' There was no reply. 'Not long before the Clanging Bell of Doom, Death and Destruction rings!' he called, a little louder.

What's the Clanging Bell of Doom, Death and Destruction? signed Tula.

'Frailskins would call it a kind of a fire alarm, I guess,' said Errol, over his shoulder as they did another lap of the tree. 'It gets rung in times of danger when we've got to return to the fortress. The doors are locked to keep everyone safe. Only our most skilled aviators and warriors are allowed out to defeat any threat. There are practice drills every month. I bet they'll ring it before nightfall to make sure everyone's in tonight.'

A branch creaked and rustled alarmingly as

Charlie leaned out from a wooden balcony to stare down below. 'Hey!' he said. 'We have an issue!'

'Oh no,' said Errol. 'I bet it's the rigs. What's wrong with the rigs?'

'They're gone,' said Charlie. 'I was certain I left them out here on the veranda when I was training Morty last week, but they're not here. Come help me look.' He turned away, groaning in frustration. 'And hurry, hurry,' he called, before disappearing inside. 'It's getting dark.'

Finn, Tula and Errol exchanged a worried glance. Another howl drifted across to them, louder than before, and that rotting smell drifted closer.

'How do we even get in?' asked Finn, walking round the base of the tree. 'It feels rude to just climb up into his house.'

He's rude for not inviting us in properly, signed Tula with big indignant gestures.

Errol sighed. 'So rude,' he said. 'He's behaving like a panicky three-year-old, when actually we've all got to be sensible and get back to safety.'

Tula's eyebrows twitched and her thumbs made a symmetrical movement. Tân waved his tail in agreement.

'No,' said Finn. 'Don't go getting all deep and meaningful on me. I understand that he's an orphan and living in a weird place all on his own in the middle of the scary woods, but...'

Tula grabbed Finn's arm and pointed to the trunk of the tree. She tugged him closer to it and Finn put his nose to the bark. He drew in a careful breath. Slowly and methodically, he smelled his way to a tendril of ivy branching into three. When he leaned back, Tula pounced, lifting the ivy away. Beneath it was a knot just like any other, but there was no doubt that it concealed metal of some kind.

Tula placed her fingers over it and closed her eyes. With a sound of rustling leaves, the trunk of the tree shifted open, the bark lifting away in a small doorway shape glowing with a warm, orange light. Beyond it was a tight spiral staircase of wood carved from the inside of the tree. It was lined with hundreds and hundreds of books, lit by the cosy glow of a lamp next to the door. Tula gasped with wonder, her eyes sparkling at the sight of the library stretching above them as far as they could see, and down below too, into the dark and quiet shadows among the tree roots.

'Yes!' exulted Errol. 'We're in!' He was dancing around in huge excitement, and Manchego emerged from Errol's satchel to see what was happening. 'I can't believe I'm going to get a chance to get into this place! Apparently, there are technical developments in the high branches and the roots that even the CIA and MI5 don't know anything about!'

Tula's face lit up. *Ooh! Science! Sounds grea—*

'Dangerous,' interrupted Finn, frowning, and Manchego seemed to agree because he dived straight back into Errol's satchel as they stepped through the doorway.

23

‡⚡≡◊†⅄·†⋂↖≡≡

Once they were all inside, Finn pulled the door closed behind them, and they stood still for a moment, listening, looking.

'Up we go,' said Finn, gesturing to the spiral stairs, and they began to climb. There were landings at various points, with doors to the rooms on the other side, but they climbed higher and higher, looking for Charlie, until at last they came to a tiny doorway high in the branches. It had a small window in it and pressed to the glass was Charlie's face.

He disappeared and the door opened. 'Come in and don't touch anything,' he said.

A large, shallow bowl, about two metres in diameter, took up the centre of the room. On it was a strange shifting picture. Finn looked up at the ceiling and Errol went, 'Whoa… Is that… Is this … a scrying bowl?'

Charlie nodded.

Tula was examining the image on the bowl shape. She glanced up at Finn, her face flushed. Her fingers moved quickly to him, but it was Charlie who answered.

'Yes, it's the Clifton Suspension Bridge and your Bristol house.' He flushed. 'You were watched all day and all night in the beginning when you left here, but later that only happened now and again. Mainly because by then they'd bugged the inside of your house and could hear everything they wanted to.'

Finn's jaw dropped. Tula's eyes were wide. Errol frowned.

Charlie shrugged. 'You can't blame them, really. They were desperate to work out what was in the equaliser hydrant, but everything they tried failed. Probably because Augustus knew where the microphones were. Sometimes they'd go off, you see, not in a suspicious way – just in an oh-the-tech-is-on-the-blink way – and in the end no valuable information was ever gathered.'

'Y-you've,' stuttered Finn, 'been *spying* on us?'

Charlie shrugged again. 'Only a few people can get into this treehouse. I'm one of them, and this scrying bowl works for me. Try turning the handle,' he said to Tula.

Tula looked up and grasped a heavy wooden lever

that was linked to a pole disappearing into the ceiling above. She pulled it a little to the left and the image on the bowl shifted to show the River Avon.

'Press the button at the bottom of the handle,' said Charlie.

When Tula pressed the button, the image focused in on the bridge with such clarity that it felt as if they were sitting on one of the pedestrian's shoulders.

'How is this possible?' asked Errol. 'An automated scrying bowl? Impossible!'

'Not if it's linked to specific heartstones,' said Charlie.

'You'd have to have permission!' objected Errol.

'I had permission,' said Charlie. 'Permission from Augustus.'

Tula's hands were moving quickly, and her shoulders twitched too. She did a tapping thing with her foot, and then Charlie put up a hand in the halt position.

'First of all,' he said, 'I can't see what you're saying when you go so quickly. And second of all I wasn't spying on you. I was...' He flushed. 'I was looking out for you.' There would have been a prickly and uncomfortable silence, but he rushed on with, 'And third of all, you think I *liked* watching that stupid house all the time? I hated it! There you were with your happy selves and your happy father—'

'Happy?' blurted Finn. 'We weren't happy! Our mother died—'

'Yeah, well I lost my mother *and* my father!' yelled Charlie, his face going red and his hair tufting up into messy spikes. '*Because of you!*' He stopped suddenly, looking shocked, as if he hadn't meant to say that.

'What do you mean, because of us?' asked Finn, his voice higher than he'd like.

'Because of the battle,' said Errol hastily. 'That's what he means, but that's not true...'

'Yes, because of the battle!' Charlie's hands whirled around. 'Because of Augustus making a mess of everything. *Everything*. Now I'm trapped on this island with no parents, no future. What about *my* dreams? I'm never going to be able to fly anywhere far and fast – be an actual pilot instead of just a stupid aviator with questing rules and regulations. Ever seen a turbojet? What I'd give—'

'You blame us?' Finn felt weirdly hurt.

'No. Yes. But I shouldn't.' Charlie's shoulders sagged. 'After watching you for a bit I realised you never got to leave the house. No school, no friends, no people. Augustus never let you out. You had grocery deliveries, milk deliveries, sometimes things in the post...'

Tula sat down at the scrying bowl, two or three expressions chasing across her face.

'Exactly,' said Charlie. 'So I stopped being so cross with you and felt bad for you instead.' With a heavy sigh he added, 'I liked to see you through the windows, balancing and playing. It made me feel better knowing you were having fun, but ... all day and all night in one building? I thought you'd go mad, but you're kind of normal.' He glanced at Finn. 'And for a boy who never gets out, or even for one who does, you're really fast and agile. You'll be amazing when you fly – with or without a rig. And I'm sorry I kept defeating you at Level Five on Flybynight.'

Finn's forehead shot into furrows of disbelief. 'Th-that was you?' he stammered. 'You're Flybynight Solo? Why did—?'

Charlie interrupted, saying to Tula, 'You are great with words. You will be a songstress like no other.'

Finn was startled into silence, because just for a moment he thought he'd tasted orange juice, but when he took another breath it was gone. He must have imagined it. He didn't state the obvious, which was that Tula did not speak, let alone sing, and that he had a big hunch right at the point from which fireblood wings would need to sprout.

'Well,' said Errol, 'this is not awkward for me at all.' He cleared his throat. 'We should get back to the fortress before the Clanging Bell of Doom, Death and Destruction rings. It's not safe out here.'

Charlie raised an eyebrow at Finn and Tula. 'I thought you wanted to learn how to fly.'

Finn and Tula nodded, and Errol cleared his throat again. 'Can you do it? In, like, ten minutes, like you did for Morty?'

Charlie shrugged, looking at Finn and Tula with a questioning gaze. 'I don't know about ten minutes. It's got very dark.'

'Better that way,' said Errol. 'Remember what happened with me?'

Charlie pulled a face. 'The humiliation *did* kill your street cred.' He went over to a window facing the fortress. Lights were winking on all over it, soft and warm, and the moon was hidden behind restless clouds. 'We can't do battlements here, or cliff jumping, but perhaps that's for the best. You've got the energy of the tree to help you here, and the leaves to break your fall.'

'Oh boy,' said Finn, his heart starting to hammer. 'I'm not going to fall with a rig, though, right?'

'Rig?' Charlie's eyebrows shot up under his shaggy fringe. 'No rig. I found this on the balcony.' He held up a distinctive wing feather, all green and gold. 'Meritas and her stupid brother stole them. We're going to see if that hump of yours holds any surprises.'

24

‡▽≡◊‡⅄ ⌐◻∨⌐

Finn's hump held no surprises.

Charlie's Plan A – for Finn to jump straight from the balcony thirty metres above the frozen ground, stretching his arms out wide and feeling light, and sending energy out through his shoulder blades – resulted in Finn smashing into several snowy branches and leafy clumps before hitting the earth hard.

Very hard.

Over and over and over again.

Now his glittery blood glinted all over his body from scratches and cuts that were getting slower and slower to heal, and his right shoulder was in such agony that it took a few minutes before he could sit up and croak, 'I'm okay...' in answer to Tula's agitated gestures and Errol's frantic yells.

'He's *fine*,' came Charlie's annoyed voice from above. 'Your turn, Tula. Now, remember what I said, send the energy out from your shoulder *blades*. You're not trying to grow extra arms or heads.'

'Wait!' Finn staggered to his feet. 'Tula! I can catch you if you fall.'

'Get back up here, Finn,' called Charlie. 'You'll ruin Tula's motivation.' Though he dropped his voice, Finn could still hear him clearly. 'So, Tula, you've got great form for an excellent flyer, and you're a born airhead. You'll crack this quickly, I reckon, but you gotta be braver than your idiot brother, okay?'

'I don't think Finn's an idiot,' came Errol's voice, also quiet but not quiet enough. 'It's pretty hard throwing yourself off something this high you know, Charlie, when you don't know whether you're going to live or die.'

'We are not frailskins, Errol Ember,' said Charlie. 'We self-heal. There's no dying from silly accidents.'

'There is plenty of dying. Plenty! There are only five immortals left out of fourteen originals, and that's the *immortal* firebloods! Destroyed!' Finn saw Errol make a big explosion gesture. 'And not everyone heals brilliantly. Admit it! You're the worst self-healer. You're always in the clinic with your horrible flying injuries.'

Charlie's failings made Finn feel a bit better. He stepped into the shadows of the tree and put a hand to his shoulder, breathing deeply. In a few seconds the pain had faded and he could hear Charlie telling Tula to spread her arms wider. Finn felt sick as he watched his sister climb on to the railing, and he had to clamp his hand over his mouth when she leaped off it.

'Your arms,' yelled Charlie. 'Wider! Wider! Head up! Breathe in! Shoot the energy out! *Shoot! Shoot!*' but Tula's left arm was bent, and her eyes were squeezed tightly shut and she fell like a stone. Finn caught her, winding them both, and they lay gasping on the ground for a few seconds, unable to move. There was that stink again … and another rumble from the earth that lasted longer than any of the others.

Charlie was yelling all sorts of unreasonable things from above about needing to hurry the hell up, and Errol was going, 'Calm down, calm down. Let's get back to the fortress now. The Clanging Bell—'

'Forget the Jangling Blangling Bell! They stay here till they fly!' was Charlie's retort, and Finn was surprised to see Tula smile as she finally hauled in a breath.

'You think this is funny?' he hissed, getting to his feet and pulling her up. 'Not funny and I keep smelling—'

Tula did think it was funny and was already climbing back up the tree. She tried again, this time leaving Finn on the balcony behind her, but he leapt like lightning from branch to branch and again the two of them hit the ground together after she'd hit the springy lower branches on the way down. They did it over and over. No matter how clearly Charlie described the feeling of energy in the shoulder blades, Finn just didn't get it. Tula got better at the symmetry of the jump, and Finn got better at catching her, and Charlie got angrier at Finn breaking her fall.

'She's not going to learn, Finn Firefearer! If you keep doing that, she's not going to get her wings. Stop it!'

'*You* stop it!' yelled Finn. 'Why are you getting so shouty?'

Before Charlie could reply, a strange sound filled the night air – a long, low, gonging sound, followed by another, then another.

'Oh, for snakes' sakes!' Errol exclaimed. 'The Clanging Bell of Doom, Death and Destruction and we're all the way out here! I wish I had my plane!'

'What the—' exclaimed Charlie, jumping back from the balcony edge. Something plummeted from the sky towards him in a rush of silver and turquoise that shone with iridescent beauty in the moonlight.

'Drishti?' Errol exclaimed as she unfolded from a ball in an explosion of wings. She was breathing hard, her hair standing up all around her head, curling and twisting with a life of its own. 'What are you doing up here?'

Finn and Tula were already climbing the tree, leaping from branch to branch to reach her and Charlie, with Errol following quickly behind.

'Shen sent me,' panted Drishti. 'The translation – it wasn't Russian. It was Icelandic. *Þú munt ekki ná árangri* means, "You will not succeed."'

Charlie's eyes widened with sudden understanding. 'Augustus is not in Russia?'

Drishti shook her head, and her hair whipped around in a frenzied cloud. 'I don't know why Simon said he was.'

'That means the Venomous have Dad somewhere in Iceland, not Elbrus in Russia,' interrupted Finn, his eyes ablaze. 'What does *tala* mean?'

'Speak,' said Drishti.

'They want information from him,' said Errol.

'Information,' said Drishti. 'We need more. I'm going to activate full code-red protocols and access all the frailskin systems to see if we can pinpoint Augustus's exact whereabouts in Iceland. Come to my lab as soon as you can!' And in a crackle of light, she shot into the sky, back towards the city.

Finn and Tula stared at each other, feeling fear

seep into their bones. Finn saw Tula's jaw bunch and both her index fingers curled towards her palms.

We should tell the Telling Stone to do some telling, he signed back.

Tula whirled to face Finn, and her signing went even faster. *The Stone! It's still in the watchtower!*

Charlie looked horrified. 'That Stone is the most important dragon artefact we have – it has been kept safe for *thousands* of years – and the minute I let you out of my sight you—'

'George said the Stone was safe in the watchtower,' said Finn. 'It's where Dad chose to hide the hydrant, after all.'

'Which isn't even there,' said Charlie. 'It wasn't right for Augustus to keep the alchemy to himself. Look where we are now! And it put him and you in terrible danger.'

Finn was about to say they should leave right away but at that moment a disgusting gust of stink reached his nostrils, and this time even Tula screwed up her face in distaste.

Charlie's next words jolted Finn's heart into a yammering panic. His voice was tight and low, his fingers pressed hard to the marks on his chest.

'I can hear something on the western balcony of the watchtower.'

'Someone who is not a Flint is in the watchtower?' cried Errol.

Charlie took a moment before he answered, and Errol fished out his binoculars.

'Not inside,' concluded Charlie, 'but it sounds like more than some*one*.' He tilted his ear to the air and winced. 'They're too loud for this super-hearing.'

'Charlie's right,' said Errol, adjusting his binoculars. 'A Venom is climbing the wall.' There was a frightened squeak from Manchego as he peered out from the neck of Errol's shirt pocket, whiskers trembling, and dived straight back in again. Errol lowered the binoculars. 'And all our aviators are at Mount Elbrus!'

'I'm the best aviator they've got,' growled Charlie, 'and I'm still here. I hope you lot run better than you can fly. Let's go.'

25

‡⑂≡⊖‡⋏·⌐ȝ∧≡

The smell of Venomous got worse the closer they came to the fortress building.

'Can no one else on this island smell that stink?' coughed Finn.

'Angelina can, and sometimes George, but no one else,' panted Errol. 'Looks like the villagers probably think it's just another Tuesday practice alarm, because there are no house moves occurring,' he whispered as they arrived at the fortress itself. The streets all around were completely deserted and lights in houses were turned off. 'No one's panicking.' He glanced back at Finn and Tula. 'Rule is you got to treat the practice like the real thing.'

'Well, that's the only rule that seems to have worked out okay for the island,' muttered Charlie. 'Last thing we need now is panic.'

Tân whisked himself into Tula's shirt pocket, just the tip of his nose visible, and Manchego was still hiding in Errol's satchel.

Charlie led the way through a side door, and Finn shut it carefully behind them. They sprinted up steep, narrow steps that twisted and turned, opening into dark corridors with no sconces alight at all. Charlie paused at one of the junctions, his head cocked.

'Follow me!' called Errol softly, pulling Charlie through a small wooden doorway. 'I know a shortcut!'

They ran behind him down shadowy corridors and twisting steps until at last Finn recognised where they were. He and Tula reached the spiral staircase before the others. They were at the watchtower door in a heartbeat, but the stench coming from within made Finn retch again. Tula was holding her nose, her eyes watering, and she gagged too.

'You two are going to have to *not* do that,' said Charlie joining them, breathing hard.

'It's a bit distracting when we're all trying really hard to stay alive,' added Errol in a whisper.

Tula put her finger to her lips, and she moved slowly and carefully to the door and looked over to Finn. *Ready?* she signed.

Finn nodded, and the two of them pushed the door open and inched over the threshold, cautious, wary of Venomous who might already be in there, lying in wait. Sconces flickered to life with a strange reddish-orange glow that seemed like fire, but which somehow wasn't. The room seemed to be holding its breath, all the plants unmoving, frozen in fear.

'Stop!' whispered Errol. 'Invite us in! It's not safe for you to be in there alone.'

'Come in,' said Finn, but Errol held up his hand up hastily.

'Always by name,' he added, 'otherwise any sort of creature that heard you could gain entrance under a general invitation.'

'Come in, Errol and Charlie,' said Finn. 'Please.'

Charlie barked a bitter laugh, but Finn and Tula were already turning to face the dark and frightening shapes at the far end of the room where the glass doors, windows and wall seemed as if they might be writhing snakes instead of vines and tree roots, or hunching Venomous instead of thickly leaved shrubbery and architectural foliage.

'Oh,' said Errol, 'it is not how I expected. Charlie, could you dim the lights? We need to stay hidden, especially if one of them is climbing u—'

THUD. Scrape. Scrape.

'Too late,' murmured Charlie. 'I can hear that a Venom has just landed on the roof. Besides, I didn't—'

Tula grabbed his arm and pointed out towards the darkness.

They watched in silence as another Venom

climbed slowly, awkwardly, on to the top of the balcony balustrade outside. He sat, head bowed and shoulders curved inwards, gathering his breath. His skin was maggot white, and it was deeply scarred with ridges of purple lines.

'Everyone stand absolutely still,' said Errol. 'Though their sight and hearing is limited, they've been trained to smell certain things better than we can.'

'I could fireball him from here,' suggested Charlie, still in a quiet voice.

'They are incombustible,' replied Errol. 'Or did you mean to knock him off the edge?'

'Exactly,' said Charlie, and his fingers twitched. A blue ball of roiling light appeared in his palm and he covered it quickly with his other hand, but the hulking shadow outside howled so loudly that the whole tower shook.

'Sorry,' said Charlie. 'That sense of sight must be better in the newer models.'

On the roof, another Venom hammered with what sounded like his bare fists, then paused and began to scratch at it with long talons.

Errol whimpered. 'Nothing could miss your fireball, Charlie! What were you *thinking*? Stay still!'

But it was too late.

There was another THUD and then another,

and another, and when Finn tilted his head to listen carefully he could hear the roof was crawling with figures all trying to get in.

'So many,' said Charlie grimly.

Finn and Tula moved closer together, and she grabbed his hand, pressing her fingers to the edge of his palm.

It's going to be fine, she signed. *You snuff the fire out. I'll throw up the ice.*

On the balcony ahead in the shadowy darkness, two more figures arrived to join the first, then another two, and then finally a wiry man wearing a black suit, a black shirt, a black tie and black pointy shoes climbed up over the back of one of the hulking brutes and stood poised on its shoulders. He wore elaborate eye goggles that sealed all round his head, leaving his short, bleached hair tufting above it, his pointed teeth glistening below, with just a hint of his face to confirm who he was.

Errol had his binoculars out, and he gasped. 'He's wearing night-vision goggles! He'll be able to see in the dark almost as well as we can.'

'It's Craven,' whispered Finn, 'that man from the alley in Bristol.'

He's come back with reinforcements, signed Tula, her face stricken.

'This man has come after us before,' Finn explained to Errol. 'He wants us, and he wants the Stone.'

Craven raised the whip he carried, with a small red light at its vicious tip, and all the Venomous roared, rattling every window in the room.

Errol shoved his binoculars back in his bag and swallowed hard. 'We're safe in here, right?' he queried, pushing his glasses up his nose and squaring his shoulders.

Craven added a strange piercing shriek to the noise. When it seemed the sound could get no louder, he whirled his arm back and brought his whip down hard against what must have been an invisible barrier between the watchtower and the outside. There was a cracking sound that seemed almost to tear into Finn's head, and he dropped to his knees in agony. It was the same for all of them. They clutched their ears, eyes watering, struggling to stay standing. An acrid burning smell filled the room, and the air in front of them seemed to shimmer with a strange freezing heat that tremored over their skin in waves.

In that instant, not one of them could move. The rucksack with the Stone within it seemed suddenly vulnerable on the table in the middle of the room.

Charlie groaned, fighting against the evil power of the whip. His arms and legs inched forward in slow jerks, his face was set in jaw-locked tension and his eyes had narrowed to furious slits.

'*How – dare – you!*' he ground out, striding forward step by agonised step. His voice shook with the force of his fury. 'HOW DARE YOU COME TO THIS PLACE WITH YOUR HAVOC AND HATE! I will match you with every broken atom you bring here! I will fight you to the death! I will see you returned to the infernos beneath, rotting with the corpses of which you still stink!'

The sconces around the room *whumphed* into a blaze of orange flame, and Finn gasped, his intense fear of flame squeezing his chest so he could hardly breathe. He felt himself shrinking in his skin, retreating into himself, down, down, down, when all he wanted to do was reach the bag.

Tula grabbed his arm. *It's all right!* she signed. *Come back, Finn! It's going to be absolutely f—*

Charlie drew back his arm with a manic yell, and hurled his fireball at Craven, still standing firm on the Venom's shoulders. The flames in every sconce roared high and wide, right up the walls, across the ceiling and out towards the Venomous on the balcony. The fireball sizzled through the glass without breaking it, but Craven dodged it, leaping away to land on another Venom's head. Beneath him, the Venom grunted and clutched at Craven's feet, pushing his shoes from his eyes.

Finn's throat had constricted so tightly that now he could hardly breathe. He had a dim awareness of everything around him starting to move: all the plants, the carvings on the walls, the painting on the ceiling, the inlays in the floor. The whole tower seemed to be coming alive.

'The Stone!' he gasped, struggling forward, but Tula and Errol could not move any faster.

There were crackling sounds that seemed to be more than just the result of intense heat, and over to the left of him Finn saw the enormous stone dragon carved round the banister start to writhe and twist. He drew in a scorching breath of pure fear as its massive head began to turn slowly in their direction. Its heavy stone eyelids opened, revealing bright citrine eyes that stared intently at him. From its nostrils came curling twists of smoke and its mouth began to yawn.

'No!' yelled Finn. 'Stay back!'

But the flames from the sconces burned higher still, fanning his fear and clouding his vision. Out of the corner of his eye he could see the bag on the table, and Errol on his knees, signing to them.

The Stone! The Stone!

Step by agonising step all three of them made

their way to the table, and when Errol reached Finn and Tula, he crouched down between them. 'Grab the bag. And the bottle of equaliser hydrant!'

'There is no hydrant,' cried Finn. 'Patrick already searched all the hidden places.'

Errol shook his head. 'Impossible! That human outside knows something we don't – he's cracking your dad's defences. Any ideas?'

I will throw up the ice! signed Tula.

'DIE! DIE! DIE!' yelled Charlie, hurling one fireball after another at the Venomous.

'He's not going to win that game,' observed Errol, blinking rapidly. 'Shouldn't he just help us instead?'

'We have to help ourselves,' gasped Finn, and though he felt sick to the stomach at the roar of flame and the crackle of heat, he stood, every muscle straining against the Venomous roar, and stretched towards the bag on the table.

Outside, Craven screamed an instruction to the Venomous, bringing his whip down hard, and the laser-like agony in Finn's head felt like a fist squeezing his brain. He dragged the bag towards him, clutched it to his chest and slumped back to the floor.

'Milady,' he gasped. 'I'm sorry to wake you…'

'Oh my good golly gosh,' said the Stone. 'Do not take me out of this lovely, lovely bag. I repeat, do not take me out of the bag. This fight of good versus evil has unlocked the hydrant hiding place, and you have the gift to see it now.'

Errol's mouth dropped open in shock. He drew breath, about to speak, but Tula put her finger to her mouth and shook her head. Her eyes had begun to leak with tears, which told Finn that her head, too, felt as if it were about to blow apart.

'I think Charlie is losing control of his anger issues,' said the Stone, her voice ringing out into the room. 'You really need to get the equaliser hydrant and get out of here, children.'

'I do not have anger issues!' yelled Charlie. 'DIE, DIE, DIE, YOU BLASTED MONSTERS!' He spun, and spun again, and suddenly his whole body lit up in a bright white glow and his wings flashed out taut and wide, zooming him high in the air. The infernos raging in each of the sconces snuffed out, leaving just Charlie spinning in the air in a halo of pure light.

'Wow!' gasped Errol.

'Bioluminescence,' breathed Finn.

Like the fireflies, signed Tula. *It's silenced the Venomous. We can move again!*

Finn felt the mark that the fireflies had left upon his chest heat up beneath his searching fingers. He tugged the bag on to his back and sprang to his feet alongside Errol and Tula.

'The Stone was right! The bioluminescence is showing us things!' said Errol, looking all around. 'Whoa!' he said when he glanced back at Finn and Tula, his eyebrows pushing his forehead into astonished furrows. Finn felt as if his skin was buzzing all over and saw that he and Tula were vibrating with the magical glow of fireflies too.

All around the room tiny details lit up, like neon colours under an ultra-violet light: the eyes of the carvings, lettering on the spines of books, writing on sheets of paper on the table, things on shelves, marks on the floor, a crossbow on a wall and…

'Look,' croaked Finn. 'Can you see it?' He pointed towards the banister dragon. Its mouth was now wide open, and within it glowed a blue glass bottle with gold flames wrapping round the outside. Inside it was a dark liquid that seemed to absorb all the colours of the room and the shadows of the night outside.

'Hidden in a lead-lined mouth,' marvelled Errol, his face alight. 'The equaliser hydrant! This could save us all!'

'LEAVE THIS PLACE,' yelled Charlie, coming out of his spin, still entirely focused on the attackers outside, 'before you are DESTROYED!' He drew his arm back, ready to hurl another fireball, but when he released it from his clenched fist it shrank in the air and disappeared with a sibilant hiss, his power finally all used up.

And then the turret was plunged into complete darkness and absolute silence. The only light came from the dragon's yellow eyes and the eerie blue glow of the precious bottle held between its sharply fanged jaws.

A light that all could clearly see, even the Venomous outside.

26

‡▽≡Ɵ‡⅄·Ɵ꒚𝗑

Despite the darkness, Finn could make out quite clearly the crouched and panting form of Charlie, now down on one knee, sobbing in muffled gasps. It was a sound of such agony and anguish that Finn felt his chest contract. He crawled over to him.

'The Venomous cannot get in,' he said, 'and the flames have gone. The hydrant is right there – in the dragon's mouth, which is definitely, definitely not alive.' He swallowed. 'Just a magical carving, right? I have the Stone. Simon Veritas and Shen will be here soon, won't they? We are quite safe.'

'Milady,' croaked Charlie towards the bag on Finn's back, 'Does Simon bring the mythics?'

'No. I see Simon at a labyrinth exit, far away. There are Venomous everywhere.'

As if in reply, there was another barrage of sound from the balcony as the Venomous lifted their faces to the roof and howled with everything they had. Craven added his keening shriek to the mix and then there was a most definite cracking sound. Tula jerked upright, her eyes drawn to the topmost branches of the yew tree that had grown through the window. Finn followed her gaze and saw a strange pulsing energy there, visible in an oily spread of pus-coloured yellow, and Craven began moving rapidly towards it.

'No,' breathed Finn.

With a low growl, the banister dragon twisted, turned and shut its jaws, enclosing the hydrant within its mouth once more.

Tula sprang to her feet, throwing her arms up high in front of her. There was a rushing noise, as if a thousand small streams were hurtling to her aid, and then a *CLAP!* as ice bonded in a sheet up against all the windows before them, frosting thickly around the tree.

'Oh, thank the forces,' muttered Errol, his shoulders sagging slightly as he came towards Tula. 'Activate the bioluminescence again so the banister dragon releases the hydrant again, and let's get out of here!'

'Wait,' said Finn, watching his sister sign. 'She says it's not enough.'

'They're gearing up for another howling session,' said Charlie, turning back to face them. His voice was hoarse and his eyes red. He looked exhausted. 'And I don't think even the ice can stop them.'

'We have to try,' said Errol. 'If they get in through here, they'll overrun the entire fortress!'

'Ha ha haaaa!' The manic laughter from the balcony drew all the children closer together. Gathered around Charlie, they peered out through the icy sheet that Tula had thrown up. Even though it was frosty and misted over in large patches, they could make out Craven still balanced on a Venom's shoulders.

'Ready to run, boy?' he taunted, the reflection of his goggles shifting and moving as if seeing things within their minds. 'Run, run, run, RUUUUUN? Ha ha! Yes, you should, just like your father before you, and his father before him, and we shall not –' he paused to assume a mimicry of Charlie's voice, though all he managed was a strange growling rage that did not do the boy's fury any justice '– LEAVE THIS PLACE! Instead, we shall come here in our hordes and wipe you out for all time. We shall do what we do best – incite the volcanoes, stir the levels of the planet to its very depths, exult in tornados, in the mile-high waves of the oceans, in the ash clouds that have obliterated the world before and which will obliterate it again, leaving us to command the precious metals and reach out beyond the stars. We shall rule the world in all its true glory!'

'Can you breathe more ice, Tula?' murmured Finn, and in reply he felt Tula grow cold.

Outside, the Venomous drew breath and began to howl again, with less power this time. Craven lifted his whip high, like that of a cruel circus master from times long ago, and he slashed it down, across the heads, necks and backs of the creatures around him. They screeched and yowled, and he yelled something at them that was hard to hear through the thickening ice. Up went his wicked whip again, and when it came down the Venomous voices were a union of terrible rage and pain.

'It's the opposite of fireblood melody,' croaked Charlie. 'That sound is built for breaking.'

Again came a cracking noise high above them, and Craven screeched in triumph. He leapt from the shoulders of the Venom and grabbed hold of the very tip of the tree that grew from the inside of the turret to the outside. It was as if an invisible gap had opened up around the leafy twigs, which still wasn't big enough for him to get through, and he scrabbled at the invisible edges like a demented starving dog, frantic to get in to satisfy his hunger.

'Tula,' whispered Errol. 'Tula!'

She had sunk to her knees, her arms poised just above the ground, her fingers still stretched out. Her skin had gone as white as snow and charcoal crescents furrowed beneath her blue eyes.

Finn placed his hands upon her shoulders and after a moment she threw her arms out again with a desperate force, her fingers splayed, her eyes wide. Finn felt as if the blood were rushing from his veins and pounding hard towards his fingertips, pushing, shoving, hurtling energy towards her outstretched hands. The sound of streams ran clear again, for just a moment, followed in a split second by the rush of rivers, the crash of racing ocean waves, and this time the CRACK of the ice forming was of Arctic proportions.

High above, Craven screamed in pain as the ice froze round the hand attached to the tree branch. He snatched it away and fell down, scrabbling for grip as he went. The biggest Venom of all, standing just to the left of the mob on the balcony, grabbed hold of him and set him down carefully on the balustrade.

Finn watched Craven catching his breath with great heaving intakes of air, inaudible through the ice sheets.

'Oh no,' he murmured as the evil man reached for his whip again.

Instinctively, he pulled Tula behind him, just as Charlie went, 'Brace yourselves.'

'Stand back,' said Errol. 'If he—'

The whip slashed down, the tip of it a red-hot laser, and it sliced neatly through Tula's ice. Instead of slamming it down again, Craven twitched it this way and that in a strange dance of pinprick light. Finn blinked, feeling dizzy, and hugged his sister to him.

'Don't look at it,' he said, though he could not explain why.

'Come on, Shen. Hurry, Simon,' murmured Charlie. 'We're not going to be able to hold them off much longer.' He pressed his fingers to his chest to activate his gift of endurance and his fingers grazed the firefly mark. The room lit up again, and the dragon on the banister slowly opened its jaws.

'The hydrant!' yelled Errol. Before anyone could see what was happening, he dashed up the stairs and snatched the glowing bottle of hydrant from the dragon's mouth.

'What?' exclaimed Charlie. 'He can just take it?' His voice had gone high and a little hysterical. 'What about precedents, like Excalibur, for goodness' sake?'

Errol held up the precious bottle and called out, 'I think we should use this. We could throw it at the wall like Augustus used to throw it into the volcanoes, and all the Venomous would be obliterated.' He turned to glance at the ice where Craven whirled his whip, and could not look away.

'NO!' Charlie's voice was hoarse, and he ran to Errol. 'The hydrant doesn't work like that. Give it to me, Ezza. You know how dangerous it is!'

Errol jumped on to the back of the banister dragon to get closer to the bright red orb of the demonic whip.

'No, Charlie, no, no, no,' he murmured. Then, more quietly, 'No, no, no.' His gaze was still fixed to the Venomous on the other side of the ice, and in particular on that fiery tip of the whip.

It's the whip, signed Tula frantically. *He's hypnotised by it*.

'ERROL, NO!' yelled Finn. 'Quick, Charlie!' but before Charlie could reach the boy there was a groaning sound and the banister dragon began to move, writhing its coils back into position, turning its head and closing its mouth. Charlie, already dizzy and faint from his fireball battle, lost his balance and fell to the floor, four metres below, landing awkwardly.

Leaving Errol all alone, completely exposed, holding the only thing that could save the world from total destruction.

27

‡▽≡◊‡人·θ≡∧≡◊

Errol leapt on to the banister before Finn had even blinked. In a broken heap, Charlie yelled, 'Stop him!' and Finn sprang into action, Tula still facing the Venomous on the balcony. Finn was already moving in a race of tangled arms and legs to get to Errol when his friend unstoppered the phial and drew back his arm.

'ERROL, NOOOO!' yelled Charlie and Finn, while Tula shook with the exertion of holding up the ice.

'Come and get it, you stinking invaders!' called Errol in an entranced voice quite different from his own, but before he could hurl it towards their attackers there was a blinding flash and Craven was in the room, snatching the phial from Errol's grasp. He danced in spinning leaps down the stairs to land on the big table, scattering papers and breaking glass.

'Thanks for the invitation,' he hissed, his ruby eyes

alight with triumph. 'My happy helpers will join me soon, little boy.'

'GET OUT!' yelled Charlie, now at Errol's side, grabbing his friend back by the collar of his shirt.

'Too late!' laughed Craven. He snatched at the air, and Finn saw clearly – though he was moving at warp speed – that he'd retrieved the stopper of the phial from Errol's outstretched hand. With glee he sealed the liquid safely inside and laughed again, slashing his whip from left to right. It caught Errol round the neck and spun him in a tumbling cartwheel to the floor where he landed, unconscious.

Finn rushed to his side, pulling him to safety under the table, while Craven spun high again, jumping to the floor directly in front of Charlie's bent-over body.

'Errol?' said Finn urgently, his hands shaking his shoulders. '*Errol!*'

Craven leapt back as Charlie vaulted up, his fists lashing out in a right hook, a left hook, so fast that Finn wasn't certain he'd actually moved, except that the man had sprung out of reach, laughing his mocking laugh, taunting Charlie with the precious bottle, and making his whip dance in a mesmerising sequence of glowing light.

Outside, the Venomous howled, desperate to get in.

Charlie sank to his knees and Errol blinked, as if coming out of a strange hypnosis. He took in the scene with one frightened glance. 'No...' he whispered. 'What did I do? No no nonononono.'

'It's the whip, Errol!' hissed Finn. 'Not you! We need to think! Milady,' he ground out, 'if ever you had a suggestion as to what to do next, now would be good.'

His back warmed, and Errol placed a hand on the bag as if to add his plea to Finn's.

'Erm...' went the Stone. 'A lot of peril here. Not many options.'

'Please advise of perilous options,' said Errol, his face still wet with desperate tears. '*Please.*'

Freezing air blasted in with a whirl of icy pinpricks, and the whine of the wind was loud and ferocious. There was a cracking sound from behind as a Venom smashed at the ice.

'Oh boy, oh boy, oh boy,' went the Stone.

Tula sagged, totally spent, and rolled beneath the table with Errol and Finn.

Nothing left, she signed. *So sorry.*

'Milady,' whispered Finn, holding Tula's shoulder to send her what little warmth he had left. 'What would my father do? I am not asking advice. I am asking for information.'

'He would get you to safety.'

Finn drew breath for an angry retort, but Errol held up one hand to stop him and dashed the tears from his face with the other. 'And then what would he do?' he asked.

'He'd rip the goggles from that evil man! He'd disarm him with a flourish! He'd retrieve the phial of equaliser hydrant! He'd kill all the Venomous! He'd—'

'Here I am!' screamed Craven, cracking his whip around Charlie's head. 'In the heart of the fortress! Never again will you have the power to stop the forces beneath!'

Finn could hear Charlie whimpering, curling over on himself. His pain and vulnerability sparked that white-hot heat inside Finn that he swallowed down every day, but this time he knew he needed it. The angry red pulse at the end of the whip pulled pictures from the walls, books from shelves and smashed more glass from the big table to pieces. Plants withered and crumpled and died. Outside, three Venoms were struggling to clamber up and over each other to reach the broken ice at the top of the tree where Craven had come in, and they were getting higher and higher. It wouldn't be long before they figured out the mechanics of a Venomous stepladder.

Finn bent his head to think, but snaking into his

ears came Craven's voice, speaking more loudly to Charlie now as his words dripped with menace: 'Poor little bereaved boy, bent on revenge. Everything about you is useless, you antisocial little freak. Everything. Where are your little minions when you need them? Tucked up in bed with their mothers and fathers who despise who you are and what you stand for?'

No, thought Finn. *Charlie is NOT useless.*

He is trying to break Charlie! signed Tula furiously. *Help him, Finn!*

'You are a drain on this island,' continued Craven, gathering his whip behind him. 'A blight on the efforts of these silly firebloods. Even the mythics shy away in fear and loathing when you enter the labyrinth. You are our strongest tool in this place for all the damage you wreak!' He raised his whip above his head, and Finn felt a frightening rush of intense heat powering up his insides.

He sprang to his feet and crept up on Craven from behind. For once, he felt no urge to swallow down his fury, no fear of what might happen when he vented his rage.

'Nobody loves you,' said the human, drawing back the whip, and his voice seemed to echo again and again and again in Finn's head.

Nobody loves you.

Nobody loves you.

Nobody loves you.

The words brought such an uprising of emotion in Finn that he felt he could hold his breath no longer.

As Craven brought his whip slashing down, Finn leapt into the air and the end of it sliced the front of his legs – back, forth, back. Finn bit back a scream of pain and spun right towards the man, leaping high to catch the razor-sharp whip before it could do any more damage. He timed it just right, grabbing the tip in his fist. Craven shrieked with delight, but Finn felt every one of the marks on his chest pulse on his skin as they'd never done before. He clapped a hand to the most painful of them, and a flash of extraordinary bioluminescence pulsed from him, encasing him in a bright blue light.

The whip warmed Finn's palm, nothing more.

He pulled on it with all his might, and it flew out of Craven's unwitting grasp smashing the lenses of his night goggles. Craven shrieked again, this time in surprise, and pain, whirling to face Finn, his face a mixture of confusion and darkening anger, his eyes squinting blindly into the glare.

'Charlie has more love than you will ever know!' shouted Finn, flicking the whip so that the handle flew across the room towards him. He hefted it in his other fist, keeping the dangerous tip clutched in his left hand. 'And you *do not* come uninvited to our home!'

Craven's eyes had narrowed to slits. 'Give that back to me!' he hissed, his teeth glinting in the gloom. His face flickered with a fear that Finn had not expected. He released the tip of the whip and swung it gently back and forth. The man watched it and his jaw went slack.

'Get out,' said Finn, gesturing to the balcony where more Venomous were climbing over the balustrade and beating at the ice with their massive, clawed hands. 'Go back to your twisted creatures.'

Charlie coughed and pushed himself up on one elbow. 'The bottle…' he groaned.

Craven tried to take a step towards Finn but seemed to be fighting against an invisible force. His eyes were still fixed on the laser light at the end of the whip.

'Rrrreeeeaaarrrrgh!' he growled.

'Give me back the bottle,' said Finn, feeling a strange surge of electricity zinging to his outstretched fingertips. '*Now*.'

Craven's arms clenched and shook. It seemed almost as if they might break. For a split second he was frozen absolutely still, until at last he screamed out a strangled, high-pitched sound, and flailed his arms helplessly. The liquid inside the little bottle bubbled and frothed.

'Stay back,' warned Finn. 'Throw me the bottle, and get out of here.'

Craven's eyes bulged, and his legs moved in reverse, his unwilling feet dragging on the floor. Again he windmilled his arms, as if struggling to keep his balance, and then suddenly the hydrant flew from his grasp into Finn's waiting hands. With eyes stretched into an expression of furious pain and agony, Craven screamed once more. Saliva flew out in speckles that seemed to hang in the air for too long. It was a high-pitched wail of such intensity that Tula's wall of ice cracked in several places. One of the Venomous raised his mighty fists and slammed them against the icy wall, again and again, until at last it shattered. With a guttural grunt of triumph he stepped over the threshold, shaking glittering shards from his greasy form and clenching his fists. The rest of the Venomous from the balcony hurled themselves, howling, at the fragile barrier and in an explosion of icy dust, sharp shards and demon stink, they staggered into the room.

'Tell us what to do, boss,' growled the biggest of them, the one with headphones seared to his head. 'You want us to squish them?'

Three stood behind Craven now, side by side, steaming in the icy darkness, their scars glinting in evil patterns across their warped and swollen bodies. Behind them was a heaving force of many more enormous figures, dwarfing the man with their hulking proportions, saturating the room with their stench, staring stupidly around them with a drooling rage that struck horror into Finn's very soul.

'Attack them!' croaked Craven, and the huge Venom tugged on his master's arm, shoving him out of his path to safety on the balcony outside, where he collided with the other monstrous creatures crowding there.

'Finn,' rasped Charlie. 'Wave the whip! Tell them to leave!'

But before Finn could say a word the first Venom hurled an enormous wooden mallet towards him and, though the boy had the lightning reflexes of a puma, the weapon still caught him square in the guts.

'Oof,' he gasped, and crumpled down on to Charlie, winding them both.

'FINN!' yelled Errol. 'Come on!'

But Finn could not for the life of him draw breath or speak or even stand up.

'Tula!' called Errol. 'Tell them to go!'

Tula stared ahead at the Venomous, more and

more of them advancing with a slow, stupid tread, her hands signing the command for them to leave, but to no avail. What was needed was voice, and she could not speak.

Finn found himself flapping like a fish on the floor with Charlie, watching the Venomous horde advance four metres into the room, now five, now six. His legs were not healing, and blood leaked slowly to the floor.

Errol muttered a curse, took a deep breath and shouted another word, but Finn saw to his horror that the balcony was still crowded with the warped creatures. They were coming through the ice, and it was just a matter of time before the firebloods would be completely overrun.

Tula reached back and grabbed her brother's arm in her left hand. *Come on, Finn*, she signed.

Finn felt an unlocking sensation in his chest, sucked in a desperate breath and yelled with all his might: 'LEAVE THIS ISLAND, creatures from beneath, and … and … you too, Craven!' he yelled, flourishing the whip at the scarred man.

'*Yes*,' gasped Charlie, drawing whooping breath at last. 'Leave!'

And then Tula sprang to her feet, her face glowing with realisation.

The griffin's mark! she signed, pressing her cold

fingers to her chest with one hand. Her other arm flung out, and her mouth opened wide in a magical cry of soundless intensity. One by one, each Venom dropped unconscious to the floor, ears bleeding, eyes rolling, tongues lolling, disintegrating to ash. The only creature left standing between the firebloods and the balcony was Craven. His body was rigid with rebellion, drenched in perspiration, and he gasped and groaned as his feet shuffled uncontrollably backwards.

'Whoa,' breathed Errol. 'He's going…'

Going… signed Tula.

'Gone,' said Charlie with satisfaction as Craven toppled backwards over the balustrade.

28

‡▽≡⊖‡⅄≡ȯ⊖⋔‡

harlie was shaking badly, and one of his wings hung broken and useless, leaking a lot of gold on to the floor.

'To Drishti,' he rasped. 'We need her to tell the aviators that we have the hydrant.'

Drishti's tech room was as far below ground as the island went, explained Errol to Finn and Tula. They were moving as quickly as they could, exhausted, torn and trembling, down dark tunnels hewn from black rock where Finn had not ventured before. The sconces here glowed into a brief blue light, then faded out swiftly once they'd passed.

At last they came to the end of the tunnel, looking down a steep spiral staircase that disappeared into pitch black.

'I'll go first,' said Charlie, swinging round the rail and down.

What does Drishti do here? signed Tula, already making her way down the steps.

Errol gestured for Finn to go next. 'She runs the place. She has to get the latest tech smuggled in, or she gets it made down here, and then we use as little as possible and cover our tracks so the frailskins don't ever find out we exist.'

Thirty seconds later their feet were on solid ground again. At the end of the corridor was a set of solid steel double doors. On them, in big red letters, were the words:

NO ENTRY

And beneath that:

Authorised personnel only.
I mean it!
DS

Errol hurried to the door and knocked out a quick rhythm.

'Morse code?' said Finn, surprised.

'Whoa! You guys are a *mess*,' said Drishti, throwing the door wide open. 'What took you so long? What the hell happened?'

'The Venomous were here,' said Charlie, still breathless with pain. 'Got to tell George and the aviators.'

'Venomous?' Drishti's face paled. 'On the island? Where? How?'

'Someone must have let them in,' said Errol, gesturing Finn and Tula inside and shutting the door behind them. 'We got rid of a horde up at the watchtower, but we should ask Shen to scry to check that there aren't any more, unless you've got surveillance at all potential entry points?'

'Did you tell George about Augustus being in Iceland, not Russia?' interrupted Charlie.

'I left a message,' replied Drishti, 'because I couldn't get through. They must be on the move. So just stay calm, all right?' She pointed a warning finger at Charlie. 'We don't need any explosions in here. This is our only link to the outside world.' She whirled away. 'I'll get hot chocolate going, extra chilli. You'll need it.'

'No time,' said Finn and Charlie in unison.

Drishti threw a curious look over her shoulder and hurried them further into the room. 'I've been scrutinising all geothermal patterns across Iceland. I'd bet my last cowri that Gargan is holding Augustus in the depths of Hekla, that ancient volcano near the south shore. It's been smoking and steaming like a teahouse kettle for weeks.'

She clicked her fingers, and with a *tick-tick-tick* sound the room was suddenly lit by a bright glow. Tân emerged from Tula's pocket, his eyes wide, and Finn's jaw dropped in surprise. The space was vast, and every square centimetre of the walls and floors was covered in wiring and tubing and pipes and circuitry and switches and connectors.

'So, we know the Venomous are driving recent eruptions and earthquakes, yes? Well, look at this!' Her hands moved swiftly over the desk again and a map flowed on to the screen, zooming further and further from a reddish glow in Russia, closer and closer to Iceland, showing a crimson infrared glow in one specific area.

'Magnetic activity that is completely off the scale,' explained Drishti. 'Tula?'

Tula placed her finger on the map, closed her eyes for a second, then nodded. *Dad*, she signed.

'He *is* at Hekla,' said Charlie.

Finn laid the whip down carefully on the desk but kept the bag strapped to his shoulders, leaning in to study the terrain around the Icelandic mountain. It was covered in rock, snow and ice.

'Yes,' said Drishti, 'and if we don't intervene,

there's a chance Gargan could turn Hekla into a supervolcano – which would be enough to cause another Ice Age. It would be the end of the world as we know it. Exactly what the Venomous have always wanted.'

'How do we get there?' asked Finn. 'Can we leave now?'

The griffin is not here, signed Tula. *Are there any other creatures that could take us?*

'No mythic will go anywhere near you,' declared Charlie. 'Not after what happened in the Last Battle.' He stopped and took a breath. 'I'll go. If I leave just before dawn, I'll be there by mid-morning.'

'No, Charlie,' said Drishti, panicked. 'No!' She gestured impatiently at the satellite picture on the screen. 'Look at this *and* this, and what about *that*?'

Charlie's brow furrowed. 'Bad weather isn't going to stop me.'

Drishti barked a bitter laugh. 'It can and it will. *This* is Hurricane Celeste right here. Mean and nasty and totally impenetrable. This over *here* is a cold front currently charting thirty degrees below freezing. And even your flight capabilities won't make it through this hailstorm hitting the south coast. We need to wait for Idris and the aviators, with Patrick, George and Angelina. They'll already have picked up my message and be back by tomorrow, in the nick of time because by my calculations Hekla is predicted to blow two days from now.'

'That doesn't sound in the nick of time. That sounds too late.' Charlie clenched his jaw. 'Boats?' he asked. 'What about boats?'

Drishti just stared back at him, deadpan.

'A submarine?'

She closed her eyes and her nostrils flared.

'A plane!' burst out Errol. 'My brother's turbojet! My jump jet!'

'Both are still in pieces!' retorted Drishti. 'And you know it, Errol! Come on!'

'Fine,' snapped Charlie. 'Fine. I'll go talk to the mythics,' and before anyone could say anything to deter him he'd rushed out, leaving nothing behind but the echoing clang of the doors shutting behind him.

Errol raised his eyebrows at Drishti.

'Nothing and nobody is getting to Iceland through that storm,' she muttered. 'You've got to stop him, Errol.'

Errol paled. 'Go back into the labyrinth after we sent their strongest warrior away and the Venomous have arrived?'

'You can do it, Errol,' said Drishti, spinning round to clatter away at the computer keyboard. 'Let me

check for any remaining Venomous on the island…'
Finn, Tula and Errol found themselves holding their
breath until she said, 'Sulfuric detectors and infra-red
imaging show footprints here, here, down the side of
the watchtower and we lose track when they retreat
to the ocean.' She turned and grinned at them. 'You
puny lot vanquished them! How does that feel? You'll
go down in songs for years to come!'

'Songs about doom, death and destruction,' said
Errol, 'unless we move fast. I'll catch up with Charlie
now and reassure the mythics as best I can.' He turned
to Finn and Tula. 'What's next for you?'

'Well, we have the Stone and we have the equaliser,'
replied Finn. 'No one else knows that yet. Who can
we trust?'

'With *that* information?' squeaked Drishti. 'The
hydrant? Really? You have it?' Her hair was whipping
so fast around her head that Errol and Tula took a
dubious step back. 'Where is it? Can I see it?'

Finn fished the bottle out of his pocket and held it
up to the light.

All four of them were silent, staring at the deep-
blue glass and the gold flames that circled its base.
The liquid inside moved and swirled with a life of its
own, even though Finn held the bottle still in a steady
hand.

'So powerful, but so fragile,' murmured Drishti. She turned her gaze to Finn. 'Guard it with your life.'

'Of course,' he replied.

'Go tell Shen what you have,' Drishti continued, 'but no one else. She'll help. And wait for better weather. It's more than seven hundred miles of bad storms by air and sea between here and Iceland. No mythic is going to do that, no matter how much they love the Flints. Not even Grey Griffin, and he'd die for your dad.'

She pointed back at the screen. 'Hurricane Celeste should blow over in a few hours, taking Charlie with it if he's stupid enough to ignore my advice. This cold front is moving north, so there's a chance you might run into that, but actually it's more likely you'll just be on the edge of it. This hailstorm … well, that's more unpredictable. I might have to call in a few favours from the airheads.'

'Really?' Finn asked. 'You'd do that for us?'

Drishti laughed. 'Of course. Go talk to Shen. Get some sleep while the storm passes, and for snakes' sake look after the hydrant.' Finn nodded, zipping up his coat pocket with the precious bottle within it. 'I'll keep trying to get hold of George,' she continued, her face serious again, 'and I'll let you know when it's safe to leave.'

Back on the ground floor of the fortress, Finn, Tula and Errol were hit by an onslaught of noise so loud that Tula clapped her hands to her ears, wincing.

'Many houses are moving,' shouted Errol, taking them to a window. 'Everyone, and everything, is afraid.'

And it was true. All around them, buildings were either in the process of extricating themselves from their streets or already creaking and groaning on spindly legs of brick, iron, steel or concrete as they went looking for safer places to reside, away from the fortress walls.

'I bet the harbour will be almost empty,' called Errol over his shoulder, 'even with some of the best views in town. I'm sure Rudimenta's place already went to a street on the cliff above last night. That house is really nervy.'

Two semi-detached homes were taking up the whole road, even though they were moving sideways like a pair of conjoined crabs. Another building, small and narrow, slipped off the pavement, bumping into the semi-detacheds. There was a shrieking sound of metal on metal, even though no surfaces ground against each other, and the little house leapt back on to the pavement, flapping its window shutters frantically. It bashed into a tall, skinny warehouse-looking building, which was trying to slide down a narrow side street, and there was a furious clattering sound in return that made Tula clap her hands to her ears.

'We'll get some sleep here in the fortress,' decided Finn, 'after we've talked to Shen. Will you be okay getting back to the Arsenal?'

'Of course! See you tomorrow,' said Errol, and jumped from the window on to the terrace outside. In minutes he had disappeared from view.

We have the Stone and the equaliser hydrant, signed Tula, *plus a hypnotic whip. I know you have a plan.*

Finn clapped a hand to his forehead. 'I left the whip in Drishti's lab!'

At least it'll be safe there, signed Tula. *Let's get to Shen quickly for healing tonic for your legs because Dad may need it too, and then we can ask the Stone—*

'I'd like it if you two didn't call me the Stone,' said the Stone from the rucksack on Finn's back.

Finn jumped. 'Oh, my g—'

'If ever there was a time to ask for direction, children, it's now. Why has everyone forgotten that I'm here?'

'W-what should we do?' asked Finn.

'Go to the clinic. Update Shen. Get some sleep.'

'Of course,' said Finn, shrugging at Tula. *That's what we already decided*, he mouthed to Tula.

And then we're going to find a way out of here, signed Tula. *Whatever that might be.*

30

ᚠᚪᚷᚲᛏᛉ

Outside the window above Finn's bed in Shen's medical room, the sky was dark with a thunderous storm, but it was clearly day. He pulled the bed curtain wider and saw to his alarm that the whole space was now filled with hospital stretchers. In them were wounded people, some snoring gently, some tossing and turning, one weeping and one groaning quietly. The rectangular pools around the big pool in the middle were covered up with slabs of what looked like granite, and the big pool had a glass cover over which he saw a young woman hurry with a tray.

A movement to his left made him jump.

Shen.

She smiled at him. 'You passed out when you staggered in here last night.' She sighed, fixing a spraying device to a purple bottle, and shook her head at Finn's legs laid out in front of her. 'My clinic, as you can see, is now full to the brim with wounded aviators, back from Elbrus. Patrick has only just managed to heal a nasty Venomous bite on his shoulder. He wanted to speak with you and Tula urgently. I'm waiting for George – he'll be here soon, I'm certain, but I'm wondering if I should take this opportunity to explain a few things first that have been kept from you for too long.'

A door at the far end of the room opened and Tula appeared with Patrick.

Your legs are very purple, she signed to Finn when she reached his bedside. *You feeling better?*

He nodded. 'Shen was just wondering whether we should know some secret stuff. Probably secret stuff like what happened at Elbrus.'

'What secret stuff?' Patrick asked Shen, ignoring Finn and frowning.

Shen raised her eyebrows at him. 'The boy is right. You should explain things like the ambush you just had with Venomous out at Mount Elbrus, and also the fight between you and Augustus after the Last Battle, and your disagreements about secrecy, and how you're the children's godfather, and about Charlie—'

'Okay, okay! I'm happy to talk about all this,' said Patrick, looking unhappy, 'but we need to work out a few things first. Craven was tracking the children when they first left home,' he said. 'I don't know how.

And someone in this place is feeding the Venomous information. Who?'

A bright and cheerful voice bounced across the room, followed by a short, round man who moved as he spoke with short, energetic strides.

'Yes, who, my dear boy, would you suspect of such a terrible thing? I don't think it would be wise to start any rumours of treachery at this difficult time.'

Finn and Tula recognised Simon Veritas instantly from the portrait in the Hall of Heroes. His hair was carefully combed into a precise side parting, his moustache clipped into two narrow arrowheads facing opposite ways above his mouth, and his eyes were bright and shiny, blinking quickly as he glanced around the room, taking everything in.

'Only one person has ever betrayed the people of the fortress,' he continued, and Patrick flushed, while Finn's mouth filled with the taste of rust, 'and ... well, I'm afraid history is not on your side, my dear Patrick. There are whispers aplenty here that you—'

'We do not need to speak of that, Simon,' said Shen with a frown.

Simon clapped a hand to his forehead. 'Of course not! I beg your pardon, Patrick! Bygones, bygones – forgive me. I'm flustered by all the information I must share, but also because who do I see before me? Is it truly the legendary Flint offspring?' His smile was bright and wide, and when his fingers touched Finn's wrist the rust taste faded from Finn's mouth, and he felt oddly comforted.

'Welcome!' said Simon, but his face when he looked over to Shen and Patrick was confused. 'Why were these dear children not placed in the labyrinth quarantine rooms until all proper checks were undertaken? We must remedy this immediately. They are not safe here, as evidenced last night!'

'What?' exclaimed Patrick at the same time as Shen went, 'Oh no! There's no doubting that—'

'Excuse me!' squeaked Simon. 'The minute they arrive we have a Venomous invasion! How do you explain that? People are saying the Flints let them in! We know that's not true, but we should be following all our usual rules and regulations!' His pale face had taken on a strange sheen, gleaming like the alabaster skin of a snake's underbelly. 'Sir Arthur! Sir Dornar!' he snapped. 'An escort immediately, please!'

Finn and Tula watched in shock as, with a great clanking, two figures in an odd configuration of armoured plates and chain mail came forward.

'Oh, for heaven's sake!' muttered Patrick. 'This is ludicrous. Stand down, Arthur. Drop the sword, Sir Dornar. We need these children! They are not traitors!'

'We have the hy—' croaked Finn, horrified at what was unfolding.

'Let's just get this over with, mate,' interrupted Sir Dornar from behind a helmet made of copper and steel. 'Won't take long to do the checks, and then we can sort this whole mess out properly before it escalates *as it did before.*'

Patrick was about to speak but flushed again and gritted his teeth.

'The boy is not well!' cried Shen. Her voice had gone high and quavery. She cleared her throat. 'Why don't you leave both here, under guard? The labyrinth—'

'Is the best place for them,' concluded Simon. 'We must protect them and their reputation. What if something else were to happen, Shen? Would you want to be responsible for a Portaldor uprising against our own? We must consider the big picture! Public health and safety! In George's absence, I have the authority—'

'Absolutely not!' snapped Shen, her eyes shiny with tears of frustration. 'I—'

'Tula and I are happy to do whatever checks,' said Finn quickly, watching Tula sign to him – *We shouldn't talk about the hydrant with all these people here*. She stopped as soon as Simon swung his glinting gaze her way.

Shen bit her lip.

'We promise,' Finn added. 'We just want to get Dad back as soon as possible, and arguing about everything is getting in the way.'

Shen turned from the bed, murmuring something about getting Finn's clothes, and it was some minutes of seething, awkward silence later before she returned. Tula's face was locked in silence, and Finn's throat was still tight and dry, as if hot coals were lodged there.

'I've put some more of this healing potion into your pocket, Finn,' said Shen softly, showing him a purple bottle, 'as you will need more treatments.' She tapped the label. 'Read the instructions carefully.'

'Hmm,' said Simon. 'I'm not sure he should have any—'

'Enough!' Shen did not raise her voice, but she was trembling with suppressed rage. 'I appreciate we need to protect the Flints' damaged reputation, but that is all. Let the tests commence, and then George himself will put this matter to rights.'

31

‡Ⴎᔐ·ᒃᖆ·ᐱ ·�□Ձ≡

An hour later Finn and Tula were locked in a cold, dark cell, deep underground. Finn shivered. Though Shen had made sure they were fully dressed, and that they had their bag, he wished he were wearing more clothes. He pulled Tula close to him with one arm to warm her, as she was shaking too, and he shoved his other hand into his pocket. His fingers found the little bottle of healing potion and the equaliser hydrant. It gave him courage.

'We still have the Stone and the hydrant,' whispered Finn, fierce. 'We're going to get out of here with your unlocking skills, Tula, and find a way to Hekla before it blows up.'

With Dad in it. Tula went over to the barred gate serving as the door to the cell. It had a big, heavy doorknob embedded in a lock that was two hands wide, and a hand and a half deep. When she put her thumb to the opening on the other side, a series of clicks and clanks came from the mechanism.

Looking back over her shoulder at Finn, she gestured *Come on*, turning the handle. It opened. Tân jumped from Finn's lap, scurried up Tula's jeans and hid under her shirt collar.

Finn grinned at her and pulled out the healing potion from his pocket, hastily smearing a little more on his legs as he got up.

Tula frowned. *What does that label on the potion bottle say?*

Finn teased it from beneath the twist of string that held it to the bottle. 'It's not a label. It's a note.' He moved his glowing finger wonderingly away then back again to the paper. 'The writing only shows when I use my light.'

Tula leaned closer and the two of them stared at the words growing darker in Finn's light:

Beware the mythics from days of yore;
they will not let you through the door.
Seek she of sea, thought long dead,
fast asleep on her precious bed.
Go far beneath, follow signs of old,
towards songstress call, piles of gold.
Knock and you shall enter there
where others could not, would not dare.

'Oh no,' murmured Finn. 'I'm useless with riddles.'

It's not a riddle, signed Tula, impatient. *It's a simple instruction. Don't be put off by the slanty writing and stupid rhyme.*

'It *is* a riddle,' insisted Finn. 'There's nothing clear about it at all.'

A world-weary sigh came from the rucksack. 'So it's a riddle to other people, then, but not for us, because you play Flybynight Warrior and know all about a creature long thought dead,' said the Telling Stone.

Finn frowned.

Tula's signing grew wilder. *The clue is in the songstress call. Remember Aria's ally in the battles? With the reins of fire?*

Finn's face lit up. 'I'm such an idiot. It's the water dragon.'

Yes! Now we just have to find her. You'll need to sing.

'Oh no!' spluttered Finn. 'I can't sing. I—'

A clang, the sound of metal on rock, came echoing down the passage.

'Well, you've got about ten minutes to learn,' said the Telling Stone.

Tula whirled back into the cell and extinguished the sconces of fire between her palms while Finn shoved the bottle with its note deep into his pocket. He held the door ready as Tula danced back out from the dark shadows and closed it soundlessly behind her. She locked it again with a frown of concentration and the pressure of her thumb.

Which way? she asked.

'To the left, down towards the sea gate,' whispered the Stone.

There was another clank, louder than the one before, and long streaks of light came leaping round the edges of the walls.

Finn and Tula ran. They turned the corner at the end of the corridor just as voices rang clear behind them.

'Yeah, that's right. Like it or not, Simon Veritas wants both them kids questioned.'

'Questioned?'

'*Interrogated*, like. Eejit, you are. Wants to ask 'em loadsa questions. It's 'is job, innit? Protecting us all…'

The voices faded as Finn and Tula turned another corner, the corridor becoming narrower, colder, darker.

Finn wasn't sure this passage was going to the ocean. He couldn't smell salt water at all, just dry and dusty rock. The Stone whispered directions. They took another turn, then another, not daring to slow, and then the corridor narrowed to a half-metre-wide schism in the rock. Finn couldn't see into it. He waved his hand to illuminate it, but light from his fingers whooshed out like the last, quiet gasp of air from a hot-water bottle when it's filled up. Tula touched his arm. He turned to look at her face.

Keep going.

Finn began to move again, but slowly. Tula pulled on Finn's arm, making small, quick signs.

What happened? You okay? Are you tired?

Though still breathing hard, Finn was not tired. He shook his hand, willed his fingers to warm to a glow.

Nothing.

'I don't know,' he whispered. 'It's like... It's like someone blew me out. Like I've been extinguished on the inside.'

'The water dragon,' said the Telling Stone.

'What about the water dragon?'

'Just keep going,' urged the Stone. 'Hurry!'

Tula signed, *I don't like this*, but didn't slow down. A rotten smell hung in the air and the roof of the passage was getting lower.

'You should see an entrance coming up on your left,' said the Stone.

There, signed Tula, hurrying ahead, and Finn

noticed that beneath their feet were pieces of broken wood and crumbles of thick shattered glass.

He picked his way over more splinters of wood, through a roughly rectangular hole where an oak door had once hung on enormous hinges. On the other side, he stopped and helped Tula through, then they both slowed to a halt and looked around them. The air was different here: the way it felt, the way it smelled, the way it *sounded*.

Finn's eyes shifted and adjusted to find that they were standing in the small opening to a huge cavern. The stone on the ground was covered in a light dusting of sand, and the cave roof was a hundred metres above them. The rock supporting the ceiling was worn smooth by what must have been centuries of relentless waves crashing against it, and a thick green slime grew vigorously across its surface. In front of them was a huge pool with water that was so still and unmoving it looked like smoked glass. They could not see how deep it was, or how wide.

'Can you smell the sea?' whispered Finn. 'I'm sure I can hear waves, but the labyrinth is below sea level, and I thought we'd run far below that...'

Look. Tula was gesturing ahead of them to a faint glow that seemed to move and shimmer. *We need to get over there. It looks like it goes outside.*

'Wait—' Finn whispered, but Tula was already making her way round the very edge of the water, along a narrow ridge of rock that sometimes disappeared entirely beneath the water. Finn shook his hand and muttered rude things when his fingers refused to glow then, with a frustrated sigh, he hurried after Tula, feeling off balance and vulnerable.

CLANG … clink … CLANG…

The sounds rang out from the cavern's entrance.

The guards have caught up with us.

Finn slowed his breathing and concentrated on moving silently and quickly away from the men.

Tula was going more slowly now, her hands hovering above the slime and weeds as if ready to grab hold of something should she fall, because the narrow ledge had disappeared below the surface of the water. She was feeling her way with care, her movements soundless, the water around her scarcely rippling.

Finn flung a piece of weed at her head, and she stopped still, then turned round.

Guards, signed Finn. *We need to hide behind the weeds.*

Tula shook her head. *Let's keep going.*

Finn signed *NO!* so wildly that he nearly fell into the water.

A voice from the entrance echoed round the cavern. 'What is this place?'

'The lowest salt water. It's the final resting place of Shuĭlóng the water dragon. She came here to die after the Venomous speared her in the last battle.'

Shuĭlóng! Was that who helped our mother? thought Finn.

'Whoa!' Flames from a torch danced some way around the walls and across the water but did not reach Finn and Tula. Finn gestured to Tula again, and this time she nodded. She waited for her brother to catch up, then the two of them moved forward again, searching for a niche behind the weeds in which to hide.

'Why does no one come down here?' continued the guard. 'It's epic!'

'Usually there's a door barring the way. Usually you have to knock. *Always* there's no answer and always no one can get through.'

'*Un*usually today the door lies in pieces. But I don't think those kids are strong en—'

'No, dumbo. The door was broken from the outside, to go inside.'

'Oh. Is this the southside exit from the labyrinth? Where the Venomous got in?'

Tula's arm disappeared into the wall, and she quickly righted herself, and looked back at Finn.

Another tunnel! Shall I go in?

He nodded.

There was a grunt from the other guard. 'Zackly. There's no one here. Kids must've gone the other way. C'mon. Better hurry before we lose 'em.'

Just then Tula slipped. She grabbed with one hand at the weeds on the wall while the other hit the surface of the water with a splash.

'Jacob! Wait! You hear that?' The torchlight reached higher than before and danced across the rippling water. Finn froze, pushing himself into the plants on the rock, willing himself to be invisible. Tula had disappeared underwater. The torchlight danced high in the air, flickers of light moving carefully along the opposite side of the cave. Finn moved quickly through the hanging weeds to find himself in a dark space away from the searching lights and eyes of the guards.

Holding his breath, he leaned back towards the screen of plants that hung over the entrance and listened carefully.

'Nothing there, mate,' came the voice from the second guard. 'Probably just one of them icicle thingies falling in. C'mon. This place gives me the creeps.'

'Stalactite, Jacob. Stalactite.' The voices faded as the guards turned to go. 'You know the difference between a stalactite an' a stalagmite, an' all…?'

'Can we jus' focus on findin' these kids…?' Their bantering voices faded into faint echoes.

His heart beating wildly, Finn saw a silhouette of his sister about three metres away from him, half-submerged in the water.

'Tula,' he whispered, 'the guards have gone. We need to find a way out of here.'

Tula gestured ahead of her.

'No!' said Finn. 'Not that way!'

Tula motioned with her arm again, more urgently this time, and Finn groaned.

'*I'm* in charge,' he muttered. '*I* am the oldest, but *every* time, *every* time…'

He was walking slowly through the water, which was at about waist height, and his clothes and boots were soaked. The bag on his back was still dry, thank goodness, because nobody wanted to hear the Telling Stone get huffy about being cold and wet.

Finn reached Tula, but stopped and gasped unable to move for the wonder of what he saw in front of him: an enormous cavern, glowing with a dancing golden light, even bigger than the one they'd just left behind. The water in which they were standing was held back from the cave in front by a wall of hastily assembled rocks and boulders.

In unspoken agreement, the two children

scrambled to the top of it, and then paused. Even Tula's restless fingers and face were still.

Piles and piles of gold coins were heaped on a floor of stone and dry sand that stretched away from them into the vast space as far as the eye could see. Heaped on the coins in massive piles were ingots of gold, cascades of jewels in every colour of the rainbow, strings of pearls, gold chains, precious candelabra. On the rocky walls hung paintings in heavy gilt frames, and from the ceiling swung hundreds of chandeliers dripping with faceted shapes of purest crystal. Here and there, their candles were lit, and the light that danced from the sconces filled the children with a sense of awe and wonder.

They no longer felt the gnawing burn of fear, the desperate anxiety to run, run, run. Each took a deep breath and the air seemed to fill their chests with peace and tranquillity. Each felt a yearning to lie in those great soft piles of coins, covering themselves over with the cool precious metal and to hold in their hands the pretty, pretty things.

'Come in, my lovelies.' The voice from a pile of aquamarine gems and finest jewels startled them, and Finn yelped while Tula gasped and clamped a hand to her mouth. The shimmering colours shifted, and Finn saw that part of the heap was actually the coils of an enormous serpent-like creature. It had a body as thick as an ancient oak, but must have been at least fifty metres long, with three sets of enormous fins. The head of the creature was exactly like Aria's familiar in FlybyNight Warrior. It reminded Finn of a Chinese water-dragon lizard that he'd seen on the telly with his father, but with a slightly longer jaw and iridescent scales. The big eyes, raised out of the narrow forehead, were mesmerising, and it had large, round nostrils at the end of the angular snout.

'I am Shuǐlóng, mistress of the deep,' the creature continued when the children failed to move. 'Some call me a sea monster, though really that's rather rude. Shen has sent you to me.' Tula clutched Finn's hand as the earth rattled into another tremor, and the sea monster ducked her head and squeezed her eyes tightly shut. The shaking of the world around them sighed away with a whisper of sliding coins and tinkling crystal from the chandeliers above. The sea mistress opened her eyes and cocked her head, listening. 'Hurry. We are nearly out of time.'

'Sheelon?' repeated Finn.

'You pronounce it *shay-long*,' explained the sea mistress. 'It means water dragon, though I cannot breathe fire. Come, you must hurry.'

Hurry for what? asked Tula, but the movement

of her hands was so slight Finn hardly realised she'd asked a question.

'We are nearly too late to save your father,' replied the sea mistress, 'and that would be devastating. We must leave within the hour.'

32

ꓤꓷꙅꓘ𝖥ⲁ ꓝᴠᴟ◻

Shuǐlóng turned, and with a ripple of her coils and a scattering of gold she moved further into the cave. 'Come in, Finn and Tula Flint. You are safe here.'

Finn blinked. 'Everyone thinks you were killed in the Last Battle,' he blurted.

The sea monster stopped and looked back at Finn and Tula. She smiled, revealing an extraordinary amount of teeth, but she had long, deep laughter lines round her mouth, so somehow all those teeth weren't in any way fearsome.

'Shen and Otto know I'm here. Your father too,' she said. 'It's he who hid me beneath the labyrinth all those years ago. Could you both come over here, please, and get dry? There are trunks of clothes over there. The third one along should have garments in your size.'

Tula vaulted off the wall of the watery inlet and

slipped and skidded on the treasure. She shot a look at Finn over her shoulder, her face alight with silent laughter.

Come on, Finn! This is amazing!

Finn hauled himself down the other side of the wall. His coat was sodden and heavy on his tired bones. The pockets bumped against his knees when he jumped down on to the gold and silver coins, and he shoved his hands in them to check that the equaliser and Shen's potion were still there.

Tula had already scrambled her way over to the trunk. She hauled the lid open and threw another one of her delighted looks over her shoulder.

Finn! Finn! A dress! An actual dress! She pulled out a pink floor-length, crushed-velvet dress embellished with silver beads round the neck and cuffs. It had a stiff bodice that looked somehow as if it would deflect the sharpest sword, and the long sleeves had ribbons at the cuffs that fluttered in Tula's excited sighs.

'My sister has never had a dress,' explained Finn. 'She's always had to wear my old clothes.' He drew breath to tell Tula that a flappy dress would not be practical, but Shuǐlóng spoke before he could.

'Pink is a powerful colour against your enemies. Tula has chosen well. We can leave as soon as you are dressed.'

Tula was getting changed at the speed of light, so Finn hurried over to the trunk and found it packed full of fine fabrics. Shivering with the cold and the wet, he found himself reaching for a thick cotton shirt, a furry gilet, a soft wool scarf, thick woollen trousers with silk lining and a leather coat lined with cerise satin. He chose the coat because it had deep pockets like his own, and they buttoned up tightly.

While he dressed, Tula scrambled over to Shuĭlóng, and no amount of calling from Finn would make her return to add layers of warmth to her fabulous outfit. Once Finn had bundled himself up, and pocketed the bottle from Shen in his coat with the equaliser safely buttoned into the other, he rummaged in the trunk again until he found another leather coat in a smaller size. It was made of the softest brown suede, with white fur on the inside, and had a high collar that would fasten up against the cold.

He took it over to Tula, who shook her head.

'Listen to your brother,' said Shuĭlóng, and nudged Tula so she fell in the heaps of coins.

Tula laughed, just with her breath, and turned round, batting the monster playfully on the nose. Finn swallowed hard. It was so seldom that he heard Tula's breathy laugh that it made him want to cry every time.

'Put on the coat that your brother has found you, young lady,' said Shuǐlóng. 'Both of you will find proper boots near the armoury. Please lace up while I get a midnight feast ready.'

A feast! exalted Tula. *Hurry, Finn!*

In the trunk they found knee-high boots of thick leather lined with dense wool. Straps zigzagged all the way to the top and once Finn and Tula had secured them, they were immediately warm.

'Children!' called the sea monster. 'It's spaghetti tonight with heaps of parmesan, garlic-butter bread and doughballs, and look at these salad leaves! One of Otto's speciality meals. You're going to love it. We must make time to eat as you have much to do in the coming hours.'

Finn and Tula picked their way over to where an enormous oak banquet table had been unearthed from beneath the treasure. One end of it was still buried, but the other was set with three silver platters. Cutlery of solid gold sat aside them, and huge tureens weighed down the middle of the table. Glass goblets of a deep red liquid were set to the left of each place, and the aroma of delicious, heartwarming food filled their nostrils.

'Wow,' said Finn, his mouth watering. 'Where did all this come from?'

'The kitchens.' Shuǐlóng flicked the end of her tail, creating a shallow hollow opposite a place setting, then another opposite it, before settling herself at the head of the table. 'Otto always sends food to the mythics in the labyrinth. He keeps my secret from them too.' She bowed her head gracefully. 'You may start.'

Finn and Tula had cleared their plates within minutes, and they drank deeply from their goblets to find that it was a hot berry drink that warmed them from the insides and made them feel incredibly sleepy.

'These fins of mine can fly us a fair distance, children,' said Shuǐlóng softly, 'but never too far from the water, and I will need the yew tree leaves to sustain me.' She nudged Finn with her snout as his chin was sinking to his chest and his eyes were closed. 'Finn, did you put the equaliser bottle in your pocket?'

Finn nodded his head and yawned. 'I promise.'

Shuǐlóng laughed. 'Good, and I promised your mother that I would share with you the final secret ingredient of that powerful potion.'

Tula frowned. *Final? It's not complete as it is?*

Shuǐlóng shook her head, rippling the scales all across her skin. 'It needs a drop of your father's blood, otherwise it will not speak to the earth as you wish.'

Finn and Tula exchanged worried glances.

'Now come here and show me your shoulder,' said Shuĭlóng.

Finn pulled his shirt across and looked at her with a question in his eyes, but she just pressed one of her nostrils to his skin and huffed out a breath. It burned, but only for a second. She did the same to Tula. They blinked blearily at the newest mark in the line of symbols on their skin there – a perfect circle like the dragon mark, but hollow – and had no energy to ask what it meant.

'Climb on to my back, just above my fins,' said Shuĭlóng.

Finn and Tula touched her skin, marvelling at its soft warmth, and clambered up to just below where her neck would be if she had shoulders. 'Take a deep breath,' she suggested. 'I have marked you with my power to keep you dry, and to breathe and see underwater, but it might take a little getting used to.'

And then Shuĭlóng took them skittering over the treasure, through the secret space they'd found just an hour earlier and out into the underground lake. Water splashed up around them, and the water dragon sank beneath the surface, taking the children with her in a rush of bubbles.

She took them up, up, up through wet channels, then dry tunnels, Finn and Tula getting used to the cold sensation of underwater air in their lungs, until finally they were bursting out of a waterfall that spouted from the fortress walls into the ocean far below.

It was the darkest night outside – no stars, no moon – and only the lights from the fortress behind them came flickering over the softly swelling waves. They were flying north-north-west, and Finn felt a lifting of his heart at being so free. Tula looked back at him, and he could see the joy he felt to be racing towards the rescue of their father at long last reflected in her face.

We're getting closer to him, Finn! she signed. *I can't feel it, but I know it. I just know it!*

33

ᚦᚨᛋᚱᚦᛘ·ᛏᚨᚱ==

Finn and Tula woke as the sun rose behind them. They were skating low over the ocean now that the hailstorm was behind them, and Shuǐlóng was singing something to herself in a soft, whispering breath that seemed to speed her on and lift her from the surface of the sea. But, even so, water was splashing her belly and she was going slowly now. Not far away, a great buttress of land rose from the ocean. It was covered in ice and snow, and above it the air was filled with low cloud.

'Where are we?' he asked, squinting ahead.

Tula stirred behind him, and her breath sighed from her in a slow waking.

'Good morning, children,' said Shuǐlóng. 'This is Iceland. The clouds you see before you come from the volcano.'

'Are you okay?' asked Finn.

'I need the yew branches I put in your bag,' said

Shuǐlóng. I can just about make it to the shore, I hope, and then you'll need to get them out for me, Finn. The Telling Stone said to tell you your father will need the potion you carry, so don't cast it aside.'

Finn felt his throat tighten. 'He's hurt.'

'Nothing the potion can't fix.'

It seemed Shuǐlóng would have said more, but she was using every scrap of energy to move them forward. Her belly hit the surface of the water again, and she skidded along fifty, sixty metres, before rising even slower than before. Finn touched his forehead to her skin and imagined golden waves of energy rising up from his stomach and passing through to her.

'No…' whispered Shuǐlóng, her voice disappearing into the icy wind around them. 'You'll need that for yourself … and your … father … your sister.'

Finn lifted his head and saw the shore just two hundred metres away now. He pressed his hands either side of Shuǐlóng's neck, and breathed warmth onto her skin.

'You should have woken us to feed you,' he whispered. 'Nearly there…'

A hundred metres away, Shuǐlóng's belly grazed the water again.

Now fifty metres. Her tail flashed back and forth, propelling them forward, even as they sank. Now just fifty. And then with a messy splash and a crunch of pebbles, Shuĭlóng came to a halt on the shore, her head still partly submerged in the last ripples of the shallowest waves. She sighed and lay still, the waves gently waving her fins back and forth. Finn leaped into the water and ran to lift her head from the ripples.

'Are you all right, Shuĭlóng?' he asked. 'Shuĭlóng?'

Tula was already tugging at Finn's bag, and he released it from his back. They both dived into it to pull out the cloth bags of yew fronds.

'Please, Shuĭlóng,' urged Finn. 'Open your mouth.' He and Tula splashed to stand beside her head, Finn tugging at the top of her jaw. Her mouth parted slightly, and in an instant Tula had pressed the fronds between her teeth, on to her tongue.

Finn released her jaw and nodded at Tula. 'Again?'

Tula nodded and gave her more, but her previous mouthful was still uneaten.

Shuĭlóng! Tula signed the monster's name, pulling her eyelid up. *Look at me! Eat! The sun is rising. They'll see us, standing out here like this.*

Finn saw Shuĭlóng's jaw crunch once, twice, and her throat moved. When she opened her mouth, Tula was ready with more, but Shuĭlóng was whispering, 'Run … I have had enough … They are coming … Run…'

Finn tasted orange juice, but the stench of drains burned his nostrils. He turned and saw a dark cloud emitting a putrid yellow haze rolling steadily towards them. Closer and closer it came. It was about ten minutes away.

'Shuïlóng,' begged Finn. 'Please! We can help you!' His voice was desperate.

The monster's whisper, when it came, was barely audible: tired and raspy.

'Your family has already helped me more than you could know, children. You must run now. The leaves are already working their magic. In minutes I will be able to slip away, but by then it will be too late for you. *Go*.'

Finn's mouth flooded with the taste of hot orange juice again.

Shuïlóng, signed Tula, leaning close to her. *We cannot leave you.*

'You *must* go now, or all is lost for the world,' Shuïlóng whispered. She turned her head and began to sink slowly back into the waves.

Soon she was hidden in the water, leaving Finn and Tula to run for their lives.

Finn and Tula leaped over the frozen scrub and icy stones to get to the waterfall that lay about a hundred metres ahead of them.

'We've got about five minutes before they're here,' gasped Finn. 'Think we can make it?'

Tula's reply was a burst of speed that overtook Finn's scrambling run through the thick snow. He threw a look over his shoulder, and what he saw drove a shaft of fear hard into his chest. Just half a mile away, yellow plumes of dragging smoke raked through the sky, leaving a filthy residue hanging in the cold, misty air.

His sharp eyes could now make out monstrous shapes of Venomous small and large within the boiling cloud. Some rode elephantine beasts with sharp tusks and armour bristling with lethal spikes and gun barrels, some whipped smaller creatures to move faster and some were so large they did not need steeds at all. All had horny protrusions sprouting from their heads. All had murder on their minds – he could see it in their glowing eyes. He could hear it in their rumbling war cry, growing louder with every second.

Finn's muscles were straining, and his breath was beginning to rasp in his throat and chest. The bag on his back was thumping painfully against his spine with the weight of the Telling Stone, and he wished he had a moment to check his pockets for the bottles of potion and equaliser. He didn't dare look behind him again but focused instead on catching up to his sister. When he did, it was all he could do to gasp, 'We're not going to make it!'

She threw him a glance that didn't need any signing to interpret further: *Shut up and RUN!*

To the left of them was a wide rush of water that washed into the sea behind. The closer they got to the cliffs, the deeper this water became, filled by a colossal waterfall that plunged to the shore from the rock face in front of them.

Finn threw another panicked glance over his shoulder and saw that the yellow cloud was only a minute from swallowing them up. He leaped round a boulder and slipped on the ice to the side, nearly abreast with Tula now, but with a graze on his cheek that he didn't think would heal any time soon. The backpack thunked hard on the boulder before he could push himself away, and the Telling Stone went, 'Ow!'

'Really?' gasped Finn. 'How the—'

'Up ahead,' called the Telling Stone. 'Hide in the water!'

Tula grabbed Finn's forearm and pointed at the deep pools formed by the rushing water that had reached the ground from the cliffs above.

Brother and sister slipped and slid over the ice into the closest pool. Cold water flooded over their heads and tingled their faces, and Tula hit her head hard on a branch floating on the surface. Her mouth opened underwater in an expression of pain, but she snapped it shut again and tugged at the neck of her dress to show Finn the mark from Shuǐlóng glowing on her skin.

Finn stilled and sank lower into the pool with Tula floating down beside him. He took a cautious sniff through his nose, and the water that seeped in through his nostrils felt like cold, slippery air.

His chest pulsed. *Shuǐlóng's mark...*

A long, low *BOOM* thudded through the water, causing it to shimmer and shake all around them. Above their heads, a wave crashed from the direction of the sea towards the cliffs, then another, and another.

The Venomous are here! signed Finn. *We need to get under the waterfall and then find a way across the land to the volcano.*

Just then there was an enormous splash just behind them, and Tula's mouth opened in a soundless scream. Finn whipped round to find one of the elephantine beasts deep in the water only two metres away, reaching for him with its trunk. Three enormous Venoms peeled off the beast's back towards him with spears raised and teeth bared. Finn kicked his legs hard, propelling himself towards Tula, and together they sped away.

When the elephantine beast let out a bellow of rage, releasing a cloud of bubbles, Finn glanced behind to see that one of the Venoms, in its panic, had speared it just below the eye. The beast swiped out at the Venom with its lethal trunk and sent it rolling to the bottom of the pool where it landed in a cloud of mud and sand. Of the two remaining, one had struggled to the surface – to gasp air, no doubt – whereas the other was still determinedly coming at them through the water, teeth still exposed in a sharp-edged grimace. He was swimming like an awful toad, legs frogging out behind him and his wide webbed hands savagely scooping the water in front, so that in seconds he'd caught up to Finn and Tula.

He made a grab for Finn and caught his foot for one heart-stopping moment, slicing his skin with a claw before Finn kicked away again. The Venom would have snared Finn again in his next lunge, but there was another *BOOM!* and a second elephantine beast landed in the water in front of Tula, carrying even more Venomous this time. They exploded off the beast's back in a confusion of froth and bubbles, and the huge wave knocked Finn and Tula straight back into the creature behind them.

A series of images flung through Finn's head like Polaroid pictures: the large snakelike trunk wrapping round him and Tula; the wide, frightened eyes of his sister; the freezing numbness of his whole body; the terror of no power in his fingers; the pain of a thump from a spear handle on his hunched back; the taste of metal in his mouth; the roar of water and battle cries in his ears…

In the next instant, Finn was flung high into the air with Tula spinning up with him. They were caught on the bank of the river in the huge snake-like trunks of two beasts, Finn howling in horror, unable to blast anything, as Tula was ripped away from him.

Her face was still frozen in a soundless, terrified

scream. Finn kicked and yelled, his voice a wild cacophony of threats and demands and fury and frustration. He strained with every cell of his being against the trunk wrapped round him, but Tula gradually stopped moving until finally she hung limp, her head sagging to her chest.

Finn felt pure fear close up his throat, and he screamed her name over and over, watching her with an icy terror creeping over his heart. In his peripheral vision, he realised the yellow cloud was dissipating, revealing more of their captors. There were four massive beasts in total, and it was the one larger than the rest that dangled Tula from its trunk. It was approaching him with a heavy tread, swinging his sister from side to side in a slow, cruel taunt. On its head was a leather skullcap from which protruded vicious spikes. Roped to its neck just behind the clump of evil edges was a large, ornate chair upholstered in luxurious satins and suedes and silks and velvets, all of the deepest black.

Sitting in the chair was Craven with his whip – *How did he get his whip back?* thought Finn – and behind him, clinging to the beast's back from ropes and chains, was a gang of slavering Venoms, all wrestling for a space to sit.

None of the other beasts carried a throne-like

construction like this. One had, instead, what looked suspiciously like a cannon, manned by two grinning Venoms who had about four teeth between them. Another had an enormous catapult held in place by thick ropes, and all along its sides were big baskets of round projectiles covered in long, sharp spines. The beast holding Finn had three Venomous crowded on to its head, each of them heavily armed with strings of bullets and belts of knives and guns.

Finn stopped calling Tula's name, breathing heavily and thinking fast instead.

It seemed then as if the wind dropped. At the same time, the churning water of the river ceased and the beasts stopped their huffing and heaving, and the Venomous seemed to hold their breath too. Then every last one of them cowered in fear as the ground beneath them shook with a ferocity that Finn and Tula had not felt on the fortress island. With it came a roar from the volcano that they could see in the distance, and a blast of putrid air that stank of sulphur and hordes of Venomous. It lasted longer than any quake they'd felt before.

A flock of soot-black ravens barked alongside a great skua flapping through the air, shouting its outrage with loud ARGH! ARGH! ARGH! calls that echoed all around even when the shaking of the earth had subsided.

Craven stood slowly.

'You want us to shoot 'em, boss?' called a Venom from the head of the beast holding Finn.

Raising his hand in the stop position, Craven cocked his head slightly, as if he were listening to something just that little bit too quiet to hear.

Finn's eyes stayed fixed to Tula's drooping form, but he did not blink when she raised her head ever so slightly and turned her face to his. Craven did not see her move. He was still listening. Finn kept carefully still when he felt Tân's little feet reach his ankle and start climbing up his trouser leg.

Though hair hung across Tula's cheek and obscured one eye, he could see her sign, *Errol is coming. Get ready to jump.*

Even before her fingers had stopped moving, Finn had heard it too: the thin high-pitched drone of an old-fashioned aeroplane. One with power and intent.

35

‡⊦Ɑϟⵑ‡⅄·ᒣϟ⅄≡

Ready, Finn signed back with a twitch of his thumb. He took a calming breath, expanding his chest, trying to stoke the furious fire that flickered in his belly at the sight of his sister rendered so lifeless by Craven.

Come on, he told himself. *Breathe*.

'Can you idiots and cretins not hear it?' yelled Craven. 'There is an aircraft headed our way.' He muttered something under his breath that made the Venomous around him grind their teeth and pound their chests. The beast holding Finn turned its head to see what all the fuss was about, and as it did so the coils of its trunk shifted ever so slightly.

Just enough for Finn to huff out his breath in one sudden rush, his chest instantly ten centimetres narrower. Though the beast tried to clamp at his falling body, Finn was too fast, curling into a ball, hitting the ground hard and rolling away. Tula meanwhile had turned her head and blasted the beast holding her with icy breath. It staggered one step, then two, three, four. Finn ducked and danced between the beasts' enormous legs, afraid he'd be trampled at any moment, but unable to run for safety without his sister.

Craven was halfway out of his throne, yelling for calm, and his face had gone an ugly purple. Tula blasted again, and the beast threw up its trunk in automatic defence, flinging Tula free of its coils as it screamed in pain. She, too, tucked into a ball, just as Dad had shown them, but Finn was there to break her fall before she hit the ground.

He scrambled after his sister, narrowly avoiding a ball of rock flung at them from the catapult beast, and leaping over the metal-barbed lines of a vicious whip that cut the air with a hiss.

'Catch them!' screamed Craven. 'Get them NOW!'

With a chilling roar, the Venomous began to swarm down off the backs of the massive creatures to give chase to Finn and Tula.

But the children were making the most of their head start and pulling away.

'Tula!' panted Finn. 'I've got no power in my hands!' He made a quick sign and she nodded and turned to face Craven's beast. She took a deep breath in through her nose, and then sniffed again, opening her eyes wide. Thundering towards them, its tentacles outstretched, Craven's beast showed no sign of stopping. He was still standing astride it, holding on to its bony ruff with one hand, and screaming instructions.

The aeroplane was nearly upon them now, and its engine seemed to shift gear. It hovered in the air a little distance away, further up the shore, before descending like a helicopter, making straight for the ground. It was so close that the wheels were visible. They could even see the helmet of the pilot in the cockpit.

The running Venomous were twenty metres away, now fifteen, now ten, and Tula turned her blast on all of them. Finn felt a sudden craving for yew needles, desperate to help his sister, desperate for his power to return. Her blast crackled all their predators into frightening statues that threw up sprays of ice as they slid to a halt.

Behind them, they could hear the jet landing, but the children did not run towards it. Finn was pointing, wordless, at Craven, who was not frozen at all, but standing slowly.

He began to move, ice crackling from his black suit, and raised his whip.

'Tula,' whispered Finn, 'again!' and Tula blasted him with such force that he spun like a top across the ice.

Finn grabbed her hand and together they sprinted for the jet. The glass dome over the seat behind the cockpit was already open and Finn heard Errol's voice shout, 'Get in! Get in!'

Tula ran and jumped, her fingers only just reaching the edge of the opening, but she lost no time hauling herself in and squishing to the side to make room for Finn who was right behind her. Errol was already snapping the switches in front of him, this way and that, as Finn pulled the cover down over Tula and himself. There was a roar of powerful engines and the jet swung into the air just as the first of the Venomous arrived.

Errol said something that Finn could only just hear, but when the cover snapped shut he heard him add, 'Why?'

'Why what?' asked Finn.

'You two are crazy!' yelled Errol. 'Why did you leave without me? You were so unhappy when Grey Griffin, George and the aviators left you behind! Why would you do the same to me?'

Sorry, signed Tula miserably. She reached back for Tân, who hopped to her hand from Finn's shoulder and curled into her neck, patting her skin with his tiny foot to give her comfort. *We didn't have much choice but we're not like George. We'd never underestimate you.*

'Underestimate?' yelped Errol. 'You think that's

what George did? You think he underestimated you?'
He half twisted in his seat to look at Finn and Tula,
his eyes wide. 'He was *protecting* you, you idiots! You
cannot fly! You cannot defend yourselves! You are,
actually, quite useless! You—'

He stopped, suddenly stricken at what he'd said.

'You're right,' said Finn, 'I'm useless, but Tula isn't.
She's—'

'No,' said Errol, turning back round. 'I was wrong.
You're not useless. You're brilliant, but George hasn't
seen your brilliance yet like I have, so don't be cross
with him. He was just trying to look after you and
save the world at the same time.'

'I get that now,' said Finn. 'I'm not angry any more.'

Nearly dying all the time, nodded Tula. *It gives you
a clearer understanding.*

'Yeah,' said Errol, pulling his goggles down over
his eyes. 'Nearly dying definitely brings a different
point of view.' He huffed a heavy sigh then shook his
head and asked more quietly. 'Do you even know
where you're going? Charlie is going to be so furious.
He was supposed to come with me, but Rudimenta
got hold of him and he couldn't get away.'

'So *you* left without *him*?' asked Finn. 'Really?'

'He told me to go,' said Errol, tipping the plane
slightly to the east.

'No way.' Finn looked at Tula and she raised an eyebrow. 'No way,' he said again.

'Yes way,' said Errol. 'He did that thing with his finger that you two do when you mean "everything is okay".'

'Um,' said Finn, 'this...' he flicked his finger '... does not mean "it is okay for you to head off without me". It probably means nothing, in this context. It probably means...'

'That he just flicked his finger?'

'I think you know that,' sighed Finn.

'I am in so much trouble.'

'So much.'

Tula nodded and bit her lip, peering out through the windscreen at the scrambling Venomous and beasts below.

'They move fast,' observed Finn.

'We move faster,' said Errol, adjusting the throttle. 'Fast enough to get to Hekla, grab your dad and get back to the fortress just after sunset.'

Finn sank back in his seat, and gradually he felt his heart rate slow though he was still shaking with cold and there was no warmth in his fingers at all.

'Now rest,' said Errol. 'In about twenty minutes you're going to need all the fire power you've got.'

36

$‡Ո̄ȝ̄ſ‡⅄·θȝ̄⋉$

Finn did not sleep. He watched Tula doze beside him. He watched Errol hard at work with the complicated dashboard of the Harrier jump jet, muttering to himself. He watched the sun climb just a little higher off the horizon. And he watched that horizon change from a flat line into a vast mountain growing bigger the closer they got to it.

Errol noticed him sitting forward, his eyes zeroing in on what lay ahead.

'Nearly there,' he said. 'According to Drishti's calculations...' he tapped a square of paper taped to the dashboard '...Augustus should be at these coordinates, twenty metres below sea level.'

Finn squinted harder. 'Is ... is the earth ... *cracking*?' he asked in disbelief. Tula stirred beside him.

'Yup,' said Errol. 'The rest of the world is in a bit of a panic. If Hekla blows, then—'

'Then there will be devastating consequences,' interrupted Finn, anxious for Tula not to hear all this again. 'I remember.'

Tula's eyes flashed open. *How close can we get to Dad?*

'Errol,' said Finn. 'How close can you land to those coordinates? Do you—'

'Not at all close,' said Errol with certainty. 'We're going to have to park a bit away to protect the plane from the shifting earthquake area over there...' he pointed to the cracking earth to the west just ahead '...and we're going to have to get underground as fast as we can.'

Finn blinked. 'Are there caves? Tunnels? Will they be affected by the quake?'

'Ask the Stone because I don't have a map,' said Errol, tipping the plane into a slight turn towards the western base of the volcano. 'But I do have a secret weapon,' he said, almost to himself, and began the descent.

In minutes, the jet had landed with a gentle thump, and as soon as the engines had begun to quieten Finn released the glass hatch. Tula pushed out quickly, shimmying down the side of the plane, across the wing and dropping to the ground in seconds. She stayed crouched down in the snow, looking around her. Finn followed more slowly, and the minute he breathed the outside air he knew why Tula was hiding, fiercely pinching her nose. He swallowed down the nausea and hurried to join his sister.

Errol locked the hatches and scrambled over. 'You guys okay?'

'Venomous stink,' croaked Finn, and gagged.

Errol flipped open his bag and retrieved tissues. 'How far away?'

Finn shrugged, taking the tissues gratefully and giving one to Tula. 'No idea,' he said, keeping his nose covered while Errol rummaged in his bag and pulled out a small cardboard box. It was old and battered and covered with what looked like bloodstains. Rough knotted string held it all together.

'This is a wyrm,' he announced dramatically. 'Our secret weapon. It is one of the mythic beasts. I stole it from the labyrinth when I heard your father was missing.'

Finn's eyes were huge. '*You*? You stole a *creature*?'

'My sister is one of the best scryers on the whole island. She said Augustus was in big trouble even before we discovered he'd gone missing. I knew we'd need help from something magical that we could trust.' He held up the tiny box and smiled. 'A wyrm can track anything within a hundred miles. It's amazing! It just needs to smell something from its target, so it will take us to your father, provided you have something of his for it to scent him out, and I knew there'd be something.'

Errol's eyes fell to the bandanna tied round Finn's wrist, then to the amulet that swung from Tula's neck.

'I don't know if it'll work,' muttered Finn, struggling to undo it. Tula caught his wrist and began unknotting with surprising strength in her small fingers. 'It must smell more of me than him now.'

'The wyrm will have you here as reference, so that won't matter,' said Errol. He tugged at a cord round his neck, pulled out a compass and sighed heavily. 'Augustus is under all of that lot,' he said, gesturing with his head towards the cracking surface of the mountain ahead of them. 'Messy.'

Tula pulled the bandanna free from Finn's wrist and held it out to Errol. *Here you go*, she signed.

'Hang on to that just a second,' said Errol, and he tugged the string from the box. 'Wow,' he said in a strangled voice, placing the box hurriedly on the ground.

'What's wow?' asked Finn.

'The wyrm,' said Errol. 'It's desperate to get munching underground.'

Just underground, signed Tula, *not us?*

'Ready?' asked Errol, ignoring the question, his right hand upon the lid of the box, the string undone all around it. He was crouched down, the base of the box in his left hand just above the snow.

'Ready,' said Finn, flexing his fingers, feeling not at all ready.

Errol opened the box to reveal a pale, fleshy tube of a creature, all squished into the small card rectangle with fragments of eggshell still sticking to its skin. It had waving tentacles all in lines down either side of its segmented body, and the minute it smelled the fresh air it writhed like a mad thing, desperate to get out.

'Hello, wyrm,' said Errol, placing the box on the snow and holding his left hand out for the bandanna while keeping the index finger of his right hand on the twisting folds of the strange creature to stop it escaping right away. Tula gave him the bandanna. Errol released the wyrm and waved the fabric in front of its head, which suddenly appeared from beneath the writhing tube of its coiled-up body. The writhing slowed for a moment as it lifted up to smell the fabric. It had two enormous black ovals for eyes that took up most of the head, two small holes for nostrils and what looked like a small opening for a mouth. A few of the tendrils around the head touched the material delicately, and the eyes blinked.

'Whoa,' breathed Errol, leaning closer. 'It has eyelids. Did not know that.'

The head of the wyrm retreated, as if it had had enough of the bandanna, and in an instant it spilled out on to the snow. Errol stood and took a step back.

'Watch out,' he whispered.

The wyrm seemed to anchor its mouth into the snow, and then its body began to move round the head, scuffing the surface in a circle, which widened the faster it went, probably because the wyrm was rapidly expanding and lengthening too. It got bigger and bigger as it ate frantically at the snow then the earth. In a few seconds it was moving so fast that it was simply a blur and the circle had widened to at least a metre in diameter and was now gaining significant depth. Within a minute a perfectly round hole had been formed, at least a metre deep.

'What the...' Finn swallowed.

'It'll go faster and faster, but that's about the size of the tunnel,' said Errol. 'It starts off using mostly its tentacles, but it grows exponentially until it fills the space it's made, and by then it's mostly eating its way through to the scent you've given it. If it smells another tunnel or an underground river course, it'll head for that for an easier journey, but otherwise it generally goes in as straight a line as possible.'

Tula signed something frantically.

Errol's forehead creased in confusion and then he went, 'Oh no. Definitely won't want to eat your dad. Unlike the Venomous.' He squeezed his eyes shut in remorse. 'Sorry. Shouldn't have said that...'

'Why does the smell get it going like this?' asked Finn.

'Well, the first thing it smells and touches is generally its mother,' explained Errol. 'And instinct tells it to follow her because she'll provide safety and food for it. Like ducklings.'

'But *my* smell was also on the bandanna that it touched,' said Finn. 'Doesn't make sense.'

'It always chooses the older smell – in the person's age, I mean,' said Errol. 'Very clever because it's looking for its parent, right?' He peered down the hole. 'Time to go,' he announced. 'If you've got any other questions, they'll have to wait. You first, Finn, then Tula, then me.'

37

‡ꓵꙅꓕꓕꓯ ·θ≡ᐱ≡ꝺ

The tunnel the wyrm had made was dry and crumbly with sharp rock, and Finn, leopard-crawling along on his forearms and tiptoes, was soon cut up and exhausted. He could hear Tula keeping pace behind him, though, and Errol panting behind her, and that spurred him on.

Now and again a strange sound of scraping and sighing could be heard from up ahead, generally when the tunnel had reached a long, straight section, and a host of smells filled Finn's nostrils along the way: clay, rock, metal, water.

And fire.

Mostly fire.

Finn felt himself begin to thaw. They turned a corner and a strange dancing light shimmered into the tunnel ahead of him.

'Tula, Errol,' he called over his shoulder. 'You see that?'

Not waiting for a reply, he scrambled faster, then stopped in a rattle of loose sand and gravel, wide-eyed at what lay ahead.

The wyrm's tunnel had punched out into an enormous underground cave that felt as if they were in the belly of some massive creature because the walls were blood red and black. Here and there small flames flickered up through cracks in the ground. To the right, there lay an inky pool of water, and the ceiling of the cavern sloped down into darkness.

Tula tapped Finn's ankle, and he wriggled further along. The tunnel exit was about two metres off the ground, so they'd have to jump. Luckily the wyrm's excavations had left a heap of freshly churned soil just below, and it would break their fall.

He leaped, thinking, *Where is the wyrm?* as he landed, and then he saw its tracks down to the water. Tula flung herself out behind him, staggering off the heap to stand beside him, Tân clinging to her neck. Then Errol emerged, blinking in the flickering light and shaking soil from his hair.

'Oh no,' he said. 'Warm water.'

'Huh?' said Finn. 'Why "oh no"?'

Errol manoeuvred himself out of the tunnel and jumped carefully, his shoulder bag, compass and tool belt all bouncing around him. He stepped off the heap and gestured to the pool. 'I bet it's in there.'

As if to assure him of this, the water moved in a slow, shifting ripple and a few enormous segments of wyrm, grown to what seemed like a million times its baby size, broke the surface then submerged.

Tula took a short, sharp breath and Finn voiced her fear.

'Won't he take us to our father?'

Errol frowned and bit his lip. 'Unlikely.'

All three stood silent, watching the wyrm roll and revel in the water, all three thinking hard.

Then Tula's face suddenly brightened and she gestured to the backpack.

'Of course,' said Finn. 'The Telling Stone.' He pulled the bag off his shoulders, undid the straps and flipped open the top. Carefully, he reached inside and withdrew the Stone, which glowed with a white light that seemed completely out of place in all the red and orange around them. 'We need to think carefully about what we ask,' said Finn to Errol.

'Ask it where your dad is,' said Errol, leaning closer.

'It?' burst out the Stone, and Errol took a frightened step back, falling painfully on the gravelly ground. '*It?* You should know by now I'm a female being, and of course you should think carefully about what you ask, but don't expect miracle answers from me! Finn, you said *discussions* were the modern way forward, yes? Discussions! I thought that was working for us!'

'Yes!' yelped Finn! 'Yes, milady! I just meant that we shouldn't upset you with any references to—'

Tula grabbed his arm and shook her head frantically.

'It's just that on previous occasions,' continued the Stone, 'my insights caused … issues … of warlike proportions, so it really is best to remember that you're responsible for your own actions, and that way you'll probably come to the best outcomes, which is not to undermine my incredible skills and psychic abilities, of course.'

'Of course,' said Errol weakly. He glanced at Finn and Tula and made a funny expression that translated as *This is one crazy Stone!*

'And,' continued the Stone, suddenly sounding testy, '*and* I can see what's going on around me, and I don't appreciate that kind of "oh, you crazy Stone" kind of attitude.'

Errol clapped a hand to his eyes. 'I'm so sorry,' he mumbled, and got to his feet again.

'That's all right,' said the Stone grudgingly.

'It's just that…' continued Errol, 'can't we just ask you where, exactly, Augustus is?'

'Just think about it,' said the Stone, but her voice wasn't petulant, or cross. 'You especially, Tula.'

Tula blinked, as if suddenly recognising that she had skills, choices, a mission to complete. Shading her eyes, she scrutinised the cavern walls from where they stood, and pointed her finger at the only visible exit.

'Yes,' said the Telling Stone.

'Oh!' said Errol. 'Well, that's just logic, isn't it? What I want to know is—'

'Be careful what you ask, Errol,' said Finn, placing the Stone gently in the backpack and strapping it shut.

'This is madness,' Errol whispered to Finn as they ducked into the dark tunnel after Tula. 'Why—'

'I'm right here,' said the Stone from inside the bag. 'Don't complain about me, boy. Yep, just so you know, *right here*. Unlike that stupid worm we're leaving behind.'

'*Wyrm*,' said Errol, 'and it's not stupid.'

'Don't push me,' said the Stone.

Errol did not answer, mainly because he was distracted by frightening vibrations from the rock beneath their feet, and deep rumblings that emanated from the tunnel ahead of them. The rock in here was black as night, and the air hot and dry. Finn was certain he could hear shouting from somewhere, and the stink of Venomous was stronger than ever. His eyes watered with the effort of not vomiting, and Tula had tugged the collar of her dress up round her nose and mouth to stop the smell. Tân disappeared into her sleeve. There were no torches of flame along this cavern passage, as there were back at the fortress. Instead, fire flickered and trickled from cracks in the walls and from the ground beneath.

Finn was filled with a fear so great he thought it might burst from him in a desperate wail. He clamped his lips together, sweat trickling from his forehead and temples down his face, and he tried not to flinch every time the fire seemed about to leap from the wall across their path.

'It's no good telling Tula to think about her skills,' muttered Errol, who was tactfully ignoring Finn's erratic pace through the tunnel, 'when she cannot scent anything in all this heat and Venomous stink.'

'Are you a grumbler, Errol?' asked the Stone suddenly from the depths of the backpack again.

Errol jumped. 'Don't *do* that!' he hissed.

'Believe me, you'll be begging me to speak in ten seconds when we hit the T-junction,' said the Stone. 'And in my defence I just told Tula to *think*, not to think about her *skills*.'

Errol sighed as the path came up to a solid wall

of rock, leading down to the left and slightly up to the right. 'Apologies, Stone,' he said, and pushed his glasses up his nose, staring down to the left, then to the right.

There was a silence while Errol refused to ask the question, but the ground started to shake, and when the rumblings from beneath suddenly escalated in a long groan, as if the earth were actually begging for help, he burst out, 'Which way, please, Stone?'

'You may call me "my lady",' replied the Stone, and Finn would have laughed, but the cavern walls around them were now juddering and shaking, and it felt as if they'd be buried beneath this mountain at any moment. Whole facets of molten rock were splitting apart in gushes of flame and steam, and the rattle of falling stones and boulders was terrifying.

Errol grabbed on to his backpack straps and blurted out his question again.

'Which way, please, my lady?'

'Left, and hurry,' said the Stone. 'This volcano is about to blow, earlier than predicted, unless Tula can remember how to save us all.'

The children turned and ran as fast as they could, twisting and turning deeper and deeper beneath the mountain, the smell of Venomous and the heat of the earth growing more overwhelming with every second.

When they burst out into a crossroads of sorts, with Tula looking around wildly in each direction, Errol didn't waste a moment.

'Which way, please, my lady?' he gasped, turning, like Tula, to stare down each of the six tunnels that branched away from them.

'Um,' muttered the Stone. 'Could be one of two. Just give me a moment, please…'

Errol whimpered, tugging at his straps again and glancing behind him, as if wondering whether it was too late to run back to the jump jet.

Finn dropped his hand from his nose where he'd been keeping his nostrils clamped and took a cautious sniff. Then another and another. The acrid stench of burning and rotting came equally from each of the tunnels. They all felt just as hot and fiery. They all looked equally unstable and perilous. There was nothing to distinguish any of them from each other, but when Finn walked closer to the tunnel straight ahead he noticed that pinned to the rock above each one was a pattern of charred bones.

'What the…' he breathed, squinting in the flickering light of the flames.

The earth groaned again and Errol whimpered. 'Please oh please…'

'It says WEST,' murmured Finn, his brow still

creased. Taking another step back, he checked the tunnel to the right of it. 'And that one says DOWN.'

'Oh good,' said the Stone. 'Take the one saying down.'

'No!' burst out Errol, but when another rumble reverberated through the tunnels he and Tula hurried after Finn with no hesitation. 'We've already descended two hundred metres!' he shouted, the rock around them shaking with the forces from beneath. 'Any further and we'll be hitting the molten lava flow!'

'Good thing you lot can't burn, then, isn't it?' said the Stone sharply. 'I can tell you for nothing that you've got thirty-nine minutes before Hekla blows.'

Errol would more than likely have retorted something he'd have regretted, but at that moment they burst out onto a wide spiral of open-sided steps that wound steeply down into the Earth's core. Even from this dizzying height, they could see Venomous hurrying this way and that on the big open floor beneath them. To the west of this huge space was a long fissure cutting through the rock. It was lined with heavy steel doors on either side of it, stretching away into the distance beyond.

The children moved slowly and steadily down the stairs.

What if they look up and see us? signed Tula, her fingers trembling.

'Unlikely,' whispered Errol. 'Venomous sight is not the best.'

'This is clearly a Venomous dungeon,' whispered Finn. 'Dad must be in one of those cells.'

The three children came to a hollow in the wall of the stairs, and all pressed into its shadows. They slid down to crouching to stare at the spectacle below. Tân poked his head out of Tula's sleeve, his eyes wide and unblinking. Even from here they could see that the Venomous were terrified by the shaking earth, the shards of molten rock and sprinklings of sand that were beginning to rain down, yet they were more afraid of the most colossal Venom of them all.

'Gargan,' they whimpered. 'We should leave, O Master of All You Love and Despise!'

'The mountain will blow—'

'Blow right now—'

'We will die—'

'Please, O Master of—'

'SILENCE!' he roared, and the huge Venomous bowed and scraped before him, small in comparison with their leader.

It was not just his immense size that set Gargan apart. Whereas the others were the colour of burnt, bruised or ablated flesh, Gargan was as pale as an underground grub, though much of his skin was covered in thickly knotted purple veins through which a complex pattern of black and red tattoos scrawled. Wide-set eyes bulged in shining black orbs – two pairs either side of his face, rimmed with greasy ridges of swollen red flesh. A huge domed forehead arced into a pig-snout nose with irregular slits for nostrils that shuddered with every rasping breath he drew. His chin dripped with strings of saliva streaming from a wide, gaping mouth that revealed curved, pointed teeth set crookedly in his powerful jaws. Either side of his mouth were white tusks that curved up to just below his cheekbones, sharpened to menacing points.

He raised his huge arms above his head, holding whips and chains in his massive, clawed hands, then stamped one of his trunk-like legs, his cloven, elephantine foot thudding to the floor with a dull echo.

'Bileous! Go see if Craven is back with the equaliser! I smell human, I smell fireblood … I smell it nearby…' A slow, fat and old Venom with particularly rounded shoulders and an unusual amount of body hair all over his chest, back, legs – even sprouting from his ears and nose – grunted agreement: 'Yes, Master Gargan,' and began shuffling towards the spiral steps.

'Oh no!' whispered Errol, but as another roaring quake began to reverberate through the mountain Bileous staggered and fell over.

'Do as I say!' bellowed Gargan, striking Bileous on the head with a whip. The earth shuddered again and Gargan hollered at two guards fleeing their sentry posts from a cell in the chasm.

'Go back to where you were, you festering imbeciles!' he yelled, swinging his flail threateningly, and the guards retreated instantly, mewling and crying as they went.

An almighty *CRACK!* splintered the air, and Errol slammed his hands to his ears. Behind them, a huge wedge of the stairs sheered off from the rock wall and hurtled to the ground in an explosion of black dust, enormous boulders and rattling stones.

Tân ran out of Tula's sleeve and on to her hand, lifting his nose in the air.

The two guards back in sentry position either side of one of the cell doors, heavily armed with axes, daggers, clubs and spiky mallets and flails of every kind, shielded their faces and ears with their monstrous hands, but did not try running again. Gargan had moved closer to the chasm entrance, blocking their escape route, and had called for guards to stay at the bottom of the stairs to prevent defectors from escaping.

Finn lowered his hands from his ears and stared through the swirling dust cloud at the enormous hole behind them.

There was no going back, and no going forward because they could not get down the stairs without being seen.

Their scent had already alerted Gargan to a fireblood arrival. He would not stop until he'd found them.

They were well and truly trapped.

Finn glared at the weeping wounds on his ankle where the Venom had caught him in the river. He clenched his fists. Still no power.

38

'We should have waited for the wyrm,' whispered Errol. 'No, actually, we should never have used it until this very moment!' He thumped his forehead with his fist. 'What a waste of a mythic! Dad is going to think I'm such an idiot. We should have just gone straight to the crater and dropped in the equaliser. No! We'd never have got there, and only Augustus knows how to do that. I should have … I should never have set off alone…'

Finn took Errol by the shoulders and shook him. 'Stop it, Errol. If the sea monster hadn't taken me and Tula, we'd never have got here in time. If you hadn't left when you did, on your own, you'd never have saved our lives. If the wyrm had taken us here, every Venom under the mountain would have attacked us, because exploding out of the rock down there in our own homemade tunnel would have attracted a bit of attention, right? It's all good so far! We just need to think.'

Errol nodded, looking tearful, but was distracted by Tula. She was patting her clothing frantically, and didn't blink an eye when another quake sent more of the stairway behind them rattling to the ground amid fearful wails and cries from the Venomous below.

'Oh no!' whispered Finn. 'Tân?'

'Tân?' said Errol, sniffing and adjusting his glasses. 'Your lizard?'

Tula nodded, looking steadily more anxious.

'Shh!' said Finn, though she was making no sound. 'Stop, Tula. I bet he's gone scouting…' They each took a breath and held it without meaning to, staring at each other, then all three children peered carefully out from the shadows of the niche. Perfectly visible in their hypervision was the tiny form of the little gecko skittering at high speed down all the steps.

'Oh, bajingalingablingas,' whispered Errol. 'Should I send Manchego after him?'

Finn could feel Tula's breath quicken over his shoulder. She was holding his arm too tightly, but he hardly noticed, intent as he was on keeping Tân in his sights.

'Too late – he's on the ground now,' whispered Errol in reply to himself. Then, 'Oof,' he gasped, as the large, heavy tread of Gargan nearly caught the fast-moving lizard. Tula made a motion, almost as if she were about to leap from the niche to rescue her companion, but both Errol and Finn held her back.

'Are you *crazy*?' hissed Errol. 'Tân can look after himself! If we get spotted, we'll be obliterated.'

If Tân is spotted, he'll be obliterated too, thought Finn, but he didn't say it out loud. Down below, the Venomous were still hurrying across the open area at the bottom of the stairs, before Gargan hollered at them to move on.

'AND FIND ME THE FIREBLOOD! I SMELL IT HERE!' He turned slowly, his bulging orbs swivelling this way and that as he stared out at nooks and crannies of the cavern walls. The whips twitched at his sides. The chains jangled in his restless grip.

'Come on, Tân,' whispered Finn. 'Find Dad.'

'Oh my gosh!' whispered Errol as Tân leapt to a Venom's trouser leg then to the hem of the long, belted shirt of another Venom going in the other direction. The long-shirted Venom paused and looked around, checking to see who had bumped into him, then continued on his way, taking Tân towards the corridor of cells. When he got to the first door, he stopped to say something to a guard in his path, and Tân jumped off, running fast to the nearest wall.

A small tremor sent two more of the stairs behind

them rattling to the ground, but the three children's eyes were fixed on Tân, their hearts in their mouths.

'There he is,' whispered Finn. 'Just above the door.'

Tula squeezed her eyes shut and tucked her face into the back of Finn's shoulder, unable to watch any more.

Inching through the cracks and crumbles of the rough-hewn rock, the little lizard moved so slowly that even the fireblood vision found it hard to keep him in focus.

'Open your eyes, Tula,' urged Errol. 'You've got to see this! He's amazing! He's hanging from that bit of rock by his tail to see through the window!'

Tula's head jerked up.

'He's moved on to the next door, Tula,' said Finn. 'Can you see him?'

This time Tân swung himself back up from looking through the door window and stayed hidden on a ledge jutting out just to the left of it. He did not move to the next cell but moved his tail back and forth over and over, staring fixedly in their direction.

'Find Craven!' roared Gargan. 'Or whichever slave he has sent! The stench is strongest by the stairs!'

Finn took a short breath in and held it. His fingers tightened round Tula's and his throat felt too thick to speak.

Errol glanced at him and blinked rapidly at the expression on his face. 'Finn?' he said. 'Are you all right? Do you think Tân has found your dad? He's waving his tail left, then straightening it up. What does that mean?'

Tula huffed out a sigh of relief and smiled through the last of her tears. Looking back over his shoulder at his sister, Finn's eyes prickled, and he swallowed hard.

'Sure?' he asked her. 'Dad's in there?'

Tula nodded again, still smiling, and Finn beamed back at her.

CRACK! Three steps behind the children smashed to the ground as the earth roared louder than ever before, and rock and dust and dirt and grit rained down on every creature below, sending the guards outside the cell running and howling.

'My lady!' squeaked Errol, his arms protecting his face and head. 'How do we get over there to let Augustus out!'

'Use the diversion of the wyrm,' said the Stone, 'and don't talk to me again – I will not answer. If those Venoms get the smallest whiff of me, they'll take me away. They've already smelled you stinky lot. Good luck, kids.'

Errol drew breath to howl his frustration at the

Stone, but Tula was pointing at a cracking wall to the east of the open floor.

Gargan was shouting something, but even Errol couldn't hear what he was saying.

'What is it, Tula?' cried Finn, shading his eyes as if that would help him see through all the dust and falling debris.

'Yes!' yelped Errol. 'We're saved! It's my beautiful wyrm!'

'How the hell…!' gasped Finn as delicate tentacles appeared round the edges of the cracks. 'Do you think it's still on a mission to find my father?'

Errol grinned and nodded vigorously. 'It'll motor through those Venoms and be there in the blink of an eye.'

'BILEOUS, bring the serpents!' roared Gargan. 'NOW!'

'Quick!' decided Finn. 'Gargan will be focused on the wyrm now. I'm going to climb down the other side of the steps! Tula, do you think—'

Enough talking! signed Tula, shoving all three of them out of the niche.

Errol did a muffled squeak of pure terror, but Tula grabbed him by the backpack and hauled him off the side of the steps. Finn went too, showing him where to put his hands and feet, staying close to the wall where it was darker. Down they scrambled, as fast as they could, grazing hands, knees, elbows on the sharp rock as they went.

About two metres from the ground, there was a thunderous roar and half the ceiling above the prison-cell chasm smashed down into it. Clouds of dust and rock vaulted into the air, and with the debris came a wave of such intense heat that Finn felt his skin prickle. The force of the crash was so great he lost his grip and fell but, scrambling swiftly on all fours, he was soon up and running, reaching Errol and Tula at the cell door within seconds. Finn glanced back in the direction from which he'd come and could see silhouettes of frantic figures over near the east wall.

Gargan was roaring instructions, but it seemed as if not one of his minions were doing what they were told, and many of them were staggering back towards them as the rumblings, tremors, groans and shakes from the earth juddered through every bone in their bodies.

'Oh my gosh, I'm terrified!' yelled Errol. 'Incredibly stupid with fear! Where is the wyrm? Where is Augustus? We need to get out of here! We need to talk to the Stone!' He was leaping from foot to foot, and Tula, perfectly calm, reached for Tân on the ledge, placed her forefinger gently on Errol's forehead and blew out a short puff of air.

'Oh,' said Errol, hardly noticing, but he suddenly stood firm, standing back so Tula could look into the cell. Tân jumped down from his ledge and scampered on to Tula's shoulder, hiding beneath her hair.

Tula nodded at Finn. *Yes.* Her eyes filled with tears.

'It's him,' murmured Finn to Errol. 'Our dad.'

Errol looked behind them with watering eyes, coughing at the dust. There was a lot of yelling and commotion from the east wall. It sounded, thankfully, as if the wyrm was holding its own.

'Quickly, Tula,' urged Finn. He gestured to the lock on the door. 'Quickly, quickly, quickly.'

Tula pressed her palm to the keyhole and bowed her head. A definitive set of clicks and scrapes sounded from it and the door swung open. The children crowded inside, shutting the door behind them. The gloom was greater within and Finn's eyesight changed to technicolour night vision. The bundle of rags sat up slowly.

All the breath and heat and fury inside Finn hurtled out in a raw sob that hurt his throat.

Here in the small, dark cell it felt suddenly impossibly quiet, the tension tight as a wire. No one moved. Finn could hear a rasping breath from the bundle of rags and then…

'Finn? Tula? Charlie?' it said.

Tula raced over and flung herself at a folded-up man of skin and bone in the corner of the cell. Finn caught a glimpse of a hollowed-out face, a straggly beard and moustache, and hair longer than usual.

'Dad?' he said, and then he was across the cell in two strides and throwing his arms round his father and sister. 'I'm so glad we found you. We thought … we thought…'

'I have longed for you,' said his father, and then his voice cracked. 'I should be rescuing you, not you me.'

Tula leaned back and patted his face.

He laughed and Finn sensed tears on his cheeks.

Tula grabbed the lock that bound the chains to their father's hands and feet, and, squeezing her eyes shut, she focused on the metal mechanism. A series of scarcely audible clicks preceded a loud CLACK and the lock opened. The chains fell to the ground with a loose rattle of heavy links.

'Whoa,' said Errol, and Augustus raised his head. 'Charlie?' he said, squinting towards the silhouette of Errol against the small window of light.

'No, sir,' said Errol, coming forward slowly. 'I'm Errol Ember, and we've got to get you out of here, right now. The wyrm will not last much longer.'

Despite his weakened state, Augustus huffed

out a surprised laugh. 'I am honoured ... that you have used a ... a wyrm for my rescue. Thank you.' He took a painful breath. 'And thank you ... for coming ... to get me.' Pausing to cough, he gestured at his legs. 'However, I can no longer move. They have damaged me ... I have lost the power ... to heal myself.'

Finn rummaged frantically in his coat pockets, pulling out two bottles. 'Here, Dad,' he said, thrusting Shen's bottle of potion into his father's hands. 'Here! It will get you walking straight away.' He put the hydrant back in his pocket, but it suddenly felt small and vulnerable, as if it could fall to the ground and smash uselessly at any moment. 'Buckle this into your satchel, Errol,' he said.

Errol swallowed, but did as Finn asked, his fingers trembling.

Augustus pushed himself to sitting, and Finn's eyes prickled with tears again at the sight of his father's emaciated legs. They were cut to ribbons, oozing a colourless fluid and bruised and scraped, along with the bottom of his beaten feet.

'Walking won't help, Finn,' said Augustus. 'I need to be able to run.'

Tula snatched up Shen's bottle and began feverishly applying the potion to Augustus's legs and feet.

'Do you mean you need to fly?' Finn asked him, his voice raw in his throat.

'Ah,' said his father, leaning one hand against the wall, flinching at the sting from the potion. 'Flying. You know. So P-Patrick found you ... Or was it Charlie? Or ... George?'

'Patrick,' said Finn shortly.

'I wanted ... to ... explain.' Augustus shook his head, his speech slowing and slurring, as if he were winding down. 'I could never ... find the words. Y-your m-mother ... would have had you understanding ... everything ... straight away, but I was afraid I'd ... mess it up ... like I did with ... your brother.'

'My sister,' corrected Finn, but Augustus's eyes were closing and he did not reply.

'Oh!' yelped Errol, still at the door and peering out through the window. 'We must be at the edge of the crater wall. I can see the sky ... I can see sparks and – oh my gosh – *lava...*'

Finn whirled back round to his father. 'Dad, you can explain everything when we're out of here. Can you give us just one drop of blood?'

'I have no blood.' Augustus's head drooped to his chest. 'I stopped myself from bleeding so they could not use me to make equaliser hydrant, and it will take me days to recover. Y-you'll n-need t-to...' He stammered to a halt.

Tula looked over her shoulder at Finn, her expression panicked.

Another roar from Gargan – 'I SMELL FIREBLOOD!' – made Errol whimper, 'Please, please, please,' to the Stone, but there was no answer.

'Dad?' said Finn. 'Dad!' He shook his father's shoulder. 'Can you hear me? We must leave now! The volcano is ready to erupt! Only you can stop it!'

Augustus slumped back into the nest of rags, a last breath carrying one word to their ears amidst all the noise of impending doom.

'*Sing*.'

39

ing?' exploded Finn. 'What the... Dad! Wake up! Wake up!' He grabbed his father by both shoulders, pulling him upright, shaking him, yelling at him.

No, Finn! signed Tula. *He's not going to make it if we don't get him help NOW! We have to take him to the clinic, to Shen.*

'Take him to the clinic?' yelled Finn. 'Dad! Dad! Wake up NOW! To the *clinic*?' he repeated to Tula again, incredulous.

'Stop it!' shouted Errol. 'Stop it, Finn. She's right. We're going to have to sing like your mother used to, and hope you have some of her magic—'

With a body-juddering roar, and another wave of intense heat, a flurry of sparks suddenly lit up the small window of the cell.

Tula jumped to her feet, her expression determined and intent. With startling strength she hoisted

Augustus to her shoulder, lifting him just about upright. Errol dashed to the other side, pulling him almost to standing. 'Sing?' blurted Finn, his hands pulling his hair into frustrated tufts. 'Does he mean the ancient song of fire to fire, "*Canu I Ni*"? I can't sing that song. Not like Dad. His voice goes everywhere; the words, the melodies are perfect. It's complicated. I bet if you get even one note wrong it won't w—'

'Finn!' yelled Errol. 'Help us! Get the door!'

Finn yanked the door open and a torrent of rock on the other side shifted and rumbled in. Finn leapt aside just in time.

The three of them stared in horror at the blocked doorway, flying dust and grit making them cough and blink furiously.

Finn ran at the pile, pulling at the rocks, but another crash at the left cell wall made him whirl round in fear. 'NOOOO!' he yelled, rushing over to stand in front of Tula, Augustus and Errol, waving his arms as if they were slashing swords ready for defence, though no light came from him. Bursting in came the enormous head of the wyrm, covered in dust and grime.

'Wyrm!' cried Errol in joy, pulling Augustus closer to the doorway. 'Please get us out of here!'

The wyrm reached over Finn's flailing arms and

touched Augustus's face gently with its tentacles, smelling his filthy hair and skin. It made a whimpering sound, not unlike that of a small dog, and wriggled closer.

'Oh,' said Finn wonderingly. 'It wants to help.'

A clattering sound of hoisted rock racketed through the thick walls, and with it a muffled shout from Gargan. 'You imbeciles! And you wastes of space! Move the rocks from prison row! They are here...'

Tula reached up and touched the skin of the wyrm's body, which was surprisingly cool and dry, almost soft and velvety. She pressed her palm to it in a careful pressure and Finn saw her sign to it.

Please help us.

The wyrm's nostrils fluttered and the enormous eyes blinked. Finn saw that it had long, soft eyelashes and that its mouth was not big and scary as he'd imagined. He took his father from his sister, and she moved towards the doorway, looking over her shoulder questioningly at the wyrm. *Errol?* she signed. *Did it understand me?*

'Yes,' said Errol. 'That was perfect!' He joined Tula at the doorway and repeated her words.

Please help us.

The wyrm waved a few tentacles, and moved with surprising speed, not eating at the rocks as it had when first tunnelling, but moving everything aside with strangely elegant movements, sending igneous rock rolling across the cell floor. At last the doorway was clear from the waist up, enough space for an easy exit. It turned to face Tula, who signed *Thank you.* She looked back at Augustus and the boys. *The wyrm will protect us as we leave and will follow in her own time. She'll see us back at the fortress.*

'Back at the fortress?' echoed Finn, once again incredulous.

'You are also stupid with fear,' replied Errol. 'That's what's happened to you. That's why you keep saying the same things over and over again.'

Another roar from the crater sent both boys staggering back. The wyrm was already outside, standing guard while Tula hurried over the pile of rocks, making for the crater.

'Bileous! Put your back into it!' roared Gargan, just the other side of the rockfall.

'Hurry,' whispered Errol, and the boys followed Tula, Augustus between them, the man's feet and ankles dragging on the rock, but it couldn't be helped.

Together they scrambled away from the Venomous as fast as they could, staggering closer and closer to the blasting heat of the volcano core.

The heat was warming Finn in a strange way. He

should have found it difficult to breathe, but instead his chest felt full and deep and powerful. The sparks that landed on him seemed to ignite a wondrous energy that pulsed through his entire frame, pushing away the last of the numbness. The cuts and bruises from their journey faded to nothing. When Finn looked over his father's bowed head to his friend, Errol's forehead creased.

'Finn,' he panted. 'You can sing. Believe me, please, you can sing. I'll sing too if you remind me of the words! Come on! If you don't, this volcano is going to erupt, taking half the world with it.'

Tula, just a couple of metres ahead of them, had come to a halt, a small, dark silhouette facing a blazing inferno alive with sparks, flames, smoke and floating ash. She whirled to face them, nodding, and her lips parted. She pointed to her father, and pointed to her throat. Something occurred to Finn, and he pulled the bottle of healing potion from his pocket. Keeping his father's arm wrapped round the back of his neck, he poured the last of the potion into his hand and gestured to Tula to step forward. She came to him and took his wrist in her hand, guiding the potion to her throat.

Finn gulped. 'Tula, we did not know who we were. Not really. We did not remember what had happened to us and to those around us. Now that we know, we can untangle all the things we didn't understand that we feared.'

Tula's throat felt hot then suddenly cool beneath his palm.

'Your mother would whisper us all to sleep at night when our parents were together,' said Errol. 'Do you remember? I cannot forget the first line of her song, but the rest…' He shook his head. 'Dad said it was a powerful song that if sang at full volume with all her heart could stop the world in its tracks. He said we were lucky to hear her sing it.'

'You're sure?' asked Finn.

'The first line was "*Canu i ni*",' whispered Errol, glancing nervously behind them, then back to the crater. 'Like you said. Welsh.'

'I thought it was just a lullaby,' said Finn. 'Dad sang that to us over and over. I'm not sure I remember all the words.'

'There's a reason he sang it to you over and over.' Errol swallowed hard. 'You'll remember,' he said. As if in agreement a roll of thunder groaned out from the volcano. Finn dropped his hand from Tula's throat and stepped forward, holding tightly to Augustus. Errol shuffled with him. The air was hot enough to melt the ends of Finn's bootlaces. He watched them shrivel, and held his breath as the edge of the precipice on which they stood crumbled away into the crater.

'Tula,' he whispered. 'Tell me you can sing. Tell me you remember your voice.'

He looked up to see her mouth open, the cords in her neck taut with effort, straining, straining.

'Tula?' he said. It was the first time he'd ever seen her try to speak, and watching her unable to do so twisted at his heart.

Behind them came a familiar-sounding shout, and all three of them whirled round.

Emerging from the shadows into the hot orange light, into the air alive with flying soot and ash and sparks and flame, came the enormous Venom, now wearing body armour of gleaming metal that accentuated his indomitable size and strength. He saw them standing there and roared. Five other Venomous walked into the light beside him.

'Gargan,' whispered Errol. 'The Venomous must have got past the wyrm.' He gritted his teeth. 'We're going to have to beg for mercy.'

40
ᒋᐊᒋᐟᚴ

Finn looked at Tula and saw that her eyes were bright with furious unshed tears. His throat was hot again, tight and clenched and painful.

'No!' he growled, his fists clenched. 'We're not begging the Venomous for anything. I can sing that song.' He turned back to the precipice edge and shouted out the first line of the lullaby, '*Canu i ni!*' and then again: '*Canu i ni!*'

The volcano spat out a sparking wave of lava that reached the crater's edge.

Errol whimpered, head bowed, his hands clasped over Manchego in an effort to protect him from the heat.

'Errol!' said Finn. 'Help me sing! I can't do this alone!'

There was another shout from behind. Finn looked past Tula to see Gargan marching over fallen rock towards them, at least fifteen Venomous now at his back, a snarl on his face. He felt suddenly that Tula was standing too close to the edge. The tendons in her throat stood out like steel cables beneath her skin, and her jaw was clenched, every muscle ready for rebellion.

Gargan stopped and laughed. Though the sound of his evil humour was swallowed up in the shifting crackle of the volcano, Finn went hot all over, and the feeling prickled so painfully that the burning of his throat faded.

'I can ride those lava wavess,' said Gargan, his voice rumbling yet sibilant all at the same time. 'Give it all up now, you sstupid children. You might ssurvive the heat, but you will drown in the ssucking crater, and I will love watching you ssuffer for all you have done to our kind!'

Tula flung her arms out and breathed in. A rush of cool and healing air swept about them, despite the fire and fury that raged all around. She opened her mouth, and Finn felt the creeping sensation of a clock ticking, ticking towards sounding the alarm.

Gargan stopped in his tracks, his eyes narrowing at the sight of Tula starting to stretch forward, as if she were a bird of prey about to drop in a freefall attack. Tula's breath sighed out silently, and the voicelessness of it drew hot tears from her.

I remember my mother's song to me, my father's lullabies, and I remember how they made me feel: safe and strong and loved.

I've been too afraid to sing those feelings out to others.

Not any more.

In that moment, as the tears flooded down her face, her sighing breath found sound, a clear high-pitched note fast growing in volume, like the mistral winds, the austru, the balal, the coriolis, shrieking through the eaves, the gutters, the facias, the chimneys of a million homes.

'Tula,' whispered Finn.

She stepped towards Gargan and his horde, bringing her arms round, her palms facing forward in the *back away* position, her voice still growing, now an indescribable fury of noise. To the Venomous it was more than the wind, more than an eruption, more than the groaning of tectonic plates. They staggered and fell, their hands clapped to the sides of their head, howling in agony.

The power of all the air coursed through Tula's body, filling her with an incredible strength that bunched her muscles and lengthened her limbs. Her hair flew around her in a wild frenzy as her voice echoed in an agony of sound that caused a rockfall exploding into the lava below. In that moment, she stopped her terrible war cry and whirled to face the crater again. Before Finn could stop her, in two, three jumps she flung herself into its roaring, roiling abyss, her arms still outstretched, her head straight, her feet together, just like Charlie had taught them.

'Noooo!' yelled Finn. 'Tula!' He flung his arms wide, ready to jump, but just as he tensed Tula shot suddenly up from her freefall. Up she spun, like a drunken swan, lurching and swooping and circling higher and higher.

From her back had unfurled wings – huge, white feathered wings – bursting from her shoulder blades in an explosion of soft, snowy down, like a pillow that had been overstuffed for too long, and which had now been ripped open.

'Your arms,' croaked Finn, his throat tight. He swallowed hard, tears pouring down his face. '*Your arms*,' he cried out to her. 'Hold them out straight!'

Tula veered into a tumble turn, then one arm shot out, then the other, and her wings had space and symmetry to swoop her suddenly higher than the crater's rim. They beat hard, and another drift of down scattered into the air. Again they beat, sending a soft thump echoing off the hard rock, then another and another, and it sounded as if she were part of her own drum beat, the intro to a primal song from long, long ago. She swooped and glided down to where Finn stood, his eyes wide and shining, and she sang:

> 'Canu i ni
> gweddill eich calon anhygoel gyda'n cariad
> anadlu gyda ni
> llenwch eich enaid gwag gyda'n cariad
> cysgu nawr
> byw gyda ni...'

41

ΓΟΓ⼊·□Ꙛ≡

The lilting voice and soaring melody quenched the bloody taste of Gargan's words in Finn's mouth instantly, replacing it with the taste of sweet grass, soft rain, low cloud.

Tula sang the same words again, swooping in a vast figure of eight within the crater. The lava pelting up the sides of the volcano subsided, but the rumblings continued, and the sparks still flew high.

Tula swooped again, this time so close that the feathers of her wings brushed Finn's face. Her face was full of a joy so complete that Finn thought his heart might burst from his chest.

He laughed, uncaring of the Venomous now getting to their feet behind them. 'Tula,' he called to her. 'Sing again!'

She flew away, then back towards him.

'You sing!' she called in an echo to him, and her voice was just as he expected it to be, and it felt as if it reverberated through his whole body along with the beating of her wings:

'*Sing! Sing! Sing!*'

It *was* reverberating through his whole body. The voice was coming again not from Tula, but from the bag on his back. The Telling Stone whispered it again:

'Sing, Finn Flint! Now before it's too late.'

'*Canu i ni*,' lilted Tula, even louder than before, and a splash of molten rock caught her boot as she turned in the air. Words floated out from behind him. Finn frowned. It was the Telling Stone … definitely…

'*Canu i ni*,' she sang, and her voice trembled against the muscles in Finn's back, and the taste of fresh water touched his tongue. Behind them the Venomous crawled closer, almost as if they could not help themselves, but they were unable to stand. Even Gargan, every bit of him quivering with the strain of trying to get up and fight, was down on one knee. He thrust a mighty fist on the shoulder of his nearest henchman and began to struggle to his feet.

'Finn!' begged Tula.

Errol stood tall. '*Canu i ni*,' he began, his voice croaky, bolstered by the sweet voice of the Telling Stone.

He caught Finn's eye and Finn drew breath. He joined in on the second line, slightly out of tune, his voice also cracking, and then in the next line all four sang at once.

Gargan fell to both knees. The Venomous behind moaned – whether in pain, rage or sorrow Finn could not tell – and grovelled even closer to the ground. Every face was downturned, except for that of Gargan, whose eyes bulged, sweat pouring from his hideously tattooed and scarred face.

Finn, Tula, Errol and the Telling Stone sang the next lines louder, and then the next, and Errol stood proud, shoulders back, his cheeks wet, and Finn held his father close to him and sang every note perfectly, and Tula swooped and dived and added more complicated melodies and every word was faultless and the volcano stopped its spitting and fighting and spewing, and calmed just a little…

So when Tula flew back in her figure of eight towards them standing on the cliff edge, Finn could see her face clearly through the subsiding smoke. He saw her eyes blink wide and her face transform into an expression of terror.

'Finn!' she yelled. 'Behind you!'

Somehow Gargan had crawled all the way to where the boys stood holding Augustus, and when the monster breathed down Finn's neck, he felt the heat instantly.

The song stopped, and a faint hiss issued from the crater, almost as if the volcano were saying *I've had enough ... for now...*

Gargan put his clawed hand on Finn's shoulder. There was nowhere for him to run. He clutched his father desperately. One misstep and they'd fall over the edge. Gargan's breath was putrid. Finn could not breathe it in.

'My boss would like a word with you and your father,' he rumbled, 'but this curly-haired one can feed Hekla today.'

Finn's mouth filled with the taste of blood again. Then, with a strangled roar, still unable to stand at full height, Gargan kicked out with a powerful leg, booting Errol.

In what felt like agonising slow motion, Errol stumbled, falling towards the edge, one hand snatching desperately at the rock, one still cupped over Manchego's pocket to protect him.

'Finn!' he shouted, his hand slipping.

'ERROL!' yelled Finn, there in an instant. He grabbed Errol's hand, his father still clutched to him. A plume of smoke billowed up from the hell below, obscuring everything, but Finn held his friend's hand with every ounce of strength he had. 'Errol, hold on! Hold on to me! I've got you—'

And then it was as if something wrenched Errol from him, as if the volcano had breathed him in, because in an instant he was…

'Ha! *Gone*,' said Gargan. 'And your sssister too, but I have you now, and your father, and that's all the boss needs to take over the world.'

42

�𝈉ᚩᚱᚦᛣ·ᚠᚢᚱᛯ

'*TULA! ERROL!*' Finn's scream was so loud and so fierce that the rock around them shook and tumbled. Just behind Gargan's biggest minion, a part of the roof and wall smashed to the ground, leaving a gaping hole that stank of ancient sewers and dead things. Even the molten monsters near it howled and rolled away. A shelf of blackened rock just to the right of Finn and his father sheered off and plummeted into the smoky abyss of the crater. The urge Finn felt to leap into the void after his friend was so strong he had to grit his teeth and clench his fingers round his father and take deep shaking breaths to stop himself from jumping after them. Had Tula saved their friend? Or had both of them fallen to their deaths?

Augustus's eyelids fluttered, and he said in a voice of such tired grief that Finn's heart stuttered and thumped, 'L-let us go, or you will live with terrible regret, or die with the same.'

Gargan laughed quietly. Ignoring Augustus, he leaned in closer to scrutinise Finn's face.

'I remember you,' he rasped, flicking the bottom of the boy's chin with a clawed finger. 'You caused me a lot of trouble, back then. Don't you remember the lesson you learned that Day of Burning, you irritating little shrimp? The lesson is *do not mess with me or my kind*. You should also remember that the stupid song you just sang, while it can croooon a crater back to sleep, it doesn't last long…' He stuck his face right up close to Finn's and said, 'But what it does do, my brave little friend, is reach deep into the belly of the earth, where the fiery fire grows, and it calls … not just to the forces that move and pound and build and burn…' he slammed a huge hairy fist into the palm of his hand in time to his words '…but to all of the Underworld's Venomous. It calls, and we come.'

He stepped back and laughed again. 'And so in a few hours, perhaps even minutes, a fabulous army will be here to do my bidding.'

Finn felt the weight on his shoulder ease as his father found the strength in his healing legs to stand up on his own. He yearned to blast Gargan and his soldiers into the molten lava, but his cold, clenched fists told him he was not ready yet.

'You monster,' said Augustus in a voice almost too

quiet to hear, 'you speak of a Day of Burning – the Last Battle. But have you forgotten what happened in that fight?' Gargan bared his teeth, about to speak again, but Augustus held his hand up for silence. 'You killed my wife, slaying her in mid-air, mid-song, in the back, like the coward you are, and then you tried to turn on us—'

'I *did* turn on you!' snarled Gargan. 'You and your stupid children!' He sneered at Finn again, his spit speckling Finn's skin. Finn gritted his teeth, trying not to flinch away. 'I annihilated you!'

'Indeed, Venom,' said Augustus. 'Is it not enough that you run the entire Underworld, but that you must have the overground too?'

Gargan shrugged and curled a lip. 'We'd like a bit more variety in our landscape. A few more helping hands from the overground … maybe a few good singers, someone like this boy here who can hold a tune and light a fire.'

'Thanks to you,' murmured Augustus, 'this boy has not learned the full power of song and cannot light a fire. You took his gifts when you took his wings.'

Finn blinked. *Took my wings?*

Gargan grinned, exposing blackened stubs of broken teeth and yellowed fangs growing at unnatural angles from his wet and shining gums. 'Was tempting to crunch them up as a little snack on that fearsome day, but I kept them as pretty souvenirs,' he said, rattling something on his belt, and Finn tasted rotting oranges. 'Now what I'd like is *all* of you two as pretty souvenirs,' he sniggered, and he flicked Finn's chin again with his claw.

Finn bled and the monsters shifting closer around Gargan huffed with laughter at the sight of the boy's blood running thick and gold from his chin.

'Someone pass me the poison ropes!' commanded Gargan. 'It's time to get these two in a real cage. Hang them up on the Island of the Fort as wingless beasts for all to see. Bleed them dry whenever we like, whenever we need their tainted blood.'

There was a mutter behind Gargan, a Venom telling him there were no poison ropes, and he howled in frustration. 'Where is Raddles? Can he do nothing right? *Ever?*' he shouted, and turned to push his way back up the tunnel. 'Watch the firebloods,' Finn heard him say. 'Do not grab them. They are not afraid to fall to their deaths.'

He stomped away, and his Venomous horde shuffled closer. Finn felt Augustus reach for his hand, seeming stronger now. He focused on the cliff walls, searching for an escape route. There was only the stinking hole that had opened up near the Venomous. Could they make it there in time?

'Finn,' urged Augustus in his ear. 'Do you hear that?'

Finn saw a look in his father's eye that he'd not seen before. He took a shaky breath, cocked his head and listened. He heard the wind first, a blast of ocean fury speeding up from the freezing Atlantic Ocean in the south. Then he heard the tearing roar of something ripping very fast through the air.

Despite his desperate grief, Finn felt a lightening in his chest.

'Sounds like a turbojet,' he whispered to Augustus. 'Do you think Charlie—'

'Any parent,' said Augustus with a slow spread of a smile, 'would be proud.'

A strong taste of something fizzy and alcoholic flooded Finn's mouth, sending a bolt to his chest, and he pressed his fingers to his heart to stop it thudding so hard. Beneath his fingers, a mark on his skin flared hot. Shoving his shirt aside, he found the gift from the griffin reddening, and his words echoed through his mind:

You, Finn Firefearer, have forgotten too much. Use this gift when you are ready to remember.

'He'll need to land,' continued Augustus, 'and we'll need to get to him.' He glanced down at his legs and feet. 'I can move better now, but I still won't be able to use wings.'

Finn pulled his shirt back over his chest, his hand shaking. *Not now, not now...*

'What do you think is through there?' he asked, with just one blink in the direction of the stinking hole that had opened up at his grieving howl. 'I'm guessing the sewers...'

'It's the only way out. On the count of three, run. One...'

Gargan pushed through his obsequious crowd, muttering and growling at them.

'Two...'

In his hands he held coils of a rope that seemed to be made of living, breathing serpents. They writhed and spat, their jaws wide, tongues flicking, venom dripping from their fangs.

'Three!' said Augustus, much faster than Finn had expected, and they turned and barged towards the stinking hole, knocking two Venoms off balance. Finn's eyesight adjusted immediately to see in the pitch darkness, and his sense of smell heightened too, which was a pity because the stench was overwhelming. He heard Augustus say '*fflam tân, llosgiad tân*': fire flame, fire burn. In a series of four swift moves, he whirled his hands in front and behind him, and suddenly he was holding a blazing beam of white-hot flame. With Finn just in front of him, he thrust it at the roof of rock behind.

'STOP!' yelled Gargan, through the falling shards of stone, hurling a serpent rope with all his might. It spun through the air, spitting and writhing. 'STOP!' he roared again. The snake hit Finn with a heavy thud in the back, but it fell to the ground before it could sink its fangs into him. The rockfall from the roof of the tunnel thundered all around them, preventing the Venoms from following and trapping the serpent beneath tonnes of rubble.

Augustus could not move fast, but it was fast enough to escape the worst of the falling debris. His shambling run, favouring his right leg, was painful to watch.

'Dad!' gasped Finn. 'You okay? Do you—'

'We need to get out of here. Got to find Charlie.' He stopped suddenly at an intersection in the tunnel. 'Left or right?' he asked Finn.

'Right,' piped up the Telling Stone unexpectedly, and Augustus laughed.

'Milady,' he huffed.

'Be quiet and run,' she urged. 'Finn, follow the smells of burning…'

A shout from behind drove them on faster, through the twisted angles of the tunnel, seeming to stay on one level, yet moving deeper into the mountain then back round. At a distant sound of metal and rock, Finn threw a panicked look over his shoulder. Nothing. But then, just before they turned another corner, he glimpsed the fast-moving shadows of three, maybe four, Venomous giving chase, one holding a flaming stave that threw frightening shadows of their over-muscled forms on to the tunnel walls.

Finn gasped with fear and rushed to catch up with his father. He crashed into him as he rounded the corner.

'There's no escape route,' he whispered, 'and we've got three Venoms behind us, maybe more!'

Augustus pointed ahead. 'We're back at the crater,' he said, 'but on the other side. Ready? You're going to have to fly us out.'

Finn shook his head. 'What? Dad? No! Never in a million years! I can't fly! I can't do fire—'

His father laughed. 'You do fire better than anyone. You've just got to remember how.'

'What do you mean?'

'It's time to tell you everything, my son.'

43

ᚠᛟᚱᚠᛁ·ᚠᚪᚱ

gnoring the shouts of Venomous getting louder with every second, Augustus took a breath and said, 'You were three years old at that last battle, and Charlie was seven and Tula was one and a bit.'

'Dad!'

'Shh. Listen. The three of you were standing roaring defiance at an onslaught of Venomous so fierce that almost every last person on the island had taken cover. As a baby you were a liability.' Augustus laughed and clapped a hand to Finn's shoulder, pulling him close.

'What are y—? Dad! The Venomous are just round the corn—'

'You loved fire. Had no respect for it. Finn, you *breathed* it.' Augustus's eyes were alight with passion. 'Without meaning to, you'd burn everything in sight until you slowly learned not to.'

'What? I breathed fire?' Finn's expression was

one of surprise, then a look of broken despair flitted across his face. He held up his hands. 'You know I … I can make a – a sort of a light?'

Augustus swallowed. When he spoke, his voice cracked. 'Of *course* you can breathe fire. Of *course* I knew that.' He shook his head, clasped Finn's hand. 'That day, the day of the battle, you were standing on that balcony, roaring support for me and for your mother. In the sky battle, you saw me trapped and overwhelmed, and you saw your mother consumed by a burning beast, and…' Augustus drew a ragged breath and Finn was startled by his father's reddened eyes and shaking hands. 'Oh, my boy, you became so afraid of fire. In all its forms. Your sister had her hands pressed to her eyes so she did not see your mother burn, but she heard that song and all the noise and from that moment she did not speak again. Until now.'

His throat was thick with tears.

'Tula has faced her fear and bought us time by singing the volcano to sleep. That day, I watched you with your hands clapped over your ears so you did not hear your mother's dying song, but your eyes were wide open to all the Venomous fire that they were lashing round your mother, wide open to the vulnerability of flight.'

'Dad...' Finn's chest was tight with pent-up emotion and the mark of the griffin burned his skin.

'Listen, son. You must face these terrors you have. Of flying. Of fire. Flight and flame are your gifts. Do not let Gargan and his kind hold them in their hands. Do not let them be stolen. We need you to be brave.'

'I *am* brave,' said Finn, his voice fierce through his tears. 'But I know what I can do and I know what I can't do! I have no control over the fire! If I begin to breathe—'

'So let me finish the story.'

'Dad—'

Augustus laid a hand on Finn's arm. 'Your mother sang her last, and it is that which killed her, not the fire that was eating her up, not the Venomous trying to tear her limb from limb, and then ... *then*, son, you breathed like you have never breathed before. It was unimaginable. It was like a nuclear furnace blasting from you in a mighty column of the brightest flame.'

As if on cue, the clang and clash of approaching Venomous came round the corner of the entrance tunnel. Augustus nudged Finn to the side and flung a fireball at the roof of the tunnel. 'That should keep them busy,' he muttered as the roof smashed down, sending black dust exploding out all around them.

Finn coughed and swiped at his streaming eyes.

'And in that moment, Finn,' said Augustus urgently, ignoring the shouts of the Venomous beyond, 'all the world in front of you was obliterated. Do you remember?'

Finn frowned and shook his head.

'It was a shimmering haze of white flame and white smoke and blackened shapes all consumed by this strange fire of rage and grief and desperation and … and of … a sort of clinical justice. In an instant, everything was razed to the ground: the Venomous, the buildings behind which they skulked, the trees in which they hid, streams through which they walked…'

'What about the firebloods?' Finn's eyes were wide, and it was all he could do to ask this question. Strange images were flashing through his mind. The mark was beginning its work as his father spoke.

'That's just the thing,' said Augustus. 'I was there, in the full burst of your flame, fighting high in the air watching your mother and watching you three, and I saw everything.'

'Us three?' said Finn, his forehead wrinkling.

'Yes, you, Charlie, Tula. The fire you breathed seemed to suck the Venomous in from far and wide. Almost as if what you had within you contained some of what lies within their melting pot. They were drawn to it just as we are sometimes drawn to gold, but to an unimaginable extent – like moths to the flame, but at a hundred times the speed. The firebloods within your blast were completely unscathed, well, most of them...'

Finn swallowed hard. 'Most?' he croaked.

'In seconds it was over.' Augustus pulled Finn to him in a tight hug. 'The Venomous were gone.'

Finn pushed away, holding his head to block out the pictures of raging flame, death and destruction that were flooding his head. His mouth was so full of chaotic taste that he could barely speak. 'B-but also so m-much of our city,' he stammered, 'and the forest and the rivers and the streams, and you say *most* but that must mean that ... that I ... that I killed people.'

'Never.' Augustus pushed Finn to arm's length and stared into his eyes. 'You never killed anyone. Those found lifeless in the aftermath can only have been murdered by the Venomous. Do you understand? You, a tiny three-year-old, saved our world.'

Finn shook his head, looking dazed. 'This is why people fear m—'

'And now you must save it again.'

Finn was still shaking his head and was about to speak when a shout from high above distracted him. There on the rim, silhouetted against the darkening sky, teetered a familiar figure.

'Charlie?' breathed Finn.

And then, 'Finn!' came a bellow from across the lava pot. 'FINN! I've been looking for you! We need to get out of here.'

Shielding his eyes, Augustus peered down through the drifting smoke and ash. 'It's Idris's youngest boy, Errol,' he said with satisfaction. 'On that blessed wyrm.'

'Errol!' croaked Finn. 'How—'

'Augustus!' called Charlie from above. 'Bring Finn with you! Up here! I have the plane! Ezza, I'm coming for you! You're about to be eaten alive!'

'He cannot fly!' shouted Finn. 'His wings are broken!' but his words were lost in the *BOOM* of falling rocks near Errol and the howling rage of Venomous, who were working hard to clear the path to their target.

Errol's voice, though he was far away, was clearly audible across the lava.

'Uh oh.'

'Errol, you banana!' yelled Charlie. 'You've come out on the wrong side!' A wave of Venomous stink hit Finn's nostrils just as Charlie blanched and said, 'And now you've got a whole tribe of angry knuckleheads behind you.'

Finn gasped as Charlie dropped down into the

crater. It was clear that one of his wings was damaged, because he spun like a sycamore seed, circling slowly down towards Errol.

'Oh my gosh!' yelled Errol. 'What are you doing, Charlie? How can this be going so wrong?' The wyrm touched a tentacle to Errol's cheek and he whispered what sounded like a magical chant to it, pressing his hands to its face. It began to sag smaller, smaller, smaller … until it was tiny enough to fit back into the matchbox. Errol scooped it up carefully, putting the box safely in a pocket on his gilet. Throwing a panicked glance behind him, he shifted as far as he dared on the narrow ledge away from the tunnel entrance as Charlie spun closer to him.

'I thought you were dead, Errol!' called Finn, his heart pounding with joy. 'I thought you were DEAD, but you're ALIVE! How di—'

'Not for long if you don't do firebreathing, Finn Flint!' Errol shouted in reply, reaching out for a harness of knotted rope that Charlie swung in his direction. 'I came to tell you it's okay to feel angry and afraid and desperate and—'

And then Errol was snatched away by Charlie.

'Where is Tula?' yelled Finn.

'Singing!' called Errol, clipping his harness to Charlie's belt. 'She pulled me from the crater of doom and now she's up here with the mythics! We need your help, Finn!'

He and Charlie swooped higher in a slow, desperate spiral, Charlie's punctured wing making raspy whistling noises as it beat the air.

'Go, Charlie,' muttered Augustus, watching the boy intently, almost as if he were urging him higher with the sheer force of his mind.

'The equaliser,' called Errol down to them. 'Can you try Augustus's blood again? Ready?'

Finn stepped forward, his forehead creased in confusion, his hands ready for anything, and Errol threw the bottle as hard as he dared.

It spun through the air and both Augustus and Finn had their arms outstretched, but it was Finn who caught it.

Charlie fell and climbed, stuttered and started, and as they whirled round and up Finn caught a glimpse of Errol's face, his eyes squeezed closed now, jaw clenched, rigid with fear. Yet still he'd come in here, charging with his wyrm through rock and sewer, ice and fire, just to bring him this … this…

A sigh from the backpack warmed Finn's body. 'The answer is no,' said the Stone. 'Augustus cannot yet bleed,' said the Stone. 'Augustus, you must tell them.'

'Oh no,' breathed Augustus. 'I don't want this…'

'Don't want what?' Finn asked. 'What is this? What's going on?'

'He does not want to tell you that if his blood will not work, then the hope is that his children's blood would be enough to power up the equaliser,' said the Stone. 'But, if that is true, then all of you will be running from the Venomous all your lives, ransom to the life he's had to lead.'

The confusion on Finn's face cleared. 'We're already ransom to the life you lead, Dad!' he exploded. 'I'd rather die than go back to living night and day inside, hiding, trapped, pretending to be normal when actually we're something completely different and I don't even know what that really is any more!'

Charlie had reached the top, disappearing in a flurry of falling pebbles and rock, but no sooner had his feet vanished than his head reappeared.

'Could you please have the father-son chat later?' he called. 'Get up here now.' A loud *BOOM* sounded from somewhere far off, and he ducked and winced. 'Overground and Underground are flying towards each other out here,' he said, 'and Tula is singing her guts out, and the airheads are singing with her, and the beasts are arriving one by one, but nothing can stop this slaughter without the equaliser and without the two of you getting out of there!'

'I can't fly!' shouted Finn.

'Come *ON*!' yelled Charlie, his face turning red and his eyes awash with tears of frustration. 'Can't you taste that lie in your mouth? Can't you? No family of mine could not fly! It's in our blood, our hearts, our minds! Along with the fire that *you* can BREATHE, dammit, and *I* cannot! Do you hear me, Finn Flint?' He slammed his hand down on the ground and dry soil and rocky shards fell into the simmering pit below. 'Errol's run for help, but no one can hear him in this mess! Dad? Finn? You've got to get out of there!'

44
FORTY-FOUR

'Dad?' whispered Finn, and his mouth flooded with the taste of rain. His heart and head and body were awash with emotions he didn't understand, and his mind was filled with questions there was no time to ask.

'When we left after that battle,' said Augustus, his hands hanging limp at his side, 'Charlie could not come with us because he could not retract his wings. It broke my heart. And so I met him when no one else knew, and we talked in secret each day, and he played games with us, and he watched us from afar—'

BANG! Black smoke and soot and stench billowed from the tunnel. The Venomous were breaking through.

The sound startled Augustus into a defensive stance, pushing Finn behind himself. His legs were shaking, and his breathing rattled painfully in his chest, but even so he raised his arm with a powerful swing, about to swipe at the rock again to create another rockfall, but it was too late. Three panting Venoms flung themselves from the tunnel out on to the precipice and yelled in triumph and anger upon seeing Augustus and Finn before them.

'Finn,' muttered Augustus, 'stay behind me. If we cannot fly, we'll fight them off, then go back out the way we came.'

Two more Venoms joined the first three, panting and drooling and dripping green blood from fingers raw from clawing at the rocks. Finn whirled round to stare at the rockface around them. Could they climb it?

'You sstinking firebloodss … I'm gonna tear you limb from limb…' came a low, hissing voice.

Finn spun back round. There was Gargan, joining the five warriors on the precipice, and behind him more Venomous crowded in.

'There iss no esscape,' Gargan continued, taking a small step towards them. Finn saw that over his shoulder was the last thick coil of the writhing viper ropes. He held the end of it in one hand, and it was formed of the biggest serpent that Finn could ever have imagined. Its jaws snapped wide as Gargan lifted the coils off his shoulder, getting ready to throw them, and Finn saw bright yellow venom drip from its fangs.

'Stay back, Finn,' murmured Augustus. 'That viper poison is what killed half those who died on the day of the battle. One drop of it on our skin will bring us to our knees.'

'Sstop sspeaking!' rasped Gargan. 'Lie down on the ground, your handss in front of you, and I will sspare your livess.'

He took another step towards them, a small pair of wings dangling from his belt. When Finn saw again what this monster had ripped from him all those years ago, anger surged within him. This creature had not only damaged him forever, but he'd decimated his childhood too, forcing them to live in hiding, forgetting family, friends, their own identity...

'Get ready to climb the walls, son,' said Augustus. 'Ready? One...' He dropped to his left knee, as if complying with Gargan's demand.

'You too, boy,' said Gargan, squeezing the serpent head so that its jaws gaped wide again.

'Two...' said Augustus, and then very fast, 'Three!'

Finn was already leaping at the rock face, gripping the crevices, the tiny shards that protruded from its surface, the holes, the bumps and ledges, and in two moves he was suspended above the Venomous, looking down at the tableau below.

Augustus had sprung to his feet again and slashed

at Gargan with a strike of green flame from right to left, which should have sliced his head clean off his body, but a Venom to Gargan's right flung up his meaty hand and blocked him. Before Finn could draw breath, Gargan had already raised his arm and thrown the viper rope in a spitting lasso at Augustus, who slipped and caught the full lash of venom all over his neck and chest.

'Dad!' screamed Finn, but, soundless, Augustus flung his arm from left to right, this time the flame from his fingers catching Gargan across his cheek. The Venom did not fall. He took another step closer.

'*Noo*,' breathed Finn, and he released one hand from the rock, slamming it into the mark of the griffin on his chest, and in a split second all he'd shut out from that terrible day came flooding back. He clung to the wall, shuddering with the horror of it all, but also the power that flooded through his mind and body.

How to protect.

How to breathe.

How to burn.

Fury raged through him. White flame licked the edges of his lips. As Gargan drew back his arm to lash the viper at Augustus once more, Finn flung his arms wide, releasing himself from the rock, releasing the wash of emotion from inside him in a blast of white-hot fire. The force of it propelled him back against the rock, and the flame he breathed shot out in a searing arc at the crowd of Venomous below. Gargan spun, caught by surprise, and howled a primal yell of raging defeat. He released the viper rope in one long tether of roiling, spitting venom, straight at Finn.

Finn did not flinch. Still he hung on the rock, suspended by the power of his flame, and when the viper struck him full in the chest, right over his heart, sinking its fangs deep into his muscle and releasing a poison so strong that no one had ever survived it, he did not feel or fear it.

Before him, the Venomous fell to their knees with screams and cries of terrible pain and terror, disintegrating in the fire he breathed. Finn could not hear their shouts or understand their desperate gestures. He knew only that his father had fallen on his side and had not moved again.

Gargan staggered and fell. The intensity of Finn's breath fast reduced him and his crowd of Venomous to blackened, unrecognisable molten shapes, twisting, changing from black to grey to white until at last all that was left were swiftly disintegrating piles of ash…

And still Augustus did not move.

Finn took a shuddering breath to dive down to him, but a jolt from the bag on his back swung him dangerously out from the rocky wall and the Stone's voice within it yelled:

'NO, FINN! BREATHE FIRE NOW! BREATHE FIRE! You must burn away the venom within you or you will die!'

Finn gasped and roared out with flame again, realising from the sharp tingle of viper venom in his chest and the truth in the Stone's words that if he stopped breathing such intense heat he would freeze up and crack into a million lifeless pieces, *But what about Dad? I need to get to Dad!*

A fresh wave of Venomous crowded out on to the precipice, greedy for violence. Yet when they saw Finn's arc of deadly heat they turned and ran, and those that didn't fell, blackened, on the piles of ash already on the ground as Finn's flame found each and every one of them.

Still Augustus lay lifeless on the ground below, and even though all the Venomous had not run back up the tunnel, and even though the venom still felt cold in his veins, Finn snuffed out his flame and dropped to the ground beside his father.

The Stone whimpered. 'Finn … You should—'

He ignored her. They were out of time. This mattered more than him. 'Dad!' he said urgently, shaking his shoulder. 'Dad! We can climb the walls!'

When his mouth flooded with the taste of rust, he knew they were in trouble.

'Dad!' he said, and hot tears tracked down his sooty face. He held two fingers to his father's neck and found a pulse, slow and erratic, then pulled him across his shoulders, sobbing openly now with relief that he was alive.

'Charlie!' he shouted, then struggled to stand.

There was movement in the tunnel ahead, but none from the rim above. There were distant sounds of warfare. Shouts. Bangs. Booming noises. The rush of flame from a billion fireballs. No one could help them escape; those up there were fighting for their lives and did not know of the peril Finn and Augustus were facing here.

Finn straightened, Augustus a dead weight on his shoulders. He lifted his face and sniffed the air of the tunnel – their only way out. It was ripe with the stink of hiding Venomous. It would not be long before another wave of them braved the precipice, and Finn did not know if he had the strength to breathe fire again. He had to find an exit route.

Fast.

A weapon would be good if he was out of firepower.

Finn stepped over to where Gargan's remains lay at a little distance in front of the other incinerated heaps.

Something was gleaming in the ash. A blade, perhaps, that he could use. He reached down and though it should have been searing hot, the soft gleam of metal he found was cool to his touch. Wondering, his legs quaking under the weight of his father, he pulled the object free of the ashes and found that in his hands he held the remains of his own childhood wings. They were formed of titanium feathers so small that they felt soft in his fingers. Each wing was double the size of his forearm now, impossibly light, impossibly beautiful. Gargan had drilled into the hard nubs at the top, through which he'd looped a circle of gold that he'd hung from his belt.

Finn fixed them to a strap on the rucksack and took a deep breath. He felt a sudden warmth at his back and remembered the Telling Stone.

'Hello, my lady,' he said. 'Can I get back out of this mountain through that tunnel?'

'No,' she said.

'Huh.' Finn chewed his lip. 'Can I carry my father out of here up the walls?'

'No,' she said.

He took a shaky breath. 'Is anyone coming to rescue us?'

'No,' she said. 'But that is because they do not know where you are. Tula, Charlie and Errol are fighting for their lives.'

Finn suspected that the heat he felt from the bag was something she was trying to tell him that he had not thought to ask.

Something important.

It was hottest over the hunch in his back, and Finn gritted his teeth with the knowledge of what he knew he had to do. He stepped closer to the edge of the precipice. His heart was pounding uncomfortably and his legs felt wobbly and his vision was faceting in a strange way that showed him bits of everything around him, even views from the top of the crater, which he should not have been able to see. Mythics were flying in from across the seaward side, or running across the land with pounding hooves, clawed feet, slithering coils. He thought he could even see Shuĭlóng, but then his view shifted to the air, and he saw Charlie out there, fluttering like a broken butterfly among the fiercest and most timid of firebloods, all dodging daggers of putrid yellow flame from swathes of Venomous below.

Of every size and kind and colour and age and shape, they staggered up from crevasses in the ground, ready to do battle, ready to relish the agony they could inflict with their vipers and their toxic weapons.

Angelina hovered high above, a stark silhouette of deadly precision, picking the enemy off with arrows, two per second. She called out orders to the firebloods below to corral their efforts to best effect. Grey Griffin tore through the swathes of Venomous, snatching up dozens at a time and tossing them into a pit of bright green flame that five of Charlie's minions were building with a volley of fireballs. He did it again and again, his wingbeats never slowing.

And George.

George.

The first thought to flood Finn's mind was, *He needs a weapon*, but the old man seemed to be doing perfectly well without it. He had a long springy branch of yew, and he floated, spun and whirled his way through the younger firebloods, touching them on the shoulder, the head, their hands. Finn could see traces of pale blue energy scythe into their flagging forms, rejuvenating them instantly, protecting them from wayward claws, poisonous fumes and beams of Venomous fire. He called and urged, shepherded and nudged them on to higher ground, oxbow formations, fireball crews.

It looked, for now, as if the firebloods had the upper hand.

There was no leadership in the Venomous forces below and their numbers were dwindling, but smoke from the volcano was blackening the air, choking fireblood warriors and mythics alike, and causing problems for those on the ground. It did not seem to bother the Venomous.

The warmth from the backpack intensified and Finn's focus snapped back to the crater in which they were trapped. His hump radiated with a pain he'd never felt so intensely before. It felt as if all the pressure of Augustus's body upon his shoulders was breaking the bones in his spine.

He gasped, stood straighter to adjust his father's weight and took another step forward. Now the front of his boots hung over the edge of the precipice. Pain crackled again and he shifted his shoulders back, gasping at the waves of agony. Heat from the lava below blew the hair back from his face and warmed the icy feeling in his veins.

Heat…

'Yes,' whispered Finn, distracted from the agony in his back. 'Thermals. Of course.'

He stood straighter still, took a deep breath and breathed out, but this time, instead of ferocity and fury and fear and desperation, he breathed the words of the song he'd last heard his mother sing. Not words for the mountains of fire, not words to win battles, not words to call water. He breathed the words of love and comfort that she'd sung to those around her every day of her life.

Strength and power hummed through Finn's bones, and he shifted the grip on his father out, holding him straight across the back of his shoulders, gripping his knees and his ribs, almost as if the length of his father's body were the wings of a plane. It felt, through more pain, but just pinpricks this time, as if he were uncurling. His feet left the ground and, though his heart thumped loud in his chest, he leaned into the fiery pit below, breathing the words...

As he leaned, he felt the cushion of the heat.

Slowly, carefully, hardly daring to breath between the words of his song, Finn stepped off the edge of the precipice. And, instead of falling into the seething lava below, he felt the thermal draught push him gently up, higher and higher, and the Stone in the backpack warmed him through, and the titanium wings on the strap rustled and went still. Finn inhaled but did not fall. Over and over he sang the words his mother had taught him, with his father's body hooked into his arms, pulling his chest out proud, his back tall and strong, until at last he was up in the night sky.

Now it was so thick with smoke that all Finn could see was a bright light up ahead and the spewing droplets of lava erupting from the crater and flashes of flame everywhere from fireblood fireballs. The chaos of battle raged around him, and the words of the song quietened in his mouth, but he did not fall from the air, gliding instead towards that brave pillar of light. When he reached it, he saw that it was not one light but two – Charlie and Tula lit up like fireflies, both struggling to stay aloft in the buffeting blasts from beneath.

'About time!' yelled Charlie, but he was grinning and the expression on his face was one Finn had not seen before. If it had been anyone else, Finn would have said he looked happy and proud.

'Have you got the equaliser?' asked Tula, signing as she spoke aloud. 'I'm guessing Dad could not bleed? What—'

Finn grinned, wondering if he'd ever get used to hearing her actual voice. 'It's in my pocket. Can you reach it?'

Charlie dipped in the air, wincing with the pain in his wing, and pulled the bottle out.

'It needs our blood now, not his,' said Finn, and Tula nodded straight away, understanding, her face alight with hope.

She tugged a small blade from the belt at her waist and pricked her finger. A shimmering golden droplet appeared, and she cupped it carefully. Charlie held his hand out to her, and she pressed the blade to his thumb. He held the bottle and dribbled his blood into it, then Tula added hers.

Finn drifted closer to her, saying, 'I can't let Dad go.'

With a careful cut, Tula pricked the edge of Finn's hand, and Augustus's too, but still no blood ran from his wound. Charlie caught Finn's golden droplets in the bottle, and together the three of them flew out across the crater until they were right in the middle.

'Ready?' asked Tula.

All three held the bottle as Charlie tipped it gently over so that its precious drops spilled into the boiling ocean of lava below.

There was a strange sound, as if someone had gone *hhhp* – a gulp of startled breath. And the boiling lava flashed with the colours of the north, spraying blue, green, pink and purple light across the night sky, sucking all the acrid smoke back into itself and leaving just the cold air and stars and moon of a world saved in the nick of time.

45
ᒥᓍᒧᖏ·ᑭᒾᐱ≡

Finn, Tula, Charlie and Errol stood guard at the north-west corner of the ramparts upon their return, though they were dead on their feet. They took it in turns with all the firebloods of the fortress to sleep, then wake, then sleep, then wake, guarding the city in case the Venomous dared to launch another attack.

People from the town drifted to the children in couples, in families, in groups of friends to thank them. Some came to apologise for distrusting Augustus, for fearing Finn, some to celebrate their hard-won triumph, asking questions, smiling, telling them about themselves. Some were shy and wary, others joyful and loud. Many were bruised and battered, and there was a long queue outside Tahira's Tonics, which had moved into where Rudimenta's house had been, just the other side of the piazza from where the children kept watch. There was no sign of Idris, who was far below in the labyrinth, working with Francis the unicorn to heal the injured mythics.

When the bell to her shop door chimed as she opened for business, none of her customers grumbled as Tahira hurried away from them across the piazza towards Errol and the Flints, with a bright red bottle in her hand.

'Hello,' she said, coming to a breathless halt. 'What marks did you gain from the battle?'

Charlie pulled his shirt aside to show the seed of the plane tree beneath the neat row of other symbols imprinted on his chest. Tahira nodded approvingly. 'For your helicopter action with that holey wing. I like it.' She pulled out a square bundle of gauze tied with string and gave it to Tula with the purple bottle. 'Can you patch him up? I know your energy has gone, but these should work without it.'

Then she turned to Finn with a bright, brave smile. 'Ohhh,' she said, her smile fading, looking confused. 'What the…' She walked slowly round him and then her face broke into a smile that lit up her face. 'Well I never,' she breathed. 'Your hunch…'

'… has changed,' said Finn. 'Feels weird.'

'Was it Augustus?' asked Tahira. She gestured to the two fist-sized knuckles of softly gleaming titanium-like steel that now protruded from Finn's back: sheered-off wing stubs. The skin around them was pink and new but healing quickly. 'I hear you carried him across your back. Did his powers rip your scars apart? Or … or was it the Venomous poison?' She nudged his shirt aside, and clear for all to see at the end of Finn's row of marks was the snakebite where the viper had struck him.

'Venomous poison?' asked Charlie, his brow furrowing into his customary frown. 'What Venomous poison? Did those snakes bite you, Finn?'

Tahira glanced at Charlie. 'I still sense viper toxins in his veins.' Her eyes were very wide. 'You should be dead,' she murmured to Finn.

Finn swallowed. 'Well, I feel good,' he said, and smiled reassuringly.

Tahira chewed her lip. 'The Venomous get a small dose of Gargan's viper poison before they go into the boiling pot that turns them into the force they are. It helps to melt their skin before they simmer into their monstrous forms. It could be—'

'It was Dad,' said Tula quickly. 'Most definitely. That's why Finn's wing stubs revealed themselves properly.'

'Or maybe it's just that Finn learned to fly,' was Charlie's quiet suggestion.

'I didn't learn to fly,' said Finn. 'I've told you a gazillion times that it was the thermals.'

There was a pause, then, 'Perhaps all of these,'

decided Tahira. The air seemed to crackle with an energy that hadn't been there before. 'Flying without wings. Wow.'

'No, I was riding thermals,' countered Finn. 'I don't think—'

'Nonsense,' declared Tahira. 'Let Charlie teach you his loop-the-loop.'

'Yeah,' said Charlie.

Finn looked at his smile and thought back to when they'd first met him, and he'd thought this boy would never look truly happy.

Tahira grinned round at them all. 'Well, thank you again, brave children. I'd better get back to the other war heroes.' She blew them kisses and hurried away across the square just as Otto approached.

Though the children had been grateful for the delicious gifts the islanders had brought them from their own kitchens, Otto's basket brought actual squeals of delight.

'I know what you like,' he said. He pointed at a rock cake on which Errol had been gnawing for some time. 'Your mother cannot bake,' he declared. 'No offence.'

'She's *busy*!' protested Errol.

Otto ignored him. 'She spend too much time...' he made big slashing and banging gestures '...melting, sharpening. Me, I focus on the tasty.'

'Thank you, Otto,' said Tula before Errol could defend Edith more vehemently. 'Ooh! Peaches!'

Otto grinned. 'I know you like them, and freshly sliced mango for him...' He winked at Finn. 'It is the sweet taste of victory. Thank you, *helden*. Rest and regain your strengths.'

Errol waved goodbye with one hand while lifting out sandwiches of the freshest bread with the other. He found crisps, grapes, cheeses, cakes, crunchy salads and roasted morsels that had been burnished by Otto's very own gourmet flames. He was muttering to himself and whimpering in delight. Gently, he nudged his pocket and gave Manchego some Cheddar. He ate it fast, his whiskers quivering and his eyes bright.

The best food of all came a few moments later, when Rudimenta brought Charlie pepperoni pizza – speechless, with welling eyes and a jubilant Morty at her side, the mark of George's yew upon his proud young chest.

Now it was sunset, and most of the island were in their homes preparing for a celebration of the Venomous defeat. The air hung quiet and still and cold.

Finn shot a sideways look at Charlie. 'So you're not just a spy for the fortress,' he said.

Charlie, his mouth full, caught Finn's eye and shook his head.

'You're not just some kid that Dad remembered from before.'

Charlie's chewing slowed, and he shook his head again, still staring intently at Finn.

The stars were coming out one by one and the ocean breeze was fresh and clean. Finn's heart beat faster, his mind going a million miles a minute. 'You're not an orphan, you're not a bad sort, you're not a troublemaker.'

Charlie shrugged. 'Well…'

'You have actually got a dad, a brother, a sister…'

Charlie swallowed. 'Yeah.'

Emotion prickled at Finn's nose and he rubbed it furiously. 'You … you are our … *brother*.'

Charlie did not cry, but his eyes were very bright.

'Yes, Finn. I'm your brother.' He slung his arm round Tula, who turned and smiled widely at Finn.

'You are so slow, Finn.'

Finn swallowed hard at the teasing voice of his sister. He didn't think he'd ever not feel joy at hearing her speak. His mouth was filled with a dozen flavours, all of them mingling in a heady taste that made his head swim and his eyes fill up again: the dry fizz of champagne with the sweet softness of mango were the strongest of all, but there was sadness there too, and regret, and the dark intensity of a rare cocoa that he knew was love.

'She's a cheeky one, your little sis,' said Errol, winking at Tula. A pair of firebloods approached to take the next lookout shift, and he got to his feet. 'I need to go help my dad with the mythics. You guys gonna check on your dad?'

'Yep.' Tula stood and pulled the boys to their feet either side of her. They clasped each other in a three-way hug, and Charlie's pale-blue flame crackled all around them.

Finn nodded at the fire. 'You going to show us how you do that?'

Charlie grinned, squeezed their shoulders, and pushed away with a laugh. 'Nope. Never. Let's go see Dad.'

They crossed the square to the fortress. Up the stairs they climbed, out onto the terrace facing the ocean. Guards in old-fashioned Turkish clothing with small black serpents for hair stood either side of the door. Both nodded at the trio and opened the door without being asked. The Flints walked in, and it was only when the doors had closed behind them and they were halfway across the entrance courtyard when Charlie said, 'Wish Dad had seen that. Automatic entry, no questions asked.'

'Is Dad okay, do you think?' asked Finn, fear crunching at his stomach. 'And the aviators?'

'Everyone's okay,' assured Charlie. 'You think we've been sitting around doing nothing since the Last Battle? We've been drilled to within an inch of our lives every day since then. We're all okay.'

He shoved through the doors to the pool room.

Shen and George were standing at a bedside on which lay a motionless shape. Their expressions were worried, and they were talking in quiet voices, but they stopped when the children hurried over to Augustus.

Shen put her finger to her lips, but Tula stared down into her father's face and asked loudly, 'He gonna be all right?'

Shen laughed.

'Course he's gonna be all right,' said Charlie.

'The antidote we made from Finn's blood is what really saved him,' said Shen.

Augustus lay rigid on the bed, eyes wide open, yellow, unshaven, hair lank and greasy. Soft light poured in through the clinic windows, but it did not seem to warm his skin.

'I wouldn't say he's been saved,' whispered Finn, the only one still looking anxious. He walked round the bed and stared down at his father, angry that he'd kept them from this place of like people, upset that he hadn't been entrusted with the secrets, worried about the future of the world if Augustus faded away. The future of *them*, him and Tula … and … Charlie.

'Oh, he's been saved.' George gave Finn a reassuring nod and sighed. 'I'm so sorry to have left you children behind, young man. Flying into the Venomous ambush at Elbrus was a devastating reminder of how even the best plans can go so badly awry. I won't make that mistake again.'

Finn swallowed. 'I didn't get it at the time, but I know you were just looking after us, and trying to get to Dad as quickly as possible.'

There was a moment of silence as they all took in the deathly pallor of Augustus lying unmoving on the bed.

George came over to stand next to Finn. 'Have you said hello to your father properly, young man?'

Finn shrugged, his throat tight.

Tula, on his other side, elbowed him. 'You haven't actually, Finn.'

Finn frowned.

Tula's fingers fluttered towards Augustus and her heart before doing a complicated movement near her face.

He loves you, Finn. And me. And Charlie. He was just trying to do his best.

Charlie, on the other side of the bed, nodded at Finn. 'Yep,' he said. 'Adults are mostly a bit messed up.'

'Except for Augustus,' said George, smiling gently at Charlie, then Finn and Tula. 'He knows what he's doing, really, though it might not seem that way just now.'

Tula shuffled closer to her father, putting her palm carefully on Augustus's forehead and whispering something in his ear. Charlie cleared his throat, grabbed Augustus's right hand, and squeezed it.

Finn sighed and took his father's left hand in both of his. As his fingers wrapped round Augustus's palm a cold sensation flooded up his arm and jolted him in surprise. Tula's eyes widened and so did Charlie's.

'That's what was missing,' she whispered. 'Can you feel that, Finn?'

'Don't let go,' said Charlie, his voice urgent, tight with anticipation.

Finn leaned forward, pushing his hand down on his father's chest. Heat shot up his arm. His first instinct was to pull away, but Charlie said, '*Don't let go*,' again, and his words made him hold on.

George exclaimed, using words of a language from a long time ago. Shen whispered something Finn didn't hear, and all of them shifted closer together, as if channelling all their energies at once.

Come on. Come back to us. We need you. The world needs you.

Augustus blinked once, twice, and slowly, slowly, and while everyone held their breath, not daring to move, the yellow staining in his eyes slowly faded. His body trembled, as if fighting off the remaining toxins from the viper venom. He drew a shuddering breath and then the intense gaze that Finn and Tula knew so well was back: ocean blue sparkling in ice white. He blinked again, then his eyes moved to Tula, to Finn, to Charlie.

'Thank God,' he whispered, his voice hoarse and broken.

George laughed. 'Welcome back, Augustus. Your children just saved the world.'

Augustus's face lit up. 'Yes, Gargan is defeated. And Tartarus?'

'Ah,' replied George. He patted Augustus's shoulder gently. 'No.' His eyes looked suspiciously shiny. 'But *you're* alive, and that's more important than the chaos of the Underworld.'

Finn and Charlie released their grip as Augustus sat up, weary and clearly in pain. 'Only just alive, Sir George.'

'But it's enough,' croaked Charlie, and he blinked furiously.

'For now it's enough, my boy,' said Augustus. He swallowed hard, staring at Charlie as if he couldn't believe he was so close to the son from whom he'd been apart for so long. 'But now the Venomous know about the equaliser activator in you three. And they won't stop until they have it for themselves, until they have taken it from us.' His hands were curled into white-knuckle fists above the blankets, and his jaw was tightly clenched.

George shrugged. 'That is tomorrow's problem, Augustus, and we'll tackle tomorrow when it comes. For now, the whole island would like to celebrate the reuniting of your family and the defeat of the Venomous.'

'My family,' said Augustus, his voice croaky again. His eyes were bright with unshed tears. 'The islanders no longer fear our fire? Our song?'

'You have the fire that keeps the Venomous beneath, the earth in balance.' George patted Augustus through the bedclothes again. 'We do not fear that. You have been missed, my old friend, more than you could know. And as for song, have you really forgotten the power of our melodies?' He cocked his head and cupped his hand to his ear, his eyes sparkling. Finn thought he could hear snatches of music from somewhere, and there was a taste in his mouth of champagne and mangos that fizzed with a sharp dryness that he knew now meant triumph and celebration.

'Time to get up,' Finn said to his father.

Charlie strode to the southern wall and drew aside

the curtains to reveal glazed doors that he opened onto the balcony.

'Dad,' he said, 'you've got to see this.'

Finn and Tula helped their father from the bed to where Charlie stood outside.

The mist that hung perpetually over the island had billowed to wider borders, revealing vast sparkling views of sea and sky. Just to the east of them Shuǐlóng played in the waves, splashing huge plumes of water at the aviators, who zoomed across the setting sun in triumphant arrowhead formations, dipping, wheeling and diving. The arch of rock in the ocean below was busy with children tumbling and swooping too, showing off flying skills that made Charlie beam with pride.

On the square below, snow had been swept away and people were gathering, mingling with mythics, talking, laughing, singing. The only part of the town that seemed to be motionless were the buildings, which stood still, peaceful.

In the distance the Flints could see the road out of the town curving across the slopes of patchy snow and ice of dry brown grass. It meandered close to a tree standing a little distance away from the blackened forest that spread into the valley behind it.

'Your house, Charlie,' said Finn, pointing to it. 'We can see all the way, and beyond!'

Augustus took a shaky breath. 'You lived in the obscura tree?' His voice was cracked and broken, and he seemed to stoop a little lower.

Charlie swallowed. 'I didn't want to tell you – I knew you'd be worried – but I could see you better from there. Every night and every morning. I kept hoping you'd come back...'

'Oh, my boy...' Augustus pulled Charlie close to him. He was trembling with emotion. He held him close and Charlie's body, usually so rigid with anger, seemed to melt into his father's, so that his head tucked into his shoulder in a proper hug.

Augustus took another ragged breath and pushed Charlie from him just a little so he could stare into his eyes. 'I'm sorry it took so long for us to return. It was a mistake for me to stay away, to keep your brother and sister from you. Will you come back to live in the watchtower,' he said, 'with all of us?' He looked over at Finn and Tula. 'And you two can learn what it truly is to be a fireblood.'

'Combat training,' said Charlie gloomily, but he was smiling and his cheeks were flushed with joy.

'And Physics and Chemistry and Engineering,' said Augustus, 'and my favourite, which is Study of the Mythics and Magnificents, which could be understanding how a lizard thinks' – he nodded at

Tân – 'right up to a griffin's favourite food.' He stared
out at the enormous griffin who had triumphed so
gloriously in last night's battle, who perched on
the ramparts to the west, his gaze fixed firmly on
Augustus. He had not moved in all the time they'd
been standing there.

'There are many lessons to learn,' said Shen, her
voice gentle, nudging away Augustus's sadness. She
gestured to the horizons that stretched in blues, purples
and greys far beyond the forest. 'Grey will come back
to you, Augustus,' she said. 'Just give him time.'

'I think he is Angelina's familiar now,' said Augustus,
and the taste of ash in Finn's mouth was so strong he
winced.

It started as a breeze, little more than a breath, but
Finn knew it came from the griffin:

'No...' came the creature's voice, sighing across
Augustus's face.

And then the griffin stood, spread his wings
and leapt from the ramparts. He dived down to
the ocean, and when he swooped back round,
higher, higher, higher, the crowds below yelled
their approval. Morty had leapt on to Rudimenta's
shoulders, punching his fist in the air and yodelling
so loudly that he could be heard above the roar of
the crowd. Then Grey Griffin turned and slowed,

dipping lower until he was gliding past the balcony on which they all stood.

'Jump,' he commanded, and Augustus staggered forward, but Grey Griffin had already flown past.

Tula frowned. 'You'll need to move faster than that.' She nudged her father to the edge of the balcony, and when they saw Grey Griffin circling back round, she, Finn and Charlie helped him on to the balustrade.

'Jump,' came Grey Griffin's voice again, and Augustus leapt on to his back.

Tula laughed and clapped her hands, her eyes shining with delight, and Finn tasted mangos again. His big brother pulled him close, and Tula squeezed his hand.

'Look,' she said, pointing to the dais on the edge of the ramparts where Grey had perched. Visible now were four women with butterfly-like wings and a lot of sequins, billed as THE SCRYER SINGERS! on a luminous banner. Even Drishti, waving up to them all with a grin, had come from below to hear their music.

'I think,' said George slowly, 'that they could do with a warm-up act.' He turned to Finn and smiled. 'Your mother used to do it for us in the springtime, but Mother Nature wouldn't begrudge us a bit of light and life earlier than usual. Ready, my boy?'

George touched his stave to Finn's forehead, and Finn had a sudden flashback to a woman he thought of often, though it was hard sometimes to remember her. He was little, holding her hand, and they were on the watchtower balcony, looking over the island. She said to Finn, 'Blow gently, from under your stomach, for as long as you can. That's how to whisper to the green. Breathe and it will come...'

With the memory warming his heart, Finn tightened his body, closed his eyes and took the deepest breath he could. His ribs hurt, his lungs burned, his head pulsed, and he thought about his mother who would never be with them, and his father and his brother and his sister, who were here now. He opened his eyes and he breathed...

Directly in front of him, all the way across the square, the blackened trunks of the twisted oaks began to creak and stretch. The townspeople gasped. Finn could hear raised voices for a moment before they hushed and watched the trees grow up and out, eight years of suspended living bursting out, standing tall and proud in the pink light of the setting sun. The last rays caught new leaves as they budded, sprouted and unfurled, sending dappled green light across the square. There were shouts of approval and wonder, a growing rattle of applause that gathered, and in the groundswell of it the four scryers on the dais began to sing.

Finn felt more heat still to come and turned his

attention to the other trees round the plaza, the silver birch near the Veritas house, the yews and acacia near the Arsenal, the holly hedges topping walls and the ginkos on each street corner. Every trunk shed its sooty shadows, stretching out of burnt bark, reaching up for the last of the sunlight.

The long road out of town caught Finn's eye, and with the last of his breath he sent a puff of warmth to the obscura tree that had stood by itself for so many years. The griffin lifted Augustus high to see it burst into even brighter green, along with the slopes and meadows all around it.

Finn's breath returned to normal as the singers below reached the crescendo of their chorus. The sun dipped below the horizon and all the gemstones of the fortress stairs began to glow, bathing the square in a swirling show of greens, purples, pinks and yellows.

'Wow,' said Charlie, but he was looking at Finn, not at the tableau before them.

'Don't give him a big head,' said Tula. 'Like George said, we've still got things to sort out, like defeating the Venomous for good, and how to keep the Telling Stone safe.'

She jumped up on to the balustrade, her wings flashing out behind her. Charlie's were already stretched taut and ready. The two of them shouted, 'Come on!' to Finn, and they swooped away.

'Keep the Stone safe?' Finn held tight to his backpack straps, whirling round to George and Shen, his face tight with worry.

'Don't worry, Finn Flint,' said the Telling Stone. 'Listen to me for once, instead of always bombarding me with questions. I say to you: *do not worry*. I say to you: *sing*.' Her last word seemed to echo louder, then louder still: *sing*, **sing**, **SING**…

The crowd roared and sang:

> *'Canu i ni*
> *gweddill eich calon anhygoel gyda'n cariad*
> *anadlu gyda ni*
> *llenwch eich enaid gwag gyda'n cariad…'*

And Finn roared and sang with them. He leapt from the balustrade, the song in his heart and pouring through his voice:

> 'Sing to us!
> Fill your heart with our love.
> Breathe with us!
> Fill your empty soul with our love…'

Down below, the melody of so many nations and many more magics united in their celebration of a world saved. Finn floated down with his sister and brother to stand side by side with their father on the griffin.

'Too cold for thermals,' said Charlie when he landed. 'It *is* impressive – flying without wings.'

'I'll have to teach you how,' laughed Finn, thinking there'd definitely been thermals, otherwise how would he have been able to ride the air? But he shrugged and grinned at his brother and sister, and they grinned back, each of them knowing a little about each other that they didn't know themselves.

Now that we're home, signed Tula, *there'll be plenty of time for loop-the-looping.*

Home, thought Finn, and though he knew this life would not be one of peace and tranquillity, he felt his chest warm with all the wonder that lay ahead, with the sense of finally belonging somewhere, with people who needed him, who loved him. Grey Griffin brushed his cheek with a soft feather, as if he could hear his thoughts, and Finn held his family close as they sang their hearts out in the starlight of the northern skies.

I'm truly home.

ACKNOWLEDGEMENTS

I feel very grateful for the support from these remarkable people: Shannon Cullen and Julia Bruce, whose writing soirées keep me full of joy; Megan Kerr, Felix Kirby and Matilda Kirby, trusted experts who read early drafts; David Barron, who helped me believe in big things; my literary agent Lucy Irvine, whose editorial expertise knows no bounds; and all the team at Firefly, who are so passionate and innovative: Leonie Lock, the wondrous person who first read the manuscript, and who copy-edited the final draft so carefully; Penny Thomas, my editor, who talked me down from a fair few cliffs; Becka Moor, who has been very patient with my design wobbles; Karen Bultiauw, whose energy and marketing expertise is so inspiring; Elaine Sharples, who typeset the pages so expertly; Rebecca Lloyd, who proofread the final pages; Keith Robinson, who created the compelling cover art; and Guy Manning, who illustrated such a fabulous map.

Immense thanks to Matt Kelly for finessing the final cover design and for his absolutely brilliant typography, and to David McDougal, who helped me see things differently. Thank you also to the very talented Andy Hastie for web design and authorial motivation, and to Michael and Lesley Richards, who give me more than there is space to write here.

I am indebted beyond words to my most beloved characters, Calla, Torin and Grace, who have lost hours of my time to the firebloods, and to John Richards, my adored champion in all the real and imaginary worlds.

And nothing would have been possible, of course, without my heroic mother, and my dad too – thank you, thank you – who rescued me and my baby sister from the first fire I lit all those years ago.

(Dear reader: don't play with matches.)

MAGICAL MYSTERIES
AND HIDDEN HISTORIES

By now, you will have translated the secret story of how the firebloods came to be. Congratulations! You are now a verified confidant with the knowledge that each of the knights once splashed with Oriel's golden blood inherited her magical gifts. Some gained more than others, all were immortalised.

Eventually, the firebloods, exiled by frightened frailskins, left for the hidden island of Portaldor, far off the north-west coast of Scotland, where they could live without fear.

As the years passed, the knights' gifts were passed on to their children, and children's children. Those sharing similar powers would meet, live and train in each of the four towers – Vulkan, Brann, Siarad and Kellan.

It was the mighty St George who trained the knights and their descendants to protect the world from the greedy forces beneath, as dragons had done for thousands of years. This was Oriel's wish. George had always protected dragonkind and knew more about their magic than anyone.

Turn the page for the information from secret files held by Augustus in the Bristol Observatory...

Would you train in the House of Vulkan?

Vulkan was a fireblood descendent of immense power who George found abandoned near Scafell.

Her house is a turret of granite and iron facing west, towards the sun. She was a young woman with bright orange hair and emerald eyes. Those with Vulkan heritage are frugal people, trusted with the protection of the earth. They love gold more than most, and are excellent hoarders. They are called the terrors, because they're territorial – of the earth.

Depending on the strength of their magic, they have the ability to grow plants in any circumstances, to taste metals within the earth to seek them out for hoarding or mining, to crack or shake the surface of the world or bring it together, depending on their strength, to sense paths and openings ahead.

Most firebloods with earth skills are wayfinders like Charlie Flybynight.

Do you have the magic of the House of Brann?

Brann was found by George, abandoned as a baby in a Norwegian fjord. He could fly before he could walk and had the biggest wings of any fireblood.

The Brann turret is made of crystal and glass. Those invited to the house have all the powers of the air. They can control it to create mist, winds, clouds, and thermals to aid flying.

They can breathe underwater. By creating thick banks of mist and cloud, the breathers, which is what those in the house are called, keep Portaldor hidden from frailskins and enemies.

Patrick belongs to the House of Brann, and loves to show off his wings.

Do you belong to the House of Siarad?

Siarad, the founder of this house, is a grey-bearded man found by George washed up on a beach in Wales.

The House of Siarad is a tower of glass and mother-of-pearl, encrusted with shells and seaweed and barnacles. It stretches from the sea high into the air. It's built to the south of the fortress with the lowest foundations, right down near the island walls, constructed in the cliffs. Siarad people are most often scryers, with exceptional control of water, which is why they're nicknamed 'torrents'. They can breathe below water, and can control water to create rain, floods, tides and waves of immense proportions.

Shen is a torrent, and she has exceptional scrying abilities.

Do you have the power of the House of Kellan?

Kellan was the smallest of the firebloods that George found, but she had astonishing power. She could do anything with fire.

Kellan's family brought her to George all the way from Africa – she wasn't abandoned like so many others. The Kellan house is a black tower to the east, and those within it are called flamers. Flamers have the ability to create heat, fire and light from their palms and fingertips, sometimes even from their entire body. They can control heat in all its forms, from lava flows to soft light.

They are excellent warriors with high healing capacities.

Everyone seems to think Finn is a flamer, but he's certain he's not.

MAGICAL MARKINGS

Sometimes a creature will gift a fireblood with their special skill. In *The First Flight*, Finn, Tula and Charlie are given the gift of bioluminescence by fireflies, which allows them to see hidden magical objects. Grey Griffin gave each of them the power to hear across great distances too. Each of these gifts comes with a mark placed near the shoulder or collarbone. Patrick is covered in them! Can you guess which of these gifts are marked on Finn, Tula and Charlie?

claw of the dragon: *secret dragon powers*

wing of the owl: *silent flight*

tongue of the snake: *magical healing*

eye of the fruit fly: *magnetism*

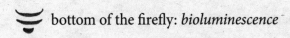 bottom of the firefly: *bioluminescence*

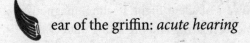 ear of the griffin: *acute hearing*

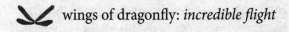 nostril of the water dragon: *breathing underwater*

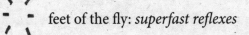 wings of dragonfly: *incredible flight*

whiskers of catfish: *taste of truth and emotion*

feet of the fly: *superfast reflexes*

seed of the sycamore: *single-wing flight*

feather of the peregrine falcon: *exceptional speed*

bite of the Venomous serpent: *undiscovered powers*

Magical markings – answers:

Tula's dragon mark has given her ice-breathing as a skill, and she also has the powers of silent flight, healing, magnetism, bioluminescence, acute hearing and breathing underwater.

Finn's dragon mark and serpent bite have given him secret powers that we have yet to see, and he also has the powers of incredible flight, magical healing, taste of truth and emotion, bioluminescence, acute hearing and breathing underwater.

Charlie's dragon mark has given him undiscovered powers, and he also has the powers of incredible flight, superfast reflexes, exceptional speed, bioluminescence, acute hearing, single-wing flight and breathing underwater.